W9-ANM-154

He was a hero, a mercenary.
And he'd come back to his hometown
to find her missing brother. But he was about
to find a lot more in Annette Broadrick's
Lean, Mean & Lonesome.

"Annette Broadrick always tells a great story."
—Bestselling author Ann Major

Did they *have* to get married?
Well, it sure looked that way. But could this
marriage, begun for the sake of propriety,
end in love? Find out in Cathy Gillen Thacker's
A Shotgun Wedding.

"Cathy Gillen Thacker's fans…
enjoy her combination of warmth and romance!"
—*Rendezvous*

Western ROGUES

They were knights in shining…Stetsons!

CRITICAL ACCLAIM FOR
ANNETTE BROADRICK

"Her books make you feel good when you read them.
She's one terrific writer."
—International bestselling author Diana Palmer

"Annette Broadrick's glorious love stories
always sparkle with irresistible joy and grace."
—*Romantic Times*

"[Annette Broadrick's books] make me laugh and cry
and then laugh again as she takes me on a whirlwind
ride toward a wonderfully happy ending."
—Award-winning author Paula Detmer Riggs

PRAISE FOR CATHY GILLEN THACKER

Of Cathy Gillen Thacker, *Rendezvous* says:

"Hats off to Ms. Thacker for an uplifting romance."
(On *The Bride Said, "Surprise!"*)

"Cathy Gillen Thacker fans can enjoy her
combination of warmth and romance!"
(On *The Virgin Bride Said, "Wow!"*)

"Cathy Gillen Thacker fans will enjoy."
(On *The Bride Said, "Surprise!"*)

Western ROGUES

ANNETTE BROADRICK

CATHY GILLEN THACKER

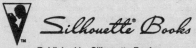

Silhouette Books

Published by Silhouette Books

America's Publisher of Contemporary Romance

If you purchased this book without a cover you should be aware
that this book is stolen property. It was reported as "unsold and
destroyed" to the publisher, and neither the author nor the
publisher has received any payment for this "stripped book."

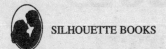 SILHOUETTE BOOKS

ISBN 0-373-21729-3

by Request

WESTERN ROGUES

Copyright © 2002 by Harlequin Books S.A.

The publisher acknowledges the copyright holders
of the individual works as follows:

LEAN, MEAN & LONESOME
Copyright © 1999 by Annette Broadrick

A SHOTGUN WEDDING
Copyright © 1995 by Cathy Gillen Thacker

All rights reserved. Except for use in any review, the reproduction
or utilization of this work in whole or in part in any form by any
electronic, mechanical or other means, now known or hereafter
invented, including xerography, photocopying and recording, or in
any information storage or retrieval system, is forbidden without
the written permission of the editorial office, Silhouette Books,
300 East 42nd Street, New York, NY 10017 U.S.A.

All characters in this book have no existence outside the imagination of
the author and have no relation whatsoever to anyone bearing the same
name or names. They are not even distantly inspired by any individual
known or unknown to the author, and all incidents are pure invention.

This edition published by arrangement with Harlequin Books S.A.

® and TM are trademarks of Harlequin Books S.A., used under
license. Trademarks indicated with ® are registered in the United States
Patent and Trademark Office, the Canadian Trade Marks Office and in
other countries.

Visit Silhouette at www.eHarlequin.com

Printed in U.S.A.

CONTENTS

Dear Reader,

I enjoy writing about tough heroes who have a vulnerability that can be reached only by the heroine. Writers call that sort of hero a wounded warrior.

In *Lean, Mean & Lonesome* I decided to explore what happened to Rafe to cause him to be so distant with people. Unfortunately too many of us have been exposed to the ravages of alcoholism. I thought that would be a good place to start. Rafe was tough because he had a tough childhood, but other things happened along the way that helped to form him. He needed to know what love was all about.

I've known people like Rafe, and my heart ached for the hard lessons they learned so early in life. We all want to think that every child is nurtured and loved, but that isn't always the case.

Rafe is one of the lucky ones. He found redemption. I hope you enjoy Rafe and Mandy's story.

Enjoy!

Annette Broadrick

LEAN, MEAN & LONESOME
Annette Broadrick

This book is dedicated to

Candy Kacena
1954–1998

I will always treasure your
beautiful gift of friendship.
You will not be forgotten.

One

A friend in need is a real pain in the ass.

Rafe McClain had muttered the thought to himself more than once in the past few days, but the utterance did nothing to change the present situation. Until the letter had arrived, Rafe hadn't given friendships much thought. He'd been a loner for a long time, which was just the way he liked it.

Then Dan Crenshaw's letter had turned up in mail that had finally found its way to him. As soon as he read the letter Rafe had been forcibly reminded of another life and time, one he'd dismissed from his conscious mind years ago.

The letter had been a plea for help and Rafe had known that, inconvenient as it was—and it was damned inconvenient—he couldn't ignore Dan's request. Thus, Rafe now battled jet lag on this, the final leg of a journey that had started many hours and time zones ago.

He scratched his cheek and made a face at the feel of the rough surface against the pads of his fingers. He should have shaved during that last layover in Atlanta on his way to Texas. It was too late, now. They'd be landing in Austin in less than an hour.

He'd been flying for two days—waiting around in airports for the next available flight. Killing time. Wishing he knew what the hell was going on to cause the summons he'd received. He was long past being tired. Hell, he didn't even know what day it was in the Central Time zone.

None of that mattered. He was doing what he could to respond to a friend's summons.

Texas.

He hated the place. He hadn't been in the state of his birth in twelve years. Not a hint of nostalgia stirred within him at the thought of his return. When he'd left with his high school diploma stuck in his back pocket, he'd vowed never to return.

So much for pledges. Dan Crenshaw was his best friend—probably his only friend if he were to be honest. They'd met in the fourth grade. The unspoken message in Dan's note was that he knew he could count on Rafe, just as Rafe had always known that Dan would be there for him if he ever needed him.

He wished Dan had been a little more specific. Other than mentioning that he could use his help and hoping to see him at the ranch soon, Dan hadn't indicated what kind of assistance he wanted or needed.

Rafe felt badly that his mail hadn't caught up with him right away. The postmark showed the letter had been mailed five weeks ago. For all Rafe knew, he could be too late with whatever help he was supposed to be offering.

He'd tried to call Dan as soon as he got the letter, but there had been no answer, no answering machine and no way of knowing whether Dan was working somewhere on the ranch or actually gone.

Rafe had seen no other choice but to head back to the states. He had no idea whether or not his showing up at the C Bar C Ranch would accomplish anything positive.

He could think of a hell of a lot of negatives that could occur.

For one thing, he'd been warned by old man Crenshaw never to step foot on his ranch again. Of course, Dan's father had been dead for the past five years, so he supposed he could ignore that particular threat.

So, here he was, landing in Austin at ten o'clock on a hot and muggy July night, rushing to the rescue like some damned knight.

If he weren't so blasted exhausted, he'd laugh at the picture that came to mind. His armor was rusty and dented, his steed gone long ago and his lance had been smashed to smithereens. But he was there.

Once on the ground, Rafe grabbed his bag and picked up the rental car he'd reserved. Within the hour he was headed west out of town, following road signs on thoroughfares that hadn't existed when he'd lived in the area.

The ranch was located about thirty miles southwest of the state's capital in the rough and rugged hill country of Central Texas. As he drove, he was amazed to see how much expansion had taken place as civilization moved westward to claim ranch country. He noticed a Polo Club on the way, for God's sake. Polo? In Texas?

He shook his head in amusement. The times, they were definitely a-changing.

When he finally pulled up at the entrance to the ranch a while later, Rafe was more than ready to find a bed and crash for a few hours. Whatever the reason for his summons, he had a hunch it could be postponed for at least long enough for him to get some rest.

He got out of the car to open the gate and found it was padlocked. There was a large sign on the gate:

Private Property
No Trespassing

The sign and padlock were new. In the past, the combination lock had been easily opened if you knew the birthdays of Dan and Mandy, his sister.

Amanda Crenshaw. Rafe hadn't thought about her in years. She'd been fifteen the last time he'd seen her— a gangly, coltish girl with russet colored curls and an infectious smile. He had a hunch she would have as little use for him as her father had…with more reason.

Dan mentioned once that Mandy lived in Dallas, which was just as well. It would be much better for all concerned if they didn't run into each other while he was in Texas.

He studied the sign and the lock, then glanced at his watch. It was close to midnight. He could either sleep in the car and go on foot to the house in the morning, or he could make that multi-mile hike now.

Neither option particularly appealed to him.

Oh, what the hell. He returned to the car and grabbed his bag—thank God he traveled light—locked the car and climbed the fence.

He knew he was taking a chance going on the property at this time of night. In this part of the world trespassers could get shot before they had a chance to explain their presence on the premises.

If Dan wanted to shoot him he'd have to spot him first.

Rafe smiled to himself at the thought of putting into practice the training he was paid to teach in Eastern Europe. He'd see just how good he really was.

By the time he reached the ranch buildings, Rafe had slipped by two armed guards. What in the hell was going on? Rafe was beginning to get a bad feeling about all of this...a really bad feeling.

Yard lights surrounded the house. There was no way to approach it without being seen.

The house was a single story, Texas-traditional style home. Made of limestone, it had a tin roof that seemed to stretch over several acres. A long, covered porch graced the back of the place. Rafe knew the interior well, unless the family had done major renovations. Mexican tile covered the floor in most of the rooms except for the bedroom wing. A luxurious, deep-piled carpet covered the bedrooms, baths and hallway.

He recalled his youthful dreams of one day having a similar home and a loving family. Rafe was amused by those boyhood dreams, now, but they had served him well at the time, getting him through the bad patches when he was growing up.

Well, standing there admiring the place wasn't getting him any closer.

The area around the house looked free of guards but he wasn't taking any chances. He stashed his bag in some brush and began the intricate and laborious approach that would keep him from getting spotted and shot. By the time he reached the comparative shadowy area on the back porch he was royally pissed off. Mostly at himself. Why hadn't he just called and had Dan pick him up at the airport? That would have circumvented the necessity for all this sneaking around.

Suddenly all hell seemed to break loose inside the house. A large-sounding dog began a barking spree that was guaranteed to wake the dead. Rafe leaned against the wall next to the kitchen door and waited for Dan to check on why his watchdog had suddenly gone ballistic.

Amanda Crenshaw bolted out of bed as soon as Ranger started barking. Someone was out there. He didn't bark at animals. He was a trained watchdog who was now making it clear there was an intruder on the premises.

She peered out the window of her bedroom. The canine alarm should have some of the men coming to check on her soon. In the meantime, she slipped on her robe and shoes and silently made her way down the long hallway to the main part of the house.

Ranger was at the kitchen door, barking loudly. She heard a low, male voice talking in a soothing tone to him. She froze, her mind unable to accept what her heart had immediately recognized. She knew that voice. It was a voice she hadn't heard in years, one she'd never expected to hear again.

With something like panic, Mandy peered through the glass of the back door as she turned on the kitchen light.

A tall, lean man stepped away from the side of the house when he saw her at the door. The illumination from the kitchen revealed him to her slowly, as though her senses would go into overload if she were presented with his entire presence at once.

"Rafe," she whispered to herself, trying to come to

grips with his unexpected presence. She cleared her throat. "Ranger, that's enough!" she said firmly. The dog stopped barking, but continued to growl. She opened the door and motioned for Rafe to come inside. Her heart felt as though it was going to jump out of her chest.

As he moved into the light she saw his boots first— working boots that should have been retired years before. The light moved up his frame, slowly revealing him to her. Faded denim jeans lovingly clung to his long, muscular legs and emphasized his masculinity. A faded denim shirt that looked strained across his broad chest was open at the neck to reveal a strong column of dark skin at the throat. She saw a well-defined jawline bristling with a couple of days' growth of beard.

He definitely needed a haircut, she thought, noticing how his dark hair fell across his forehead to his brows. The last to be revealed as he stepped past her into the house was the expression in his black eyes.

She shivered. "What are you doing here?"

A glint of white showed when his lips turned up in a half smile. "I didn't intend to frighten you. I'm looking for Dan."

"Dan?"

"Yeah. He asked me to come back."

She placed her hand on Ranger's head. "Enough," she said to the rumbling dog. "You've made your point." She spoke without taking her eyes off Rafe.

The light mercilessly showed her that the man before her was no longer the boy she remembered. There were creases in his cheeks that bracketed his mouth. More creases covered his forehead. Deep lines were around his eyes. Whatever he'd been doing since she'd last seen him, Rafe's life hadn't been easy.

The shock of being awakened from a sound sleep to find Rafe McClain had suddenly leaped back into her life had her reeling. "How did you get here?" she asked. What she really wanted to know was if this was some stress-induced dream she was having. Could she find a way to wake up and discover she was still tucked in bed with only Ranger for company?

He leaned back against the door and allowed Ranger to check him out. When the dog appeared to be satisfied, he said, "The usual way. Plane and car—until I got to the ranch. Then I had to hoof it the rest of the way. Why does Dan have the gate padlocked? Does that have something to do with why he sent for me?"

She shook her head, trying to clear it. None of this was making any sense.

Rafe McClain was back in Texas. He was here because of Dan.

Dan. She shivered. "When did you talk to him?" she asked.

"I haven't. He wrote me a letter a while back. It took some time to catch up with me. Said he needed my help." He shrugged his shoulders. "So I'm here."

She spun away from him, needing some space from the roiling emotions he provoked within her. Peering out the window, she said, "I don't understand how you reached the house without someone seeing you."

"I didn't figure getting myself shot was part of the deal. So I was careful." He stretched and smothered a yawn.

She forced herself to face him. She leaned against the kitchen cabinet and asked, "Where have you been? I mean, where were you when Dan's letter caught up with you?"

"The Ukraine."

That surprised her, although she wasn't sure why. "What were you doing there?"

He lifted one of his eyebrows into a quirk. "You writing a book or something?"

Some things never changed. Rafe had always had a sarcastic comeback when he didn't want to answer personal questions. As far as he was concerned, every question was personal.

Why hadn't Dan ever mentioned to her that he was in touch with Rafe? The man's name had never come up in all of these years. Now she finds out Dan had contacted Rafe. Why would he have thought Rafe could help him? So many unanswered questions. They continued to race around her head.

She had to make a decision. Did she call the foreman and have Rafe evicted from the place? Surely she wasn't expected to welcome him, despite the fact that the ranch belonged to Dan, who appeared to have invited him.

Rafe drew up one of the kitchen chairs and sat down with a sigh. Mandy knew she was being rude. She could feel the hated color creep across her throat and cheeks.

She'd often envied Rafe his beautifully tanned skin that darkened into a burnished copper in the summer. In the sun she turned an angry red and peeled. She'd long since decided she needed to stay in the shade. There was nothing she could do about her thin skin that reflected her embarrassment at the most inopportune times.

This was one of them.

He must have recognized her discomfort because he decided to answer one of her questions. "I'm a consultant."

A consultant. Somehow she had trouble seeing him in a suit and tie working for a corporation.

"What kind?"

His white smile flashed across his dark face. "Believe me, you don't want to know." He looked around the room. "I like the way this place has been updated."

"So do I. Dan had it redone a couple of years ago."

"Do you live here now?"

She paused. "No. I live in Dallas. I've taken some time off."

He glanced at her hands and she realized that she was clenching them tightly. She deliberately placed them behind her and leaned against them and the cabinet.

"You're not married?" he asked, sounding surprised.

She shook her head without quite meeting his gaze. "No."

"Why not?"

It was all right for him to ask personal questions, she noticed. "Why aren't *you* married?" she replied, carrying the inquisition into his corner.

"I never stayed in one place long enough, I guess. Most women I've met tend to want their husband at home with them."

She couldn't imagine Rafe in the role of husband. He was too untamed. "I suppose," she murmured, wishing she knew what to do with him now that he was there.

"So what's your excuse?"

Her gaze darted to his. She raised her chin. "Maybe no one has asked me," she replied evenly.

He grinned and her stomach did a somersault. "I don't buy that one," he said, his gaze sliding over her in an intimate perusal that made her shiver in response.

She lifted her shoulder in a shrug. "No one that I wanted to marry, anyway." She straightened and crossed her arms over her chest. "Dan says I have lousy taste in men."

Their gazes met and held for a long, silent moment before each looked away.

"You never told me where Dan is," he said.

"He—he isn't here right now."

"Well, where in the hell is he, damn it? You keep avoiding my questions. I came a long way to find out why the hell Dan needed me here. So where is he?"

She had known that she was going to have to answer his questions and had hoped that she could talk about Dan without breaking down. But the lateness of the hour and her sense of vulnerability where Rafe was concerned weren't helping her deal with the situation.

She attempted to swallow around the lump in her throat. It was hard to put her thoughts into words. She wanted so much to be wrong.

"I think Dan's dead," she said, her voice breaking on the last word.

Two

Rafe studied the woman before him. She no doubt believed what she was saying, but it had no meaning to him. None at all.

"Dead?"

He repeated the word as though he'd never heard it before. He shook his head. "He can't be. I'd know it if something had happened to Dan. He..." His voice trailed away. He knew how stupid that sounded. He, better than most, knew how easily a life could be snuffed out. Rafe wiped a hand across his face, ignoring his exhaustion. "You'd better start at the beginning, Mandy, and fill me in on what the hell's going on around here."

Mandy picked up a glass and absently filled it with water. He thought about asking her for a drink, then decided against it. At the moment he had more important things on his mind. She faced him once again, but her lustrous gray eyes stared past his shoulder and he knew she no longer saw him sitting there.

While he waited, he looked for the young girl he'd known in the woman standing before him. There were traces of her in the way she stood, the way she moved. He still had the same strong reaction to her, he was sorry to discover.

Although she was still slender, she'd added curves that would make any man take a second look. Her satiny smooth skin made his palms itch, wanting to touch her cheek. She still wore her reddish-brown hair long. Tousled waves tumbled around her shoulders, unnecessarily reminding him that she'd just come from her warm bed.

She focused on him once more and swallowed painfully. He found her nervousness around him troubling, but he wasn't surprised.

"I haven't seen Dan in a couple of months. We've both been busy, although he usually calls me every week or so. About ten days ago I received a call from Dan's foreman, Tom Parker. He asked me if I'd seen or spoken to Dan."

"Why would he call you?"

"Because he said he'd checked with everyone else— including Dan's business partner—to see why Dan had left without letting anyone know."

"You mean he just disappeared?"

"Tom said he spoke to Dan late one afternoon. He told Dan he needed to talk to him about moving some of the cattle to a different feeding area. Dan told him he had a meeting that night, but would meet with him the next morning. However, the next morning Dan wasn't to be found."

"Does anyone know who he was meeting or where?"

"Unfortunately, no. I think he must have met someone at the airstrip and left, because his car is still in the
garage and Tom found the Jeep parked at the airstrip."

"What airstrip?"

"Dan had one built on the ranch about three years
ago. He and his partner were thinking of buying a plane
together. According to the partner, they never did, but
they rent planes from time to time and use the strip on
a regular basis."

Rafe shook his head. "This is all a jumble to me. I
guess I'm going to have to get some sleep before I can
make any sense of it."

"I hope sleep helps. It hasn't helped me, although I
have to admit I haven't been sleeping too well since
Tom called me. I came down immediately to see if I
could help figure out where he'd gone. I'm so frustrated
because outside of Tom and me, no one seems to be
concerned—not Dan's partner nor the sheriff's department. His partner said that Dan would be back in his
own good time. I don't believe that. I don't believe that
Dan would just disappear like that, especially after ar-
ranging to meet with Tom. I also think he would have
called someone if he ran into some kind of a delay so
that we wouldn't worry."

"So do I. Dan is one of the most responsible people
I know."

"Exactly." She studied him for a moment. "You're
right, Rafe. You need to get some sleep. You're out on
your feet. Go on to bed. We'll discuss this in the morning."

He knew that she was right. He could feel weariness
claim his body now that he'd finally reached his desti-
nation. He stood and stepped away from the chair.

"He's been missing this long. I don't suppose another few hours will matter."

She entered the hallway and spoke as she moved away from him. "You can sleep in Dan's room."

Rafe waited until a light turned on in the hall before he turned off the kitchen light. Ranger watched him without blinking.

"I'm glad you're watching out for her," he said in a low voice.

Ranger didn't change expression. Rafe got the feeling that Ranger didn't particularly care what Rafe might think about anything.

Smart dog.

Rafe followed Mandy into the hallway.

"Dan moved into the master bedroom after Mom died," she said, motioning to the end of the hall.

Rafe paused beside her. "I was sorry to hear about your mother, Mandy. She was always kind to me. I've never forgotten that."

"It was quick," she replied, her gaze on her arms, folded across her chest. "At least she didn't suffer."

"Her heart?"

"Yes." She looked up at him. "Dad, on the other hand, lingered months longer than expected with his cancer."

He didn't want to talk about her father, not now, not ever. He stepped past her and entered one of the few rooms in this house he'd never been in before. Mandy followed him into the room and glanced into the adjoining bathroom. "There are plenty of clean towels and things," she said. "I'll talk to you in the morning."

With that, she quietly left the room, closing the door behind her.

Only then did Rafe remember that his bag was still

hidden outside, but he wasn't about to go back out there tonight to look for it. He glanced around the large room. A king-size bed was on one wall. Another wall was lined with bookshelves, filled with a mishmash of fiction and nonfiction. He smiled, thinking of Dan and his love of reading.

His smiled faded when he remembered what Mandy had told him. Dan couldn't be dead. There was no way Dan would allow himself to get into a situation that was life-threatening. But accidents happened all the time, Rafe reminded himself.

Where was he? If Dan was alive, why hadn't he returned?

Rafe walked over to the third wall, next to the door leading to the bathroom. This wall was filled with photographs, large and small, of varied subjects. Most of the photos had been taken at the ranch. There were shots of longhorn cattle, deer, family pets, and many pictures of family members.

Rafe was surprised to see that he was in many of them. He hadn't remembered being that thin, or looking so grim.

As he turned away, he paused and looked again at photographs that must have been taken at the party the Crenshaws gave the night that he and Dan graduated from high school, the last night he was on the ranch.

There was a picture of Mandy in a cotton-candy-colored dress with a full skirt and sleeves that rested just off her shoulders. He still recalled, without the need of a photograph to remind him, how she looked at the party with her glowing eyes and her contagious smile. She'd looked much older than fifteen that night and had delighted in her newfound ability to attract admiring gazes. He touched the photograph lightly with his forefinger, tracing the curve of her lips, the shape of her shoulders.

He could still remember how her mouth had tasted, how smooth her shoulders had felt, how much he'd wanted to make love to her that night.

Rafe deliberately withdrew his gaze from Mandy's photo and focused instead on another one taken the day they graduated of Dan in his suit, looking solemn enough if you didn't look too closely at the amusement in his eyes. The one of Rafe alone caught him by surprise. He'd filled out from the earlier pictures Dan had on display and wore the first and only suit he'd ever possessed. Rafe looked closer at the boy he had once been. He'd had his hair cut and looked equally solemn. However, there was no amusement twinkling in his eyes, just a firm resolve to make something of himself.

He'd managed to do that, all right, with the help of Uncle Sam.

Rafe continued into the bathroom and shucked off his clothes. He stood under the hot, steamy water and let it massage the soreness from his body. He could scarcely keep his eyes open. Once the water began to cool, he turned it off and grabbed a towel. He didn't need anything to sleep in tonight. He'd raid Dan's closet in the morning so he could pick up his bag outside. Now all he wanted was a few hours of oblivion.

After Rafe closed his bedroom door, Mandy returned to bed, Ranger padding softly behind her until she turned off the light and crawled beneath the covers. Then he stretched out on the rug beside her and gave a deep sigh.

She wanted to echo that sigh.

Having Rafe McClain show up like this had been a

shock she could have done without. However, now that
he was here, she had to admit to herself that if anyone
could solve the mystery of Dan's disappearance, it
would be Rafe. She should be relieved that he had
shown up. Just as important, knowing that Dan had notified his friend strengthened her belief that something
in Dan's life had gone wrong. Why else would he have
contacted Rafe?

Her thoughts kept circling back to the man. How
could a person she hadn't seen in twelve years still have
such a strong effect on her?

She would never forget the day all those years ago
when he showed up at the ranch for the first time. He'd
been fourteen, Dan's age. She'd been eleven.

He'd worn ragged clothes, much like what he'd had
on today. He had needed a haircut, as he did now. Not
much had changed in his overall appearance for that
matter, she thought to herself.

He'd been thinner then. Much thinner. He'd still had
bruises on his face, bruises he hadn't chosen to explain.
Her mind drifted, returning to those long-ago days when
she had been a child filled with curiosity, eager to learn.

Mandy was in her room on a Saturday morning, trying to decide if she was ready to pack away her dolls
and other childhood things. She enjoyed playing with
them once in a while, when she knew Dan wouldn't
catch her at it and tease her for being such a baby.
However, she could use the space they took up for other
things. School started on Monday and she felt the need
to organize her room and get ready to face the new
school year.

It was tough being too old for toys, too young for
boys.

She heard the yard dogs clamoring outside and peered out her window to see what had set them off. She saw a tall, skinny boy standing beside the gate of the fence that protected the lawn from the rest of the ranch. He stood as still as a statue, while the dogs carried on all around him.

Dan's voice carried ahead of him as he dashed out the back door, the screen slamming behind him. "Hey, Rafe! How ya doing?" Dan chased the dogs off and invited the boy inside the stone fence.

Mandy vaguely recognized the boy. He'd gone to the same elementary school in Wimberley that she and Dan had attended. Of course now the two boys would be starting high school this fall. Except maybe Rafe had dropped out of school a couple of years ago. Either that, or his family had moved away. She hadn't seen him in a long time.

Now he was back. Curious—as usual—Mandy raced downstairs and walked out on the porch. She was surprised by what he said.

"I'm looking for work."

Dan laughed. "You serious? Aren't you going to school?"

"I intend to enroll on Monday, but I need a local address. So I thought maybe I could work here on the ranch for your dad evenings and weekends until I finish up with school."

Dan reached over and touched a gash just above Rafe's eye and Rafe flinched. "What happened?"

"It doesn't matter."

"Your dad?"

"Forget it."

"Are your folks still living in East Texas?"

"Yeah."

"Do they know where you are?"

"No." He frowned at Dan. "You gonna tell 'em?"

"Not if you don't want me to. Won't they be looking for you?"

Rafe laughed, but he didn't sound amused. "Not hardly." Rafe looked past Dan and saw her watching them. He looked away. Dan turned around and saw her.

"Quit being so nosy and go back into the house," he yelled.

Without a word Mandy went back inside. She went looking for her mom and found her in the front yard, working in her flower garden as usual.

"Mom, there's a guy here wanting a job."

Her mother sat back on her heels and looked quizzically at Mandy from beneath her wide-brimmed straw hat. "Why are you telling *me,* honey? Your dad handles that."

"He's just a kid."

Her mother grinned. "Really? How old is he?"

"Dan's age. They used to be in the same class until Rafe moved away or something."

"Rafe?"

"That's what he goes by."

Her mom got up, dusted her knees, removed her cotton gardening gloves, straightened her hat and walked around the house. She saw the boys sitting on the back steps and joined them.

Mandy followed her, daring Dan to say anything about her presence.

"Hello. I'm Dan's mother, Amelia Crenshaw," she said, holding out her hand to Rafe. Mandy noticed that her mother acted as though there was nothing unusual about his appearance.

He looked at her hand uncertainly, then reluctantly

took it, shook it quickly and released it. He bobbed his head without meeting her gaze. "Hi. I'm Rafe McClain."

"Amanda tells me that you're looking for work. Is that right?"

Dan glared at Mandy. She gave him a sunny smile in return.

Rafe cleared his throat. "Yes, ma'am."

"After school, of course."

"Yes'm."

She smiled. "Why don't you come inside and have something to drink? Dan's father should be coming in for dinner in an hour or so. You can join us and discuss the matter with him."

Mandy sensed Rafe's embarrassment. He kept looking at everything but her mom. "That's all right," he mumbled. "I can come back later."

"Nonsense," her mother said gently, smiling at him. "You have to eat like the rest of us. Dan can show you around the place after you get something to drink." She walked up the steps and across the porch as though there was no doubt in her mind the boys would follow her into the house.

"Snitch," Dan muttered, walking past Mandy and pulling her hair.

"What's so secret about wanting a job?" she asked him, swatting at his hand.

Rafe glanced at her and smiled. "Nothing. There's nothing wrong." She smiled back, liking the boy with the black, sad eyes.

Later, over the noon meal, her dad asked Rafe a bunch of questions about what he was trained to do, but nothing about why he needed a job and a place to stay.

Mandy had a hunch Dan had already filled him in on that part when she wasn't around.

And so it was that Rafe McClain made his home on the ranch on that day in late August. There was a small cabin—really only a large room with a bathroom added off the side—that was just over a rise from the house and barns. A small creek ran nearby and the place was shaded with large—and obviously old—live oak trees.

Her dad had suggested that Rafe move in there.

Nobody talked about the fact that he didn't have any belongings. He just showed up at mealtimes wearing some of Dan's old shirts and jeans. Her dad insisted on paying him in addition to his room and board—and gradually Rafe acquired a pair of shoes that weren't falling apart and had his hair cut. He worked from dawn until time for school, then from after school to dark or later.

Sometime during the following four years, Mandy developed a crush on Rafe. She could still remember the pangs of adolescent angst where he was concerned. He, on the other hand, hadn't known she existed as anything but Dan's pesky little sister.

Too bad she hadn't left things that way. Life would have been so much better for both of them if she had.

The sounds of voices and the routine of activity around a working ranch roused Rafe the next morning. He opened his eyes and lay there, remembering why he was back in Texas. He sat up and groaned, feeling the stiffness in all his joints.

He forced himself out of bed and stalked over to the dresser in search of some briefs. When he pulled the drawers open, he let out a silent whistle. These were not discount store items. He picked up a pair of silk boxer shorts and smiled. The kid certainly believed in his comfort. He'd have to give Dan a rough time the next time he saw him.

If he saw him.

Damn. He hated the not knowing. He opened the closet door and stepped inside a spacious walk-in area. Racks of suits, dress shirts and shiny shoes were on one side. Jeans, Western-cut shirts and boots were on the other.

Interesting. It looked to Rafe like a town and country wardrobe to fit any occasion.

He tried to remember the last time he'd talked to Dan, or heard from him before this letter that had finally caught up with him. He'd gotten a short letter a couple of years ago mentioning an engagement and that he expected Rafe to show up and be his best man.

Before Rafe had found the time to respond—and he'd put it off, admittedly, because he didn't know how to remind his old friend that he wouldn't be welcome around the Crenshaw family—Dan had written an equally terse letter saying the engagement was off.

What Dan hadn't told him now spoke volumes. What did he do that called for suits, dress shirts and a wide assortment of expensive ties?

Rafe pulled one of the work shirts off a hanger and put it on. The fit was fine. He didn't have as much luck with the jeans. It seemed as though Dan had put on a little weight around the middle since high school. Rafe rooted around until he found an old pair of jeans that would fit him.

They were worn white at the knees and the seat of the pants. Hell, for all he knew they may well *be* jeans from high school.

He grabbed a pair of socks before putting on his own

boots. Then he went in search of some coffee with which to start his day.

There was no sign of Mandy but she'd left evidence of her passing. A pan of biscuits sat next to a plate filled with crisply fried bacon. He couldn't remember the last time he'd eaten. His stomach growled at the thought. He poured himself a cup of coffee and stuck a piece of bacon between two halves of a biscuit. By the time he'd finished his coffee, he'd made a large dent in the biscuit and bacon supply.

He peered outside, but there was no sign of Mandy. One of the first things he needed to do was to get his clothes out of the brush where he'd hidden them. After that, he'd talk to someone about getting his car back to the rental place. He walked to the back door and eased it open. In addition, he wanted to hunt up the foreman and get his view on what might have taken place here the night Dan disappeared.

He stepped off the end of the porch and started toward the gate. He was almost there when a slight noise at his back caused him to glance around, but he was too late. He felt a blinding pain directly behind his ear.

His last memory was a vision of the limestone walk rapidly coming up to meet him.

Three

Rafe knew that he was getting too old for this business if someone could take him out in a friend's backyard in the middle of the morning. He sat in the kitchen holding a cold compress to the back of his head while Mandy apologized to him and explained to the foreman that he wasn't an interloper and shouldn't have been ambushed.

From what Rafe could gather as he sat nursing his goose egg and bruised ego, Tom Parker wasn't any too pleased with Mandy's explanations. He appeared to be upset that all of his carefully planned security measures hadn't prevented Rafe from reaching the ranch house undetected last night.

At the moment, Rafe was having some difficulty working up much sympathy for the man.

"I'd intended to introduce Rafe to you this morning, Tom," Mandy said in a conciliatory tone that wasn't improving Rafe's mood of the moment. Hell, she didn't need to apologize for him. "I wasn't aware he was awake or I would have invited you to the house for coffee so the two of you could get acquainted."

"So introduce us," the man replied in a gruff voice.

Mandy rolled her eyes. "Rafe McClain, this is Dan's foreman, Tom Parker. He's worked for Dan for several years." To Tom she added, "Rafe is a family friend."

Rafe wasn't in the mood to be polite, damn it. Getting his head bashed in wasn't on the top of his list of ways to start the day. Hell, Ranger had been better protection for Mandy than all the armed guards. Where was this character last night when Ranger had carried on so loudly?

Rafe leaned back in his chair and looked over the man who was propped against the cabinets with his arms folded, glaring at him from across the room. He wasn't particularly impressed with the man or his glare, although he might have been more tolerant of the man's attitude if this was the first time they'd had occasion to meet.

"A little quick to take a person out, aren't you?" Rafe drawled, holding Parker's gaze with a steady look.

"You're a stranger on the property. As far as I'm concerned, you have no business being here. I have zero tolerance these days."

Rafe carefully touched the knot behind his ear. "Yeah. I noticed."

"Hope you're not waiting for an apology," Parker growled. "With Dan missing, I'm not willing to take any chances where Mandy's safety is concerned."

Mandy interrupted. "Tom, I've already explained that…"

Parker ran his hand through his hair in a frustrated

gesture. "Hell, I know what you said, Mandy. Has it occurred to you that if this guy—"

"Rafe—" Rafe reminded him softly.

"—If *Rafe* could get on the property without any of us seeing him, so could anyone else. Until we locate Dan, we don't know what the hell is going on. For all we know, this guy could have something to do with Dan's disappearance."

Rafe chuckled, then groaned, holding his head very carefully, afraid it might tumble off his shoulders at any moment. "I'm not up to laughing at your absurd accusations just yet, so try to hold back on the humor for a little while, okay?"

He was amused to see that this Tom character was actually grinding his teeth. I bet his dentist was going to love him for that.

Parker straightened. "I've got to get to work. I need to—"

"—show me around the place?" Rafe inserted. "Thanks, I'd appreciate it. Now that I'm here, I can relieve you of some of the burden of figuring out what's going on."

A rush of emotions seemed to sweep across Parker's face—disbelief, anger, with more than a hint of bewilderment. "Just who in the hell do you think you are?" he finally managed to get out through clenched teeth.

Rafe continued to lean back in his chair. He smiled, feeling better by the minute. "The man who's going to find out what happened to Dan."

"I see. You think you can do any better than I have, or Mandy, or the sheriff's department?"

Rafe shrugged. "Won't know 'til I try."

Mandy spoke up. "Look, Rafe, you don't have to

stay. Just because Dan contacted you doesn't mean that you have to—''

"Dan contacted him! When?" Parker turned and looked at Rafe. "How come I've never heard of you, if you're such good friends with the family?"

Rafe scratched his chin thoughtfully. "Tell you what, Parker," he finally drawled. "The minute I finish my autobiography, I'll make damned sure you get the first copy off the press. Until then, I don't owe you any explanations about anything, you understand me? I'm here now. I aim to stay until I get ready to leave, and not one minute sooner." He studied the other man thoughtfully before adding, "Unless you're already seeing yourself as the boss around here now that Dan isn't around."

Parker straightened and took a step toward him before Mandy stepped in front of him. She placed her hands on Parker's chest. "Look, Tom, I know Rafe very well. You aren't going to win this argument. I'll talk to him…try to get him to calm down—''

"Calm down?" Rafe repeated. "Hell, Mandy, if I was any more calm at the moment, I'd be comatose."

She ignored him. "Why don't you give us a few minutes," she said to Parker. "Rafe and I will be out later. I want to show him the airfield and other things that weren't here the last time he was here. I'd like you to go with us."

Rafe idly noted that Parker contented himself by giving Rafe a hard look. Rafe assumed it was supposed to make him tremble in his boots. Parker nodded to Mandy and left the kitchen, allowing the door to slam behind him.

"His mother must not have taught him much manners, slamming the door that way," Rafe commented.

He got up and went over to the coffeepot and carefully poured himself another cup. His head hurt something fierce, but he'd be hanged before he'd admit his pain to Mandy.

Part of the macho creed, he supposed, amused at himself.

"Oh, you're a great one to be spouting off about manners. You practically accused him of doing away with Dan so he could run the ranch!" Mandy turned away and quickly scrambled some eggs and placed them on a plate along with what was left of the bacon and biscuits. She set the plate hard enough down at the table where he'd been sitting that Rafe feared for the safety of the china plate.

"Eat," she said tersely.

"What about you?"

"I've managed to look after myself just fine for all these years without your help, McClain. I don't need you or any other man looking after me, have you got that straight?"

"Look, Mandy, I'm not sure why you're upset, but I—" But he what? Was he sorry for anything he'd said or done? Not only no, but hell no. So what did he say to her? "I don't want to see you upset," he finally muttered.

"Then sit down and eat your breakfast," was her only reply.

He sat down and ate his breakfast, which he found a little tough to do since he'd already helped himself to a large portion earlier. But he figured it wouldn't hurt to pacify her at the moment. She seemed to be just a mite touchy. Maybe he should have taken into consideration all she'd been through these past few days before he let loose at the foreman.

"You had no reason to accuse Tom of trying to take over the ranch," she finally said from across the room, where she busied herself loading the dishwasher. He tried not to wince when breakables collided.

"Didn't I? Well, that's good to hear."

"He and Dan are very close."

"So?"

"If you think that he might have had anything to do with Dan's disappearance—"

"Whoa! Now wait a minute, Mandy. That's quite a leap you've made between the two subjects."

"Is it? I don't think so. You're implying that Tom has something to gain if we can't find Dan."

"Am I? Funny, but I don't see it that way. In the first place, I don't know enough about what has happened to start coming up with conclusions about anything."

"Then what were you implying by your out-of-line comment?"

He grinned. "I figure he was making damned sure that I understood he'd already staked his claim where you're concerned and he didn't like the idea I might be trespassing on that claim."

"Me?!"

"Aw, come on, Mandy. You're not that naive. The man is obviously playing the protector role where you're concerned. Not that I blame him. In his place I'd be doing the same thing. After all, if Dan hadn't been worried about something several weeks ago, he never would have sent me that letter. The fact that he has now disappeared and no one seems to know why or where, or even—God forbid!—if he's even alive tells me we've got something serious on our hands. If something *has* happened to Dan, that leaves you in a very vulnerable position.''

She stopped what she was doing and looked at him. ''In what way?''

''You're a very attractive woman, Mandy, as well as being the only family member left to inherit the ranch if something *has* happened to Dan. Don't pretend not to see what a sweet setup that would be for some unscrupulous male.''

''Ah. I see. You think Tom hopes to acquire me and this ranch in one neat package. How gracious of you to believe that a man would want more than just me in a relationship. Not only that, you've already managed to figure out that Tom is just unscrupulous enough to make a play for me based on those terms.'' She crossed her arms and glared at him from across the room. ''What sort of stuff are you smoking these days, Rafe? I swear, you must be downright delusional!''

He certainly wasn't making any points at the moment, Rafe decided. So maybe he'd better get started on his plans for the day.

He got up and carried his dishes to where she stood. Nudging her aside, he rinsed his plate, utensils, cup and saucer and quietly placed them in the dishwasher. He looked down at her, suddenly amused at the fiery glints shooting from her eyes. He'd forgotten how much fun he'd had as a kid teasing her in order to provoke just that expression.

He had a sudden urge to kiss her, just to provoke another reaction. He leaned toward her, wondering if she would taste as sweet as he remembered. She'd been staring past him, looking out the window. When he leaned toward her, she glanced back, focusing on him once again.

Their eyes met and he realized how much trouble he'd be in if he actually followed through on the idea. Man, what was he thinking!

He immediately straightened and turned away. He had already learned one thing since he'd returned to Texas. Mandy Crenshaw affected the grown man just as strongly as she had the young boy. This time, he was supposed to have enough self-discipline not to succumb to the temptation she presented.

Four

Rafe walked over to the door and looked outside, watching the activity in the ranch yard and concentrating on why he was there. "You mentioned Dan's partner last night," he finally asked when it became obvious that Mandy wasn't going to speak. "His partner in what?"

"He and James Williams started a business with computers. I think they met in college. They make circuit boards for computer companies who want to hire that part out. I guess they've been fairly successful. I know they have a small factory with over fifteen employees. James takes care of running the plant—he's some kind of computer whiz—while Dan's been handling sales and contacting potential clients."

She walked over to the table and sat down. Rafe glanced around and saw what she had done. With a certain amount of reluctance he decided to join her. He needed whatever information Mandy could give him. The sooner he resolved the matter, the sooner he could hightail it out of there.

He crossed the room and sat down across from her. "Which would explain why he spends his time traveling," he replied, thinking out loud.

She nodded.

"But this Williams—he doesn't know where Dan could be?"

"No, but he said he isn't worried. He said Dan travels all the time. When I pinned him down, he admitted that Dan usually lets him know when he's going to be out of town for any length of time." She hugged her waist. "He's never been out of touch for this long."

"When is the last time either the foreman or Dan's partner saw him?"

"It's been almost two weeks now since July 1. Tom said he spoke to Dan that evening, but he wasn't around the next morning when he came up to the house for their meeting."

"Any of his clothes gone?"

She shrugged. "I have no way of knowing. Plenty of his things are still here. I don't know what kind of luggage he kept, so I have no way of knowing if he has bags with him."

"You mentioned last night that you reported this to the sheriff. What sort of response did you receive from that avenue?"

"A deputy came out to talk to me. He was very patronizing. Asked a lot of personal questions about me and my interest in my brother and his possible disappearance. Wanted to know if I was his heir if something had happened to him. He was a real jerk."

"Do you remember the deputy's name?"

"Oh, yeah. I'd never forget it. Dudley Wright. I think of him as Dudley DoRight. Treated me like some kind of neurotic female who needed to get a life instead of trailing along behind my brother, asking inane questions." She looked at Rafe for what seemed to be a long time before she asked, "Do you think there's a chance Dan could still be alive?"

"Will you stop thinking that way?" Rafe replied in a growl. "Just because we don't know where he is doesn't mean he's dead. There could be all sorts of explanations why we haven't heard from him. Let's don't start jumping to conclusions."

"Then why hasn't he been in touch with anyone?" she replied with some heat. "Why is it I'm the only one who sees something strange about the fact that he hasn't gotten in touch with me, or with Tom, or even James?"

He shook his head as though he wasn't sure what she was implying. "You think it's a conspiracy?" he finally asked. "You think everyone else knows where he is but no one is telling you?"

She glared at him. "Oh, puleeze. So now you're agreeing with the good deputy and think I'm neurotic as well?"

Rafe took a deep breath and let it out very slowly. "For what it's worth, Mandy, I think you're a tad sensitive about what others might or might not think of you. Like you, I'm puzzled about how a person could disappear like that without somebody, somewhere, knowing what happened and where he is now. It's possible someone knows more than he or she realizes he knows." He rearranged the salt and pepper shaker, moving them around each other. He glanced up at her. "When did you last speak to him?"

Mandy was quiet for a moment. When she spoke, she sounded calmer. "About a month ago. He'd been checking on me more often than usual. During that particular conversation he suggested that I might want to take my vacation early and come to visit him." Her voice wobbled and she swallowed before continuing. "He said we hadn't spent much time together since Mom died. He thought I could use a break."

"From what?"

She nibbled her lower lip. "I recently broke an engagement."

"Seems to run in the family." He smiled, trying to put her at ease. "Dan wrote me about his engagement. Then later let me know there was not going to be a wedding."

She shook her head. "That was Sharon. He seemed to be crazy about her. All she wanted to do was party. I wasn't sorry to see her back out of their engagement, although I think Dan took it hard at the time."

"Could his disappearance have anything to do with her?"

She looked at him, startled. "Oh, I don't think so. That was a couple of years ago. He's dated several women since then."

"Any seriously enough that they might have some idea where he would be?"

"I don't know. I could talk to James about it." She hesitated, then said, "Better yet, I'll let you talk to him. He makes me uncomfortable."

"How?"

"Every time I see him, he makes a pass at me." She shivered, as though repulsed by the idea.

Rafe smiled. "The man shows good taste, at least."

She frowned. "Very funny."

He could see he wasn't going to win any points around her at the moment. He shoved back his chair and stood. "I'm going out to get my bag. Is the cabin in use these days? If not, I might as well bunk down in it." He moved rapidly toward the door, but came to an abrupt halt when Mandy spoke.

"Uh, no. The cabin burned a few months after you left here."

He turned around.

"Really," he said softly. "How did that happen?"

She shrugged. "One of the hands got careless, was my dad's guess. Left a smoldering cigarette too close to something flammable. By the time anyone saw it, the cabin was in full blaze. It was too late to do anything but keep the fire from spreading."

Rafe looked out the window for a moment before returning his gaze to her. "Then I'll find a motel in town. I have a rental car parked outside the gate that I need to return. I figure there are enough vehicles around the ranch for me to use one of them while I'm here."

"Of course you can use one of the pickup trucks and there's no reason why you can't continue to stay here at the house. Dan isn't going to mind your using his room and you know it."

Rafe knew that he would get little rest staying in the same house with Mandy. He needed all the distance he could muster between them. However, his choices at the moment were limited. In his opinion, the ranch held the key to Dan's disappearance. It made more sense for him to stay put.

"What about Parker?" he finally asked. "He's not going to like us sleeping under the same roof."

"And whose fault is that? You certainly didn't put yourself out trying to get along with him."

"Yeah, I'm funny that way. Somebody slugs me from behind with no warning, I become very judgmental about his character."

"You know why he did that."

"I know why you think he did it, but I'm not buying his explanation. He could see I was making no effort to hide, for God's sake. I was no threat to any one. It's my guess he doesn't want anyone hanging around you. He might have figured that taking me out would discourage me from lingering for more than a brief visit."

"Will you please stop it! Tom isn't interested in me...*or* in acquiring this ranch through me. Really, Rafe. I don't remember you being so cynical."

"Right. I always waited around for the Easter bunny every spring." He walked out the door and let the screen slam behind him. He strode across the porch shaking his head at his juvenile behavior.

What did it matter to him what kind of relationship Mandy might have with the foreman of Dan's ranch, anyway? Maybe he was still reeling from too many hours of travel. Mandy had nothing to do with the reason he was here. He needed to remember that.

"You looking for something?"

He stopped in his tracks and slowly turned around. Parker stood a few feet away, his hands on his hips. Damned if he didn't look like a gunfighter waiting to draw on him.

"I left my bag out there," he said, nodding toward the thick foliage across from the house. "Thought I'd go pick it up. You got a problem with that?"

Parker ignored his question and asked one of his own. "How long you intending to stay?"

Rafe turned back and continued to walk toward the brush, forcing Parker to follow him if he intended to continue the conversation. "Until Dan shows up. Why?"

"Then you think he's still alive."

Rafe stopped. Why in hell was everyone so willing to think that Dan was dead. "Don't you?" he asked pointedly.

Parker shifted his feet, removed his hat, smoothed his hair, replaced his hat, then looked toward the rolling hills that surrounded them. "I don't know what to think," he finally admitted. "He's never just disappeared like this before. He'd know we'd be worried about him and would do everything in his power to let us know if he was all right. If he could. I think something's happened to him. I'm just not sure what. It's been too long now. Much too long."

"Tell me about the airstrip."

Parker looked at him, surprised by the shift in subject. "What about it?"

"Can you hear when a plane lands or takes off from the ranch buildings?"

"Sometimes. When the wind's right."

"Did you hear a plane the night Dan disappeared?"

"I don't remember."

"Mandy mentioned his Jeep being found down there. I figure that's how he left the place. Which reminds me, I need to turn in my rental car. Is there someone who can follow me into Austin?"

Parker took his own sweet time about answering. "I can send Carlos," he finally said.

Rafe nodded in acknowledgment of the foreman's reluctance to accommodate him in any way. "Thanks," he said wryly. Rafe pushed through the thick undergrowth and picked up his bag. When he came out, Parker was still standing there.

"You made my efforts at security look pretty bad, coming in like you did. How did you manage to do that?"

"I'm professionally trained to get in and out of places without anyone knowing about it, courtesy of the United States government. So don't feel too bad, okay? Unless enemy infiltrators decide to take over the country by starting with this ranch, your security is just fine."

He turned away and left Parker standing there, a frown seemingly etched permanently on the man's face.

Rafe figured it probably wouldn't hurt for him to brush up a little on his people skills now that he was back in the States. He could see that he certainly wasn't winning many points around here. Then again, he had no plans to teach any Dale Carnegie courses as a second career, either.

His immediate plans were to find out what had happened to Dan.

Mandy watched Rafe slam out of the house. What was she going to do if she wasn't able to better handle her reactions to him? It was obvious that he had no intention of leaving until the mystery of Dan's disappearance was solved.

She should be feeling relief that she could turn the matter over to someone as capable as Rafe appeared to be. There was nothing to be gained by her continuing to stay on at the ranch. Her life was in Dallas, after all. She could go home, return to her job and wait there for developments.

She had come to the ranch when Tom first notified her about Dan's disappearance, thinking it would help her peace of mind to be closer to where he had disappeared. She had thought that if and when Dan did show

up, he would return to the ranch. Unfortunately, now
that Rafe had arrived there was no more peace of mind
to be found.

This morning had certainly proven that. They
couldn't be in the same room without arguing. Which
was ridiculous. She generally got along with everyone,
but Rafe seemed to deliberately bait her with his caustic
remarks.

As if his attitude wasn't irritating enough, there had
been a moment there when she'd suddenly felt as
though he was about to kiss her. She'd looked up at
him and seen something in his eyes that had started her
heart racing. She must have imagined it, though. He'd
turned away as though nothing had happened.

Oh, but something *had* happened to her. She'd been
thrown back into all those confusing feelings she'd had
for Rafe McClain when she'd been a teenager.

Her thoughts drifted back to that time in her
life…when she had been fifteen and in love for the first
time.

After weeks of feverish anticipation, the night had
finally arrived for the big barbecue celebrating the high
school graduation of Dan and Rafe. Mandy could
scarcely contain herself. Her mother had allowed
Mandy to choose the dreamiest dress she'd ever owned
to wear to the party. She loved the soft pink color, but
more important to her was the fact that the neckline
barely hung on each shoulder, the sleeves puffing out
and thereby disguising her rather bony shoulders. The
dress accented her small waist, then flared in a full-
skirted way to her knees, with flouncing petticoats beneath it.

Mandy took a last look at herself in the mirror before

going outside. She no longer looked like a child. In this dress, she appeared to be a full-fledged woman— attractive, seductive and alluring. She leaned closer and slowly smiled at her reflection…and blinked…startled at the sensuality she portrayed. Wow, she scarcely knew herself.

She patted her hair, swept up in a coil with an ornamental comb, blew herself a kiss and strolled out of her room.

She paused once she reached the patio. There had never been a more beautiful Texas night, she decided. The stars looked as though they'd been freshly polished and hung, glittering on the black velvet backdrop of sky.

She breathed deeply and smiled. The giant barbecue smoker had been going long enough that the scent permeated the area.

A large dance floor had been laid down on the back lawn, surrounded by the live oak trees that shaded the house and surrounding area from the blazing Texas sun. Lines of Chinese lanterns stretched from tree to tree, casting colorful lights and adding a festive atmosphere.

People would soon be arriving, bringing casseroles, salads and desserts. Her mom and dad had been planning this party for weeks. Their friends, neighbors and all the members of the graduating class and their families were invited. Her dad was in charge of seeing there was enough barbecued brisket, ribs and chicken for everyone.

Mandy wondered if her folks would do this again in another two years when *she* graduated. If so, she hoped that Dan and Rafe would be there to help her celebrate.

Rafe had mentioned the possibility of his going into the military sometime this summer, but Dan wanted him to stay at the ranch and go to college. Dan had talked about possible scholarships that were available. Rafe would certainly qualify because his grades were excellent.

Mandy didn't want Rafe to leave. Her dad had promised her that as soon as she turned sixteen he would allow her to go on single dates. He was still living in the Stone Age, insisting that she could only go out with a group until that time, preferably one that included Dan. Neither she nor Dan liked that idea at all. But once she was sixteen, she hoped that Rafe would ask her out on a date.

Of course he had no idea how she felt about him. She'd made sure that no one did. If Dan got a hint that she had a crush on Rafe, he would never let her forget it. He'd taunt and embarrass her every chance he got.

People would be arriving any minute, but for now it was just her parents and the hands making sure there were enough tables, chairs and picnic tables outside for people to have a place to sit and eat.

Mandy wandered away from the lights so that she could enjoy the luminous heavens. She loved living on the ranch away from the city lights. It gave her a sense of belonging to the land that she had never felt whenever she visited anywhere else.

From her sheltered position, Mandy spotted Dan and Rafe when they came out of the house. They looked so grown up in their Western-styled summer suits. She'd never seen Rafe dressed so formally. He'd chosen a light beige, which set off his bronzed skin tones. Rafe and Dan were opposites in coloring, opposites in personality, but were as close as brothers, closer, even, because they never really quarreled.

Dan had been the team quarterback for the past two years. Because of the extra time it took for him to practice and play, Rafe had covered for him here at the ranch, doing the work they'd both been assigned without complaint.

Rafe showed no interest in sports. He'd always been a loner and seemed to prefer his own company even when he was on the ranch. He probably wouldn't have come to the party if her mother hadn't insisted that the party was for both of them.

A couple of hours later Mandy found herself on the dance floor, having the time of her life. It must be the dress. All of Dan's classmates seemed to suddenly discover her tonight and were giving her the rush.

She loved the attention. She hoped Rafe had noticed.

When she looked around for him, she saw him standing with her dad and some of his friends, listening to them talk. With newfound courage, Mandy walked up to him and in front of her dad and everyone else said, "When are you going to dance with me, Rafe?"

His ears reddened and one of the men chuckled, causing Rafe to stiffen slightly. "How about now?" he replied in a husky voice.

He held out his hand.

Mandy couldn't believe it. He was actually going to dance with her. She almost laughed out loud, but that wouldn't do. She smiled, the smile she'd been practicing in front of the mirror, and grasped his hand.

He felt warm, which wasn't surprising. Even though it was after ten o'clock, it was probably still eighty degrees outside. He looked as if he'd like nothing more than to remove his Western string tie, unbutton his collar and toss aside his jacket.

That was the first thing she asked him when they started to dance to the slow, melodious music from the tape deck that had been set up for the party.

"Why don't you get comfortable? It's too hot for a jacket."

He glanced around at the other males, young and old, dancing nearby. "I don't know. I guess I thought I was supposed to wear it all evening."

"Naw. Dan had his off fifteen minutes after the party started."

He smiled. "You look cool enough, like cotton candy."

"Yuck. That stuff is so sticky it gets all over you."

"I was thinking about your bared shoulders. That dress makes you look years older."

Ah, bless him. What a wonderful thing for her to hear. "Thank you." She took a breath, then blurted out, "I think you look very handsome in your suit, Rafe. I've never seen you in one before."

"That's for sure. And I doubt you'll ever see me in another one." He reached up and unbuttoned his collar. "I feel like I'm in a straitjacket."

"Then you sure don't want to go into the Army. They always have to dress up like that."

"Good point. Actually, it looks like I'm going to be staying here after all. After Dan nagged me into it, I applied to Southwest Texas State University in San Marcos earlier this spring. I didn't tell anyone because I wasn't sure if they'd take me or not. I just found out that I've been accepted. It's close enough that I could continue to work and live on the ranch. There are a couple of scholarships that are going to pay for books and tuition for the first semester. We'll see how I do after that, but at least it's a start."

"Oh, Rafe, that's wonderful. I'm so proud of you!"

His grin flashed in his dark face. He smiled so seldom that she felt a pleasurable rush to be able to witness it now. "Well, it's not exactly Harvard, but it's a fine school and I'm looking forward to it."

"I think Dan is so dumb, wanting to go to Harvard. He should be going to Texas A & M. After all, he's going to be running this ranch someday. He should be learning how to do that instead of taking some silly business courses."

"Dan knows what he wants. Besides, your dad has taught us both a great deal about ranching."

"So maybe you'll end up being the foreman here. Wouldn't that be neat?"

"No. After I get a little more education, I want to get out and see something of the world."

"Will you take me with you?" she asked, feeling oh, so daring.

He laughed and swung her around the dance floor. The first song had ended and another one immediately began. She sighed, and stepped in closer to him. When he finally answered her, she was disappointed to hear him say, "I don't think you'd want to travel the way I'm planning to go about it."

She tilted her head up slightly so that she could see his eyes. "Oh, really, and how's that?"

"I want to hop a freighter and work my passage. I want to visit different countries, learn new languages, get to know different people and their cultures."

"I could do that, too, you know."

"They don't let girls do that. It's too dangerous."

"Well, maybe so, but you would be there to protect me."

He hugged her to him. "You're so sweet. Has anyone ever told you that before?"

This close to him, she could feel his heart thudding in his chest, as though he'd been running. She liked being so close. It was as if their bodies had been designed to fit together. Rafe slid his hand down her spine to her waist, then took several fast, turning steps which she followed as though they'd been practicing together.

"You're a good dancer, Rafe," she whispered. "The best I've danced with tonight."

"Believe it or not, they made us learn in gym class during one of the semesters last year. I found out it was fun once you learned the steps."

"When I get older, will you take me dancing in Austin and places?"

"Sure. If I'm still around."

She rested her head on his shoulder and they continued to dance together as the evening wore on. People began to drift away as the evening grew later. She heard the sound of slamming car and truck doors, engines revving up, tires throwing gravel, but none of it could spoil the mood she and Rafe had found, dancing under the Texas stars on a summer night.

Eventually her mom called her to help with the cleanup. She and Rafe pitched in, gathering trash and carrying food to the house. By the time everything was put away in the kitchen and Mandy looked for Rafe again, he was nowhere to be found.

She didn't want the night to be over. There was magic in the air and she wanted to share it with someone special. She wanted to share it with Rafe.

Mandy checked inside the house first, just in case he was there with Dan. When she didn't find him, she decided to follow the dirt track to the cabin where he lived.

He had left without telling her good-night.

He'd left without giving her a good-night kiss.

She had known that he'd wanted to kiss her while

they were dancing. She also had known that he wouldn't attempt to do so in front of everyone.

How could she forget how he had looked at her, how he'd held her pressed against him, so that she felt his body as an extension of her own?

She arrived at the cabin breathless, not all of it caused by the fact that she had hurried. She knew her parents would not approve of her being there. Maybe it was wrong, but it felt right to her. There was no way she could go to bed now and expect to sleep—not without seeing Rafe first.

There was a light on inside. She smiled to herself. He was home. With more than a hint of bravado, she tapped on the door and waited expectantly.

There was a pause before she heard him say, "Who is it?"

"It's Mandy," she said, still trying to catch her breath.

In her nervousness, it seemed to take hours for him to open the door. When he did, she was surprised to see that not only had he removed his jacket and tie, but he'd also unbuttoned his shirt so that it hung open, revealing his bare chest. He stood there in the doorway barefoot, obviously getting ready for bed. At that moment Mandy knew he was the most gorgeous male creature she'd ever seen.

He stared at her in disbelief. "What are you doing here?"

"You disappeared without telling me good-night."

"Oh. Sorry. Good night." He started to close the door.

She quickly pushed it open and stepped inside. "And…I wanted to give you your graduation present from me."

He looked at her as though wondering if she'd slipped a mental cog or two. "You gave that to me this morning, Mandy. The wallet. Don't you remember?"

She smiled. "This one is a little more personal than that." She stepped closer to him and put her arms around his neck. Leaning into him, she said, "I wanted to give you a graduation kiss," she whispered, pressing her mouth against his.

His mouth felt warm and firm beneath hers. He'd caught his breath when she threw her arms around him. She wasn't sure whether out of shock or surprise. He put his hands on each side of her waist as though to push her away. But he didn't push her away at all. Instead Rafe began to kiss her back, slowly, sensuously, as though there was nothing else in his world but her, nothing else he needed to do but kiss and caress her.

All of her girlish dreams were coming true right then and there. She was finally in Rafe's arms, kissing him. What was even more wonderful to her way of thinking was that he was kissing her back.

He held her as he had during their dances, still swaying slightly. He nibbled on her ear and down her neck before returning to her lips. She could almost hear the music and feel the beat, although the strong, steady rhythm could be coming from her heart.

"Ah, Mandy, you rip me up inside," he whispered. "I want you so much and you're such an innocent. You're too young and I can't—" He groaned and kissed her again, holding her so tightly that she knew without a doubt exactly how strongly he wanted her. Instead of frightening her, the knowledge made her feel very adult. Her crush wasn't so absurd, not if her feelings were returned.

She slid her hands from around his neck and rubbed

them over his bare chest. He shivered without breaking the kiss. He coaxed her with his tongue to open her mouth and she felt as though he'd taken possession of her in the true sense of the word, the kiss being a silent vow each of them made. She belonged to him.

"Mandy!"

She jerked her head toward the open doorway. She had forgotten about the door when she came in. Now her father stood there staring at them, his rage growing.

Rafe dropped his arms and stepped away from her. She realized how this must look to her father, with Rafe half dressed. She was completely clothed, but that made no difference to her father. He must have decided that Rafe's state of undress showed his intentions.

"What the hell do you think you're doing!" her father bellowed at Rafe, storming into the small cabin.

Rafe never changed expression. He looked first at Mandy, then her father. Finally he said, "Kissing your daughter." He sounded quite calm, particularly when compared to her father, who was getting louder with each word.

"You keep your stinking hands off her, do you hear me? Is this the way you repay me for giving you a home, by seducing my daughter?"

Rafe gave her father a long, silent look before he said, "I was under the impression that I've earned everything I ever received on your ranch, Mr. Crenshaw."

"Well, if you think you've earned the right to paw my daughter, you're dead wrong. I gave you a chance to make something of yourself. That's what I gave you. You're damned lucky you haven't been living on the streets for the past four years." He looked at her. "Go home, Mandy. Your mother will want to talk to you."

Mandy knew that she had to explain, that she had to

tell her father the truth—Rafe had nothing to do with her being there. Only she'd never seen her father so angry before and she was frightened. In a panic she darted out of the cabin, hoping that once he calmed down she would be able to explain to her father that Rafe hadn't invited her to his cabin. That she had come on her own.

Her attempted explanations made no difference. Rafe left the ranch that night and she never heard from nor saw him again.

Until last night.

Five

Mandy walked outside and looked around. There was no sign of Rafe but Tom was over by one of the horse corrals. She walked over to him. "Did you happen to see where Rafe went?"

Tom resettled his hat on his head before he replied, "He and Carlos went into town."

"Oh, that's right. To return the car."

"Yeah." Tom leaned on the fence and looked at her. "How well do you know this guy, anyway?"

She bristled. "What do you mean?"

"You said he was a friend of the family, but I've never heard of him and I know everyone you call friend in these parts."

"He used to live on the ranch years ago, when we were in high school."

"What's he been doing since then?"

"I have no idea."

"Then why do you trust him?"

"Because Dan does. If Dan wrote him asking him to come back, that's good enough for me."

Suspicion was written all over Tom's face. "Did you see the letter?"

She smiled. "Do you really think Rafe would lie?"

"How the hell should I know!" he said, throwing up his hands. "That's why I'm asking you. For all I know, he may have had something to do with Dan's disappearance."

Mandy nodded. "You're right. You don't know Rafe at all." She leaned against the fence next to Tom. "Rafe's the reason I now work for Children's Services. Not that he knows that, or would care if he heard it. Looking back, I'd have to say that Rafe McClain influenced my life as much if not more than any other person did. I don't think I ever really saw that until right now." She glanced over at him. "Funny how much of what we do is unconscious, isn't it?"

Tom raised his brow. "How did he have any influence over your choice of a career?"

"He came from an abusive home and ran away when he was barely fourteen. Given the chance, he worked hard both here and at school to make something of himself. I decided that I wanted to help others who, like Rafe, weren't given an even start in life." She looked back at Tom. "I know if I told him he would not be impressed. He was quite something, even back then."

"Did a little hero worship maybe get mixed up in there somewhere?"

"More than a little. I wasn't aware he and Dan had stayed in touch all this time. Dan has never mentioned him to me. Not once in all these years. If asked, I would have said that I never expected to see him again." She brushed her hair off her forehead and sighed. "It was quite a shock to me for him to show up so unexpectedly in the middle of the night like that."

"It was a shock for both of us, let me tell you. I've been sleeping easy thinking this place was protected by tight security. It didn't help matters any for me to realize I'd been kidding myself. It bothers me to know you were up there at the house with so little protection."

"Don't worry. Ranger did fine last night. He would have stopped anyone from coming in if I hadn't reassured him that Rafe was a friend. He's a good deterrent to trouble. You've trained him well."

"Yeah, too bad Dan didn't have Ranger with him that night. Things might have worked out differently."

"Let's see what Rafe comes up with, Tom. I have a hunch that if anyone can find Dan, Rafe can."

Mandy returned to the house, poured herself a cup of coffee and sat down. Somehow she was going to have to come to terms with Rafe's return before she saw him again.

She found it difficult to believe that he had shown up so suddenly in her life. The shock of seeing him had thrown her into her past to one of the most painful times in her memory.

She'd been crying when she reached the house that night. Her mother waited just inside the kitchen.

"Sit down, Amanda," she'd said, causing Mandy to cry harder. "You were at Rafe's tonight, weren't you?"

Mandy nodded. Her mother handed her a box of tissues. "You know better than that."

"We weren't doing anything wrong, Mom. Honest. I just wanted to tell him good-night and to—well, to…" How could she tell her mother that she'd wanted to kiss

Rafe? Her mother was too old to understand how important Rafe was to her.

"You had no business going down there."

"And Daddy was saying su-such aw-awful things to him," she sobbed. "He was making it sound as though Rafe had done something wrong and he hasn't." Her anger began to assert itself. "He hadn't done anything. It was me who went down there…he didn't know I was going to do that."

"So you got him in trouble."

"Yes! And I didn't mean to. Now Daddy's mad at him and it's all my fa-fault." She buried her head in her arms resting on the table.

Her mother patted her shoulder. "Your father is very protective of his children. You know that. I'll talk to him when he gets back. I'm sure this will all blow over."

When Mandy discovered that Rafe had left, she was filled with guilt and shame. She'd knocked him out of a place to stay while he went to college. In the following weeks she asked Dan if he'd heard from Rafe, but he hadn't. She told him about Rafe's acceptance at the university and his need to stay on the ranch and work.

Dan had no sympathy with her. He gave her a chewing out for being so stupid and said she didn't deserve having Rafe for a friend. She wondered if Dan still felt that way. Was that why he'd never told her that he knew how to contact Rafe?

Just seeing him again brought back all her old feelings of guilt and shame. Seeing him again also forced her to look at why she had broken off her engagement, why she'd never allowed herself to become close to another man. Somewhere deep inside, she'd judged herself as undeserving of a relationship. Look what she'd

done to the first male she'd ever fallen in love with—
knocked him out of going to school, forced him to leave
the only stable home he'd had.

Mandy rubbed her forehead. She'd had no idea that
she had harbored those feelings for so many years. In-
tellectually she could shoot all kinds of holes in the
logic, but it wasn't her intellect that had made those
judgments. It was her emotions.

Without her being aware of it, she had given Rafe a
great deal of power over her since that night when she
was fifteen years old. Too much power. Yes, she had
been wrong to visit him and place him in the position
of having to defend her presence in his cabin. Yes, her
father had been wrong to believe that Rafe had lured
her down there for his own purposes.

Her mother had been quick to put him straight on
that one! By the next morning he had gone back to the
cabin to apologize for his knee-jerk reaction, but it had
been too late.

Rafe disappeared that night. He didn't go to San Marcos that fall. He made no effort to contact any of them,
or so she had thought. So he had made some choices
of his own. He could have gone to school. He could
have returned to the ranch and faced her father with the
truth of what happened once her father had calmed
down.

She sighed. She'd had enough on her mind worrying
about Dan. Now she was going to have to deal with
Rafe. She felt like being a coward and running back to
Dallas to wait for news of Dan.

Mandy reminded herself that she was no longer fifteen years old. She was an adult and would have to deal
with the situation she found herself in. However, she
didn't have to like it.

* * *

Rafe returned to the ranch mid-afternoon and went looking for Tom. Instead, he found Mandy.

"I was waiting for you," she said, when he found her in the barn. "I'll take you to the airstrip in the Jeep now, if you'd like."

"Where's Tom?"

In a flat tone Mandy replied, "After your warm and friendly treatment of him this morning, Tom had a tough time forcing himself to get on with the work he'd scheduled for today rather than wait for you to show up. I know he was looking forward to an afternoon of bonding with you, no doubt certain the two of you were going to end up being best friends."

He studied her for a couple of minutes in silence. "Funny, but I don't remember your being quite this sarcastic when you were growing up."

"I'm surprised you remember me at all," she said, glancing around the barn before meeting his eyes.

"Uh-huh." The look he gave her made her drop her gaze.

She knew her cheeks were turning red. "Let's go," she said, motioning to the Jeep. He walked over to the driver's side and crawled in. Why didn't it surprise her that he chose to drive? Rafe was definitely a man determined to be in control of his environment.

Mandy figured it was up to her to let him know he wasn't in charge of her. However, she intended to choose her battles, and driving the Jeep wasn't even a respectable skirmish.

She spoke only to give him directions. He didn't speak at all. Instead he studied the terrain around them as he drove. The path to the airstrip was well-worn, which surprised Mandy. She had no idea that Dan spent much time out here.

When they reached the area, Rafe pulled over and parked beneath the shade of one of the large trees that dotted the range. He turned off the engine but didn't move to get out. Mandy remained in the bucket seat beside him, listening to the ticking sounds made by the hot engine cooling off. She was determined to ignore the heat.

There was very little breeze moving across the land. The temperatures were flirting with the hundred-degree mark. Nothing was stirring. Besides the lack of shade, Mandy knew that Dan didn't allow any of the cattle loose in this pasture because of the airstrip.

"How long has this been here?" Rafe finally asked, breaking the somnolent silence between them.

"About four years, I think."

"Why?"

"Why did he build it? Originally it was because he intended to buy a plane. But when he and James looked into the upkeep of one, plus the need to build a hangar to protect it, they chose to rent whenever they needed one."

"I need to talk to this Williams guy to find out what he knows."

"Good luck. There's no doubt you'll have more luck than I did if he'll talk to you at all. He made light of all my questions."

All the while they spoke, Rafe surveyed the area. "I've never been to this part of the ranch before. As I recall, your dad didn't use it much."

"No. Dad never liked to run cattle in here because of the breaks and hollows in the land back over there."

She nodded with her chin. "They were too hard to get to if any of them wandered into those arroyos."

"This is where you found the Jeep?"

"According to Tom. He finally had one of the men bring it back to the ranch by the time I arrived. No reason to leave it sitting here."

"Unless Dan flew back in and needed a ride back to the ranch. He might not appreciate the long hike."

"It sat here for a week. Dan would have called by then."

"Maybe."

"You know where he is, don't you?"

He looked at her in surprise. "Of course not! Why would you say that?"

"You have a rather grim expression on your face."

He shifted in his seat and adjusted his hat. "I don't like what I see," he finally said.

"What is that?"

"We aren't more than a few hours flight time to the Mexican border. This is a hidden spot. Anyone could fly in, land, load or unload, and take off with no one being the wiser." He looked around. "Is there another way to get here besides the way we came?"

"No. Boulders and gullies surround this flat area on three sides. The only way to reach it on land is the way we came."

"That's good to know."

Mandy thought about what Rafe said. Finally she asked, "Do you think Dan was involved in some sort of smuggling?"

"I sure as hell hope not, but at this point, we can't rule out anything. You have to admit the set-up here would be tempting to anyone moving drugs, aliens, even arms across the border."

"Dan would never do that and you know it."

"People change, Mandy. Maybe the Dan I knew wouldn't consider getting involved in the smuggling business, but his disappearance casts some real doubts in my mind."

"What if this site was being used without Dan's knowledge? Maybe he stumbled across trespassers or contraband and they caught him?"

Rafe studied Mandy's expression. "Is that what you think happened...why you think he's dead?"

"Oh, Rafe, I've come up with all kinds of ideas about what might have happened. I always come back to the same thing—if Dan was alive, we would have heard from him by now."

Rafe took her hand and said, "I hope to God you're wrong, Mandy, but I promise you this. I'm going to find out what happened to him. When I discover whoever was responsible for his disappearance, they'll answer to me."

He reached over and turned on the key, starting the engine. "I'd like to have some idea of how widely known this place happens to be."

"Tom may be able to give you information on that. Or James."

He turned the Jeep around and headed toward the house. "Then I'll talk to both of them. First thing in the morning I'm going to be out here exploring those arroyos. All sorts of things could be hidden in there. In fact, I may plan to camp out here for a few days and see what I can find out."

"I'll come with you."

He smiled. "No, you won't. I can move around by myself and no one will know I'm out here. Two people, unless they're both highly trained, would give my presence away."

"I want to do something to help."

"Then help keep Tom and his men away from the area. I don't want some innocent bystander stumbling around down here. It wouldn't hurt to run a background check on the help, as well. It's possible that one or more of them aren't all that innocent."

"You think he was kidnapped?"

"It's a possibility."

"Wouldn't someone be asking for ransom?"

"Not if they're holding him to ensure his silence."

"Then wouldn't they just kill him and be done with it?"

When he didn't answer, she realized that she'd once again voiced her biggest fear. Rafe's silence indicated to her that he couldn't argue with her logic.

Rafe pulled the Jeep into the driveway. "Do me a favor," he said once they entered the house.

"What's that?"

"See if you can contact James Williams for me."

She glanced at her watch. "He should be at his office."

"Make certain. If he is, we'll go in to see him now."

She was put through immediately.

"How's my favorite female?" James said, when he answered.

Mandy made a face. "Hello, James. I was wondering if I could come into town to talk to you this afternoon, if you have time."

"Honey, I've always got time for you. You know that. How about dinner? I could have it catered at my place. Of course, if that makes you uncomfortable we could—"

"Uh, James. I have someone with me I want you to meet."

There was a pause. "Someone? As in a male someone? As in a special male?" Each question was delivered in a frostier voice.

She glanced at Rafe who couldn't hear James. Maybe this would be a very good way to discourage James without committing herself. "Rafe and I go back a long ways," she finally replied, allowing James to read whatever he wished into her statement. She watched as Rafe rubbed his knuckle across his lips, hiding a smile. He might find it amusing, but she disliked James's manner toward her.

"Maybe you'd better meet me here at the office."

"Fine. We'll be there within the hour." She hung up and waited for Rafe to comment on the conversation.

Instead he said, "Let's go before the traffic gets too bad."

They drove to Austin without speaking. Mandy realized that she was getting used to Rafe and his long silences. The boy she remembered had always been quiet, but back then she'd talked enough for three people. Now, she discovered she had very little to say to the man. If she was honest with herself, she was a little intimidated by his quiet air of competence. He was definitely a person who she would want to have on her side and not working against her.

Mandy directed him to the plant that Dan and James had started several years ago. As they turned into a circular driveway, Rafe saw a wooden sign framed by limestone. Deeply etched into the wood was the name of the company—DSC Corporation. The new building looked like what it was—a warehouse with offices in front. The landscaping had been chosen to withstand the hot Texas summers.

The parking lot for employees was filled with late-model automobiles. In short, the business gave off an aura of efficiency and success.

"What arrangements has Dan made for the business, in case something happens to one of the partners?"

She glanced at him in surprise. "I have no idea."

Rafe got out of the truck and came around to help her out. She was surprised at his courtesy, then ashamed of her reaction. Rafe had always been courteous to her and to her mother. It was just that his politeness toward them didn't fit his overall image.

Rafe could feel Mandy's nervousness. He couldn't figure out if she was uneasy around him or uncomfortable with the upcoming meeting. He saw no reason to question her. He wasn't certain that she was conscious of her behavior at the moment.

He offered her his hand to step down out of the truck. She took it willingly enough, but as soon as her feet were on the ground, she quickly stepped away from him.

He almost smiled. Her instincts were good; he'd give her that. If she had any idea how much he wanted to scoop her up in his arms and carry her off for a few days of intense lovemaking, she would be even more skittish than she was now.

How could he fault James Williams's reaction to her when his was just as strong? He deliberately placed his hand at the small of her back and guided her to the front door of Dan's business.

As soon as they stepped inside the refreshingly cool office, the receptionist smiled and said, "Good afternoon, Ms. Crenshaw. Mr. Williams is expecting you."

She eyed Rafe uncertainly. He smiled at her as reassuringly as possible and wondered why her face flushed in response. She smiled in return and ducked her head.

Rafe waited while Mandy tapped on the door. He heard a strong, masculine voice respond and Mandy opened the door and walked into the office. Rafe followed.

James Williams looked to be thirty or so, the same age as Rafe and Dan. Of medium height, he possessed a slender build and wore a suit obviously tailored to fit. Success radiated from the man.

"James, this is Rafe McClain. He, Dan and I grew up together." She turned to Rafe. "James Williams, Dan's partner."

James stood and walked around the desk. "I'm pleased to meet you, Rafe. Any friend of the Crenshaws is automatically a friend of mine." James had a narrow face, with a silver gaze that seemed to take in and process data with lightning speed. Rafe shook his hand, noticing the firm grip without responding to it.

Rafe acknowledged the greeting with a nod, allowing Mandy to control their side of the conversation. He watched James as he returned his attention to the woman. His smile became more intimate. James took Mandy's hand and said, "It's good to see you, Mandy."

She cleared her throat. "Rafe wants to talk to you about Dan's disappearance, James."

The smile faded. "I wish you wouldn't worry so, Mandy. Dan has taken these long trips out of town before. I've explained all of that."

Rafe spoke from behind them. "Then explain it to me, if you will."

James tensed at his tone. With a show of reluctance,

James stepped back from Mandy and said, "Why don't we all sit down if we're going to visit a while."

Visit, huh? Interesting take on their sudden appearance, Rafe decided. More polite than to call it an interrogation, perhaps. Rafe knew quite well that James didn't consider their showing up at his office a friendly get together.

The office wasn't large. Besides the desk and chair there were only two other padded chairs in the room. It wasn't difficult to decide who sat where.

Once ensconced behind the desk, James folded his hands and confided to Rafe with a man-to-man condescension that set Rafe's teeth on edge, "I've been doing my best to reassure Mandy that there is no reason in the world for her to be concerned about Dan. I'm sure that he will—"

"When's the last time you spoke with him?" Rafe asked bluntly.

James's head jerked as though he'd been physically struck. He cleared his throat before glancing down at his desk calendar. "I'm not really certain."

"Today, yesterday, last week, last month?"

James frowned. "Obviously it has been a week or more." He looked at Mandy. "When did you come down here?"

"I arrived ten days ago, three days after Dan turned up missing."

James shook his head in obvious concern. "I really do wish you'd stop referring to Dan as missing, Mandy. Just because we don't know where he is at the moment doesn't mean anything is wrong."

"Mandy tells me that you generally hear from Dan when he's traveling. Now you're saying you haven't heard from him. I have to agree with Mandy's take on this situation. From what I can gather, no one has heard from him. I consider that serious enough to start looking for answers.''

Mandy looked at Rafe. ''Not to mention that you received—'' Rafe gave a quick shake to his head causing Mandy to stop speaking.

James didn't miss the byplay. ''You received something?'' he asked. ''From Dan?''

Rafe smiled. ''Nothing recent, I assure you. Dan and I aren't the best of correspondents.'' He continued to lounge in his chair without taking his eyes off the other man. ''Do you have a calendar of his appointments?'' Rafe asked.

''I'm afraid not. He kept his calendar with him since he moved around so much. He made his own appointments. He really wasn't here in the office all that often. We communicated mostly by phone.''

''So you have no idea who he might be seeing if, as you say, he's on an extended business trip.''

''That's right. We each have our own area of the business for which we're responsible, which seldom overlaps. It's a good working relationship.''

''Had he leased a plane?''

''No. I would have had to okay an expense of that nature.'' He smiled. ''It's a checks-and-balances sort of thing, you understand.''

''Then how do you suppose he left the ranch, if not by plane?''

''Oh, he probably did leave by plane, just not one that we leased. One of our clients probably picked him up there. It wouldn't be the first time.''

''Do you ever have supplies shipped for the factory via the ranch?''

James paused just a little too long in Rafe's estimation before answering. "Sometimes. Not often."

"Does anyone else use the airstrip?"

"Not that I'm aware. Of course, I have no way of knowing."

Rafe continued to watch James. The man was one cool customer. He could see what Mandy was talking about. He was being a little patronizing, which always put Rafe's teeth on edge. "I think that's all my questions for now," Rafe finally said. "If I have any more, I'll give you a call."

James eyebrows went up. "Then you're going to investigate this so-called disappearance?"

"Yes, I am." He chose not to reveal anything more. He didn't like this man's attitude. It was too cavalier, considering he hadn't seen or spoken to his business partner in some time, had no idea where he might be and showed little interest in finding out. He also conveyed annoyance that someone else was going to investigate. On a hunch, he said, "Would you show us Dan's office? I assume he has one."

James shoved his chair back and stood, a picture of impatience and irritation. "I suppose. But whatever it is you expect to find there, I'm afraid you're going to be disappointed. As I said, he was seldom in the office."

He walked over to another door, not the one they had entered, and opened it. Waving his hand with a flourish, he said, "There you are. Look all you want." He glanced at his watch. "If you'll excuse me, I need to get back to work."

Rafe stepped back and allowed Mandy to walk into the room before he followed and closed the connecting door. The office had an unused air about it, which wasn't surprising. It was clean and uncluttered, with the usual desk items neatly aligned in front of the large, comfortable-looking chair. Rafe went over and sat down. It was every bit as comfortable as it appeared. He leaned back and put his hands behind his head. "Nice. Dan certainly believes in his comforts."

Mandy sat down in one of the visitor chairs. "Yes." She smiled. "He was so proud of setting up his own office and being in business for himself."

A quick glance around the walls revealed Dan's academic credentials. He'd graduated from Harvard with honors and picked up a master's degree in business, as well. Good for him.

Rafe checked the drawers and was surprised to see they weren't locked. He found some files with lists of businesses, no doubt customers or potential customers.

There was no calendar of appointments, no diary of events, nothing that would give him a clue to Dan's whereabouts. Everything he found was typical…except for the newspaper jammed in the back of the file drawer. He pulled it out. It was the Austin daily paper, the first two sections, which included national and local news. Rafe glanced at the date. June 29, two days before the date Dan had spoken to Tom.

He stood and held out his hand to Mandy. "Let's go." He took the paper with him. Dan might have stored it away because he hadn't finished reading it. However, there was a slight chance that there was something he might have wanted to save. Rafe would go over it once they returned to the ranch.

Rafe walked around the desk, took Mandy's hand, and they returned to the reception area. He nodded to the eagerly smiling receptionist, who fervently wished them a nice evening. Rafe made a mental note to return to Dan's office to speak to some of the employees when James wasn't there. He had a hunch they might be more cooperative than James had been.

"Not much there," Mandy said, once they left the building.

"I'm not so sure," Rafe replied. "Sometimes you learn more from someone by what he's not saying." They walked to the truck. Rafe unlocked it and helped Mandy inside. Once he joined her and turned on the engine to get the air conditioner to cool the hot cab. "Personally, I think he's lying."

"About what?"

"I'd be willing to bet a bundle he either knows where Dan is, or knows why Dan disappeared. In fact, I have a strong hunch he's actually behind Dan's disappearance."

Six

Heavy traffic surrounded them once they returned to the thoroughfare that led out of town. After waiting in a long line through two signal light sequences without reaching the intersection, Rafe said, "Let's grab a bite to eat and wait for the traffic to thin out. I can't believe this congestion."

Mandy glanced around, only now becoming aware of her surroundings. Her mind had been replaying Rafe's remarks, wondering if James was trying to hide something. "Austin's been growing while you were away. Unfortunately the highways haven't kept up."

He pulled into a restaurant on South Lamar Street and waited until they were inside, seated, and had given their orders before he said, "I'm beginning to get a bad feeling about this. It isn't natural that James isn't worried about Dan, unless he knows where he is. There's no reason to keep his whereabouts a secret unless they're involved in something illegal. If so, I wish I knew what.''

"You mean because of the airstrip?''

"And James's attitude.''

"Then do you think the ranch is being used for some kind of smuggling?''

"The little I've learned is pointing in that direction.''

"What do you think is being smuggled? Aliens? Drugs?''

He rubbed his forehead and sighed. "It might make it easier if I had a clue.''

Now that she was facing him, Mandy studied Rafe, adjusting to the man he had become. He looked tired. Was it any wonder? He'd flown in from Eastern Europe late last night. Even with several hours' sleep, his body must still be complaining, but he hadn't stopped all day. She watched him pick up his glass of water and drink. She had a sudden urge to stroke his jaw and attempt to ease his weariness. All her lectures to herself dissipated when she was in his presence.

There had always been something about him that drew her. She would be lying to herself if she pretended that magnetic force wasn't still working.

"It's tough, coming back after all these years, isn't it?'' she asked.

He set the glass down with a careful movement. She knew Rafe never liked talking about himself. He may have changed over the years since she'd last seen him, but the boy she remembered was very much present in the man across from her.

"Yeah,'' he finally said, admitting what they both knew.

Mandy wanted so much to break through the shell in which he encased himself. Even Dan, admittedly his best and perhaps only friend, had never been able to draw Rafe out. Well, she was going to give it her best shot. For some reason she couldn't quite explain even to herself, Mandy sensed that Rafe was feeling his isolation today in ways he'd never faced before.

"I have a hunch it was no accident that you stayed away from this part of the country," she said, offering him an opening to discuss his feelings.

The waiter arrived with their iced tea and salads. When he left, Rafe picked up his iced tea. He paused with the glass halfway to his mouth and said, "I had no intention of ever coming back to Texas when I left here."

There it was, what had been between them—unspoken—since he had arrived.

Mandy leaned toward him. With an intensity that made her voice quiver slightly, she said, "If I could redo what I did that night, Rafe, I would. Please believe that, if nothing else. What happened was all my fault. I've lived with that guilt. I was so ashamed of the way my father behaved, the way he automatically blamed you, the way he treated you."

He shrugged. "Don't be." He picked up his fork and began to rearrange his salad. "If I had been in his shoes, I would have done the same thing. You were an innocent young girl and you had no business being with me that night."

"But it wasn't your fault I was."

"You think not? You think I didn't know what I was doing when I danced with you, encouraged you? I wanted you that night, Mandy, don't ever doubt it. I knew how I felt was wrong, but when you showed up at my door, I didn't turn you away. I didn't stop the kiss. If your father hadn't shown up when he did, I can't say, even now, that I would have stopped in time. Your father could see how close to being out of control I was. He was right. That was a lousy way to repay his hospitality and he had every right to kick my ass off the property. I deserved it.''

She couldn't believe what she was hearing…what he was admitting. Her body responded to his words as though he'd caressed her. "I always thought it was me," she whispered, her heart racing, "imagining things that night about how you felt."

He shook his head, frowning at her words. "It wasn't your imagination. I'd been aware of you for a long time. I kept telling myself to ignore you, that you were just a kid. I made myself adopt Dan's attitude toward you and treated you like a sister. But I couldn't carry it off that night. You looked so grown up and you felt so good in my arms. I lost my head."

"Thank you for telling me this, Rafe. That scene has haunted me for years."

"Be glad your dad came looking for you when he did. He did the right thing."

She propped her chin on her hand. "I tried to explain to him the next morning what really had happened, you know, but by then you'd already left. I guess my mother was the one who thought I might have gotten carried away that night, watching us dance, and sent him to look for me. I heard her talking to my dad the next day, after he'd calmed down. She was taking up for you, talking about hormones and youth and reminding him of when he was that age." She smiled. "That's probably why he reacted so strongly. He'd been that age once, himself."

They ate their salads in silence before Rafe said, "I got over all of that a long time ago, Mandy. Things worked out the way they needed to for both of us. You hung on to your innocence a while longer and I didn't have to live with the burden of being the man who took it from you. I got on with my life."

"But you didn't go on to college, did you?"

He suddenly became engrossed in setting his empty plate aside and she thought he wasn't going to answer her. He took a breadstick from the basket and broke it in two before he said, "No, I didn't go to college. Under the circumstances, I thought it better to leave the area."

"So I knocked you out of your education, as well," she said with self-disgust.

He shook his head. "Don't take all the credit. Remember that I was going to try it. I might have dropped out after the first semester, anyway. I was rarin' to see the world back then. Too impatient to wait."

"Did you hop an ocean freighter?"

He looked at her in surprise. "You still remember that?"

He really didn't have a clue. For some reason she felt it was important that he know the truth about her feelings. It was the very least that she owed him, as far as she was concerned. "I have never forgotten anything about that night, Rafe. There were times when I fell asleep remembering each dance, the song that was playing, what we said, the way you looked, the way I felt. I would lie there wondering where you were, what you were doing, and if you ever thought about me."

He swallowed, then looked around as though hoping their food would arrive to distract her and the present topic of conversation.

"Where did you go after you left the ranch?" she asked when it was obvious he wasn't going to respond to her admittedly provocative statement.

"I walked to Austin. I tried to catch a ride at first, but no one was going to stop and pick up a hitchhiker at that time of night."

"Oh, Rafe. That was much too far to walk."

"I didn't have anything better to do at the time. It took a couple of days. I found a barn to sleep in. I could have gotten a ride the next day, but I needed the time to rethink my plans."

"What did you end up doing?"

"I joined the Army. I needed the security afforded me in the service. I ended up writing Dan when I was in basic training and he answered. He left for college right after that, so we kept in touch."

"Did you like the Army?"

"Like it?" He considered. "It made a man of me. I went into Special Forces. You grow up quick. Actually I managed to get several college credits while I was in the military. I did all right."

"And you were good at what you did."

He gave her a level look. "Yes."

Their orders appeared and Rafe looked relieved. They ate with little conversation. Over coffee and dessert, he asked, "So what do you do in Dallas?"

"I work with Children's Services. I'm a licensed psychologist and I do evaluations on children and their living conditions. Suggest changes in their environment if I feel a child would be better served. It's no longer automatically assumed that a child is better off with his or her parents."

Rafe thought back over his childhood. He wondered if his mother and two sisters were still alive, or whether his father had succeeded in destroying them as he'd tried so hard to destroy him. Rafe had made no effort to contact any of them once he was safely away. He wondered if any of his family still lived in the East Texas area he had left at fourteen. Maybe he'd check into it while he was in the state, just for the hell of it.

"What are you thinking?" she asked.

"Nothing worth repeating." He reached for his wallet and picked up the ticket. "Ready to go?"

Once back in the truck, they followed highway 290 west out of town.

"Are you still with the Army?" Mandy asked after a few miles.

"No."

"You said last night you were a consultant."

"Uh-huh."

"What kind?"

"I teach people how to stay alive in less than hospitable surroundings."

"You learned that in the military?"

"Oh, yeah."

"You like what you do?"

"Well enough. As you suggested, I'm good at what I do."

"Have you ever thought about moving back to the States?"

He glanced at her and smiled. "There's no real demand for my kind of work in the States, Miss Mandy."

"Which means no."

"Pretty much. Yeah."

She sighed. Well, at least she knew Rafe's intentions. He would do what he could to find out what had happened to Dan and then he would disappear once again. That shouldn't surprise her.

The sun was setting when they pulled up in front of the ranch house. Mandy got out of the truck and waited while Rafe parked in the long storage shed near the barn. She watched him as he stepped down from the truck, pocketed the keys and then leisurely walked toward her.

She could feel her heart thumping in her chest, her pulse singing and a tingle of anticipation and expectancy flood her system. Once he joined her at the gate to the inner yard, they strolled up the walkway together.

Ranger came tearing around the corner to greet them, his tail wildly lashing. Rafe knelt and loved on him, murmuring something to him that Ranger seemed to enjoy. Mandy had a hunch Tom may have lost Ranger's loyalty for the length of Rafe's stay.

Once inside, Rafe said, ''I think I'll go take a shower. Maybe I'll be able to cool off. Guess I haven't adjusted to the humidity as yet.''

Mandy nodded, unable to say a word. Her feelings for this man were tumbling out from wherever she had stored them years ago. She felt inundated with emotion. Rafe was back, was all she could think. He was back temporarily, but he was here now. The question was, what did she intend to do about it?

Mandy wandered restlessly through the house, trying to deal with her tumultuous feelings. Having Rafe back in her life, even temporarily, was a turning point for her. Being able to talk about what had happened twelve years ago had given her the opportunity to release all those pent-up emotions that had kept her so locked up inside.

The question was, what could she do about it?

Mandy walked outside and sat down on the front steps. Ranger trotted up and stretched out beside her.

She had been in such turmoil these past few days that she needed some time to think about what was happening. Her safe little world had dissolved so that nothing seemed real anymore.

Dan was gone. That thought was always there, lurking. What was she going to do without Dan in her life? She didn't care if he'd done something wrong, if he was in trouble. What she wanted to know was that he was alive. Everything after that could be dealt with.

Now Rafe had suddenly appeared in her life again and their talk today had cleared away so much of the baggage that she had carried for years. She felt lighter, freer, more willing to let go of all her old perceptions.

Outside of Dan, Rafe was the most important person in her life. She knew he was scarred in many ways because of his childhood. She had worked with many children from similar backgrounds, children who had shut off their emotions rather than take a chance on being hurt again.

She probably understood Rafe better now than he understood himself. She could keep her distance and allow him to do whatever he could do to locate Dan. Sooner or later he would leave.

Unless…

What if she could show him another way to deal with his feelings rather than to keep them locked away? What if she could show him how deeply she felt for him, how strong her love and support could be? Would it make a difference to him? Would he be willing to open himself up to a relationship with her?

She shivered at the thought. He had admitted to feelings that he'd had twelve years ago. That was a start. Loving Rafe would be the biggest risk she'd ever taken in her life. He was no longer a vulnerable child, but a man who'd grown tougher as he'd gotten older, who knew no other life than one of being alone.

Did she have the nerve to confront him with her own feelings, to take the chance of making her hopes and dreams a reality? Because if she didn't, she knew that he would continue to keep his distance and disappear from her life once more.

She'd been given a second chance with this man. At a time when she was grieving for the possible loss of her brother, she was also faced with the almost certain loss of the man who had haunted her for years.

What did she have to lose—besides her dignity, pride and self-esteem? Was it worth the risk in hopes of gaining so much more if she could finally open Rafe up to the possibility of sharing her life, of forming a bond with her that might eventually become the basis of a family?

She could play it safe, of course, and keep her feelings to herself. She could play it safe and live with the knowledge for the rest of her life that she'd been too afraid of being embarrassed and possibly humiliated to find out if the boy she fell for all those years ago still existed within the hard shell of the man he was today.

Whatever she decided, she knew she had very little time and absolutely no idea how to go about implementing such a plan. She stroked Ranger's head and watched the sun set while she considered her options.

Rafe stood under the cool spray of water, willing his body to relax and calm down. The last thing he'd needed to hear today was that Mandy had spent any of her time during the past several years thinking of him. The thought scared the hell out of him, even if he wasn't certain why it should. There was nothing between them now. There was no reason to think anything would change during the time he was here.

At least she appeared to be more relaxed with him as the day wore on. In fact, she'd gotten downright chatty at the restaurant. She'd reminded him of the Mandy he used to know. He just wished she had chosen to discuss anything other than the last night he'd spent on the ranch.

Sure he'd been incensed by her father's attitude toward him, treating him like some kind of white trash, throwing it up to him that he wouldn't have had a place to live without his charity.

Rafe had been so angry that he'd been glad to throw everything he owned into a backpack and leave the ranch. He hadn't wanted to stick around if that was the way the old man had felt about him.

But it had hurt because Rafe had always respected the elder Crenshaw, thought him a fair man and looked up to him. Rafe had known that Mandy's father never would have struck him, regardless of how angry he was. Mr. Crenshaw had been the first man he'd ever trusted. It had shattered him to realize that the man may have been right about him. He might have seduced Amanda if her father hadn't shown up. What kind of scum did that make him?

He'd known that there was no way that he could face any of them after that. So he had left, determined never to look back. He set out to prove to himself, at least, that he wasn't a worthless piece of trash and that he could amount to something.

Writing to Dan had been against all his strongly held beliefs that he needed to forget the Crenshaws. The thing was, basic training had been hard, even tougher than he had imagined. Plus, he'd been homesick, which was a laugh. He hadn't had a home to miss, but it didn't seem to matter.

He'd addressed the letter to Dan because he was sure that Mandy wouldn't want anything more to do with him and he suspected her mom was just as angry as her dad. But Dan had always been there for him.

He still remembered the day Dan's letter arrived. It was the first time his name had been mentioned at mail call. He'd stared at the envelope with the cramped handwriting that was typically Dan and fought the tears.

Dan had remembered him. He'd written him.

Rafe carried the letter with him all that day. He waited until just before lights out to open it. Again, in typical Dan fashion, the letter was short and to the point. He chewed Rafe out for leaving, no matter what his dad might have said to him in anger. He reminded him that he'd just blown his education by taking off in a huff, and that he sure must like the idea of a uniform to have gone into the Army so fast.

He'd also told him to stay in touch and that as soon as Dan got to Harvard, he'd send Rafe his address.

There were times in the twelve years since then when Rafe had been ready to give up, times when the life he had chosen had seemed so godforsaken that he could think of no good reason why he should hang on. Then the memory of Dan would pop into his head and he could practically hear Dan yelling at him, poking at him, forcing him to keep going.

"I hope you can hear me, Dan, wherever you are," he muttered. "Whatever hole you've dug for yourself, don't give up, okay? Hang in there. I'm going to find you—some way, somehow."

Rafe dried off and tied the towel around his waist. He was too tired to do any more investigating today. Maybe he'd read that paper he'd brought from Dan's office. See if he could figure out why Dan saved it. He'd tossed it on the kitchen table when they'd gotten back from town. He would pull on his jeans and go get it.

He opened the bathroom door and stepped into Dan's bedroom…then stopped in his tracks. Mandy sat on the side of the bed, obviously waiting for him.

"Mandy?" he managed to say, sounding strangled. "What are you doing in here?"

Her flushed face seemed to grow even pinker with his question. She stood and he noticed that she had a death grip on the bedpost. She started to speak, swallowed, then tried again.

"Rafe, I—um—I'm no longer fifteen," she managed to say before running out of breath.

Her nervousness calmed him down, but her presence in his room totally destroyed the effort he'd made in the shower to convince his body she was off limits. He grabbed his towel as it threatened to slide off his rapidly changing body.

"I am very much aware of that," he said grimly, gripping his towel.

"I guess I've still not learned not to come to your room and throw myself at you."

"Is that what you're doing?" He sounded hoarse.

She nodded. "I want to make love with you. I want to erase what happened before and replace it with new memories. Is that asking too much of you?" Her voice faltered at the end so that he barely heard her.

Dear God, this was like one of the medicated, fevered fantasy dreams he'd had while recuperating from one of his numerous wounds—Mandy, offering herself to him. In his dreams, he'd never questioned the opportunity presented. He'd eagerly accepted her offer.

"I don't think that's a very good idea, Mandy. I—"

He wasn't certain what he'd intended to say. The

thought was wiped out of his mind when she let go of the bedpost and removed first her blouse, then her bra, her cheeks glowing with color.

He moved toward her as though magnetized by her presence. Her gaze locked with his and she stood there, waiting to see what he would do.

Never had he fought so hard to resist anything in his life. Hadn't he managed to prove to himself over the years that he had an infinite supply of self-control? But nothing had tempted him the way Mandy could. And like the boy he'd been, he still couldn't keep his hands off her.

He lifted his hand and brushed it against her cheek. "Aw, Mandy, you're so sweet." He saw that her gaze had dropped to the towel that could no longer disguise his reaction to her. She smiled and stepped closer, pressing her bare breasts against his chest and kissing him with an eager innocence that belied her twenty-seven years.

She'd certainly been right. She was no longer fifteen years old. Her kiss had steam coming out of his ears. He wrapped his arms around her, allowing the towel to fall to the floor.

Mandy sighed, her breath whispering over his lips. She placed her hands on his chest and lovingly smoothed them across the surface, allowing gravity to take over until her hands rested on his erection. She stroked him, her fingers barely touching the surface.

Rafe no longer remembered why it wasn't a good idea for him to make love to Mandy. All he knew was that if he didn't hang on to some semblance of control, he was going to explode right now.

He forced himself to step away from her, but he couldn't resist cupping his hands beneath her beautiful breasts and caressing them. Her whimper almost destroyed him.

He reached for her jeans with shaking hands and unfastened them, shoving them down her legs before he lifted her and placed her on the bed. She watched him, her eyes glistening as he pulled them the rest of the way off before he stretched out beside her.

"It's been too long for me," he said gruffly. "I can't hang on much longer."

She reached for him and pulled him over her. "It doesn't matter, Rafe. Just love me."

"This is what I used to dream about," he murmured, running his hand along a line from her throat to the top of her thighs. "You, lying in my bed, wearing nothing but your beautiful smile." He shifted so that he was touching her and paused only long enough to be sure she was ready for him before he claimed her. He was thankful she was ready because he couldn't wait.

In an embarrassingly short time, he collapsed against her, almost sobbing in an effort to get air in his lungs. She clung to him, stroking his back and whispering soothing words to him.

With a groan he pulled himself away from her and stretched out on the bed beside her, his eyes closed, his humiliation complete.

Well, so much for that, he thought irritably. *I might as well be a teenage boy for all the finesse I showed. Hell, I wasn't able to give her any pleasure at all.*

"I'm sorry," he finally managed to say when he was able to talk.

"Don't be," she replied. He opened his eyes. She was propped up on her elbow looking down at him. "We have all night, you know. There's nobody around to interrupt us,'' she added, with a shy but mischievous smile.

''Aw, Mandy, what am I going to do with you?'' he whispered, his chest aching with more feeling than he could possibly express.

''Love me?'' she suggested.

He didn't know about love. It wasn't part of his world. But he could be gentle with her. He could help her find some of the pleasure that his uncontrolled efforts just now had deprived her of. She didn't appear to be upset, not if that smile was any indication. He shifted so that he was facing her and felt himself beginning to relax.

''Let me look at you,'' she said, leaning over him. ''Let me feed all my girlish imaginings with real data.'' She ran her palms along his jaw, leaning down to kiss him before beginning her voyage of discovery.

During her exploration, she somehow found each and every nick in his hide and demanded to know what had caused them. He answered her by wrapping his arms around her and rolling her beneath him. Her touch had aroused him so quickly he was astounded. He couldn't seem to get enough of her.

She curled around him, her arms and legs holding him firmly against her. He traced kisses across her throat and down to her breasts, then caressed the tips with his tongue, toying with them until they became hard nubs of sensitive flesh.

By the time he joined them again, she was quivering, her breathing ragged. He moved slowly, watching her, waiting. He needed her to enjoy this. He continued exploring her body with his mouth, keeping his rhythm slow and easy. He leaned closer and kissed her, his tongue delving into her mouth with the same rhythm as his hips. His movement picked up in intensity and yet, she seemed to be resisting what she was feeling.

"Let go, Mandy, just…let go for me," he whispered. His control was gone. Again. Damn. With a sense of frustration he allowed his body to take over, moving faster, harder, mindlessly striving for completion.

Then he felt her convulse from deep inside and he breathed his thanks. Her inner muscles contracted and she let out a high moan, clutching his shoulders with a steel grip. He was right there with her each and every step of the way, making one final lunge that drew everything out of him—his heart, his spirit, his very life force—and passed them to her.

Rafe managed to hang onto enough awareness to roll to her side before he let go and sank into the bed's welcoming softness. He gathered her into his arms and held her close as he drifted into peaceful oblivion.

He was aroused sometime later by movement. He fought off the fog of near unconsciousness long enough to remember where he was. "What is it?" he mumbled.

"I'm cold," she whispered. "I was trying to get some of the covers out from under us."

They had fallen asleep without pulling the sheet and spread down. He rolled and lifted off the bed. As soon as he moved the covers, he stretched back on the bed.

"Come here," he murmured, holding out his arm where she'd been sleeping.

"You'll probably sleep better if I go back to my bed."

"Don't you dare," he replied gruffly.

She slipped under the covers and plastered herself along his side.

"Still cold?" he asked.

"Not now."

"Me, either." He was also awake enough to know that he wasn't going to waste having Mandy in bed with him by sleeping through it.

Whether it was the late hour when the night is hushed and time seems to stand still, or whether the first rush of sexual need finally had been met, this time Rafe took his time loving Mandy. He lazily explored every inch of her body, kissing and caressing her until she was sobbing with the need for completion. She stirred restlessly, her legs shifting whenever he touched her. She lifted her hips to him in a silent plea.

When he finally entered her, he moved swiftly. He'd teased them both almost past bearing. Now they rode together for the finish, both crying out when they reached that particular peak, holding on to each other as though fearful of being torn apart.

They lay there in the darkness, still entwined, while they slowly regained their breath. Rafe had no idea of the time, but he didn't care. He hadn't planned to return to the airstrip until daylight. He had time to lie there and savor the experience of having Mandy in his arms.

"Rafe?"

"Hmm."

"Tell me something."

He released a contented sigh. "What do you want me to tell you?"

"About your parents."

He lay there staring into the blackness. "My parents? What about them?"

"I want to know about you. You never talked about them in all the years you lived here. Would you tell me about them now?"

"What do you want to know?"

"Mmm…names? Where they're from? How they met? Those kinds of things."

He was too relaxed to get uptight thinking about his parents. Nothing could touch the cocoon of contentment he was presently enjoying.

"My father's name is Luke McClain. My mother is Maria Teresa Salinas. My dad was in the military and stationed in South Texas when they first met. Mom was seventeen."

When he didn't say anything else, she prompted him. "They met, they fell in love, they got married. Right?"

"I don't know about the falling in love part. Mom got pregnant. Her father was ready to kill somebody from what I understand, so my father married her."

"You were born then?"

"No. She gave birth to a boy. He died when he was two."

"Oh. Do you have any other brothers or sisters?"

"Two sisters."

"You are their only son."

"Yes."

"What is your full name?"

"Raphael Lucas McClain."

"Raphael. Like the angel."

"Yeah. People get confused about that all the time."

She chuckled, then nipped his shoulder with her teeth.

"Ouch!"

"What does your dad do?"

"Besides drink? He always worked in construction, but had trouble holding a job. He was good with his hands…when he was sober. Actually he was good with them when he was drunk, too. I learned to stay out of his reach about the time I learned to walk."

"When did you move to this part of the country?"

"I was eight and in the third grade. That's when I met Dan. We were in the sixth grade when my dad took a job in East Texas. We moved around a lot when I was growing up, but I really enjoyed living in this area. That's why I decided to come back here when I left East Texas."

"What did your mother say when you left?"

"I don't know. I just got tired of my dad knocking me around. I left in the middle of the night and never went back."

"Just like when you left here."

He was silent. "Yeah, pretty much," he finally said.

"I want you to tell me goodbye when you leave this time, Rafe. Don't leave in the middle of the night. Promise me that."

"Why? What difference does it make? I'm still leaving."

"Yes, I know. But I want to be able to tell you goodbye."

He turned to her. "I'm not leaving just yet, though," he said, nuzzling her ear and stroking her breast.

"I know," she replied, her lips searching blindly for his.

He hadn't promised her he wouldn't leave without telling her goodbye, but she had given him some things to think about…when he was in the mood to think.

Seven

The sound of steady knocking on a door somewhere finally roused Rafe. He rolled over and discovered Mandy throwing the covers back and getting out of bed, muttering something under her breath.

"Who is it?" he mumbled.

She glanced over her shoulder, then shrugged her shoulders and headed out of the room, saying, "Tom, probably."

"I hope to hell you don't intend to answer the door that way!" he growled, sitting up in bed. She had on as much clothing as he did. Zip. He heard her closet door slam and he grinned. She'd at least stopped for a robe.

He yawned, wondering what time it was. Didn't look as if the sun had been up long. He'd taken off his watch before his shower last night and had been too distracted to put it back on.

What had taken place last night wasn't at all smart on his part. As he recalled, he had made some sort of heroic effort to say no, but he'd been lying and he knew it at the time.

Now he was faced with the consequences, and he knew they would have lasting repercussions—on his peace of mind if no other way. He hadn't asked her about birth control, an oversight he'd never been guilty of before. His brain had rolled over and played dead from the moment he stepped out of the bathroom and found her in the bedroom. His body and emotions had taken over from there.

So what did he intend to do about the possibility of a pregnancy? He groaned at the thought of creating a similar situation to the one his dad had created thirty-five years ago. He wondered if we're destined as human beings to repeat the sins of our fathers down through the ages.

Rafe decided on a quick shower. If that was Tom, he needed to talk to him about his plans to go out to the airstrip and look around the area, possibly stay out a night or two. After what had happened last night, the safest thing he could do for everyone involved would be to stay away from the ranch house.

It would also be the hardest thing for him to do. He didn't have much faith in his willpower or self-control after last night.

Mandy was still tying the sash to her robe when she reached the back door and saw Tom through the glass. She threw open the door and said, "Mornin', Tom. Come on in."

She turned away and went over to start the coffee.

She heard Tom enter the room behind her and close the door.

"I was worried about you, Mandy. You didn't have Ranger in the house last night. I was surprised to find him sleeping on my porch when I left my place this morning."

She continued to gather the necessary items for coffee without turning around. "I guess I should have mentioned it to you, but I figured he would be a better watch dog outside and I feel safe enough with Rafe sleeping here."

"Ah."

Mandy turned around and saw that he was standing in the middle of the large room, watching her. "Sit down, Tom, and have some coffee."

Reluctantly he moved over to the table and sat down. "Sorry about waking you up," he finally said when she made no effort to speak.

"No problem. It was time for me to be up, anyway." She was uncomfortably aware that she had on nothing beneath the thin cotton material of her robe. She set out three cups, then said, "I'll be right back. Help yourself to the coffee."

She hurried down the hall in time to hear the water cut off from Dan's bathroom. Good. There would be some water pressure. She quickly went into the hall bathroom and started the water, took a quick shower, dried and threw on her robe once again before dashing across the hall to find some clothes to put on. By the time she was dressed and headed back to the kitchen she heard the rumble of deep male voices.

Both men were seated at the table with a steaming cup in front of each of them. Rafe was telling Tom his plan to scrutinize the area around the landing strip when she walked in.

He interrupted himself and said with a smile. "Good morning, Mandy. Hope you slept well last night."

"Just fine," she muttered without looking at him. She poured herself a cup of coffee and joined the men at the table. Tom was watching them closely, looking at first one, then the other. She felt as though anyone looking at her would know that she'd spent the night making passionate love to Rafe. Not that she cared if Tom figured that out, but it was no one's business. Certainly not his.

"What are you expecting to find?" Tom finally asked Rafe when it became obvious that no one else was going to speak.

She tensed, waiting for Rafe to make a flippant comment. Instead he was quiet for a minute or two, obviously thinking. When he did respond, he sounded serious.

"I'm not really certain, but it makes sense to thoroughly check out the area where Dan was before he disappeared. Maybe I'm grasping at straws, but at the moment there's nothing else to go on. I spoke with Dan's partner yesterday." He sipped on his coffee before asking, "Do you know him?"

Tom shrugged. "I was introduced to him, once. That's about it. He doesn't come out here much."

"I find it strange, and a little suspicious that he's not concerned about Dan's continued absence."

"I had the same reaction. I waited a couple of days, and when I didn't hear from Dan, I thought maybe Mandy might have heard from him. Frankly, I don't trust his partner."

"Me, either." Rafe smiled. "At least we found something we can agree on."

Tom glanced at Mandy, then away. "I have a hunch there's several things we may agree on."

"Have you had breakfast, Tom?" Mandy asked, pushing away from the table.

He smiled. "Yeah, a couple of hours ago."

Mandy knew she was blushing. It couldn't be helped. Without saying anything to Rafe she got up and busied herself with preparing bacon, eggs and toast.

"How many hands do you have working full-time on the ranch?" Rafe asked.

"Three besides me."

"How well do you know them? Did you check references, that sort of thing?"

Tom scratched his ear. "They're all local, if that's what you mean. Guess I've known them most of my life."

"You're from around here?"

"Yeah. Grew up in Dripping Springs. Went to school there."

"Dan and I went to school in Wimberley. Is that how you met him? Through living so close to the ranch?"

"No. When he let it be known he was looking for someone to run the ranch for him, word got out and eventually I heard about it. I was raised on a ranch west of here. My family sold it when I was away at A & M. All I ever wanted to do was ranch. So taking this position worked out well for me."

"Do you know if any of the men working for you have any serious problems—drug addictions, heavy gambling, messy divorce—anything that would cause them to look for extra money?"

"Not that I know of. Why?"

Rafe shoved his hand through his hair before answering. "Hell, I don't know. It just seems to me that if someone on the ranch could set up a system of contacting others, the ranch could be used to smuggle items in and out of the country with relative ease."

Tom straightened. "Is that what you think is going on?"

"It's a theory I'm working on. What if Dan heard a plane the night he disappeared and decided to go and investigate? In doing so, he might have found out more than someone wanted him to know. So he was taken on board before he could talk about what he'd seen."

"They could have just killed him right there, if that's what they wanted to accomplish."

"But they didn't. And I think that's significant. No one wanted an investigation to be brought here to the ranch."

"Who or what is behind this?"

"There's the big question. It could be so many things that I don't want to hazard a guess." Mandy set a steaming plate of food in front of him. Rafe looked up at her and smiled. "Thanks."

His smile had the capacity to make her knees buckle. Mandy didn't trust herself to answer, so she nodded in response. She placed another plate where she'd been sitting, refilled everyone's cups, then sat down, concentrating on the food in front of her and not the man sitting so close beside her.

Tom spoke. "You think it's someone here on the ranch?"

"Not necessarily. I'm just covering all possibilities."

Tom nodded. "I'll check the men out and get back with you."

"I'd appreciate it."

"In the meantime," Tom said, rising, "I'd better get back to work." He looked down at Mandy and gave her a haunted smile. "I'll check on you later. If Rafe's going to be away, I'd feel better if you kept Ranger nearby."

Tom had never looked at her quite like that before, or if he had, she'd never noticed. Was Rafe right? Did Tom consider her more than just Dan's sister?

She liked Tom. He was a good man. Unfortunately she'd given her heart to Rafe on a summer night many years ago. Last night, she'd just made it official.

"I appreciate your concern for me, Tom," she said gently, touching his sleeve. "I'll make certain that Ranger is with me while Rafe is gone."

He nodded briskly. "Thanks. I'll see you later." He glanced at Rafe and nodded, then left, closing the door quietly behind him.

Now that they were alone, Mandy was nervous. She didn't want to start building pipe dreams just because Rafe had made love to her last night. That would be worse than foolish. After all, she was the one who had gone to him, just as she had before. Okay, so he'd admitted that he'd deliberately stirred her while dancing with her all those years ago. She couldn't accuse him of having done that yesterday. His focus had been on Dan's disappearance.

She wondered if he was going to say anything about last night.

She wondered if she should make some lighthearted comment to let him know she wasn't going to make a big deal of it.

She glanced over at him and realized that he was reading a newspaper that had been lying beside his plate. Oh, that was touching. All the time she was agonizing over how he might be feeling about last night and he'd already dismissed it and moved on to other things.

Mandy hopped up from the table and took her plate to the sink. "Are you finished with breakfast?" she asked in a carefully neutral voice.

"Mm-hmm," he absently replied.

"More coffee?"

"Uh, sure." He didn't look up from the paper.

She was tempted to pour the coffee over his head, but he might think she was upset about something... when she wasn't. Not at all.

As soon as she had the dishes taken care of, Mandy left the kitchen without saying another word. After all, what was there to say? Rafe had plainly showed her by his actions that he had no intention of allowing their lovemaking to make a difference between them.

What had she expected? When she looked back over the evening, she realized that he had opened up to her in ways he'd never done before. She'd found out about his childhood, although she hadn't been surprised by what she'd heard. What she found so disheartening was that, even as a young boy, he had the capacity of walking away and never looking back.

She hoped that just maybe she had made a dent in his armor by what they had shared last night. It hadn't just been the lovemaking, although that had been beyond belief. She'd had no idea she could feel so much pleasure with someone. He'd taught her things about herself she'd never known.

Hopefully she had done the same for him.

Perhaps he hadn't known what to say to her this morning, which is why he'd immediately become engrossed in the paper once the buffer of Tom's presence had disappeared.

The first thing she needed to do was to cultivate some patience. She was trying to undo a lifetime of self-protective training. Last night hadn't been a bad first step.

With a grin on her face, Mandy returned to Dan's bedroom and stripped the bed. She'd keep herself busy with household chores today and wait to see what happened next.

Rafe was ready to toss the paper aside, convinced there was nothing of particular notice when he spotted a small article at the bottom of page three of the first section.

"Police responded Saturday morning to a security alert from DSC Corporation. Company officials state that 1000 of their new A71-E Firestorm 900 MHz microprocessor chips had been stolen from their high security warehouse.

Company officials estimate the value of the chips to be in excess of one million dollars. Police say that in today's market, the chips are actually worth more than their weight in gold."

This article must be the reason Dan had kept the paper. Rafe considered the significance of this new information. It might have nothing to do with Dan's disappearance. But what if it did? And wasn't it odd that James made no mention of any theft problems the company had been having?

Microprocessor chips. The more he thought about it,

the more he could see a possible link-if not with Dan's disappearance, at least with the idea of smuggling.

Just think of the possibilities. There were several foreign leaders he could list, barred from doing business with the U.S., who would pay mega-bucks to get their hands on some highly-advanced technology.

James and Dan were sitting on a gold mine.

Suppose the chips hadn't been stolen at all, just reported stolen, so that they could be sold to much higher bidders?

Rafe reminded himself that Dan had contacted him, asking for his help. Dan knew very well that Rafe wouldn't go against any government sanctions. At least he hoped Dan knew him well enough to know that.

What if Dan happened to discover that the missing components and his ranch were connected to illegal activities and he needed Rafe's help to stop it? That was more like the Dan that he remembered.

He had to find Dan in order to get answers to these questions. And it was obvious he would get no help from Dan's partner.

He threw down the paper and strode through the house to the bedroom. Mandy was finishing making up the bed. He had a pang of remorse that he hadn't been able to greet her this morning the way he'd wanted to, but he knew she wouldn't have appreciated Tom witnessing his ardor.

He walked over and wrapped his arms around her from behind and kissed her on the ear. "I wanted to do this as soon as you walked into the kitchen, but I figured Tom wouldn't be amused."

She turned in his arms and draped her arms around his shoulders. "That's very thoughtful of you," she replied, returning his kiss.

Rafe had to keep his mind on what he was supposed to be doing. Reluctantly he stepped away from her. "I've got to go, Mandy. I'm going to spend most of the day at the airstrip, looking around those canyons. I'm not sure when I'll be back."

She smiled. "Wait a minute. Let me put some sandwiches together for you," she said, and hurried out of the room.

He slowly followed her down the hallway. Damn, but he was in big trouble. He had to concentrate on Dan for now and he was having a tough time distancing himself from all the emotions that had been stirred in him last night. He still couldn't believe Mandy's loving and generous gift.

He'd always told himself that nothing could be as good as his fantasies about her, but they faded into insignificance compared to actually making love to her. He knew he was in danger of losing his perspective on things. It was a good thing he was going to be gone today. It would give him time to regain his equilibrium.

After placing the lunch package in his backpack, Rafe gave Mandy a wave and quickly stepped outside. The ranch yard appeared to be deserted.

He struck out down the road that eventually led to the landing strip.

"Need a ride?" Tom called.

Rafe paused and looked around. Tom stood in the doorway of the barn.

"No, thanks. I need the exercise."

Tom was the kind of man that Mandy needed. It was obvious to Rafe that Tom was more than a little interested in Mandy, regardless of her protests to the contrary. Maybe the man hadn't spoken up, yet.

Rafe didn't want to get in his way. He knew that he

would be no good to her. Mandy deserved so much more than he was capable of giving. He needed to remember that and not take advantage of her nurturing nature.

Whatever had possessed him to talk about his family after all this time? They were part of his history, a part that didn't touch on the present time at all.

If you drop your guard you'll get hit in a vulnerable spot, he reminded himself. The problem was he hadn't been aware he had any vulnerable spots until Mandy showed up in his life again.

Who was he kidding? He was just as vulnerable where Dan was concerned.

"Come on, Dan," he muttered. "Give me some clues. Help me figure out what the hell is going on."

Out of habit he soon left the road and made his way through the cover of trees and foliage. If anyone was out there, he didn't want them to know he was, too. Not that he expected to spot anyone, but he was used to taking no chances.

By the time he reached the landing strip Rafe was focused on the job at hand. He circled the area until he got into the breaks in the land, a tumbled mass of granite, rock and shale. He jumped into one of the gullies and followed it, looking for anything that hadn't been placed there by Mother Nature.

He stopped about midafternoon to eat the lunch Mandy had prepared for him, drank water from a thermos and looked at the inhospitable terrain—rugged hills, faults in the land, granite outcrops. From where he sat, it looked as though there was an indentation in the rock face about halfway up the wall of this particular dry wash.

He decided to investigate.

He'd walked past the place earlier but had missed it. The angle of the sun and ensuing shadows caused a brief illumination of the area, highlighting what looked to be a deep recess in the wall. Rafe's heart picked up. He wasn't sure what he thought he'd found, but his increased heart rate told him he was hoping for something.

There was no way to the place from down here. It took him a while to circle out of the gully and locate the same place from above.

Because he was watching so closely, he spotted a thin trail leading down over the side. An animal could be using it for a lair. It could also house a nice nest of rattlesnakes.

Once he was on a level with it, Rafe could see a cave that seemed large enough for a man to stand upright. It could be filled with bats, since the Hill Country abounded in bat caves, but he doubted it. By now, he would have gotten a whiff of the distinctive—and exceedingly unappetizing—scent to indicate their presence.

There was a small ledge in front of the cave that hadn't been visible from either above or below. Moving with deliberate stealth he edged closer until he could see inside.

He let out a breath and stepped into the cave. The roof rapidly lowered toward the back, but the livable space was about eight-foot square. Livable was the operative word. There were supplies here. Human supplies. A few canned goods, traces of a fire, a couple of small pots and a battered bedroll occupied the area.

Could this be where Dan was hiding?

Rafe couldn't buy that. It wasn't his style. No, this was someone's living quarters. But why?

There was only one way to find out. He would have to find an observation point and watch to see who returned to the place.

Within minutes he was back on level ground, looking around for a likely place to set up a stakeout.

He spotted a cluster of live oaks approximately fifty yards away. The trees were probably a hundred years old or older, thick enough that he could climb high enough to be comfortable and set up a temporary aerie while he waited.

After reconnoitering, he chose a likely looking place high up in one of the middle trees. He would be effectively camouflaged but would have a clear view of the area where a person would have to go down to the cave.

He settled back against the trunk of the massive tree and waited.

Eight

Rafe had plenty of time to think while he waited. He'd been trained to do this sort of thing, so he ran on autopilot, watching for any movement that was not in keeping with the lazy summer day.

It was after six, but the sun wouldn't set for a few more hours. There were some clouds forming across the hills to the south which could mean rain moving in. Rain could cool things down considerably. It might make who ever was staying there a little less wary.

He mulled over everything he'd learned since he'd arrived in Texas. Some of those things would have been better left untouched. He'd been content with his life, content with his solitude and content not needing anybody, not wanting anybody.

All of that had changed since he had returned.

Now he knew what it was to wake up with Mandy in his arms. He knew the scent of her, the taste of her.

He knew the little sounds she made when she was aroused, the look of wonder on her face when she achieved her first sense of fulfillment, the feel of her arms holding him so tightly he could scarcely get his breath.

Being with her last night had been the culmination of every fantasy he'd ever dreamed since he left Texas. After this trip, he would no longer need his imagination to conjure up the experience. Memories would haunt him.

She'd made him feel things he'd never known he was capable of feeling. He didn't thank her for that. Talking about his mother and sisters last night had ripped open a wound that had long been scabbed over.

He didn't thank her for that, either.

The one thing he knew about himself above all others was that he was a survivor. He would survive this trip, as he had survived numerous wounds, raging fevers and the threat of amputation.

However, the pain would be every bit as intense.

His thoughts turned to Dan. Thinking of Dan didn't cheer him up any. Had his friend decided he could make more money smuggling computer parts out of the country than running a legitimate business?

He hoped to God that Dan wasn't doing business in that way. If he was, James Williams knew about it and was profiting from it.

But what if it was James who was involved in the theft, not Dan? And what if Dan had tried to catch the shipment before it went out? Rafe could come up with no good reason why Dan would be left alive to ever talk about it.

The occupant of the cave might be able to shed some

light on what was going on out here. Now all he could do was wait to see who showed up.

Many hours later, Rafe's vigil paid off. The threatening rain had held off, but rumbles of thunder had punctuated long stretches of silence. Clouds covered most of the stars. The sliver of moon disappeared early in the evening.

He raised his night binoculars and sighted in on the moving figure, keeping the figure in sight until whoever it was went over the ridge and was no longer in view. Rafe waited another hour before quietly coming down the tree. He left his gear, knowing he could move more silently without having it accidentally brush against something.

Once on the move, he covered ground quickly. A dim light shone from the cave as he neared the opening. He took a quick peek inside, then leaned against the wall. A young boy had his back to the entrance, digging through a sack he'd brought in with him. He was alone.

Rafe stepped into the entrance of the cave and said, "Got enough food for two?"

The kid let out a shriek and whirled around, his eyes wide. As soon as he spotted Rafe, who had hunched down and was resting on his heels, he stiffened, staring at him defiantly.

"I'm not going to hurt you, you know," Rafe offered in a soothing tone. "Tell me why you're living out here in a cave, son."

The boy didn't respond. He just stood there warily watching Rafe.

He looked to be ten or thereabouts. Much too young to be out here on his own. And it was obvious he was on his own. His clothes were ragged and too small for him. His running shoes looked like someone's cast offs. His hair was shaggy, falling across his forehead and into his eyes.

Rafe was surprised that the boy looked fairly clean, as though he was making some effort to keep up his appearance. Seeing him like this had Rafe's stomach churning. It brought back too many memories.

Rafe eased down so that he was sitting on the floor of the cave. He leaned back against the wall. "You've got this fixed up really nice, you know. Hope water doesn't come in when it rains. Looks like we're going to get a gully washer before morning."

The boy just looked at him.

Rafe sighed. "Son, I figure that right about now you think I'm going to try to make you do something you don't want to do. You're wrong. In fact, I have a hunch, depending on how long you've been living here, that you could help me out on a matter."

The boy shifted his weight from one foot to the other. "How?"

He sounded so young it almost broke Rafe's heart but he knew he couldn't show his concern for the boy. He needed to get their conversation on an impersonal subject in hopes of getting him to relax.

Rafe reached into his shirt pocket and pulled out a package of jerky he'd opened earlier. He helped himself to one of the sticks, then held out the package. "Care to join me?"

The boy looked at him suspiciously, then at the jerky. Rafe waited patiently, as though he was coaxing a hurt critter from the wild. The boy watched him. Rafe took a bite of the jerky and chewed without dropping his extended arm with his offering.

Eventually the boy inched closer until he was able to

touch the package. He grabbed it and hurriedly backed away. He glanced down, then back at Rafe who still chewed. Finally the boy took one of the sticks and started to return the package.

"Keep it. I've got more."

The boy carefully placed the remaining pieces in the pocket of his shirt.

Rafe smiled.

"What did you mean, I could help you?" the kid finally said after they continued to eat the jerky in silence. He sat down on his bedroll, his back to the wall of the cave.

"Have you ever had a friend, somebody you played with, hung out with, did things with?"

The boy frowned. "Not anymore."

"But you've got friends like that. You know how much they mean to you, right?"

The boy looked down at his legs folded cross-legged beneath him. "Yeah," he whispered.

"That's the way Dan is. He's my friend. Dan and I have been friends since we were eight years old. That's a long time, you know...more than twenty years."

The boy kept his gaze on him. Rafe had managed to catch his interest.

"So when I got a letter from my friend a few weeks ago saying he needed my help with something, I came to find out what I could do. Because that's what friends do." Rafe looked around. "You got anything to drink? This jerky will sure make a person thirsty."

The boy scrambled up and went over to his sack. He pulled out two cans of soda pop. Showing a little less wariness, he handed one to Rafe.

"Mmm. Still cool. Thanks." He popped open the top

and took a big swallow. The boy did the same once he was back on his bedroll.

"Anyway. When I got here I found my friend was gone. And nobody knows where he is. And I'm really worried about him. The last anybody knows he must have been out here because that's where they found his Jeep."

He watched closely and saw the boy give a brief nod.

"So I'm looking around, trying to figure out if I could find a clue where he might be. I happened to come across your place, and it occurred to me that you might have seen something that would help me find him."

"They shot him," the boy said in a small voice.

The words slammed into Rafe with such force that he had to pause to catch his breath. He wanted to grab the boy and shake more information out of him. Instead he drew on years of experience of learning how to become detached from his feeling in order to get a job done and force himself to appear calm.

"Who shot him?"

"I don't know."

"Can you tell me what happened?"

"I heard the Jeep drive up and I went up there along the ridge to see what it was doing there. Nobody got out, but I knew someone was there. I could see his shadow. So I watched and waited. Then I heard this airplane flying low. It circled that runway thing and then landed. It never shut down though, it just rolled to a stop and a couple of guys got out and walked over to the Jeep."

Rafe took another drink of the slightly cool cola, focused on the boy's story and not what happened to Dan.

"The guy in the Jeep got out. They all seemed to be

talking at once. I heard part of what they were saying, but it didn't make any sense to me.''

"Tell me what you heard."

"The men from the plane sounded like they were getting angry. The man from the Jeep just kept saying it wasn't going to happen."

"What wasn't going to happen."

"I don't know."

"He told them to go back to their boss and tell him the thing was over. He began to walk to the plane and they followed."

"Is that when they shot him?"

"No. One of them swung at him and he hit the guy, knocking him to the ground. Another guy still in the plane jumped out and pulled a gun. He shot the guy from the Jeep and he fell. The man with the gun yelled at the other two to get him in the plane. So they did."

They sat there in silence. Rafe mulled over the story. He shouldn't be surprised but the pain in his chest was growing stronger as each minute ticked away. Now he knew why Dan hadn't contacted anyone.

"Do you think that was your friend?" the boy finally asked.

Rafe took a couple of deep breaths before he replied. "Yeah, son. That's what I think."

"I'm sorry."

"Me, too."

After a while the boy said, "I don't think it killed him, though. I think it may have hit him in the arm or shoulder, because it spun him around. And when they were moving him, I saw him lift his head. So maybe he's just hurt."

"I'd like that to be true."

"What's your name?" the boy asked.

"Rafe. What's yours?"

"Kelly."

"That's a nice name."

"So is yours."

"How long you been living here, Kelly?"

Kelly shrugged. "A while."

"How'd you find the place?"

"I was just looking for a place where there wasn't people."

"You don't care for people much, huh?"

"Not much."

"Me, either."

"Have you ever had to live in a foster home?"

Rafe thought about that one. "No, I haven't," he finally said. "How about you?"

"Once. I didn't like it."

"So you left."

"Yeah."

"What do you do for food?"

Kelly looked up at him, his blue-eyed gaze old. "I steal it."

"That can be dangerous." Rafe looked around at the things there. "You steal the sleeping bag?"

"No. It was mine. From before."

"How about clothes?"

"I don't steal clothes. Just food."

"Tough way to live."

"I don't mind."

"What if you get caught?"

Kelly shrugged.

"Have you ever thought about working on a ranch?"

Kelly blinked. "What could I do on a ranch?"

"All kinds of things. I used to work on this ranch when I wasn't much older than you."

"Really?"

"Uh-huh. I guess we have several things in common. I didn't like where I was living back then, either. So I left."

"You did?"

"Yep. I was lucky to know Dan. He owns this ranch now. When I came to work here, his mom and dad gave me a place to stay and paid me for doing work around the place. You ever thought about hiring yourself out?"

"I don't want anyone to know I'm here."

"I can certainly understand that. Here's the thing. If you decided to work and go to school, it might be arranged where you stayed here at the ranch permanently. It's not a bad place, you know."

"Are there any other kids around?"

"Nope."

"Good."

"You don't care to have kids around, huh? Guess they can be a pain sometimes."

"They steal your stuff and lie about it and nobody believes you."

"That's tough." Rafe stretched his arms high over his head and yawned. "I don't know about you, but I'm about ready for some shut-eye. Would you mind if I sleep here tonight?"

"Here?"

"Yeah. You sleep here all the time. I figure if you can do it, it probably won't bother me, either."

"I only have the sleeping bag."

"That's okay. I'm used to sleeping on the ground." Rafe stretched his length across the entrance of the cave and gave a big sigh. "I appreciate your hospitality, Kelly. I think you'd be a good friend to a person."

"You mean like Dan?"

"Uh-huh. A friend like Dan."

He closed his eyes. A few minutes later the candle went out and there was complete silence in the darkened cave. Rafe didn't want to think about Dan any more tonight. He welcomed the oblivion of sleep.

Rafe hadn't returned to the house last night and Mandy was worried. She'd kept Ranger with her as she'd promised, but he hadn't been disturbed during the night.

She'd spent a very restless night, knowing that Rafe was out in the thunderstorm that had passed through the area. She'd tried to remind herself that he had been highly trained to take care of himself. She hated to think about what he must have gone through to accumulate the various scars on his body. It would be much better not to know.

Now a second day was almost over and she still hadn't heard anything from him. She wondered if she should send Tom out to the airstrip to check on him. She didn't want to be accused of overreacting, she decided, so she looked around to find something to keep her occupied.

She'd spent yesterday cleaning the house until it shined.

To give herself something to do today, she decided to make a big supper, maybe bake some cookies. She needed to do something with her time. She was going to have to call and extend her leave of absence in another couple of days. Either that, or go home.

But she didn't want to go home as long as Rafe was here. She wanted to spend whatever time she could with him. She hoped he felt the same way.

She had a large roast ready to come out of the oven

when Ranger suddenly growled from where he lay sprawled by the refrigerator. Mandy eagerly peered out the window. Ranger shot toward the door, barking, which bothered her. He knew and accepted Rafe. So whoever was out there in the dark wasn't Rafe.

Only it was. She heard him speak and Ranger immediately quieted, but he still stood stiff legged and rumbled in his chest. She went to the door and opened it, saying, "Rafe?"

He stepped into the light, much as he had earlier in the week. "Yeah. It's me. I brought a new friend and we're both pretty muddy."

A new friend. What was he talking about?

"Take your boots off out there, then, and come on inside," she said. "You're just in time for a pot roast and all the trimmings. They're coming out of the oven now, but you've got time for a shower."

She was nervous and when she was nervous she chattered. Mandy didn't know what to expect. Where had Rafe been that he'd picked up a friend?

She heard the scraping of boots, and the sounds of them being removed. Rafe stepped inside and smiled at her. His eyes were wary. He stepped aside and motioned behind him.

"Mandy, I'd like you to meet Kelly." He turned to a ragamuffin of a boy and politely said, "Kelly, this is Mandy, the woman I told you about. She's Dan's sister."

The boy looked too thin. His eyes seemed to cover half his face. He had the biggest, bluest eyes she'd ever seen. His hair was sandy blond with darker strands mixed in and it didn't look as if it had come into contact with shampoo in a while. He was watching her as if he thought she would immediately order him out of the house.

He was breaking her heart.

"I'm very pleased to meet you, Kelly. Any friend of Rafe's is a friend of mine. We have two showers, so if you'd like to get cleaned up before supper, you can."

Kelly looked at Rafe. Rafe nodded and said, "Sounds good to me. I'll show you where everything is." He gently placed his hand on the boy's shoulder and the two of them walked out of the kitchen together.

What in the world was going on? Mandy knew that sooner or later Rafe would explain, but for now, Kelly's appearance was a definite mystery. Since all the vehicles were still parked here at the ranch buildings, she knew Rafe hadn't left the property unless he walked, which she doubted.

So how had he found Kelly?

She hurried to her room and went to the back of her large walk-in closet. She remembered packing a box of old clothes—some jeans and Western shirts she'd worn before she moved away from home. They were too small for her now, but she hadn't wanted to throw them out, and hadn't taken the time to drop them off at the local thrift store.

Most of the stuff was unisex. She dumped out the box and pawed through the clothing, laying out what she hoped would be suitable. She sat back on her heels. She didn't have any underwear for him and anything of Dan's or Rafe's would be too big. She shook her head. At least these clothes would be an improvement over the ones he wore now.

She stopped at the hall bathroom and tapped on the door. There was a tense silence before Kelly answered.

"Yes?" he answered, sounding a little unnerved.

"I found some things you can put on when you get done so we can wash what you're wearing, if you'd like."

She waited while he thought about that. Slowly he opened the door and looked out. She handed them to him. He looked at her, at the clothes, back at her. "Thank you," he finally said.

She smiled. "They'll probably be too big for you, but at least they're clean."

As soon as he shut the door she hurried down to the bath in the master bedroom. Rafe was already in the shower. Well, that was just too bad. She wanted some answers and didn't want to ask them in front of the boy.

She opened the bathroom door and stepped inside. He had his head under the water, scrubbing it, and didn't hear her come in. She waited until he rinsed his hair and was soaping his body when she asked, "What's going on, Rafe?"

He spun around. When he saw her standing there he grinned at her. "Care to join me?"

When he looked at her like that, it was hard to keep her mind on the matter at hand. "I want to know where you found Kelly."

"Living in a cave near the landing strip."

"Oh my God."

"Yeah."

"Who is he?"

"I have no idea. But I've convinced him to trade places with me for a while."

"What do you mean, trade places?"

"I'll tell you over supper. But in the meantime, I've practically promised him a job on the ranch. Do you think Tom can use him?"

"How would I know? He's just a little boy."

"Well, you and Dan worked around here at his age. So there must be something he can do to earn his keep. Because I sure don't want him sleeping down there anymore."

"Well, neither do I." She was having a really hard time concentrating on their conversation while watching Rafe rinse the soap from his body. She had to fight the urge to run her hands over his muscled exterior to make sure he was all right. She'd missed him terribly after only two days and a night. This did not bode well for her future without him.

He turned off the water and reached for a towel. She got it first. "Allow me," she said and soon matched actions with words. When she saw how he responded to her touch, she smiled.

"Well, hell, Mandy. What did you expect?" he groused, a little embarrassed. "I'm not used to having a woman's hands on me without getting ready to do something about it."

"Do you hear me complaining?"

"No, but—"

"No, but nothing. Get dressed so we can eat while it's hot." She practically ran from the room before she did something that would embarrass her. Somehow she was going to have to learn some control around this man.

She caught herself grinning like a fool while she dished up their meal.

Mandy had all the food on the table—place settings and glasses neatly arranged—when Kelly appeared in the doorway. She paused from filling the glasses with water and smiled at him. "Ready to eat?" she asked.

As she had guessed, the clothes were too large. He'd rolled up the jeans' legs and used his belt to gather the waist in. The cuffs on the shirt were rolled up. The large opening at the throat emphasized his delicate neck. She wanted to gather him up in her arms and hug him, but of course she couldn't, even though she knew the child was in dire need of one.

"Where's Rafe?" he asked, looking around the room as though she'd hidden him away somewhere.

"Getting cleaned up, like you." She pointed to one of the chairs. "Have a seat. Would you like some milk?"

He eyed her, the chair, the table filled with food, then looked back at her with suspicion. "Who else is coming?"

"You, me and Rafe. Why?"

"That's a lot of food for three people."

She grinned. "I got carried away. But it makes good leftovers."

Mandy was relieved when Rafe appeared behind the boy. He casually dropped his hand on the boy's shoulder. "Feels good to get into some clean clothes, doesn't it?" he asked, gently guiding Kelly to the table.

Kelly sat down next to Rafe and unobtrusively scooted his chair closer to him. Rafe pretended not to notice. It was a good thing Rafe was left-handed, Mandy thought, hiding a smile. He wouldn't be able to use his right hand or arm without jostling the boy.

Mandy wasn't sure what she could say or do to make the boy more comfortable. Once he saw that they were filling their plates with generous portions, Kelly did, too. She noticed that he waited to see what the others did each time before attempting to eat.

They were midway through their meal before the stiffness began to leave Kelly's spine. He leaned back in his chair and offered her a big grin. "You're a good cook, Mandy. This stuff is great."

"Yeah, that's what I keep telling her," Rafe said. His grin was filled with mischief.

Unable to contain her curiosity a moment longer, Mandy asked Kelly, "Isn't your mother worried about you being gone so long?"

Well, you would have thought she'd suggested the two guys at the table star in a porno film, the way they froze. All right, so maybe she shouldn't have brought it up, but darn it! Kelly was such a cutie. It was obvious that someone had taught him some manners. So where was she now?

Rafe shot her a riveting frown as though she'd showed a lamentable breach in good manners, herself. It wasn't as if they were still living in the Old West where no one was supposed to ask questions about a person's past. Besides, Kelly was just a child. He had absolutely no business being on his own.

Rafe continued to eat. Kelly drank some milk. Finally he blurted out, "She died."

"Oh," Mandy replied. "I'm so sorry, Kelly. It's really tough to lose your mom. My mom died, too. I really miss her."

He nodded. "Yeah. She got pneumonia, but that's not supposed to kill ya. But the doctor who finally saw her said she was all run-down and amenic and stuff."

"Anemic?"

"Where she doesn't have enough blood or something." he explained.

"I see." Mandy met Rafe's glare with a slight nod of acknowledgment that she knew he disapproved of her questions, all the while she continued to probe. "How long ago did she die?"

Kelly shrugged. "A long time. Last year, sometime."

"Yes. That *is* a long time."

As though forestalling her next question, Kelly said, "I don't have a dad. It was just me and Mom. Mom did cleaning for people and worked in a convenience store, and did these different jobs all the time so we could stay together. She didn't want anybody to take me away from her."

"She sounds like a wonderful mom."

Kelly's face lit up. "She was! She was my best pal." He looked at Rafe. "My best friend," he added, soberly.

Rafe nodded but made it clear he wasn't part of the conversation by concentrating on his food.

Now that the dam had been broken, Kelly opened up. "Rafe says that maybe I could get a job working on your ranch. I'm a real good worker. He also told me he'd like to borrow my place for a while and that I could stay here in his place. You know, like a trade." He glanced at Rafe to be sure he was giving her the straight scoop.

Rafe smiled at him. "That's right. I figure we'll sleep here tonight. I'll talk to Tom in the morning, then while I'm sleeping at Kelly's place, he can stay here with you for now."

"I've got to make friends with your dog, though," Kelly solemnly explained to her.

All three of them looked over at Ranger who still zealously guarded the refrigerator. "I don't think you'll have any problem with that," Mandy said around the lump in her throat.

Rafe McClain could be the roughest, toughest, meanest person around. He could also offer a homeless child hope and a promise for a better future. If she didn't already love him to distraction, his treatment of Kelly would have knocked out all her defenses against him.

Rafe cleared his throat. He had a clean plate in front of him. He drained his glass of milk. "Kelly has been a big help to me," he began, cupping Kelly's nape and gently massaging. "I think I've come up with a workable plan to find Dan."

Mandy stared at him. "And you're just now telling me about it?"

He motioned to his plate. "First things first. I'm telling you now. You have a problem with that?"

She sighed. "Go on."

"Well, Kelly tells me that there are a couple of planes landing on the strip on a regular basis. He's watched them and noticed that the first plane unloads some things and hides them nearby. Within a couple of nights the other plane lands and they leave something and take what's there. It's the first plane that I'm interested in. It's the one Dan left in."

"Oh, Rafe." She looked at Kelly. "So you saw my brother the night he left! Oh, that's wonderful."

Kelly looked at Rafe before nodding his head.

"I figure that somebody set up a nice little operation using that landing strip. Probably doesn't have anything to do with Dan. There's a strong possibility the strip was spotted from the air, checked out and was commandeered because of its accessibility and relative privacy."

"Do you know where Dan is?"

"Not yet, but I'm going to find out. I'm going to wait out there until the first plane shows up with a drop. Then I intend to hitch a ride with them, much like Dan did, and see what I can find out."

Mandy eyed him uncertainly. "Won't that be dangerous? These people are obviously doing something illegal. Can't you just call the sheriff and have them picked up?''

"I could. Eventually I intend to do just that. But I want to find Dan first. Once they're in custody, they won't talk about Dan, I guarantee you."

"Oh. So you think they're holding him somewhere?"

"That's what I intend to find out."

"What if they decide to hold you, too?"

The smile he gave her made her shiver. "They can try." He looked at Kelly. "So I've asked Kelly if he'll stay here and help Ranger look after you while I'm gone, since I don't know how long this is going to take. I'll talk to Tom in the morning about Kelly's assignments." He met Mandy's gaze and held it. "I figured you could use the company."

"Yes," she managed to say. What else could she say? This was Rafe in his most in-charge-of-things attitude. Not that she minded having Kelly there. It beat living in a cave, of all things. Rafe was right. She could use the company. She needed the distraction—first from worrying about Dan, second from worrying about Rafe.

"Is Dan's old room available, the one he used when he was a kid?"

"It's become a storage room more than a bedroom these past few years." She smiled at Kelly. "If you don't mind the ruffles on the curtains, you can sleep in the room I used when I was growing up." Since that was the same room she had been sleeping in since her return, Rafe lifted one brow at her in silent inquiry.

She returned his look with a sunny smile.

When she glanced at Kelly she could see he was already nodding off. A full tummy can do that to a person. She stood and began to gather plates. "Why don't you get him bedded down while I clean up the kitchen, okay?''

"Well, I thought maybe you'd want to do that, since it's your room.''

"Oh, I'll get whatever I need out of there later.''

Kelly looked like it was taking a great deal of effort for him to keep his eyes open. Rafe got up and assisted Kelly. "Come on, sport. Time to hit the sack.''

As soon as she finished in the kitchen, Mandy went looking for Rafe. She found him in the den watching the late-night news.

"Is he okay?'' she asked, sitting next to him on the couch.

"He was asleep by the time his head hit the pillow. I think we've managed to win over his trust and when he let down his guard, his body caved. He's probably been running on adrenaline for a long time.''

"Did you find out how old he is?'' she asked.

"He says he's twelve, but I don't believe it. Ten, maybe. Eleven is stretching it. But twelve? No way.''

"Did he say why he's living out like this?''

"I think he ran away from a foster situation.''

"People are looking for him, you know.''

Rafe gave her what she always thought of as "the look.'' "Now you're sounding like part of Children's Services.''

"What a surprise.''

"If you want to find out something on him while I'm gone, be my guest.''

"He's got to be in school in September, Rafe. You know that.''

"I know you'll do whatever you think is best.''

"Yes,'' she said with a nod. "I will.''

"Why did you give up your room? We could have found him someplace else to sleep."

"Because my room is ready for him and he was ready to crash. Besides, I already have a place to sleep."

"Oh, yeah? Where's that?"

"With you."

Nine

"Uh, Mandy, I don't think that's a good idea."

"Probably not," she admitted, "but what the hell, I'll pay the price later." She leaned toward him and kissed his jawline. "In the meantime, I'm going to spend whatever time I can with you. Hang the consequences."

"You know there's never going to be a long-term relationship between us. We're too different...my work takes me halfway around the world—it would never work between us."

Mandy studied him for a long moment, reading more than he probably wanted her to see in his expression. She smiled. "Let's see now," she said, holding up her fingers. Pointing to the index finger, she said, "A, whether you like it or not, Rafe, we've been in a long-term relationship since we were kids." She saw him flinch at the statement, but he made no attempt to contradict her. Feeling a little more confident, she pointed to her second finger and said, "*B*, yes we are very different from each other. I, personally, don't have a problem with that. Sorry if you do." She gave him a quick kiss then pointed to her ring finger and said, "And *C*, I've never seen you as a nine-to-five guy in my wildest dreams, cowboy. You are who you are. You do what you feel compelled to do. I would never try to change you." She tilted her head at him and smiled.

He sighed as though carrying a tremendous weight on his shoulders. "You didn't mention the most important part—it will never work between us."

"Not if you don't want it to. But it's working now, tonight, for the next few hours. I'm willing to accept that, even if there's no more. Whether you want to admit it to me or not, what you're planning to do is exceedingly dangerous. You've got a good chance of getting yourself killed. Even worse, I may never know for sure. You're planning to disappear in the same way Dan did, and it could turn out to be with the same results."

"Which is my point. I don't want to hurt you in any way. That's the last thing I want."

"I'm a big girl now, Rafe. I told you that. I'm no longer fifteen."

"Or innocent," he added with a wicked gleam.

"I should say not, considering all the things you did to me the other night."

"With you, not to you," he whispered. "We did them together."

She draped her arms around his shoulders. "Care to show me another demonstration?" She lightly kissed him, then pulled away to watch his expression.

"Damn, woman, I've never been able to resist you."

"Then don't start trying to at this late date," she replied. She rose and held out her hand. He stood and lightly grasped her wrist between his thumb and index finger while she led him down the hall to the master bedroom.

When Tom Parker stepped out of his house early the next morning he found Rafe sitting on his porch steps. "You're out and about early," Tom said. "Did you have any luck looking around the landing strip?"

Rafe stood and Tom joined him on the steps. In unspoken agreement, they started toward the other ranch buildings. "I know how Dan left the ranch. I intend to do the same thing in hopes of finding him."

"How did you manage that?"

"I found a kid living down there. His name is Kelly and I think I've convinced him that you could find work for him to do around here."

"That's for sure. How old is he?"

"Ten or eleven is my guess. No telling what he'll tell you. Twenty-one if he thought you'd believe him."

"A runaway?"

"That's a given. Knowing Mandy, she'll have all his credentials and his history by the time I get back." He glanced at Tom, then away. "I hope you'll be able to use him. He needs looking after, despite what he thinks. He needs clothes, shoes, you name it. But he has to earn the money himself, so don't even try to offer him cash."

"Sounds like you know him pretty well."

"I've known him all my life."

"Is the kid yours?" Tom asked.

Rafe laughed. "Not with that blond hair and blue

eyes. But I understand him. If you give him a chance, he'll work his heart out for you.''

"Send him out and I'll put him to work.''

Rafe held out his hand. "Thanks, Tom. I owe you one.''

Tom shook his head. "You don't owe me a thing. But I'd sure appreciate your bringing the boss home. We need him around here.''

"I'll see what I can do.''

Rafe had cautioned Kelly not to tell anyone that Dan had been shot. He saw no reason to upset Mandy, especially, when no one at this point knew how serious the wound was. There was time enough later to fill her in on all of the events once he could be with her to deal with the news.

When Rafe slipped back into the house, he found Mandy making coffee. She glanced at him, then concentrated on the coffee. "I woke up and found you gone. I didn't think I'd see you again this morning.''

"I needed to talk with Tom. He said he'd find Kelly plenty to do around here.''

"That's good.''

He walked over to her and put his arms around her waist. "I'm sorry, Mandy.''

"For what?''

"For not being the type of man you want me to be...the kind of man you need—one who doesn't keep disappearing on you.''

She turned in his arms. "You have nothing to apologize for. Nothing. I'm glad you decided to respond to Dan's message and came back to Texas. I hope you locate Dan, but even if you don't, your visit has been so good for me.''

"I'll find him, Mandy. I'm glad I came back, too,

for many reasons. I feel as though I allowed my past to become a raging tiger that I never wanted to face. I'm discovering that, by confronting it, the tiger has become a tabby kitten, nothing so ferocious or dangerous after all.''

He heard a soft footfall nearby and looked around. Kelly stood in the doorway. As promised, Mandy had washed and dried his clothes and he now wore them. Even clean, they were pretty disreputable, but they were his.

Rafe understood.

"I figure we'll have some breakfast and then go out and talk to the foreman. That sound okay?''

Kelly grinned. "Yeah. I mean, yes, sir.''

"Practicing, are you?''

"My mom says, uh, said, that politeness is never out of place.''

"I agree,'' Rafe said, pouring himself a cup of the freshly brewed coffee. He went over to the table and sat down. Kelly joined him. Mandy poured them both some orange juice, plus filled a glass with milk for Kelly. "Breakfast will be ready shortly.''

By midafternoon Kelly was running from barn to toolshed, from tractor to backhoe. Rafe had never heard so many questions coming out of one person's mouth. It took both of them—he and Tom—to attempt to supply answers and there were times when they were both stumped.

Eventually Rafe left Kelly with Tom and went back to the house. When he found Mandy, he said, "I'm going to get a few hours of sleep, then I'll go on down to the strip. I'll take the Jeep, but make sure it's hidden from the air. Once they land, it won't matter if they spot it.''

"Do you expect them tonight?"

"There's no way to know. Kelly didn't note the nights they showed up, but he said they came regularly and he hadn't seen them in a while. I'm hoping to get lucky. Maybe they'll show up tonight."

However, it was four nights later when Rafe heard the sound of a single-engine plane coming in low. During the days he'd returned to the house and visited with Kelly and Mandy, eaten, slept and returned to the airstrip at sunset. He had enjoyed seeing the bond that Kelly was forming with both Tom and Mandy. As much as it pained him to know that he wouldn't be a part of their lives, he felt good knowing that Tom would be there for them.

Now he scrambled to the top of the gully and watched as the plane circled before preparing to land. When the plane turned away from where he was, he slid over the rim and moved into the position he'd chosen earlier.

He had done as much preparing as he could for this mission. He'd dismissed every thought but the need to get into that plane alive. He'd focused on each step to ensure the success of that goal. It felt good, finally, to be going into action.

Kelly had shown him where the drop was. It was almost too easy to step behind the man as he turned away from leaving an attaché case in the Y of a tree. He caught him in a grip that included a knife at his throat.

"You're going to be just fine," he said in a low voice directly into the man's ear, "so long as you co-operate with me. We're going back to the plane.

Whether both of us get on is up to you. I intend to be on board. Understand?''

The man shivered and gave a brief nod.

"Good.''

As soon as they reached the plane, one of the men inside said, ''What's going on?''

Rafe replied. ''Just hitching a ride, my friend.''

No one said anything when he lifted the man in front of him into the plane and climbed in behind him. Maybe it was the camouflage uniform. Or it could have been the blacking on his face. It might even have been the combat knife he still held.

"Let's go,'' he said, tapping the pilot's shoulder with the knife blade.

No one argued with him.

Once strapped in, Rafe looked around the interior of the plane. There were two men seated in front. He and his newest companion were in back. The three kept darting glances his way.

Probably wanted to know the name of his fashion consultant.

"What do you want?'' the passenger in the front seat said once they were in the air and had leveled off.

"I hate to sound like a cliche, but the truth is—I want you to take me to your leader.''

"Why?''

"My reasons don't concern you.''

"He ain't going to be happy to see you.''

"I'll try to bear up under the disappointment.''

Rafe watched the ground below. There wasn't much light, but at least there was no cloud cover. The stars looked close enough to touch.

During the time he had waited in the cave, he studied aerial maps of the area between the ranch and the border. He was pleased to see that he was right. They were crossing the border and flying into the interior of Mexico.

So far, so good.

When they finally landed at another small airstrip hours later, he noted there were landing lights and a hangar nearby, but no one waiting for them on the ground. After the landing, they taxied up to the hangar and the pilot cut the engine.

"Now what?" their spokesman asked.

"Now we go see The Man."

"He's asleep by now."

"No problem. I'll add to his pleasant dreams."

The men looked at each other, then shrugged.

Rafe knew they were armed. He also knew that if they tried anything, he could take two of them out if he was lucky. The odds didn't bother him.

He let the men lead the way into what appeared to be a large hacienda nestled in the mountains. The pilot said, "I'm going to bed. You wanna kill me, go ahead."

Rafe almost smiled. "Sleep well, *amigo*."

The pilot looked at him in surprise, then shrugged and disappeared into the darkness. Of course he could be planning to come up behind Rafe and disarm him. Rafe was willing to take that chance.

Once inside the hacienda the two remaining men looked at each other. One of them said, "We wake him up, *he'll* kill us."

The other nodded toward Rafe. "We don't wake him up, he'll kill us."

"May I make a suggestion, gentlemen?" Rafe asked politely.

They looked at him.

"Tell me where to find him. He'll never need to know how I got here."

They looked at him, then each other. The spokesman gave directions while the other took off out the front door. As soon as he finished with the directions, the spokesman followed his friend.

Interesting loyalties.

Rafe climbed the stairs two at a time, went down the broad hallway and paused at the double doors at the end. He tried the door. It silently gave to the pressure and swung open.

Rafe stepped inside and closed the door behind him.

The room had windows on three sides that let in the dim light. The bed was on a large dais in the middle of the room.

From the looks of things, the boss man slept alone. At least tonight.

He woke up quickly enough, Rafe noticed, which was good. He seemed to be alert, although he didn't have much to say. It could be because of the cold steel caressing his carotid artery.

Once Rafe was certain he had the man's attention, he said, "I won't take up much of your time. I'm looking for a friend of mine. Dan Crenshaw."

The man blinked.

"Uh-huh. Dan. I've come for him. So here's the plan. You take me to him, you put us on the plane you've got sitting out there and you fly us across the border. ¿Comprende?"

Rafe could now see the whites of the man's eyes. That's because his gaze kept darting around the room. "You want me to spell it out a little clearer for you?" Rafe asked, putting pressure on the blade.

How amazing. The man's eyes were downright el-

oquent. He didn't need to say a word to convince Rafe
he wanted to cooperate in the worst way.

Rafe removed his knee from the man's chest and
eased back. ''Get up.''

The man leaped out of bed.

''Take me to Dan.''

The man looked down at his nudity. Rafe spotted a
pair of trousers draped over a chair. He tossed them to
him and kicked a pair of huaraches, a sandal common
to Mexico, toward him.

Damned if he didn't act grateful.

''Lead the way,'' Rafe said. The man looked at him
as though he was dealing with a crazy person. He
wasn't far off at the moment. Rafe's blood was pumping and so was his adrenaline. His perceptions were
heightened and he was more than ready to take someone out.

The man must have sensed Rafe's mood, or, like his
henchmen, was dazzled by his fashion sense, because
he made no argument. Instead he headed toward the
door.

Rafe walked a step behind the man down the hallway and stairs. There were no guards waiting downstairs. They turned when they reached the bottom and
walked toward the back of the hacienda. The man went
through a door that opened onto a large patio filled
with all kinds of blooming flowers and shrubs.

The man walked faster through an archway built into
the adobe wall around the place. He followed a grav-
eled path that wound through the trees. Rafe could see
small cottages among the trees, no doubt where the
workers lived.

The man kept looking over his shoulder as though
to make certain Rafe was behind him. Maybe he hoped

he was just having a really scary nightmare and would wake up at any moment.

When the man paused, Rafe almost stepped on him. The pause was to open a wrought iron gate. Rafe looked around and realized where they were.

He'd been brought to the family cemetery.

Ten

Rafe wanted to scream with rage. He grabbed the man, ready to slit his throat for what he had done to Dan. He forced himself to hang on, searching for some self-control deep inside.

Yes, he'd known the chances were good that Dan hadn't survived the gunshot wound. But he hadn't wanted to believe it.

I came as fast as I got your message, he said to Dan in his head. *Why did you have to try to play the role of hero? Why couldn't you have waited for me? You knew I was coming, damn you. You knew that I wouldn't ignore your summons. If you'd waited two more weeks we could have done this together with a different outcome.*

He still wasn't going to leave him here. He had come to bring Dan home and he was going to do it, if he had to dig with his bare hands.

Slowly he unclenched his fingers from the man's neck. The man hurried along the pathway inside the cemetery and Rafe numbly followed him. No wonder nobody argued with him on this trip. Hell, it hadn't mattered. Dead men don't talk.

Rafe heard the sound of another gate opening before he understood that the man he followed had opened the second gate, the one leading out of the cemetery, and was continuing down the path.

What the hell was going on? Rafe glanced over his shoulder. They had followed the most direct route from the hacienda, which happened to be through the family's resting place.

He picked up his pace. Was it possible that he had misunderstood? Please, God, let it be so.

They must have walked close to a mile before the path led them to an isolated cottage in the woods. The man pounded on the door and called out in Spanish.

A match flared inside and an oil lamp was lit. An old woman, her gray hair streaming around her shoulders, answered the door. She stared at them with a wide, frightened gaze.

The man said something low that Rafe didn't hear. The woman nodded vigorously several times, then opened the door wider. Rafe motioned the man to enter ahead of him. Once inside, he found himself in a two-room cottage, sparsely furnished. There was a bed in the far corner of the room he had entered. The woman walked over to it, holding the lamp high so that he could see.

Dan Crenshaw lay there, a sheet pulled up to his waist, his chest bare except for the bandage wrapped around it. His shoulder was also bandaged, but the white dressings couldn't hide the inflammation radiating around the wound.

"You've left him this way for weeks? Can't you see the damn wound's infected? It wasn't enough to shoot him, you have to let him die by degrees?" He touched Dan's forehead, unsurprised to feel the heat. He was burning with fever.

"You're going to help me carry this man to the plane," he said to the man beside him. "If you try anything, I'll kill you, do you understand?"

The man nodded.

Rafe began to question the woman in Spanish. She rattled off her answers. She had tried to care for the man. She'd removed the bullet, tried to cleanse the wound, but sometimes infections occur, no matter what you do. She had kept him fed, changed his dressings, made him herbal teas. She had done all she could.

Rafe motioned for the man to sit down in the chair beside the bed so he could see him. He sat on the edge of the bed and took Dan's hand. "Is this any way to greet me, good buddy?" he asked. "What the hell were you thinking, anyway? Did you forget which one of us was the Commando, which one the Harvard grad?"

He checked Dan's pulse. It was light and racing, but by damn he had one.

Rafe could work with that.

He tucked the sheet around Dan and motioned for the man to help him. Between the two of them they lifted him from the bed. The old woman hurried to the door and held it open for them. Rafe shouldered his way through, careful not to jar Dan any more than he had to. Every step of the way back to the hacienda Rafe prayed that God would spare Dan's life. He had kept him alive this long. Dan was a fighter. Always had been. If anyone could pull through, Dan would.

Both of the men were breathing hard when they reached the hacienda. For the first time since Rafe had arrived, the man spoke to him.

"We can put him down here while I go for the plane." He motioned to the chaise lounge on the patio.

Once they had stretched Dan out, the man stepped back. "I'm going with you," Rafe said. "You and I are going to get that plane. You'll have your men *carefully* bring him to the plane. If anything goes wrong, know that you won't live to see the sun, amigo."

"If I wanted him dead, he would already be dead," the man said, turning his back on Rafe. Rafe grabbed the man's arm and lifted it high on his back.

"Why didn't you bring him home?"

"I planned to, when he got better."

"You know him?"

"Yes."

"You've been doing business with him?"

"I thought so, until he was shot. He was not the man I knew as Dan Crenshaw. I never saw this man before, but his identification showed me that I had been misled."

"But you were still intending to let him go, huh? Out of the kindness of your heart?"

"I do not deal in violence, despite what you think. The man who shot your friend no longer works for me."

"Aren't you afraid of what Dan can tell us about you?"

The man tried to straighten, but the arm hold kept him bent. "No one can prove anything about me or my business. We are in Mexico. Your authorities have no jurisdiction over me.''

"So you're feeling safe enough.''

"If not, you would have been dead before you stepped into my plane tonight.''

"So you know how I got here?''

"Don't make the mistake of thinking me stupid.''

Rafe released his arm. The man rubbed his shoulder. "On second thought, let's you and I take Dan on to the plane. I think it would be a good idea for you to fly back with us.''

"That isn't necessary.''

"I think it is.''

"If you think you can hold me there, you are wrong.''

"I'm not interested in anything but getting Dan back to Texas. I just want a little insurance that we'll make it there. You being in the plane gives me a better sense of safety, somehow. You'll be my security blanket.''

The man shrugged and returned to Dan's side. Once again they lifted him and followed the path to the landing strip. No one was there when they arrived. The plane was empty.

"Do you know how to fly this thing?'' The man nodded. "Then let's get Dan in the back and get it ready. You'll need more fuel.'' He watched the man go through the preflight check. They got into the plane and taxied over to where the fuel supply was.

It was while they were refueling that Dan finally stirred and opened his eyes. He stared at Rafe watching him from the front seat of the cockpit without blinking.

"So you finally decided to wake up and join the party, huh?''

Dan closed his eyes for a moment, then opened them

again. "Rafe?" he whispered. He lifted his hand as though to touch Rafe's face.

Rafe grinned. "Yep, it's me under all this paint."

"Thought I'd died and gone to hell," Dan mumbled.

"Our host has agreed to fly us out of here. You ready to go home?"

Dan nodded and closed his eyes.

So was Rafe.

The sun had been up several hours by the time the plane landed at the ranch. Rafe hadn't said anything more to the man who had flown them there. He felt that they both understood each other without further communication.

By the time the plane stopped rolling, Rafe had the door open. He lifted Dan out and started running toward the Jeep without looking back. By the time the plane took off, Rafe had Dan in the back of the Jeep. He headed back to the house, his foot on the accelerator and pressed to the floor.

Tom must have seen him flying over the last hill as he approached the house because he was standing in the driveway when Rafe came barreling up.

As soon as Rafe braked beside him and he saw Dan in the back seat, Tom said, "My God, you did it." He sounded incredulous.

"He's got to have immediate medical help. Take him to the nearest hospital while I go get cleaned up. I'll follow as soon as I can." He leaped out of the Jeep and sprinted toward the house.

Tom yelled the name of the nearest hospital and where it was located and Rafe waved without stopping. When he reached the house, he slowed down and walked in calmly.

His restraint was wasted. No one was there.

He hit the shower and scrubbed the paint off his face. Within minutes he was dressed and ready to leave. He took time to leave a note for Mandy, then took off in his borrowed truck.

By the time Rafe got to the hospital, they had admitted Dan. Tom waited in the hall for him, a grin on his face. "They're pumping him full of antibiotics, they've cleaned out the wound and done some fancy dressings, and they've got him on a drip to rehydrate him."

"What do they say about his chances?"

"Nobody's saying. They're just working on him, doing what they do best."

"Did he ever come to?"

Tom's grin widened. "Yeah. He recognized me. Looked surprised to see me. Then asked if he'd been hallucinating or whether you were actually here."

Rafe laughed out loud. "Yeah, I think I scared the religion out of him, or into him, I'm not sure which." He looked around the hallway. "I could use a cup of coffee. Do you know where I could find one?"

"Yeah. Unfortunately I've had to come in here on a disgustingly regular basis. Somebody's always getting hurt and needing to be patched up." Tom took him to the cafeteria where they were able to get coffee and Rafe some breakfast.

"By the way," Rafe said, once they were seated, "Where are Mandy and Kelly? I didn't see either one of them when I was at the house."

Tom shook his head. "That little guy didn't know what he was in for when Mandy got a hold of him."

"Yeah? What happened?"

"She's been getting bits and pieces of information out of him all week. Did she tell you?"

"No. We haven't had much of a chance to talk. If I wasn't asleep he was right there catching me up on his day and Mandy hadn't mentioned anything about his past to me. So what's been going on?"

"She finally got him to tell her where he and his mother lived, then managed to get in touch with Children's Services and got all the rest of the information she needed. She's already talking about petitioning for custody of him. She was told that, with her background, she wouldn't have any problem getting temporary custody, although she'll be taking him back to Dallas with her eventually."

"So they're dealing with paperwork this morning?"

"Nope. They were getting an early start on shopping."

"Shopping?"

"Yep. She informed Master Kelly that he had to look like he was cared for and loved and that she was taking him shopping whether he liked it or not. She also found out that he had a birthday last week—you were right...he just turned eleven—and she convinced him that most of what they were going to buy was going to be birthday presents. The rest he could pay out of his wages."

"I see."

"She's a formidable lady."

"That she is."

"So what are you going to do about her?"

Rafe had finished his food and was now reaching for his coffee when he froze with his hand halfway to the cup. "Me? I'm not in charge of the woman." He took a sip of the coffee and sighed. "Thank God."

"She's in love with you," Tom said.

Damn, but the man liked to be blunt.

"No she's not. We've just been friends for a long time."

"I've known her for a long time as well. I see the way she looks at you, the way she talks about you. I know what I'm seeing."

Rafe shook his head. "Whatever you're thinking, it's wrong. Can you see me a married man?" He laughed, even if it did sound a little hollow. "And now she's asking for custody of Kelly. She needs to find a good father figure, an example for kids. That's not me."

"Whatever you say."

"Come on. I want to go check on Dan."

The hospital staff finally let him in to see Dan a couple of hours later after reassuring him that Dan was responding satisfactorily to the medications. When he walked in, Dan was asleep. Rafe didn't care. He would sit there for a while and look at his friend…his living, breathing friend. That was good enough for him.

He sat down in the large, upholstered chair beside the bed and rested his head against the back. Dan's color was already better, his breathing eased. The marvels of modern technology, he thought, had saved Dan's life. He would have died in that little Mexican cottage for lack of antibiotics readily available here.

Another day, maybe two at the most, and the medical profession might not have been able to bring him around. Rafe recognized his reaction for what it was. He went through the shakes after every mission, successful or not. This one had been particularly difficult because he'd had to concentrate on keeping his focus on the job he'd set for himself.

He'd lost his concentration for a time in that cemetery. He closed his eyes. Yeah, he'd lost more than his concentration. He'd almost killed the man he held responsible. He smiled grimly to himself. For that moment in time, the mission had become extremely personal to him.

Rafe didn't realize he'd drifted off to sleep until several hours later when he heard Mandy's voice. He opened his eyes and found her hanging over Dan's bed, hugging him. "Oh, Dan, I can't believe it. I was so afraid you were dead."

Rafe stretched and stood so that he was on the other side of Dan's bed. Dan spotted him and held out his hand. "You can thank this guy that I'm not," Dan said to Mandy. "At least, that's what they tell me. I'm afraid I don't remember much about it."

Mandy glanced at Rafe, then back at Dan. "What happened to you? Why are you in the hospital?"

"Oh, a minor wound got infected, that's all," Dan replied. He looked from one to the other. "I can't believe you're both here. Hell, I can't believe I'm in an Austin hospital. Nobody's bothered to tell me how I got here from some little room in the mountains somewhere."

Mandy smiled at Rafe. "Rafe found you and brought you back."

"Still playing the hero these days, are you?" Dan said, squeezing Rafe's hand. Rafe could feel the tremor that denoted how weak Dan was.

"When did you get here, Mandy?" Dan asked. "I thought you weren't going to take your vacation until next month."

"Do you really think I could work when nobody

seemed to know what had happened to you? I've been staying at the ranch for the past week or so.''

''What did you do, get a hold of Rafe and tell him I'd disappeared?''

''She didn't have to. Your letter finally caught up with me. I got here as soon as I could. Obviously not soon enough.''

Dan gazed at him as though he still found it hard to believe Rafe was there. ''I'm glad you're here.''

''Me, too.''

''Dan,'' Mandy said, ''there's somebody waiting out in the hall who wants to meet you. Would you mind if I bring him in?''

''I don't mind. Don't tell me you got yourself engaged again. Man, if I don't keep an eye on you every minute, you get in some of the craziest situations.''

She dropped her gaze to her folded hands. ''Well, actually, I *have* asked him to live with me.''

Dan rolled his eyes. ''For God's sake, Mandy, when are you going to learn not to step in over your head? How long have you known him, anyway?''

''Not long. In fact, Rafe introduced us.''

Dan looked at both of them as though convinced they'd lost their collective mind. ''I thought better of you, Rafe. I really did. In my absence, you should have been looking after her, not encouraging her to go off the deep end.''

Rafe still held Dan's hand. He patted it and said, ''I really think you need to meet him before you start making all these judgments about him.''

''Yeah, fine. Bring him in,'' Dan said, frowning.

Mandy went to the door and leaned out. She signaled and came back in the room, smiling.

Rafe did a double take when Kelly appeared in the

doorway. He'd gotten a haircut since Rafe had seen him, almost military in appearance. He wore a chambray shirt, new jeans and a pair of cowboy boots. He saw Rafe and hurried over to him. "Look at my boots, Rafe. Mandy got them for me for my birthday."

"They're pretty sharp, son. You look like you're ready to throw your leg over a pony any time."

"Tom said he'd teach me to ride, but right now I have to learn how to take care of a horse first." He looked up at Dan. "Hi." Suddenly he was shy.

Rafe took over. "Dan, I want you to meet Kelly. He's the one who told me where you were. If it hadn't've been for Kelly, I'm afraid I wouldn't have found you at all."

Dan had been staring at Kelly in amazement since he'd walked in the room. He took turns staring at first Mandy and then Rafe. He shook his head. "Okay, guys. You suckered me in on that one."

"You did it to yourself, Dan," Mandy replied. "You were the one jumping to conclusions. We just gave you more room to keep leaping."

"So you're Kelly," Dan said. "I'm glad to meet you." He held out his hand, which happened to be his left, and Kelly took it and gingerly shook it.

"I saw them shoot you," he said in a small voice.

"What?" Mandy exclaimed. "You were shot? And nobody told me?"

Dan replied. "It wasn't serious until infection set in. I'm going to be okay."

She looked at Kelly. "You knew and you never told me?"

Rafe spoke up. He could see the anger and confusion in her eyes. "I told him not to mention it, Mandy. There was no reason to upset you at that point."

Dan returned his gaze to Kelly. "Where were you? I didn't see anyone else around."

"I was watching from the edge of the gully."

"And you told no one?"

Kelly hung his head. "No, sir. I was afraid. I wasn't supposed to be there. I didn't know what they'd do to me if anybody found out I'd been hiding in the gully."

"How long had you been there?"

Kelly shrugged his shoulders. "I dunno. A long time, I guess."

Rafe spoke up. "He was living in a cave. I happened to run across it."

Dan closed his eyes and mouthed the word "cave."

Kelly turned back to Rafe. "Guess what? Mandy says that I can come to Dallas and live with her. She knows these people and she talked to them about me and she said she'd be 'sponsible for me."

"That's very generous of Mandy," Rafe said.

"Yes. I told her I could help pay some of her bills if I got a job, but she said I have to go to school. She said there aren't any ranches in Dallas for me to work on."

"Well, maybe Dan will let you work on his ranch during the summers. That might work."

"Where will you be, Rafe?"

"I'll be back at my job overseas."

Kelly's face fell. "Oh."

Mandy spoke for the first time since she'd learned about Dan's injury. Rafe could see she was still upset with him for keeping the news from her. "We need to go and let you get some rest, Dan. Have they said when they're going to let you come home?"

He frowned. "When my temperature's normal, whenever that is," he said, sounding disgusted.

"I'll stay until you can get around all right," Mandy said.

Dan looked at Rafe. "How about you?"

"It's your call. You wrote the letter."

"Right. We'll deal with all of that once I'm out of here."

"I'll see you later, then." He looked at Kelly. "You want to head back to the ranch with me, cowboy? Tom's probably got all kinds of work for you to do."

Kelly pulled on his belt, settling his jeans on his hips. "I'm ready," he said with just a hint of a swagger.

When Rafe reached his side, Kelly confidently took his hand and they walked out together.

Mandy could feel Dan's eyes on her. She turned to him and smiled. "I guess reaction is setting in now that I know you're okay. I was so scared when you disappeared. Then I found Rafe's note when we got home that you were in the hospital. I didn't know what to think." She took his hand in both of hers. "Are you sure you're all right?"

"I will be soon enough." He shifted and with the obvious intent of changing the subject, said, "It's good to see Rafe again, isn't it? It's been a while."

"Yes."

"He's looking good."

"Uh-huh."

"And you're still in love with him," Dan said.

She dropped his hand. "Don't be silly."

"You think I didn't feel the sizzle between the two of you? Remember, I'm the guy lying on the bed between you. It's a wonder I didn't get electrocuted from all the electricity rushing between you."

She rested her palm on his forehead. "Yep. Still feverish…and delusional. Rafe is a friend. You know that."

He sighed and closed his eyes. "He is that. He saved my life."

"I'll always love him for doing that."

"So why don't you convince him to stay here and help you raise that boy?"

She'd been under too much emotional strain for the past several hours—days—weeks—to be able to control the tears that suddenly filled her eyes. "Can you really see Rafe finding a life here in the States, Dan?"

"Once he's faced his demons, yes I can. He can't keep running from them forever. This trip back to Texas was a start. Can't you see that the man is crying out for a home and a family? Did you see how he was with the boy? As for Kelly, he's got a bad case of hero worship going there. He was even mimicking the way Rafe walks, did you see that?"

The tears spilled over. "I saw it."

"So what are you going to do about it, sis? Are you going to let him walk out of your life like he did twelve years ago without making damned sure he knows how you feel?"

"I love him enough to want to see him happy. He seems to be happy doing what he's doing."

"Yes, because that's the only life he's really known. He's alone. He figures that's the way life is. It's up to you to show him he could have another life."

"I'll try."

"Uh-oh. That's a waste of energy. If you try, you fail, because you're leaving room in there to fail. Don't try. Do it. Give it all you've got. I'm not blind, Mandy. The man loves you so much it's eating him up inside.

You've got to convince him that he's husband and father material. Right now he hasn't a clue.''

She smiled. ''How can he be so blind?''

''Because part of him is still that little kid that got knocked around by a father who convinced him he was worthless. He's needed this time on his own to learn that his father was wrong. It's time for you to help him take the next step.''

Eleven

The house was quiet when Mandy arrived back at the ranch. During the time Kelly had been with her she had turned the storage room back into a bedroom for him. It hadn't taken much, since the furniture was still in place. She'd washed the curtains, found fresh linens and had the room ready for him the second night he was there.

She'd returned to her bed, knowing she wouldn't be able to sleep in the bed she'd shared with Rafe when he wasn't there.

Now she checked the rooms out of habit. Everything was as she had left it this morning, except for Dan's room. Rafe had fallen across the bed and was sound asleep. She'd noticed the dark shadows beneath his eyes at the hospital.

He'd definitely earned his rest. She wanted to hear the details of where he'd found Dan and how he'd managed to get him home. However, she'd probably get more information out of him if she let Rafe get some sleep.

In the meantime, she would keep herself busy planning a hearty meal for her guys.

By the time Kelly showed up to eat, the meal was warming in the oven and Rafe hadn't stirred.

"Hi!" Kelly said. "I went with Tom to look for cattle. Boy, was that fun. There's lots of things to do on a ranch, isn't there?"

"Yes, there is. Are you ready to eat?"

He looked down at his dusty clothes. "Maybe I should get cleaned up first."

"That's a good idea. When you've showered and changed, why don't you wake up Rafe so he can eat."

"He's asleep? Already?" He looked at the clock.

"Remember he was up all last night. I have a hunch that cave isn't real comfortable to sleep in."

Kelly grinned. "Not as comfortable as a bed."

"That's what I figured."

She finished setting the table and took the food out of the oven and placed it on the table. She enjoyed preparing meals for hungry appetites. It got so lonely cooking for one. She was looking forward to having Kelly with her.

Her thoughts returned to her conversation with Dan. Don't try, he'd said. Do it. Don't give yourself an out. Convince Rafe he deserved a family.

The question was how.

She heard voices and knew that Rafe was now up. He paused in the doorway and looked at her. "Why didn't you wake me up sooner?" he asked a little sheepishly. "I didn't need to sleep all day."

"I have a hunch your body thought differently.

You've been under the strain of looking for Dan for several days. With that worry gone, you were ready to crash." She nodded to the table. "Sit down. Everything's ready."

Mandy watched Rafe and Kelly interact all through dinner. Rafe patiently listened to Kelly's interminable stories about everything he had seen and everything he had done and everything he had thought about doing since the last time he'd seen him, which was only the day before. Mandy wondered what Kelly would do if he had to catch him up on months...or years?

Rafe listened with a keen ear, asking a question now and again, helping the boy to find a word to describe something. Mandy wondered if Kelly had ever had a male figure in his life. What kind of mother had he had? Was she one who got involved with a man, then moved on to another one? Or had her experience with Kelly's father discouraged her from seeking out further male companionship?

She would probably never know. Kelly had talked about his mother a lot once he opened up, but he had never mentioned a man in their lives. She knew that it was going to be a real wrench for Kelly when Rafe left.

At least she'd had years to learn to cope with those feelings, plus an education in a field that offered additional tools. She still wondered how she could let Rafe walk out of her life for the second time without emotionally falling apart.

"Right, Mandy?" Kelly asked, looking at her for confirmation.

"I'm sorry, Kelly. I guess my mind was drifting."

"You told me that maybe when we go to Dallas that I could have a dog like Ranger."

"Well, maybe not exactly like Ranger. He's a big

dog, and big dogs don't like to stay in apartments. They need plenty of room to run and play.''

"So do little boys," Rafe quietly added.

"Good point. Maybe I'd better be thinking about finding a larger place…a house, maybe, with a yard.''

He smiled at her and went back to eating.

By the time dinner was over, Kelly's nose was almost resting on the table.

"Why don't you go on to bed, Kelly?" Rafe said. "Morning comes awfully early these days.''

Kelly nodded, his eyelids drooping. He slipped out of his chair and headed for the door. "'Night, Mandy. 'Night, Rafe," he said over his shoulder.

When Mandy began to clear the table, Rafe helped. Between the two of them, the kitchen was gleaming in no time at all.

Mandy followed Rafe into the den where he generally watched the news. She waited for a commercial break and said, "Have you noticed that Kelly very rarely touches anyone?''

Rafe glanced at her and smiled.

"Oh, I noticed.''

"I keep wanting to hug him.''

"He's got his own space that he guards. He feels that's what keeps him strong. He's not quite ready to lose it. He's feeling his way with all of this. Actually you've worked miracles on the sullen boy I found hiding out in a cave.''

"Sullen? Kelly? He could talk the ears off a row of corn.''

"You're really good with children, but I guess you already know that. Why else would you have chosen the field you did?''

"Why else, indeed?'' She smiled at him. "You're

looking a little more rested. I want to hear all about how you did it.''

''Did what?''

''Found Dan.''

''I hitched a ride down to where he was and brought him back. End of story.''

''There's got to be more to it than that. I mean, these are the same people who shot him, from what I can gather. They're dangerous people.''

''I suppose.''

''Did they give you any trouble?''

''None.''

''You just waltzed in and found Dan and waltzed out.''

''You got it.''

She laughed. ''Oh, Rafe, you are too much.'' They were seated on the sofa. On impulse, she leaned over and kissed him. Impulse or not, it was what she'd been aching to do ever since she saw him asleep in Dan's hospital room.

He pulled her into his lap and leisurely kissed her back. Predictably Mandy was soon fretting because she couldn't touch Rafe through all of his clothing. She worked the buttons loose on his shirt so that she could touch his smooth skin.

''I missed you,'' she admitted between kisses. ''So much.''

He looked at her in surprise. ''You saw me every day,'' he said as though reminding her of the obvious.

''But I couldn't touch you. Kelly was always there. I would peek in sometimes and watch you sleep. It was quite a temptation not to crawl into bed with you and wake you up.''

''Maybe you should show me what you had in

mind,'' he said, lifting her off his lap and standing. He walked over to the television and turned it off, then held out his hand to her. He raised his brow in silent inquiry.

She didn't consider saying no.

Being with Rafe was like watching a brushfire explode with energy and movement and power. She lost all sense of self when she was with him. She teased and tormented him because he'd taught her how. He'd taught her about her own sensuality and how to use it. Their coming together seemed to ignite both of them, driving them to an explosive finish.

Some time later they lay in the darkness, limbs intertwined. Mandy was content to lie with her ear pressed against Rafe's chest, listening to the steady thud of his heart. She could think of no other place she would rather be.

For the first time in a long while, she was at peace. Her worry for Dan was now eased, she was in the arms of the man she loved with all her heart and she had a young boy to care for and tend.

''Mandy?''

''Mmm?''

''Dan probably won't be coming home for a few days.''

''I know.''

''I've been thinking about leaving in the morning for a couple of days.''

''Oh.''

''I've got some things I need to do.''

''Okay.''

''I want you to know how much being here with you has meant to me.''

''I'm glad.''

"You're one of the warmest, most generous people I know. You always have been."

"Thank you."

"You deserve so much. A good man. A loving family."

"And what is it you deserve, Rafe?"

"I have what I deserve. I make a good living."

"You don't want more than that? Do you ever get lonesome?"

"Me? Hell, I'm too mean to ever get lonesome."

"They aren't mutually exclusive, you know."

He chuckled. "I see you aren't going to argue with me about the mean part."

"It's part of your character. It makes you who you are. You may not want to hear this, Rafe McClain, but I love every ornery inch of you—good and bad—I know your moods and your attitudes, your hard side and your soft side. You are tough, that you are. But you are also a very, very gentle man."

"Sounds like a lot of contradictions to me."

"They all make up the man I love."

"I didn't ask you to love me, Mandy."

"I know you didn't. I couldn't help it. It's like a disease…once I caught it, it's in my blood forever."

"Wow. That makes my heart beat faster. I'm like some incurable disease. You really know how to win a man over with your poetic turn of phrase."

She caught his ear lobe in her teeth and gently pulled. "I never said I was the romantic type," she reminded him.

"No, you never did. But you are, sweetheart, in every bone of that luscious body of yours."

She stroked her hand down his body and nudged him

in an intimate spot. "You really think my body is luscious?"

"Mmm." He cupped her breast in his palm, flicking his thumb across the tip. "You turn me on like no woman ever has or ever will. I spend my time around you in a half-aroused state."

"Oh, that explains how you catch fire so quickly."

"I haven't noticed a slow burning fuse around you, either."

The flame they were discussing quickly stirred from its embers, catching them both in its heat. Mandy felt helpless to fight her feelings. She didn't even want to.

Rafe was the man in her heart, the one who had never moved out. She could deny him nothing.

However, he was amazingly predictable. When she awoke the next morning, he was gone.

At least he had warned her that he was leaving. He'd mentioned a couple of days. That was a start. He hadn't just disappeared into the night. She noticed while making breakfast for her young cowpoke that the truck Rafe had been driving was gone.

He'd be back.

Her problem was that she had to do something about getting back to work. She needed her job more than ever now that she had Kelly to care for.

She called her office and explained about Dan's condition. She also contacted the local office and made an appointment to see about having Kelly officially released to her.

The rest of the time she waited for Dan and Rafe to return.

And dreamed about Rafe at night.

Twelve

It took Rafe longer than he expected because he was following a cold trail. A week later, he knew he was finally on the right track. He'd been as far south as Corpus Christi, as far east as Beaumont, as far north as Tyler. The trail finally led him to a little town nestled in the tall pines of East Texas called Eden.

How ironic.

He parked Dan's pickup in front of a tidy-looking duplex. The lawn was neatly trimmed, and there were flowers bordering the sidewalk leading up to the porch. Hanging baskets decorated the entire length of the porch. There was a porch swing at one end near the door with the number he was looking for.

He paused before knocking and looked around. The neighborhood was quiet, with large trees providing shade for the sidewalks and street. It looked like a movie set, not like a place he'd ever lived in before.

Rafe knocked on the door and waited. There was no sound from within. No radio or stereo playing, no television. That, too, seemed strange to him.

The sound of a light step preceded the door opening. A small woman with a liberal amount of gray hair interspersed with dark peered through the screen at him. She smiled politely and said, "Yes?"

He hadn't tried to imagine how he would feel at this point in his search. In fact, he hadn't expected to feel much of anything.

Which showed how little he knew about his emotions.

Rafe stood there, trying to say something. Anything. When his throat finally worked enough for him to swallow, he said, "Hello, Mama."

The woman stared at him in shock. She touched her throat with her fingers. "Rafe?" she whispered. "Is it you?"

"It's me, Mama." He fought the emotion down. "You're looking good."

They stared at each other, the screen door and sixteen years separating them—half his life.

She pushed the door open and with innate dignity nodded and said, "Please come in."

He walked into a room that was familiar in some ways because he recognized some of the family possessions and yet different from what he remembered. The furniture was new to him—well made, comfortable looking and lovingly cared for.

There were framed photographs, large and small, on every surface of the room. Sheer ruffled curtains covered the windows without cutting out the light from outside. Scatter pillows added touches of color, as did the braided oval rug that dominated the central area of the room. He stood in the center of that rug and slowly turned, taking it all in.

"Have you eaten?" she asked and he smiled. His little mama always showed her love with food.

"Yes, Mama, but I could use a cup of coffee if you have it."

She waved him to a large, overstuffed recliner. "Sit. I'll bring you some."

Her dignity never left her. He watched her leave the room, her spine as straight as ever, graceful in her flowered housedress and her neat little shoes.

He should follow her and offer to help but the truth was, he didn't trust his legs to carry him much farther. After all this time he was back home, but it was like no home he'd ever had.

Within minutes she was back, carrying a small tray with two steaming cups on saucers. She set the tray down beside him and perched on the end of the sofa nearby.

"You have gotten so tall," she said, her gaze avidly going over him. "I don't believe I would have known you."

"I would have known you anywhere, Mama. You are still as beautiful as ever."

Her cheeks reddened and she waved him away. "There is so much to ask, so much to try to understand, so much to explain. I'm not sure…" She stammered to a stop, no doubt thinking of the enormity of trying to bridge the lost years between them. Rafe was overwhelmed by the thought.

"I wondered if you were still alive. You were so young and so—"

He waited and when she didn't finish, he offered his own word. "Angry?"

She nodded. ''Where did you go?''

''I ended up back near Austin. I looked up a friend from my elementary school when we lived near Wimberley. His family hired me to work at their ranch. I went back to school and stayed until I graduated.''

She beamed. ''So you finished your schooling.''

''I did that.'' He looked around at the pictures. He recognized the smiling faces of women he recognized as his sisters. ''Tell me about Carmen and Selena. Where are they now?''

''They live in Eden, too. Carmen married six years ago. Her husband comes from here. He has a large extended family that lives in the area. He does quite well. They bought me this duplex a couple of years ago. We were living in Corpus Christi at the time. So Selena and I moved here. She met a cousin of Timothy's—that's Carmen's husband—not long after we moved to town and married him six months ago.''

''So you finally left Dad?''

She didn't answer him right away. When she did, it wasn't the answer he'd expected. It was the last thing he'd expected.

''Your father was killed in an automobile accident. He was a passenger. A semitruck crossed into their lane and hit the car your father and his fellow worker were in. They were on their way home from work there in Corpus. There was a lawsuit. The surviving families were given a large settlement before the case went to court.''

Rafe tried to feel something at this news, but he felt numb. ''When did this happen?''

''Ten years ago in May.''

His father had died when Rafe was twenty years old. That was the reality. He'd died while Rafe was overseas, hating him. Rafe had carried that hate with him for all these years, long after the object of it no longer existed.

His hate had kept him from his mother and his two sisters for all this time. "You must have moved to Corpus not long after I left," he said.

She nodded. "The following year." She looked down at her folded hands resting in her lap. "Your dad was never the same after you left. He knew that what he had done was wrong, but you know how he was when he drank." She paused, thinking about it. "He went into himself after that, as though nothing much mattered to him."

"You continued to move around."

"Yes. He was restless, you see."

"And probably couldn't hold a job for very long."

Her black eyes glistened with moisture. "I tried to find you but I didn't know where to look."

"Did you think to check my school records? I had to have them forwarded in order to enroll. I figured you knew where I was all along, but just didn't care."

She let out a soft cry. "Oh, Raphael! No, it never occurred to me to check with the school. I wonder why they never notified us?"

"Probably because they thought you moved when I did."

"Oh. All these years you must have thought we didn't care."

Rafe absently rubbed his cheek. "I was tired of the way Dad showed how much he cared."

"He should never have treated you in such a way."

"Amen to that."

"I am sorry you are so bitter."

"I'm sorry you picked that man to be my father."

"So the anger is still there."

"Alive and well."

She got up and walked over to the mantel where more pictures were displayed. "I am sorry for many things that happened in my life. I have had many years to reflect on those decisions I made that I later came to regret." She turned and looked at him. "I lost my son, which is a very heavy price to pay for choices made."

"I lost a family."

"Yes, but it was your choice to leave. I'm sorry for the way your father treated you. When he was drinking he was a stranger, not the man I married. When we discovered you were gone he seemed to lose interest in much of life. He knew that I was very angry with him. I was also angry with myself. I should have stood up to him when he was so harsh with you."

Rafe shook his head. "You'd already learned your lesson. I haven't forgotten how he treated you when I was smaller. I figured it was better for me to be his punching bag than you and the girls." He looked away. "But I finally realized that if I stayed I would kill him." He returned his gaze to hers. "That's when I knew I had to leave. I could only hope he wouldn't turn on you and the girls."

"No. He never did."

"That's good to hear."

"He continued to drink, but not as much. In his own way, I know he grieved the loss of his only son."

Rafe tried to remember the man who had been his father when he'd been sober. He had trouble remembering anything but his drunken rages. They were stored with crystal clarity in his memory. Now that he worked to recall other images he remembered a man who had played with him, threw balls with him, took him fishing.

He remembered a man who took his family with him everywhere he went, a man who bragged about his children and loved to gently tease his wife.

He shook his head. "It feels strange to consciously recall the past. I'd shoved so much of it to the back of my mind."

"It is only the past if it's no longer affecting the way you live today."

"I'm sorry I stayed away so long, Mama."

"So am I, Rafe."

He stood, walked over to her and put his arms around her. She clung to him. When he eventually eased his hold and took a step back, she looked up at him, her face wet with tears. "You're tall, like your father. He would be so proud to see how you have turned out."

"Will you forgive me for not getting in touch with you before now, Mama?"

"You've already punished yourself far more than you ever deserved, my son. It's time to let go of the bitterness and hate. It is time to accept the love that has been waiting for you all of this time. Welcome home, Raphael."

Two weeks after he'd left Dan recuperating in the hospital Rafe drove into the ranch yard once again. He looked around the place where he'd spent four formative years of his life.

He'd come to realize that perspective is everything. When a person's perception changes, his world shifts. He knew that he would never view anything about his life in exactly the same way again.

He was eager to find Mandy and tell her what he had learned since he'd seen her last. She would understand more than anyone how he felt about what he had recently experienced.

As soon as he parked the truck Rafe saw Tom walk out of the barn. He waved and got out while Tom walked over to greet him. The two men shook hands.

"Good to see you back," Tom said.

Rafe grinned. "It feels good to *be* back. I'm hoping that Dan's home by now."

Tom laughed. "Oh, yeah. The nurses begged the doctor to dismiss him before they tossed him out on his ear. He doesn't make the best patient from what they told me."

Rafe laughed. "Neither did I." He glanced at the house. "I suppose Mandy's looking after him."

Tom scratched his head and said, "Actually she was until three days ago. She and Kelly headed north. She said she needed to take care of everything up there. She's been away for quite a spell."

Rafe felt disappointment wrap around him like a cloak. "Makes sense. If Dan's recovered, there was no reason for her to hang around."

Tom clapped him on the shoulder. "Dan's been watching for you. He'll be glad to see you made it back in one piece."

Rafe grabbed his bag from the cab of the truck and strode to the house. What had he expected, after all? He'd made her no promises. In fact, he'd made damn sure he hadn't made any promises.

She needed to get on with her life and they both understood that it didn't include him.

He opened the kitchen door and stepped inside. He could hear the television going. He set his bag down and walked into the living room where Dan was stretched out in his recliner, flipping channels with his remote.

"Can't find anything better to do in the middle of the day but watch television?"

Dan's face split into a big grin. "Well, *there* you are, you ornery cuss! It's about time you showed up."

"Were you about ready to report your pickup stolen?"

Dan laughed. "Hell, I'd forgotten you had my truck. Sit down and keep me company."

Rafe stretched out on the sofa. It felt good to kick back and relax. "You're looking good. How's the shoulder?"

"It's healing, but it's sure taking its own sweet time doing it."

"You're lucky you didn't lose your arm. That was quite an infection you'd picked up."

"The doctor said the same thing, so I'm trying to sit here and remember to be grateful." He pointed to his cell phone. "Actually I'm back to work, doing my networking, that sort of thing. I just can't do much traveling yet."

"You ready to explain how you got that wound?"

Dan frowned. "I don't know all the details as yet, but I've given the authorities what I know and they're working on the matter."

"So tell me who the man was who flew us back."

"Carlos Felipe Cantu."

"Means nothing to me."

"From what I can gather, and none of it is hard evidence, Señor Cantu is an intermediary. For a substantial fee he moves products from the seller to the buyer."

"What sort of products?" Rafe asked.

"My take on it is whatever the market is demanding.

At the moment the foreign market is looking for the latest computer technology. Someone in this area is helping to supply that need.''

"Any idea who?"

"Wish I did. I do have my suspicions."

"James Williams, perhaps?"

Dan stared at him in surprise. "James? My partner? You're kidding, right?"

"He wasn't at all curious about your disappearance. I found that peculiar, given the circumstances." He eyed Dan for a moment, then asked, "What were you doing at the airstrip at that time of night?"

"One of my clients from Dallas had scheduled a meeting for that evening. He intended to fly down at the end of the business day. I told him I'd meet him at the airstrip with the Jeep. He planned to stay over and fly back early the next morning."

"He never showed?"

"No. I found out while I was in the hospital that he'd tried to reach me to tell me he couldn't get away, but didn't get an answer."

"So you were at the airstrip waiting, and..."

"And a plane landed. But instead of the engine cutting off, the plane taxied to a stop and two men got out with the engine still going."

"You spoke to them?"

"Yes. When I told them they had no business on my land, they laughed. They said I was getting my cut for the use of the place. My memory gets fuzzy after that. I think I took a swing at one of them. I remember seeing the glint of a pistol, hearing the report, feeling a sudden fiery pain in my shoulder. After that, things faded in and out."

Rafe said, "Hold on. I'm going to get us some coffee. This thing is getting more and more interesting."

Dan sat up. "We might as well adjourn to the kitchen, anyway. I'm tired of hanging around in here." He turned off the television and picked up his portable phone.

They were sitting at the kitchen table with steaming cups of coffee in front of them when Rafe asked, "So what's the next thing you remember?"

"I woke up in some cottage where a woman was bandaging my shoulder. Carlos was behind her, watching. When she left he demanded to know if I was really Dan Crenshaw. Since I'd carried ID with my photo he couldn't deny the evidence. He said I wasn't the man he'd met in Laredo to set up the use of my ranch."

"Did he describe the man?"

"It was no one I recognized."

"Not Williams?"

"No. Carlos apologized for my wound. He kept telling me he would find a doctor. When it became obvious that the wound wasn't healing he said he would arrange for me to get back home. I have a hunch he didn't intend for me to leave that place alive."

"That's what I was afraid of," Rafe said. "I'm not certain why he changed his mind."

Dan chuckled. "Then you have no idea how intimidating you appear in that Commando outfit of yours. I thought I'd died and was being greeted by the devil himself."

Rafe smiled. "So you said at the time."

"I bet ol' Carlos was only too glad to get us both out of there. You know, he doesn't have much of a staff there, just a few retainers to run the hacienda. I think he figured he was safe enough from any direct involvement—he was just making the arrangements and setting up payments. The thing is, he knows the big guys, but I'm not sure there's any way for our law enforcement people to get information from him. He knew I couldn't tell them much. I don't even know where we were."

"Neither do I."

"Carlos also told me that he would find out who had been impersonating me because whether or not I liked the idea, I was involved in his operations up to my eyeballs."

"That's what I was afraid of. You say you contacted the authorities?"

"Yes, before I left the hospital. One of them told me this was another piece in the puzzle they've been working on for some time."

"So you're not being held for anything?"

"Me? I was kidnapped. I haven't done anything wrong."

"Except own the ranch being used for a drop site for who knows what."

Dan shrugged. "Well, there is that."

"So is this the reason you contacted me to come back?"

Dan laughed. "Hell, no. The two aren't connected." He paused. "I don't think."

"Tell me."

"As a matter of fact, it was about my plant security." Dan grimaced. "I don't know what's happening there, but something screwy is going on. I thought I had an excellent security system at the plant, but things keep turning up missing."

"Like microprocessor chips?" Rafe asked.

"Did James tell you?"

"No. I happened to read an article in the paper. It

sounds like quite a lucrative pastime. When I saw the article, I was wondering if that was what was being moved out through the ranch.''

''Who the hell knows at this point. If so, that points suspicion back at me since I own the plant.'' Dan dropped his head into his hands and rubbed his face. ''I've stayed in touch with the local investigators, offering whatever knowledge and suggestions I might have. The sooner this is cleared up, the sooner my name will be cleared.''

''So how did you figure I could help you?''

''Well, after talking to all kinds of security companies I realized I was way over my head. I needed an expert I could trust. So I thought of you.''

''Me!''

''You betcha. You've been taught how to get around the best systems invented. I figure you could come up with something that even the experts couldn't get around.''

''You mean you got me back here to offer me a job?'' Rafe asked incredulously.

''Sounds like a plan to me.''

Rafe scratched his chin. ''I think you've been on pain medication too long.''

''Well, at least kick it around a while and see what you think.'' He glanced at the clock. ''Mandy cooked up a bunch of casseroles and froze them for me before she left. Let's go find one and heat it up. After dinner you can catch me up on everything you've been doing. Your letters never told me much.''

''*My* letters,'' Rafe said, watching Dan get up and go to the refrigerator. ''All you ever did was give me hell in *your* letters.''

Dan opened the freezer and took out a covered dish. "Well, somebody had to keep you in line."

Rafe thought of his recent visit with his mother and sisters. "That's true. Somebody did."

Later that evening Rafe brought up the subject of Mandy. "I'm sorry I missed seeing Mandy. My business in East Texas took me longer than I expected."

"Yeah, things are really changing in her life these days," Dan said, settling back with a beer in his favorite chair. "Makes a person's head whirl."

"She's taking on quite a responsibility with Kelly."

"Hell, she's doing a damn sight more than that, didn't Tom tell you?"

Rafe got a sinking feeling in his stomach. "Tell me what?"

"I guess he finally got up the nerve to let her know how he feels about her. She's thinking about his offer. So she may end up giving up her job and moving back down here. Wouldn't that be something?"

"Uh, yeah."

"Probably not right away. She says she has quite a caseload that she needs to handle before turning in her resignation. But she thinks Kelly would be better off living down here and going to one of the local schools."

"Makes sense."

"You know, I had a lot of time to think, lying up in that hospital, and before that, when I was stuck in the mountains in Mexico. It does give one pause when he thinks he might be checking out."

Rafe nodded. "Been there. Know the feeling."

"Yeah. I got to thinking about something that Mandy and I talked about when she first got into this business of working with kids. As big as this ranch is, there's no reason why we couldn't build a center for kids like Kelly who don't have a decent place to grow up."

Dan continued. "With Mandy's credentials and with the money I've been making in the computer business, we could set us up a first-rate home for kids who don't have one. What do you think?"

"I think it sounds like a fine idea. I know what it meant for me to stay here and feel that I was contributing to something worthwhile."

"The thing is, Rafe, we could certainly use your help here with the kids as well as with the security business. You would understand those kids. Mandy tells me you knew just how to handle Kelly and get him to relax and trust adults again. I have a hunch you could do the same with others. Besides, we could keep you so busy you wouldn't have time to miss all those war games you Commando-types like to play."

Rafe thought about seeing Mandy every day, knowing that she was another man's wife. He shook his head. "I can't, Dan. I've got my own life going elsewhere. You and Tom and Mandy will be able to handle everything just fine without me."

"It will take a hell of a lot of work," Dan said, expanding on his idea. "We'll have to get somebody to draw up the plans, decide on how many kids we think we can handle, that sort of thing. Then there's the actual building of it all. I figure while we're at it, I need to see that the foreman has a larger home. A man with a family needs more space."

"So have they set a date—Mandy and Tom?"

Dan shrugged. "You'd have to check with Mandy. I haven't heard her say."

Rafe nodded. "Actually I was thinking about maybe going on up to Dallas and checking on her and Kelly.

I need to get back to work, myself. I still have a contract over there to fill. I could fly out of Dallas just as easy as Austin.''

"I'm sure she'd be pleased to see you. And that Kelly—now there's a kid who can talk your leg off, I swear. He's a character.''

"Yeah. I've really missed him.''

"I'd say the feeling was mutual.''

Rafe went into the kitchen to get another beer and worked to convince himself that marrying Tom was the best thing Mandy could do for herself and Kelly.

Thirteen

"**M**andy, where did Rafe go?" Kelly asked for what seemed to Mandy to be the hundredth time since they'd come to Dallas.

Mandy had been trying to concentrate on making a grocery list when Kelly chose to return to his favorite topic of conversation. She sighed, took hold of her patience and said, "I don't know, sport. He didn't say."

The condo no longer reflected the life of a single woman—neat, polished and subdued. In just a few days Kelly had managed to put his imprint everywhere and to claim it for his own. Mandy was thankful that he seemed to be adjusting so quickly to a more stable home life. She just wished she could reach inside his little head and erase all knowledge of Rafe McClain.

"He just left?" he asked. Now this was a new question he hadn't thought of earlier.

His question forced her to remember her last time

with Rafe. "Not exactly. He said he had some business to take care of and he'd be back in a couple of days."

"A couple means two."

"That's right."

"But he's been gone for weeks and weeks. Do you think he forgot about us?"

She hoped her smile seemed genuine enough for a young boy. "Oh, no. Rafe would never forget his friends. Remember what he told you? He's a forever kind of friend."

Kelly scuffed his toe on the carpet, studying the track it made. "Well, that doesn't seem to be a good way to treat friends. If you're a friend you come to visit."

"Don't forget that Rafe has a job he has to go back to, now that you helped him find Dan. Even heroes have to get back to work and to school."

Kelly grinned. "Yeah, but I like school, so that's okay."

"And Rafe likes his job. See how much alike you are?"

Mandy knew that if she didn't get him off this subject, she was going to end up in a puddle of tears. The truth was that Rafe was acting very much in character and she shouldn't be at all surprised. And she wasn't. Not really. It was just that she had hoped for so much. She'd thought that loving him would be enough to help him drop some of his shields. Plus, she'd thought that Kelly's presence had given him a greater insight into his own childhood. It was true that Kelly's mother hadn't abused him, but the system hadn't been there for him and he'd been traumatized to a certain extent.

Kelly's file was a good lesson for her in her own performance. No matter how hard you tried, there seemed to be some who fell into the cracks and weren't cared for in the way that was needed. She had to remind herself from time to time that it was why she chose her profession—to see that as many children could be helped as possible.

"You want to go to the grocery store with me?"

"Yes! It's fun to go with you. You don't have to count up the cost of everything we buy like Mom always did. 'Course she did a good job of feeding us, but we didn't get to buy many extras."

"Oh, and that reminds me. You remember those snapshots you showed me of your mom and of you with your mom? Well, I took them in to make prints and enlargements and we can pick them up today. Then we'll get some frames so you can keep them in your room."

Kelly nodded. "Yeah, I'm glad. I don't want to forget what my mom looked like."

"This way you'll always have her picture."

He studied her for a moment, then carefully walked over to where she sat at the kitchen table and put his arms around her neck. "Thank you, Mandy. I'm glad I got friends like you."

Dan had insisted that Rafe drive his truck up to Dallas. He said that he or Tom would bring it back on one of their trips to visit Mandy.

After spending another week with Dan, Rafe knew that it was time for him to return to his old life. The problem was, he could scarcely relate to it anymore.

Another perception shift.

Dan had been right. They'd had a great many things to catch up on. They'd sat up several nights into the wee hours swapping stories and sucking on longneck bottles of beer.

It was during one of those nights that Rafe had shared with Dan what he had discovered when he'd gone back to confront his past in East Texas. It had been tough to talk about. He'd had a lot of strong feelings to get through. He'd also had some time to think of all that had happened from his mother's point of view.

He hadn't been fair to her. She hadn't deserved his treatment. Nor had his sisters. He'd denied himself the opportunity to watch them grow up. All of that he'd shared with Dan. They'd talked about everything under the sun.

Except Mandy.

Rafe didn't want to discuss Mandy. Or Tom. Or their future.

Dan acted as though he didn't notice that her name never came into the conversation after that first night.

He knew he was being stupid, looking her up like this, but he remembered that she had asked him not to just leave, but to tell her goodbye first. He better understood why that was necessary. For closure, if nothing else.

He also wanted to see Kelly. Damn, but he'd missed that kid. When he'd seen his nephew and two little nieces, he'd found himself telling them about Kelly, just as if he was his kid, just as if he'd known him forever.

There was no reason why they couldn't keep in touch. He'd get Mandy's address and at least write to Kelly. He didn't want to cause any trouble between Tom and Mandy.

He thought about that first day when he'd been accusing Tom of going after her. He hadn't been all that far off base. She could do a lot worse than Tom. A lot worse.

Rafe followed Dan's directions and found the street

where Mandy lived with no difficulty. She lived in a condominium, Dan said, so she would have to put it on the market when she moved.

Since it was after eight o'clock in the evening, she should be home. Maybe he should have called her first but he hadn't wanted to hear her make excuses for not seeing him.

He hadn't gotten around to scheduling his return flight. He had an open return ticket, so he could travel the same way he came back—on standby, if necessary.

After he pulled up in front of her place, Rafe realized that, just as he had in Eden, he was hesitant to get out of the truck and meet the woman inside. He was dealing with his past with a vengeance on this trip.

"Kelly, you need to start getting ready for bed now," Mandy said for the third time.

"Aw, Mandy, it isn't even dark yet. I've got plenty of time."

"Uh-huh. But it takes you an hour to put all those toys back in their box."

"They aren't toys. They're soldiers. Like Rafe."

"Right. Well, they've pretty much taken over the living room and are now laying siege to the kitchen."

He grinned. She grinned back.

"I tell you what," she said, a sudden thought occurring to her. "You can play for another half hour if you'll give me a hug."

He stopped and looked at her with those big blue eyes of his. So expressive. "A hug?" he repeated as though he'd never heard the word.

"That's right. Just like the one I got this morning. I've discovered I'm getting an addiction for the things."

He looked at her with a very sober expression. Then

he grinned widely. "It's a deal!" He dashed across the room and threw his arms around her waist. She hugged him back. Then he raced back to his soldiers and was immediately engrossed in his games once again.

Maybe he'd lived out in the wilds too long. She wasn't sure what had gotten him so interested in the idea of soldiering. She knew that Rafe hadn't told him much about what he did, but he had spent time with Dan. She'd have to check with her brother to see what kind of tales he'd been feeding Kelly.

Mandy sank down on the couch, content to watch him play while she was supposed to be going through some of her case files.

She'd forgotten how noisy and hot and humid the city was. The traffic made the Austin congestion seem a dream. How had she managed to live here for so many years?

Now she couldn't wait to get her affairs in order and move back to the ranch. Kelly was already talking about the kind of dog he was going to get as soon as they moved.

She hoped to get him settled in school in Wimberley, but that was going to be cutting things close to get moved so quickly.

Forcing her attention back to the open file in front of her, Mandy began to read and make notes. When the doorbell rang, she jumped. She rarely had callers, especially at this time of day.

"I'll get it," Kelly said, racing toward the door. He never walked anywhere when he could run.

"Oh, no, you won't," she said firmly, rising. "We don't know who it is, so we don't open the door until we find out, remember?"

"Oh, yeah."

She went to the security view and peered out. No. She couldn't believe it.

"Who is it?" Kelly demanded to know in a loud whisper.

She unlatched the door and opened it, standing back so he could see for himself.

"Rafe! You came to see us!" Kelly launched himself at Rafe. Obviously surprised, Rafe caught him up in his arms and gave him a big hug.

Mandy grinned and said, "Come on in. No need to let all the cool air outside."

Rafe stepped inside and she closed the door behind him.

Kelly bombarded him with questions while she tried to calm the butterflies that had suddenly taken up residence in her stomach.

Rafe laughed and swung Kelly around, setting him on the floor. Kelly immediately grabbed his hand and dragged him over to see his strategy with all his soldiers.

Something was different about Rafe, but she couldn't quite put her finger on what it was. He looked more relaxed, more…at peace. That was it. He seemed to have come to terms with something and had accepted it. There was a serenity about him she'd never seen before.

Maybe he was looking forward to going back overseas.

Well, that was fine. She'd come to terms with that. She'd always accepted Rafe for who and what he was. She'd just decided that it was time for her to make a life for herself now and not look over her shoulder at a young girl's dreams.

"It's good to see you, Rafe," she said smiling. "When did you get to Dallas?"

"Just now. Dan loaned me his truck. Said I could leave it here with you and he'd pick it up later."

"That's fine. I have a two-car garage. I'll just have you pull it in. Have you had supper?"

"Not really. I snacked on the way up."

"Let me get you something. We have plenty if you don't mind leftovers."

"I would never complain. Not with your cooking."

Kelly chuckled. "She's making me fat."

Rafe reached down and rubbed Kelly's stomach. "I thought you looked a little heavier."

Kelly followed them into the kitchen until Mandy reminded him that he needed to start putting his men away for the night. With dragging feet, he returned to the living room.

"You've done wonders with him. I couldn't believe the hug I got," Rafe said, sitting down at the small table in the kitchen.

"I see changes in him every day. He really is putting on weight."

"He needed it. He was definitely underweight when I found him."

"He's loosening up with people more. I guess he's feeling more secure."

"Dan told me your big news."

"My news?"

"About using part of the ranch for a special home for kids like Kelly."

"Oh! Well, that's going to take some hard work before we can turn it into a reality, but it's been a dream of mine for some time. Eventually I hope we can pull it off."

"And Tom," he added.

"Well, sure, Tom's going to be a big part of it."

"I'm glad. I really like him."

She smiled. "He's one of the good guys, that's for sure."

"I, uh, need to call the airlines and see about getting a reservation. Do you mind if I use your phone?"

"Go ahead. There's one in the den. I hope you aren't planning to leave tonight. You can sleep here and I'll take you to the airport whenever you need to go."

She faced him calmly, determined to show him that she wasn't going to ask more of him than friendship.

"Thanks, Mandy. I'd appreciate that."

"That's what friends are for."

"You've been a good one."

She turned away. Calm was one thing, but when he looked at her like that, she felt like throwing herself around his neck and begging him not to leave. So much for all her resolutions.

She finished making a plate of food for him and placed it in the microwave to warm it. It seemed as though she had spent most of her time since Rafe had showed up at the ranch getting him to eat.

They had come full circle, she and Rafe. She refused to waste an ounce of energy regretting anything that she had shared with him. She had loved and nurtured him as much as she now loved Kelly and intended to continue to nurture him. Maybe that was her calling in life—to make a home for those tough guys who didn't believe they needed anyone.

Only Rafe had convinced her that he was right. He truly needed no one.

While Rafe ate, Mandy went to oversee Kelly's evening ritual of bathtime and making sure his things were put away for the night.

It was at times like this she thought of his mother. Kelly had confided several of the rituals he and his mom had had, asking if they could do them, too. Whoever else Elaine Morton might have been, she'd been a good mother to her son, even if she'd severed all contact with any family she might once have had.

Now Kelly was truly alone in the world...except he had her...and Rafe.

It was a beginning.

When she returned to the living room Mandy found Rafe stretched out in one of her chairs, looking contented. He looked up at her when she walked in. "You are one fine cook, Mandy, in case I've forgotten to mention it." He rubbed his lean belly, at just the spot she loved to kiss.

"Thank you."

She returned to her place on the sofa.

"Looks like you've brought a lot of work home with you."

"Yes. I need to get caught up on what's been happening while I was gone."

"You're going to miss your job, aren't you?"

"A little, perhaps. I'll be doing related work in the Austin area, until we get everything up and running at the ranch."

"Did you ever find out anything more about Kelly while I was gone?"

"Some. We know when he was born and where, from his birth certificate. His mother is listed as Elaine Morton. A father is not listed. Elaine was sixteen when Kelly was born and from what we can tell, she was completely on her own at that time."

"Sounds like she had a rough time."

"She could have been a runaway. The medical records at the hospital don't give much and no one remembers her particular case from that long ago. Kelly has no memory of anyone but his mother. He said she didn't date, but she worked a lot. I can well imagine."

"Poor kid. Not much of a life for a young girl."

"It's obvious she took her responsibility toward Kelly seriously. He had a few photos of her that I had framed for his room. He'd kept what he could of theirs, which is where his birth certificate turned up. She'd kept a baby book on him and carefully recorded each step of his development."

"Kelly's luckier than he knows."

"I'm just thankful that you found him before he got caught stealing. He remembered every item he took and where he got it. As soon as Tom gave him his first paycheck he asked me to go with him to pay the store-keepers for what he'd done. He walked up and apologized to each manager of the store as though they were equals. He explained that he hadn't had any money and he was hungry, but now he had the money and he wanted them to have it."

"I know of very few adults who are that honest, forget children."

Mandy smiled. "I know. I was so proud of him I could scarcely stand there and watch without crying."

Rafe sat forward in his chair and rested his elbows on his knees. "One of the reasons I wanted to come by was to explain where I've been for the past few weeks."

"You don't owe me any explanations, Rafe," she said. "I placed no strings on you. I'm so grateful that you were able to find Dan and rescue him. You have my undying gratitude for that."

"I'm glad I had the chance. However, if I hadn't spent time with you I doubt I would have given a thought to looking up my folks. So I thought you might want to find out what I discovered."

Her eyes widened. "You went back home?"

He shook his head. "It was never home to me…not like the ranch was. The family had moved not long after I left. In fact they moved several times, which was why it took time to follow their trail. I finally found my mother living in East Texas."

"And your dad?"

"He was killed in a wreck ten years ago, which means my mother and sisters were left alone. I could have been there to take care of them if I'd known."

"But you had no way of knowing."

"I guess what I'm having trouble with is that I never made an effort to get in touch with them, despite how I felt toward my father. The news really jolted me."

"I can see that. However, I think it was a wonderful thing that you found them now. Is your mom all right?"

"Oh, she's fine. My sisters are married. The older one already has three children. The younger one just announced that she's pregnant as well. I like their husbands. They're good men. Everyone treated me so well. I—uh—it was tough trying to let go of all this time when I could have—" He stopped talking and she knew just how tough all of this was. But it explained the difference she saw in him.

She left him and went into the kitchen to make some coffee. He seemed more composed by the time she returned. He thanked her for the cup and said, "Tom's a lucky man, Mandy. I know he'll treat you with all the love and consideration you deserve."

She set the tray down on the coffee table and stared at him. "What are you talking about?"

He shrugged. "Maybe Dan wasn't supposed to have told me, but he said that Tom had asked you to marry him."

She sank into the chair opposite where he sat. "I wasn't aware that Dan knew about it."

"Tom probably mentioned it to him."

"I don't understand why. I told him that I thought the world of him and would do most anything for him, except marry him." She looked at Rafe in dismay. "Did you honestly believe that I could agree to marry someone else when you know how I feel about you?"

He looked at her as though in shock. "You're saying you aren't getting married?"

"No. I finally understand myself well enough to know that trying to find a substitute would never work."

He closed his eyes. "Mandy, you devastate me with your fearless honesty."

She glanced at her watch. "Look, it's getting late. I'm sorry I only have the two bedrooms. Under the circumstances, it would be easier—for me at least—if you slept here on the sofa. I don't like lingering goodbyes, myself. If you'll tell me when you have to be at the airport I'll set my alarm and see that you get there in plenty of time." She went to the linen closet in the hall and pulled out bedding. When she returned she found that Rafe hadn't moved.

Mandy set the pillows and sheets on the end of the couch and turned away.

"Mandy?" His voice sounded hoarse.

She turned. "Yes."

"I have to go back to my job."

"I know."

"I signed on for two years. I still have six months to go."

She felt no need to comment and wondered why he felt the need to explain.

"The thing is…well, I've been thinking. A lot. Dan has offered me a position with his company, quite a well paying one as a matter of fact."

Mandy stared at him, her heart suddenly forgetting its rhythm. What was Rafe saying?

He suddenly took a keen interest in studying his hands. He kept glancing up at her for a second or two, then looking back down. "I need to be as honest with you as you've always been with me."

"All right," she managed to get out around the lump that seemed to have lodged permanently in her throat.

He raised his head and looked directly at her, his gaze intense. "I love you, Mandy, more than I ever thought it possible to love anyone. Being with you these past few weeks was like a dream come true for me…and I don't want it to end."

She was dreaming. None of this was happening. Rafe McClain hadn't shown up at her door. She was going to wake up soon and discover this had been a dream, but oh! she hoped she didn't wake up any time soon.

"The thing is, Mandy, I've discovered some things about me that make me really ashamed of the way I've behaved in the past. I grew up hating my dad and yet in many ways I've been turning into him. Not that I will ever drink the way he did, but I seem to have adopted many of his attitudes without realizing it."

"Rafe," she said softly. "Please don't beat up on yourself. You are a wonderful man. I wish you could see the man I know and love."

"Well, my world has been pretty black-and-white. I've never let many people close to me for whatever reason. There's been Dan. And you. I don't want to lose either one of you."

She smiled. "I don't think you could get rid of either one of us if you tried."

He took a deep breath. "I was wondering…I know it sounds crazy, even to me. But I was wondering if there's a chance in hell you'd consider marrying me once I can get my contract taken care of and get back to the States."

Mandy was too stunned to think for a moment. She had never expected to hear the *M* word come out of Rafe McClain's mouth.

She'd be waking up any minute now.

A tremor had started in her body. She wanted to leap off the couch and into his arms. Rafe was asking her to marry him! The fifteen-year-old within her was exuberant. The twenty-seven-year-old was just as excited.

"Oh, Rafe," was all she could think of to say before she launched herself at him.

A slow smile began to spread across his face. It grew and grew, much like watching the sun peek over the horizon, then spread its light across the world. The brilliance of Rafe's grin could have illuminated an entire universe. In a quick movement, he was up and had her in his arms, kissing the daylights out of her.

She certainly saw no need to struggle. This was exactly where she wanted to be.

He finally raised his head so that they could catch their breath. "May I take your response as being a yes?"

She laughed. "You'd better believe it."

"I don't know the first thing about being a husband," he reminded her.

"Well, I haven't any practice being a wife, but I'm looking forward to learning."

"I'll be back a quick as I can."

"I'll be waiting." She took him by the hand and led him down the hallway to her bedroom, turning off lights as they went. "I'm going to set the alarm but I have a hunch neither one of us is going to get much sleep tonight," she said, once she'd closed the door behind them.

He hugged her to him. "Damn, Mandy, I can't believe my luck. How could you want someone as mean and ornery as me?"

She went up on her toes and gently kissed him. "Because I love you. I never want you to be lonesome again."

Epilogue

Rafe pulled up to the entrance of the C Bar C Ranch, punched the combination into the keypad and waited for the gate to swing open. Once inside the fence, the gate closed behind him as he continued on the road to the cluster of buildings that made up the heart of the ranch.

There had been many changes in the two years since he'd moved back to Texas. It was difficult for him to relate to the closed-off, bitter man he'd been back then when he showed up on the ranch looking for Dan.

Today had been a tough one, but he'd made sure that Dan knew he was there in the courtroom to support him during his testimony. The authorities had eventually arrested James Williams for the theft of various computer components, including microchips from DSC Corporation, and he'd been charged with selling them illegally overseas. That had been nine months ago. The trial was now nearing completion.

Dan had been devastated by the news. Rafe had felt badly that his friend had to discover how his long-time friend, college roommate and business partner had worked behind his back not only to make money but also to place the suspicion on Dan.

Rafe had spent the remaining six months he'd had to work overseas going over the evidence he'd uncovered and shared with the authorities before he left. In his mind, everything pointed to James Williams. He had the opportunity, greed was a universal motive and he could use Dan to hide behind. He'd passed on his theories to the authorities. Once he returned to the States and began working the security detail around the plant, the investigators suggested he help them set up a trap for whoever was responsible for the disappearance of the computer components.

He hadn't been able to discuss any of it with Dan, not because he didn't trust him but because he knew that Dan trusted Williams and might accidentally give something away.

As Carlos had predicted, the only evidence they had on him was that one of his henchmen had shot Dan. He willingly gave the authorities the man's name but there was nothing anyone could do about Carlos except to file a trespassing report against him.

The Mexican authorities refused to extradite one of their prominent citizens for such a minor offense.

Dan had been shocked and dismayed when he discovered that Rafe had been part of the trap set up to catch James Williams until Rafe sat him down one night and explained that what he had done was to clear Dan's name. Up until Williams was arrested, Dan was their prime suspect, despite his wound. His disappearance actually added to their suspicions.

Rafe left Dan at the office today after they left the courthouse and came back to the ranch. He knew that Dan would have to deal with all of this on his own. He also knew that Dan knew that Rafe was his friend.

Friendship sometimes led to unlikely situations. If someone had told Rafe that in less than three years after he responded to Dan's plea for help that he would be a contented husband and besotted father, he would have laughed in their face.

He turned off the main road onto the new one that led to his recently completed home. He wasn't out of the truck before the back screen door slammed and Kelly came bounding down the steps, racing toward him.

Kelly looked like a typical gangly adolescent with lanky arms and legs. He was going to be tall from the looks of things. He'd taken on a recent spurt of growth that kept them hustling to keep him in clothes that fit.

"Hey, Dad, how's it going?" he asked, sounding a little breathless from the sprint he'd just made. He threw his arms around Rafe in an unselfconscious gesture that never failed to touch Rafe's heart.

"Fine, son," he replied, giving him an equally strong hug. "So is school out for the holidays?"

Kelly grinned. "Yep. And I was wondering if it would be okay if I spend the night with Chris. Mom said it was up to you."

Rafe smiled. "Oh, she did. So what is it that I don't know about?"

Kelly's eyes widened innocently. "I don't know what you mean."

"Oh, yes, you do. Mandy generally gives you permission to do what you want unless it's something she's unsure about—generally having to do with your safety. Now, what's going on?''

"Nothing. Really. Chris is just having a few of the guys over and we're going to watch videos and stuff."

"Uh-huh. And does anyone of your friends happen to drive? And do you intend to be out checking on girls?''

Kelly rolled his eyes. "Boy, you're sure suspicious."

"Which doesn't answer my question."

"Okay, so Larry has his license but we weren't going to go out anywhere."

"I'm glad to hear that. And if you promise me that you won't be leaving Chris's house unless an adult is driving you, then you have my permission to spend the night over there."

From the look on Kelly's face, Rafe realized that this wasn't exactly the permission he'd been looking for. But then his face lightened, and he grinned. "All right, Dad. I promise. I may be the only one sitting there watching the videos at times, but you have my word."

"No doubt they're going to be R-rated videos, right?''

"Dad! Everybody knows those things aren't that bad. C'mon."

Rafe laughed and patted Kelly's shoulder. "Let me know which ones I'd like to see, okay?"

They had reached the house at this point in their conversation and Kelly dashed inside to get ready for his overnight. Rafe paused inside the kitchen to survey the scene.

His mother was placing something delicious-looking into the oven while Mandy was sitting in front of the high chair trying to interest Angie in trying something new. From the yucky green of the stuff Mandy was holding hopefully near Angie's mouth, Rafe thought his daughter showed remarkable intelligence by studying it skeptically.

"How are my girls today?" he asked, taking turns kissing all three of them on the cheek.

Mandy rolled her eyes. "Nothing pleases her. I think she may be starting a new tooth. I swear, she reminds me of you when she gets that stubborn look on her face. Just look at her."

Maria, his mother, chuckled. "Oh, she is definitely her father's daughter."

"Now I'm really feeling picked on," he complained. He turned to his daughter and asked, "Would you like your old man to feed you, sugar?" He took the spoon from Mandy and eased it into Angie's mouth. "You see, ladies, that's all there is to it. You just have to use a little charm to—" He stopped to wipe off the bite of peas that had just been sprayed all over him. "Now, Angie, that wasn't nice," he pointed out while his wife and mother cackled like a couple of hyenas. "Do you want your dad to look bad here?"

Angie gave him a toothless grin and banged the top of her high chair.

He nodded, "Great. Well, maybe we should try something else, huh?"

Mandy said, "Don't bother. She's been in this mood all day. I'll go ahead and nurse her and put her to bed." She wiped his face with a damp rag, then gave him a leisurely kiss. "At least you tried."

"Mama, what have you made for dinner tonight?" he asked, audibly sniffing.

"Just a recipe I found in the paper. Thought I'd try it out."

"I told her she didn't have to be cooking while she's here, but you know your mother," Mandy said. "She can't sit still." She picked up Angie and left the room.

"Once you get the big kitchen finished, I'm hoping you'll have me come help with meals when the children start arriving."

Rafe looked at her in surprise. "Are you serious? You'd consider moving here, Mama?"

Maria nodded vigorously. "There's a nice large suite built off the kitchen area that would be perfect for me. I could still visit the girls and their families but they don't need me and I'm bored sitting around all day. Being over here will keep me young."

Rafe grabbed her and hugged her tightly. "Oh, Mama, I'd love to have you here. I had no idea you'd consider such a thing."

"Well, Mandy's going to need some help…and I want to be here to watch Angie grow up. I missed so much of your life. I don't want to miss any of hers."

Rafe couldn't speak. He just nodded and walked out of the room. He walked into Angie's room where Mandy sat in a rocking chair, nursing their daughter.

"How did Dan do today?" Mandy asked him when he sat down in the recliner nearby.

"He was good. Answered questions clearly, handled the cross-examination questions without getting flustered. The defense is still trying to implicate him on everything that happened. I'm glad we were able to gather enough facts to refute that. I guess Dan needed to see that James is determined to bring him down with him in order to realize that man is no friend."

"Do you think the jury will convict him?"

"I can't imagine anything that would sway them to believe he's innocent. Dan's testimony really ties it up, which is why the defense went to such lengths to discredit him. Instead they made themselves look worse.''

"Dan's working too hard, trying to do both jobs. He's going to have to get some help.''

"I know. He's got employment agencies looking across the United States trying to find the most qualified person to take over James's position.''

They became quiet and watched Angie eat, then fall asleep. Mandy put her to bed and they left the room. Once she closed the door, Mandy turned to Rafe and said, "Please don't punish yourself for any of this, Rafe. You probably saved Dan from being arrested. He knows that.''

"I hate to see him so torn up.''

"Dan's strong. He'll work through it.''

She kissed him. Rafe wrapped his arms around her and returned the kiss. Mandy certainly knew how to distract him. His brain went dead whenever she touched him, while every other part of his anatomy came to startling life. He edged her down the hall to their bedroom.

When she finally pulled away from him she was breathless and laughing. "Rafe! Dinner will be ready in a few minutes. Besides, it's not nice to leave your mother alone.''

He sighed. "You're right. I guess I thought that being married would cool down my response to you. But it hasn't.''

"You don't hear me complaining,'' she replied with a grin. She took his hand. "Your mother offered to keep Angie for us tonight if we want to go somewhere.''

"Mmm. Okay. But the only place I want to take you at the moment is to bed.''

"Hold that thought. We'll get there soon enough," she said heading back to the kitchen.

Rafe shook his head, amazed at his own reactions. He was acting like a randy teenager. He had a hunch that Mandy would always provoke that kind of reaction in him.

Who was he to complain?

* * * * *

Dear Reader,

I'm a real enthusiast of love and marriage in general. (There's nothing that can make you happier than building a life and family together with the person of your dreams.) And there is nothing like being a newlywed for guaranteed passion, drama and excitement.

And that's exactly what Zach Grainger and Sunny Carlisle find when they are forced into a shotgun wedding by Sunny's grandfather.

They don't want to be married. And despite their "I do's" they have no intention of making a real or lasting commitment to each other. But a funny thing happens when they spend so much time together. They begin to see each other for who they really are, and discover things about each other that no one else knows.

They're both sure it can't be love. After all, this is just a temporary arrangement until tempers cool and the scandal surrounding them dies down. So what if they happen to find a little passion and fun along the way? They are simply living in the moment, not creating any kind of lasting tenderness or joy. But a funny thing happens when they try to say goodbye....

I hope you enjoy reading this book as much as I enjoyed writing it.

Best wishes,

Cathy Gillen Thacker

A SHOTGUN WEDDING
Cathy Gillen Thacker

Prologue

Here Comes Temptation

She was a vision, with her angel's face and her glorious mane of curly hair streaming down her back and gleaming red-gold in the sunshine. Her slender curves were encased in knee-length khaki hiking shorts, a powder blue-tan-and-white plaid shirt and powder blue vest. Thick white knee socks came halfway up her long, spectacular legs. Serious hiking boots were on her incredibly dainty-looking feet.

Not ready to leave his unexpected find just yet, Zach braked his truck and paused for a second leisurely look.

A backpack slung over one shoulder, the angel in the meadow resembled a classy ad for ultraexpensive camping gear. The only exception in the picture of beautiful woman and nature at its alluring best was the clipboard and pen in her hands. She appeared to be writing something down as she went from tender sapling to sapling, moving among the wildflower-strung Tennessee property with unexpected grace.

Unfortunately, Zach thought with a frown as he took in the rest of her surroundings, he wasn't the only one who had noticed the pretty lady, and he was quite sure she had no idea she was being followed. Since he was the only other person within miles of the rural mountain property, he figured it was up to him to warn her. Scowling at the potentially risky nature of his mission, he steered his pickup to the side of the narrow country road, parked and got out. He shut the door quietly, then moved around the front of the truck.

The angel had her back to him. She was busy checking out leaves and scribbling on the clipboard in front of her.

For safety's sake, Zach decided to head north of her. He hopped the fence stealthily, giving the pending disaster wide berth, then moved to the north. He wished he could just shout, tell her not to move, but a call from him was liable to startle her, and given what was at stake—for both of them now—he didn't want to chance it.

His strides long and easy, he closed the distance between the woman and him. Behind her, to Zach's growing chagrin, disaster closed in, too. He was already beginning to regret his gallant actions. Doing his best to blend in with the environment, he whistled "Bob-white, Bob-white."

To his frustration, the angel didn't look up.

So much for ye olde Mother Nature approach. Zach reached into his pocket. He withdrew a dime. Aiming carefully, he tossed it at her shoulder. It hit her, bounced off and fell to the ground. She frowned and rubbed her arm without even looking up from the tree she was examining.

Zach swore softly. The woman was right in the middle of disaster and she was too absorbed in whatever she was doing even to realize it.

Knowing speed was of the essence now, he withdrew

a quarter and aimed this coin at her clipboard. It bounced off the paper. She glanced up in alarm, stepped back quickly, saw Zach and let out a piercing yelp of surprise.

"Don't move!" he mouthed silently, letting his eyes convey the immediate physical danger she was in. But it was too late; her assailant was already zipping into action. Heart pounding, Zach knew there was only one thing to do. He called upon his years of high-school football, dashed in and grabbed the angel about the middle. To his chagrin, they were both hit with gargantuan force, even as he knocked her aside. Teeth clenched, Zach swore like a longshoreman. His first job in Carlisle was more than he bargained for.

Chapter One

You Done Me Wrong (And That Ain't Right)

"Arrggh!" Sunny Carlisle screamed as the horrible skunk spray assaulted her with hurricane force. Choking on the tear-gaslike fumes, she extricated herself from the big stupid oaf who had tackled her and stumbled to her feet. Dimly aware that he was yelling, coughing and choking, too, she grabbed her backpack and clipboard and headed for the ice-cold mountain stream at a run. She had to get this stuff off of her!

She reached the stream first. Without a glance at the hopelessly inept good Samaritan behind her, she dumped her gear on the bank, waded blindly in up to her waist and then knelt to submerge herself to her shoulders.

He came in right after. "Sorry about that," he apologized, right before he went under. He came up, his ash blond hair slicked back, his face all red from the fumes. After several more dunkings, he introduced himself. "I'm Zach Grainger."

"I'm Sunny Carlisle," she sputtered grimly, barely able to believe she was in such a predicament. "And if I didn't know better, I'd think you were yet another decoy sent to distract me," she muttered. After all, she huffed angrily to herself, the other interlude had started out almost exactly like this—minus the misguided attempt at heroism, of course.

"What are you talking about?" Zach demanded, flinging the water from his face.

"My parents. Do they know you're here?" It was possible they'd found out Zach was coming and had bought him off, too. She knew they hadn't given up getting her out of Carlisle altogether.

To his credit, though, Zach looked thoroughly confused.

"Who are your parents?"

"Elanore and Eli Carlisle."

"Sorry, I haven't met them. Yet, anyway." He paused. "Should I have?"

"No!" Sunny said. She studied Zach Grainger a moment longer. He seemed to be telling the truth. And given that he'd been born and raised in Tennessee, unlike her, there was little chance he'd ever met her parents, never mind agreed to one of their well-meant schemes. She was just overreacting, she assured herself boldly, because of what had happened before. Deliberately Sunny pushed her past romance and the humiliation she'd suffered at the hands of her ex-fiancé from her mind.

Still a little befuddled, Zach watched as she washed herself vigorously through her clothes, then followed suit, scrubbing uselessly at his own shirt and jeans. To Sunny's chagrin, they both smelled to high heaven and looked even worse. Realizing they were both using up tremendous energy with little result, she stopped what she was doing and glared at him. "I can't believe this," she muttered to no one in particular. "My life has turned into an episode of 'I Love Lucy'!"

He reacted defensively. "Well, so has mine, and don't stare at me like that," he counseled sternly. "I was trying to do you a favor by alerting you to the danger you were in!"

Well, that made all the difference. "Some favor. You got us both sprayed," Sunny grumbled, trying hard not to notice how devastatingly handsome Zach Grainger was in person. The black-and-white photo he'd sent in with his application did not convey the windblown appeal of his straight ash blond hair, long-lashed blue eyes, athletic build and all-American face. He was sexy in a very clean-cut, outdoorsy way.

"How long is it going to take for the skunk smell to go away?" Zach asked.

Sunny sighed pragmatically and tried to compose herself. "It won't. It's on our clothes. We'll have to burn them."

"What about us?" he inquired dryly. "We can't exactly set fire to ourselves, can we?"

Actually, Sunny thought, he had already done that to her senses, first with the tackle and then when he'd given her the once-over, but he didn't need to know she had personally reviewed and approved his application for employment. "No, I guess we can't," she said sagely. She gave him a brisk, purposeful smile.

"So what are we going to do next?" he asked.

Good question. "We're in luck. I have a can of vegetable juice in my backpack."

"What good will that do?"

"Boy, you are a greenhorn, aren't you?"

"Give me a break. I'm a complete novice when it comes to skunks."

"How well I know that."

"I'm also the new physician for the area."

"I know that, too," Sunny retorted, and then wished she hadn't.

Zach edged closer, his brawny shoulder temptingly near.

"How do you know that?"

Sunny paused uncomfortably as she tore her eyes from the broad, muscular planes of his chest, beginning to feel a little guilty, although there was no reason she should, she told herself stubbornly. Her part in bringing Zach to Carlisle had been completely aboveboard. "Carlisle is a small town, with a population of just 317."

Deciding they were standing much too close, Sunny stepped back. "Although they'll be changing the sign to 318 if you plan on staying."

Zach shrugged and kept his eyes on hers. "I don't really have much choice, since this is where the state assigned me to go," he said. He regarded her curiously. "Are there many people our age in Carlisle?" he asked.

Again Sunny had a tinge of regret. This was something she felt Zach should have been told up front. The other people on the selection committee had disagreed with her, and the majority vote had won out.

"Actually, there are very few people our age in the area," Sunny admitted. "Almost none of them single. So it can be hell trying to find someone to date." That was one of the few serious drawbacks to living in the small Tennessee mountain town. But to Sunny, it was a manageable situation, at least for the time being. Since her failed engagement six months earlier, she hadn't wanted to date.

"I assume you live in Carlisle, also."

"Yes, I work there, too."

Zach tilted his head and studied her silently. "You any relation to the Carlisle Furniture Factory?"

Sunny nodded, unable to prevent her pride from bubbling forth. "I run it—for my grandfather."

Zach nodded, impressed. "So what do you do for entertainment on Saturday nights?" he asked, after glancing at her left hand and seeing no wedding ring.

"Usually I work."

"Oh." Zach felt a little disappointed.

Deciding they'd chatted long enough, Sunny began to unbutton her shirtsleeves. Zach turned his back to her. "I suppose you've got a spare set of clothes in that backpack," he said hopefully.

"Unfortunately," Sunny said tightly, "no." She was just going to have to make do. Determined to get on with this and do what absolutely had to be done, she tore off her clothes and hurled them into the bushes one by one. Then she popped open the can of vegetable juice. Using the hem of her bandanna, she saturated it with the juice and began rubbing it all over her body.

"Are you sure you should be doing this here and now?" Zach asked, glancing over his shoulder in the opposite direction, toward the road. "I mean, what if someone comes by?"

Sunny blew out a breath. "We've already established who you are and that you're a gentleman, if a novice at living in the country and knowing how to properly handle skunks. Besides, one false move and I'll hit you with the pepper spray I've got in my backpack."

Zach sighed. "If only you had used that on the mother skunk first," he lamented.

"I might've, had you given me a proper signal so that I'd known she was there."

"I tried. I whistled."

"Well, I didn't—wait a minute." Sunny paused and did a double take. "You did the Bob-white thing?"

"Yes."

"That was pretty good," Sunny admitted reluctantly. "So good, in fact, that I paid no attention to it. You should have tried some other kind of whistle."

"Such as?"

"I don't know." Sunny noticed the back of Zach was every bit as sexy and enticing as his front. "You could have whistled a country song."

Zach swept his hands through his hair, the muscles in his back rippling as he moved. "I'm not that good a whistler. I can only manage a couple of notes."

Sunny watched as he began to slowly unbutton his drenched cotton shirt. "I bet you could have fired off a wolf whistle, though," Sunny countered.

Zach did not deny experience in that regard. "Good point."

Sunny became unaccountably aggravated again. "Yeah, well, remember it next time," she muttered, just loud enough for him to hear.

"Believe me, I will," Zach muttered back, mocking her cantankerous tone.

Silence fell between them. Sunny finished scrubbing herself from head to toe. She'd need to soak in a tub of vegetable juice before the skunk smell dissipated. But at least it was to the point where her eyes were no longer burning and she was able to breathe without coughing and choking.

She set the half can of precious juice aside and ripped a red-and-white checkered tablecloth from her backpack, then began to dress. Already the sun was beginning to set. Thank goodness. They could head back to town under the cover of darkness. And then this whole sorry episode would be over. "Okay," she said, "your turn."

ZACH SWIVELED AROUND. Sunny Carlisle was up on the bank above him. She had a red-and-white checkered tablecloth wrapped around her, toga-style, and secured in a knot behind her neck. She still had her hiking boots on. Her glorious hair was streaming over her shoulders in a mass of thick curls that, when wet, looked dark red.

"Strip down and use the vegetable juice all over you," Sunny instructed calmly. "The tomato juice in it will help neutralize the smell. Then we'll head back to town."

Zach had no qualms about stripping in front of a woman, but he decided to have a little fun with Sunny. He grinned at her, glad he was not in the market for romance. "Turn your back first."

Sunny shot a droll look at him, then turned around. Zach kept his eyes on her as he hurled his clothes into the bushes on the opposite bank, just as she had done. Damn, but she was beautiful. Feisty, too. But she appeared awfully young and somehow *innocent* beneath her sage country ways. "How old are you anyway?" Zach asked, as he climbed down from the bank and kicked off his soggy tennis shoes. Naked, he began rubbing the juice all over him, savoring every drop.

"Twenty-four. How old are you?"

They weren't so far apart in age after all. "Twenty-nine."

Sunny peered at him from beneath a fringe of red-gold lashes. "Why did you want to know how old I am?" she asked.

"I just wondered." Zach shrugged. "You seem a little young to be running a factory."

"I'm old enough," she said. "Are you done yet? I want to get back to town."

Zach emptied the can. "Unless you've forgotten," he deadpanned, "I'm still buck naked. What have you got in that backpack of yours that I can wear?"

"Nothing," Sunny said. "Surely you have something in your pickup truck," she insisted blithely.

"A chamois." A used one, Zach thought grimly.

She made a sweeping gesture in the direction of his pickup. "Have at it, then."

"Sunny, you *want* me to run buck naked through that field over to my truck," Zach drawled.

"Want to borrow my clipboard?"

"What if someone drives by and sees us together?"

Sunny shrugged, unconcerned. "No one has yet."

Nothing seemed to bother Miss Carlisle, Zach thought.

"What were you doing out here today anyway?" Sunny asked.

"I got here a few hours ago. I dumped my gear at the clinic and decided to go for a drive to see the countryside." And that decision had led to his introduction to the angel with the feisty spirit. Zach grinned. Life in Carlisle was definitely looking up.

"WHAT DO YOU MEAN we can't ride in your pickup?" Sunny asked ten minutes later, as she and Zach rejoined each other and squared off next to his shiny new truck.

In hiking boots and a tablecloth, she knew she looked ridiculous. He didn't look much better in that soft clinging chamois. She had expected him to put in on diaper-style or something. Instead he had ripped it in two, torn off a strip and secured it like a loincloth around his waist. It dipped just low enough to allow him some modesty, but not much, and made him look like one of the warriors in *Last of the Mohicans*. All tanned, muscular and so very male. Just seeing him made her pulse jump.

"Zach, we have to take your truck," Sunny continued. It was beginning to get dark.

"We still smell pretty bad." Hands on his hips, he leaned down so he and Sunny were nose to nose. "Or hadn't you noticed?"

"I know how we smell," Sunny said, exasperated. She stepped back and waved her arms at him. "That's why I want to go home. So I can soak in a tub of pure tomato juice."

Zach regarded her with all the sensitivity of a rock.

"Well, we're not getting into my truck smelling this way," he said firmly, carefully extracting a flashlight from the glove compartment and then locking his vehicle up tight as a drum. "This truck is brand-new and I'll be damned if I'm going to see it ruined with the aroma of skunk."

Sunny folded her arms in front of her. "You're being ridiculous," she fumed.

Zach gave her a complacent smile. "I may be a greenhorn, but I know how long the smell of skunk lingers wherever it's sprayed. Besides, I don't see you offering your vehicle," Zach continued irascibly.

"That's because my Land Rover is parked another two miles from here on an old logging road," Sunny said hotly.

Zach shrugged his broad shoulders uncaringly. "So let's start walking," he suggested.

It did not appear Sunny had any choice. Her mood souring even more, she fell into step beside him and hoped for the best.

"Isn't there a house near here?" Zach said after a while, as they kept to the other side of the ditch and followed the road.

"Nope. We're on company land."

His brow furrowed. He turned toward her slightly. "I thought Carlisle Furniture Factory was on the other side of town."

"It is. We grow the trees for the furniture here."

"Is that what you were doing today? Checking out trees?"

Sunny nodded. "We replant at three times the rate we harvest, but we're thinking of upping that to maybe five times if the land will support it."

"You really know your business," Zach said, looking a bit surprised.

"It's my job to know about reforestation," Sunny said as they approached her vehicle. Like his truck, her Land Rover was brand-new and sported four-wheel drive. She unlocked the door and climbed in. Tossed her gear in back.

Zach studied the pristine interior. He was feeling a little guilty about not using his truck. "You're sure about this?" he said. "You know, we could just keep walking. It's only another five or six miles to town."

Sunny shook her head. "The later it gets, the more likely we'll run into traffic on this road. The kids come from miles around to park out here. The sheriff drives by on a regular basis to catch them."

Zach groaned. That was all he needed. Because they had no choice, they both got in. Zach arranged his loincloth to give him maximum coverage and folded his arms in front of him. He felt ridiculous.

Sunny drove toward town. "What time is it?" she asked after a while.

Zach looked at his watch. "Nine o'clock."

She scowled. "Damn, that's awfully early."

"Drive by the clinic. I'll see if I can sneak in."

Sunny tightened her hands on the steering wheel. "The clinic is on Main Street!"

"So drive around the back," Zach suggested affably, his gaze discreetly following the movement of one sensationally curved leg from accelerator, to brake and then back again.

"No." Sunny blushed at just the thought of being seen like this. "No way. Not with streetlights. I'm not going to be seen driving you around town like this. We'll just have to go to my house, over on Maple Street, sneak in the back and wait until later to drop you at the clinic."

"Fine, whatever." Zach was really at his breaking point. Every time she moved, he could see the fluidness of her breasts beneath the thin cotton cloth, a more revealing slip of thigh.

"Do you think it's hot in here?" He rolled down his window a little more.

"I think it's freezing."

Zach glanced at her. He could see that, too. She had goose bumps everywhere.

They hit the edge of town. "Oh, damn, here comes another car. Get down!" Sunny said. As Zach bent out of sight, she turned off on a side street.

Finally the Land Rover stopped. Zach stayed where he was. His face just inches from the soft skin of Sunny's knee, he wondered what kind of perfume she wore. The prospect of finding out conjured up many exciting thoughts.

"We're here," Sunny whispered, relief quavering in her voice.

Reluctantly Zach straightened and moved away from her soft knee. He looked at the small, neat, two-story red brick house with the ornate white gingerbread trim and glossy pine green shutters. Leafy trees and neatly kept flower beds inundated the yard. A stand-alone garage in matching red brick was behind the house, at the end of a long drive.

"We're going in the back," Sunny said. "And don't slam your door," she commanded.

They crept out of her Land Rover. In the distance, a dog barked. The sounds of a television floated out from an open window across the street. Sunny moved stealthily from the cover of a shade tree, to a lilac bush, to the back door. Zach followed. She was fumbling with the lock, when another car hit the drive.

Sunny swore and dropped her keys. "Duck!" she ordered. "Maybe whoever it is won't see us!" Too late. They were caught in the headlights of a sedan. She swore and slowly straightened as the motor died and a car door opened.

Grimacing his displeasure, Zach straightened, too. He wasn't pleased to be in this situation, but he figured he might as well face it like a man.

"What in tarnation is going on here?" a raspy voice demanded.

The voice belonged to a tall, fit man in his early sixties. He had short red-gold hair that was laced with gray, piercing whiskey-colored eyes and a familial resemblance to Sunny Carlisle that was unmistakable. He carried a shotgun in his hand.

Sunny blanched. "What are you doing here, Gramps?"

"You were supposed to meet me for dinner tonight, remember? When you didn't show up or call, I knew something must be wrong. I called the police station to let them know there might be trouble and came out looking for you." He eyed Sunny sternly. "I can see it's a good thing I did, too."

"Now, Gramps, I can explain all this!" Sunny admonished with a nervous little laugh. "It's all quite amusin—oh, no!" She moaned as a second car pulled in her drive.

Two patrolmen jumped out, their guns drawn, and ran toward Sunny and Zach. "We got here as fast as we could, Mr. Carlisle!" one of them yelled. "What the heck—"

The other cop stopped short as he got a good look at Sunny and her tablecloth.

"We got hit by skunk spray," Sunny said to one and all.

"I can smell that," Gramps admitted grimly. "The question is," he continued, glaring at Zach, his distrust evident, "what were *you* doing when the two of you got hit?"

Zach had learned in medical school that there were some people you just didn't mess with, particularly when they were upset. Augustus Carlisle was apparently one of them. He was not only the town mayor and the owner of the largest business in town, but his company was paying half Zach's salary, with the state and the community picking up the other portion. Keeping his hands high in a gesture of surrender, Zach said calmly, "I was trying to warn Miss Carlisle that she was about to get sprayed."

"As you can smell, we got sprayed anyway," Sunny said. "We had to ditch our clothes, since they bore the heaviest concentration."

"You sure you're okay, Miss Carlisle?" the patrolman asked. When she nodded, he and his partner holstered their guns.

Zach could see Sunny's grandfather was still very upset. He looked at the patrolmen. "Perhaps you guys could give me a ride back to my clinic?"

"Sure thing," one of them said.

Gramps held up a hand to stop him. "I'll admit the young fella needs some clothes. As for the rest..." Gramps looked at Sunny deliberately, then continued in a stern, determined tone as he picked up the shotgun and pointed it at Zach, "There's only one way to handle this!"

Chapter Two

Stand By Your Man

"I have this friend who's been having some chest pains every now and again," Augustus Carlisle began the moment he walked into the clinic.

Dressed in fishing gear, the scent of lakewater clinging to his clothes, Gramps made it appear as if his were a casual visit. Zach knew it was anything but.

"My question is, Doc, how would this friend of mine know the difference between ordinary chest pains that come from getting older versus those generated by something serious like a heart attack about to happen?"

"It depends." Zach sat down in a waiting-room chair. "Is your friend having any numbness or tingling with these chest pains of his? Any loss of consciousness?"

"No, not so far," Gramps said carefully, fingering one of the intricate fishing lures he had pinned to his vest. His eyes glowed with relief. "Does this mean my friend is off the hook as far as his heart goes?"

"Not necessarily. Those chest pains could be early warning signs of heart trouble. Then again, they could just as easily be something else, too. If I were you I'd advise your friend to get a physical. And speaking of physicals, when was the last time you had one, Augustus?''

"Never you mind.'' He shook a finger at Zach. "You worry about my granddaughter. I'll see to my health.'' Gramps took off in a huff.

No sooner had he driven off than Sunny walked in. The warm spring wind had tossed her red-gold hair into sexy disarray. Sunshine added color to her cheeks. But she was dressed for business, in a trim navy suit that clung to her slender curves.

"What was that all about?'' she asked a little breathlessly, flattening one hand over the jewel neckline of her white silk blouse.

"I'm not sure,'' Zach frowned. He eyed Sunny. "What's up with you?'' She sure looked pretty today, sexy in an unconscious way.

"The same.'' Sunny dropped her handbag into a chair. "Everyone thinks I should marry you.''

"Only one problem,'' Zach said dryly, ignoring the mysteriously determined sparkle in her whiskey-colored eyes. "I haven't asked.''

Sunny leveled a gaze at him as she dropped into a chair with a sigh. "Under the circumstances, Zach, maybe you should.''

LONG MOMENTS LATER, Zach was still regarding Sunny incredulously. "This is nuts,'' he said as he paced the empty waiting room restlessly.

"My parents would agree with you, I'm sure,'' Sunny murmured. "Fortunately, I am not planning to tell them about our marriage until it's legal, so we don't have to worry about them interfering.''

Zach pushed the edges of his starched white lab coat

back, revealing a pin-striped blue-and-white dress shirt, matching tie and jeans. "Listen, Sunny, I think you're a great gal, but I won't marry you! I don't care how we were undressed or dressed the night we met."

Sunny glared at Zach. "You think I want to go through with this?" She plastered a hand across her chest, aware she only had thirty-three minutes of her lunch hour left. "You think I want my reputation besmirched?"

Zach couldn't believe the town was making such a big deal out of an innocent situation. He sank down on the vinyl sofa beside her. "People have actually been giving you a hard time?"

Silence fell in the room as they measured each other. "Everyone feels sorry for me...but wants to kill you."

"I know." Zach swept a hand through his hair. "For some crazy reason they think I took advantage of you."

Sunny rolled her eyes. What an understatement that was. She smiled at him consolingly. "I know you were only trying to help me." Unfortunately, that didn't change things.

"So now what?" Zach asked wearily.

Remembering she had brought them both lunch, Sunny opened the brown paper bag by her side and pulled out two containers of frozen strawberry yogurt. She handed Zach a container and plastic spoon, then popped hers open.

"I can't go on like this. I thought—hoped it would get better if we just stayed away from each other, but it's been two weeks now." She had neither seen nor spoken to Zach, yet he had never been very far from her mind. There was just something about him that made her heart race. "And nothing has changed."

"I know." Zach considered her a moment.

"And I understand it's been worse for you," Sunny sympathized.

He nodded grimly. "Not a single patient has come to see me. I've been open two weeks, and they're still driving sixty-five miles to see another doctor."

"That really upsets you, doesn't it?"

"The success of my first assignment means everything to my future."

"Has anyone even made an appointment?"

"Your grandfather stopped by to inquire about a friend who might need medical attention. And I advised his friend to get a checkup," Zach replied. *If indeed Gramps had been talking about a friend.*

"I guess everyone else must still be driving sixty-five miles to see another doctor," Sunny said dispiritedly, feeling all the more responsible for the predicament Zach was in.

"And all because I refused to marry you, even at the end of the gun."

"I admit Gramps can be a little dramatic," Sunny conceded dryly.

"A little?" Zach echoed, the first hint of humor curling his lips. He studied Sunny with great care. "I thought he was going to shoot me right on the spot."

The scene on her porch that night had been right out of a Li'l Abner comic strip, Sunny thought. But the dramatic effect it and the resulting community concern had worked on her life was all too real. "I hate to suggest it, but maybe we really should get married," Sunny said reasonably, adding, "just for a little while." It would quiet gossip and get Zach off the hook. And it would teach her parents a lesson and perhaps head off any further matchmaking schemes on their part. She kept expecting them to turn up with another prospective beau.

Zach's expression grew stony with resolve. His amiable mood vanishing, he set down his frozen yogurt with a thud and vaulted off the couch. He stared out the window at the sparse traffic on Main Street, his expression unaccountably dark and brooding. "No one backs me into a corner or tells me what to do, Sunny. I am in control of my destiny, not the other way around."

"Look, I am not enjoying this, either," Sunny yelled. "But it's interfering with both our professional lives. People are giving me so much sympathy at the factory I can't get any work done. Like it or not, we have to do something to control the damage. Proclaiming our innocence hasn't helped. The only solution is marriage." And wouldn't her parents just faint if they found out she had married a small-town doctor, instead of a big corporate giant. It might be worth it, just to see the stunned looks on their faces. She would no longer have to worry that every eligible male she met had been sent by them.

"Then—" she took a deep breath, determined to make Zach see reason as she continued with her plan "—when we've been together a month or so and people see for themselves that it's not working—and I for one plan to vividly demonstrate that concept for all to see—we'll have our marriage annulled. You can leave and go practice medicine somewhere else—" Sunny said.

"Not for two years I can't," Zach interrupted. "I have a contract with the state government. They paid my last two years of medical school. In turn, I agreed to practice for two years in whatever rural Tennessee community they could find to cosponsor me." That community, of course, had turned out to be Carlisle.

Sunny was aware the town was paying half of Zach's current salary. Her grandfather's company underwrote the living allowance that had bought, among other things, Zach's new truck. And it foot the bill for the day-to-day operating expenses of the clinic. Without Carlisle Furniture Factory, Zach would not have a job. And that made this situation very sticky indeed. Sunny thought it best to keep the information to herself. Apparently he did not know all the specifics behind the monthly check he received from the state.

"So put in for a transfer," Sunny advised. "As soon as you get it, we'll proceed with the annulment. My reputation will be saved. You'll be free and, more importantly, out of Carlisle. No one will ever have to know our marriage was a sham."

Zach did not want to see Sunny hurt, but he also didn't want to marry. "How's your Land Rover?" he asked casually to change the subject.

Sunny strode back and forth, her high heels moving soundlessly on the carpeted floor.

Her lips curved ruefully. "I still can't drive it and I've tried darn near everything. I don't think that skunk smell is ever going to go away. But that's my problem, and not something you have to worry about, Zach. Our getting caught in flagrante on my back stoop, however, is a worry we share." Sunny whirled abruptly to face him. She pointed a lecturing finger his way.

"Look, we're young, healthy, vital. No one would believe we could strip down naked in proximity to each other and not even be tempted to kiss."

That wasn't exactly true, Zach thought. He had been tempted. He just hadn't acted.

Her solution made sense. And he had already put in for a transfer out of Carlisle. The problem was, it wouldn't come through for several months, if it came about at all. Meanwhile, he didn't want anyone in Carlisle finding out about it—not even Sunny. "I am going nuts not being able to use my medical training," Zach admitted.

"I'm really tired of this situation interfering with my work over at the furniture factory," Sunny said.

Maybe her solution was worth a shot, Zach thought. "A marriage in name only," he stipulated firmly.

Sunny nodded. "That's the only way I'll have it."

Zach paused. "What happens if we change our minds?"

"We won't," she said quickly, drawing an unsteady breath.

Zach studied her. "If we do…is there a possibility the relationship could become intimate?"

Sunny flushed, beginning to feel as though she were in an "I Love Lucy" episode again. She trembled as he neared her. "Boy, you don't pull any punches, do you?"

"I like to know what my options are. And you didn't answer my question."

Sunny had the feeling a lot was riding on her answer. "Only if it was what we both wanted. But I have to warn you, Zach, the chances of that happening…are next to nil."

SUNNY WAS FOOLING herself if she believed their marriage was going to be simple and uncomplicated, Zach thought as he dressed for the bachelor party cum poker game. Even if they were married three or four weeks, there were bound to be problems, the least of which was the mutual attraction simmering between them. Sunny might want to pretend it didn't exist, but he saw it every time he looked deep into her whiskey-colored eyes. He hadn't even kissed her yet, and he had an idea how she would taste. Sweet as sugar, hot as fire. Putting them under one roof was not a good idea, but as she'd said, what choice did they have?

When Zach arrived at Slim's grocery store everyone was ready to play poker.

One of the men, George, set out the subs and beer, dill pickles and chips. "Hope you brought your wallet with you, Doc," he teased. "We take our games serious here."

His wallet was not the problem, Zach thought. It was Gramps. Unless Zach was mistaken, he was in obvious discomfort. The glass of bicarb and water in his hand was the first clue. Zach said hello to the rest of the guys and moved over to Augustus Carlisle's side. A fine sheen of perspiration dotted his upper lip. "You're in pain," Zach said in his ear.

"So I am," Gramps admitted, taking another sip of bicarb.

"What'd you do today, Augustus?" George asked, as he pulled the chairs up around the table.

"I moved some files from my office into Sunny's," he replied.

Zach moved around so his back was to the guys. "Where does it hurt?" he asked, very quietly. Augustus looked scared.

"Here." Augustus placed his hand on the center of his chest, then over his heart, toward his left shoulder.

"Any numbness? Tingling?" Zach asked. Augustus shook his head. "I want to run an EKG on you," Zach continued.

"You can't do that now!" Gramps shot back.

"You guys about ready?" a man named Fergus asked, snapping the cards.

Zach turned around and gave the men a sheepish grin. "I left my wallet over at the clinic. Gramps doesn't believe me, so he's going with me to retrieve it." Zach wrapped an arm around Augustus's shoulder. "Back in a minute." He winked at the guys. "Don't start without us."

"YOU SEE, I told you my EKG would be normal," Gramps said, buttoning his shirt, then his fishing vest over that.

Zach folded the readout from the machine and slipped it into a file jacket bearing Augustus's name. He was relieved it was not a heart attack, too. "There's a reason for the pain you were having a few minutes ago," he said. "You need more tests, ones I'm not equipped to do here." Zach wanted to determine the cause, then treat the problem, whatever it was.

To Zach's frustration, Augustus waved off the suggestion. "More tests would be a waste of time and money."

"Sunny wouldn't think so." If Augustus wouldn't do it for himself, maybe he'd do it for his granddaughter.

Augustus's face turned dark. "I forbid you to mention it to her—or anyone else, for that matter. I'm fine. I'm just getting older, that's all. Now, let's get back to the game!"

Zach recognized denial when he saw it. He stopped Augustus at the door. "It's not good to keep secrets. Sunny has a right to know if you're ill."

"Let's get something straight, young man," Augustus lectured, his normal feistiness returning as the last of his mysterious chest pain faded. "I am not going to ruin Sunny's wedding tomorrow with any worries about me. And neither are you! One way or another, you are walking up that aisle to the altar tomorrow to say your 'I do'!''

"NOW, SWEETHEART, stop looking so nervous. You're doing the right thing,'' Gramps soothed Sunny in the anteroom behind the altar in the community church. He was dressed in his best suit and tie, and seeing his contented expression, she couldn't help but think maybe he wasn't so much angry as delighted to see her in this mess. He had wanted a great-grandchild for a long time. Sunny was his only grandchild, and therefore his only hope for one.

"Then why don't I feel more relaxed?'' Sunny asked. She didn't know how she'd let her aunt Gertrude and Gertie's friend Matilda talk her into wearing her grandmother's wedding gown, but she had. Standing before the mirror in ivory lace, a veil on her head, she was aware what a hoax she was perpetrating on the people of Carlisle.

"All brides are nervous.'' Gertie tucked a new blue-and-white hankie in the long sleeve of Sunny's gown. She fastened a borrowed antique locket around her neck. "That's just the way you're supposed to feel.''

All brides were not marrying a complete stranger, Sunny thought. Of course, her marriage to Zach was not going to be real. It was only a temporary arrangement. Once it was over, she would use her "broken heart'' to fend off any further attempts at matchmaking on her behalf.

The organist began the "Wedding March.'' "Guess this is it.'' Gramps took Sunny's elbow and led her around to the back of the church.

Zach was waiting at the altar, beside the minister. He looked resplendent in a dark suit and tie. Gazing up into his face, Sunny could find no visible evidence that he was being forced into this.

He was a better sport than she had figured he would be. Unless, she thought uncomfortably, he planned to get more out of this than she had promised him. Pushing the unwelcome thought aside, she stood next to Zach and faced the minister. Her hands were shaking as she held the bouquet in front of her. All too soon, the minister had finished his introductory remarks about the seriousness of marriage. Sunny was handing her bouquet to Aunt Gertie and turning to face Zach.

"Do you, Sunny, promise to love, honor and cherish Zach for as long as you both shall live?"

As long as it lasts, she amended silently. "I do," Sunny said. She looked deep into Zach's eyes. He looked into hers. A thrill went through her. She knew they were only doing this for everyone else, but dressed in wedding clothes and standing before a church full of people, she found it hard to remember that this was all just pretend.

"Do you, Zach, promise to love, honor and cherish Sunny for as long as you both shall live?"

Zach took her hand in his, held it warmly. As he gazed at her his eyes glinted with a subdued humor, as if he could hardly believe he was going through with this, too. "I do."

Under the minister's direction, Sunny and Zach exchanged rings. The minister grinned at Zach. "You may kiss the bride, son."

Sunny's breath stalled in her lungs as Zach took her masterfully into his arms. He lowered his mouth to hers.

Electricity sizzled through Sunny at the brief, but sensual, contact.

Appearing quite pleased with himself, Zach stepped back. The organist resumed playing. To Sunny's relief—or was it disappointment?—it was over.

"I DIDN'T KNOW it was possible for anyone to blush for three hours straight," Zach remarked in Sunny's ear after he swept her up into his arms and carried her across the threshold, into her home.

Arms still hooked around his neck, Sunny gave him an adoring look that, she assured herself, was strictly for the benefit of the crowd of onlookers who had accompanied them on the short walk from the church to her home. Smiling up at him, she whispered, "When I agreed to marry you, I didn't know a wedding was included." Then, turning to those still watching them, she lifted her hand in a merry wave. The crowd waved back.

Zach gently set her down and wrapped an arm around her waist. Tugging her close, he leaned down and whispered in her ear, "Seems like everyone in town is rooting for us." Zach glanced at Augustus in the crowd. Sunny's grandfather seemed fine this morning, but Zach was still worried. He'd have to do his best to keep an eye on Gramps from afar until he could get him into the hospital for a complete series of tests.

Sunny allowed herself to lean into Zach's side only because she was tired from all the festivities. "They want you to do right by me," she admitted. With one last wave at the crowd, they stepped back, inside the foyer, and shut the door.

Exhausted, she leaned against it. Zach propped a hand next to her head and looked down at her. For one insane second, she thought he was going to kiss her again, really kiss her. A sizzle of desire swept through her.

Zach's gaze swept her upturned face in leisurely fashion. "That's quite an old-fashioned notion, even for southern and proper Tennessee, don't you think?"

"Quite. But that's the town of Carlisle for you," Sunny said lightly. "In fact, the sense of family, community, caring and warmth is one of the things I like best about the town."

"You don't find the intrusion of others into our private life annoying?" Zach asked. He did.

Sunny apparently knew what he was referring to. "I sidestepped the invitation for the honeymoon cabin, didn't I?"

"Yes, although I don't think anyone was pleased about it."

"We can't help it. We both have to work," Sunny said stubbornly. She folded her arms in front of her, still radiantly beautiful in her veil and wedding dress.

"I don't tonight," Zach said, "unless someone gets sick."

"Well, unfortunately, I do have to work. All the brouhaha of late has left me behind."

Zach was surprised at his own unwillingness to have the festivities end. "You're not going into the office!" He had an idea what chaos an action like that would cause.

"No, of course not, silly," Sunny said, slipping off her veil. "I brought all the work home with me."

Zach didn't find that much more reassuring. "Don't you think we should get to know each other a little better if we're going to be sharing space?"

"Eventually," Sunny said with a cool smile that arrowed straight to his heart. "Not tonight." She slipped from beneath his outstretched arm. "I made up the guest room for you. Shall I show you where you'll be bunking?"

Zach nodded. He moved his arm in gallant fashion. "After you."

Zach followed her up the stairs. They creaked beneath her weight, and a little more beneath his. At the top of the stairs was the master bedroom. A large brass bed dominated the room. It was covered with a patchwork quilt and numerous pillows. Sunny moved on down the hall, past the linen closet and the bath. "We're going to have to share the bathroom while you're here," she informed him with a sigh. "This is an old house, and there's only the one."

"I think I can rough it," Zach said. But that was before he'd seen his bed.

SUNNY SPENT her wedding night in a buttercup yellow sweatsuit and white cotton socks. She curled up on her bed, writing and rewriting letters on behalf of Carlisle Furniture, soliciting more business for the company on her laptop computer. She could hear Zach roaming around downstairs. She felt a little guilty for sticking him in the tiny guest room, where the rollaway bed was half the size needed to accommodate his tall, rangy frame, but that couldn't be helped on such short notice. Besides, she reassured herself, he wouldn't be here long.

Around 10:00 p.m., Zach knocked. Sunny kept typing. "Come in," she said, without looking up from her keyboard.

Zach carried a tray in. It had a pot of tea, a sandwich and some wedding cake. "I could hear you typing. I thought you might like something to eat," he said.

"Thanks for the tray. I'm sorry if I disturbed you." A tingle of awareness rushing through her, Sunny kept typing.

Zach lingered in the doorway. "What are you working on?"

"Business letters."

"Oh."

For a second, Zach appeared so lonely Sunny's heart went out to him. She thought about how it must be for him. Newly married to a woman he didn't even know. And Carlisle wasn't exactly a hot spot. TV reception was spotty at best, and cable was not available. A few people in town had satellite dishes. Sunny wasn't one of them.

"Can I do anything to help? Address envelopes or something?"

Sunny shook her head.

"Can I get you something else to eat or drink?"

He wants company. Sunny had grown up feeling the loneliest child in the world. Seeing it in Zach made her heart ache. Finished with the letter she was working on, she put her laptop aside. "This is fine. Did you get something for yourself?"

Zach nodded. "I also did a hundred sit-ups and push-ups, put all my clothes away and read the last four issues of the *Journal of the American Medical Association.*"

"Bored out of your mind, right?"

Zach nodded. "How do you stand it here?"

"I've got plenty to keep me busy."

"That isn't what I meant."

"I know, but I'm not interested in discussing my romantic life prior to you." It was just too embarrassing.

Besides, she didn't want Zach to know how she'd been duped.

"Too late," he said smugly. "There were some hints dropped at the bachelor party last night."

Sunny froze. "Exactly what did you hear?" She was going to kill those men!

"That you were engaged to one Andrew Singleton III shortly after arriving in Carlisle to take over your grandfather's company."

Sunny felt the blood rush to her face. "Yes, well, that was a mistake."

"No one really knows what happened to break the two of you up," Zach continued.

And no one was going to know, not if she had anything to do about it, Sunny thought stubbornly. She forced a smile. "We weren't suited to each other, all right?"

"Still carrying a torch for him?"

"Heavens, no!"

Zach raised a brow skeptically, seeming to know there was much she wasn't saying. Even more disturbing was the awareness that he wouldn't rest until he did know it all.

"If you don't mind, I'd like to change the subject," Sunny said prudently.

"No problem." Zach grinned. "So how's the factory doing?"

"Okay. It could be better, though. That's why I'm writing letters to solicit new business. In the past, the company has only sold furniture to other independently owned stores in the state. I think we could do a lot better if we expanded our markets."

"Hence the letters." He nodded at the stack of neatly typed envelopes beside her.

Sunny nodded. "That's not the only change I'm making, however. I've arranged for a computer-run order-entry system that will be on-line twenty-four hours a day, and I'm also putting together a catalog of mail-order items."

"That is a lot."

"Which is why I'm so busy." Sunny took the time to show him glossy color photos of their new rustically designed Tennessee Cabin line of furniture. "I've even been thinking of purchasing a few pieces at employee discount for my house. You may have noticed my guest room needs a little work."

"I noticed."

Zach leaned against the bureau, radiating all the pure male power and casual sexiness of a big screen hero. Unbidden, all sorts of romantic thoughts and fantasies came to mind. Sunny pushed them away.

She finished her sandwich and tea. "Well, thanks for the supper, but I've got to get back to work now."

Zach moved toward her gallantly. "Let me get that for you."

Sunny caught a whiff of his brisk, sexy scent and backed away. She hoped he had no idea how much having him in her bedroom this way was affecting her. "I can handle it."

"No. Really. Let me."

"Zach," Sunny insisted, as heat began to center in her chest, then moved outward in radiating waves, "you don't have to wait on me."

They both tugged at once…and let go. The tray went crashing to the floor. And so did Sunny's china. She grabbed a wastebasket and knelt to pick up the pieces. Zach knelt beside her.

"I'm sorry," he said.

"It's okay," Sunny said, unable to keep the irritation completely from her voice. Having him in such proximity seemed to make her all thumbs. Unless she got ahold of herself, who knew what else might happen?

"Where do you keep your vacuum cleaner?" he asked.

"In the hall closet downstairs."

He retrieved it. While he started sweeping the immediate area, in an effort to pick up all remaining tiny shards of glass, Sunny carried the wastebasket of broken dishes out to the trash. As she was carefully transferring the contents, the neighbor's dog ran into her yard, barking.

Matilda followed. Quickly she took in Sunny's jogging suit, sweat socks and bunny slippers. "Sunny, for heaven's sake! What are you doing taking out the trash on your wedding night?"

Sunny felt herself turning red as she offered an airy wave. "Oh, we broke some dishes. Nothing to worry about."

Briefly Matilda looked worried. Composing herself hurriedly, she advised, "Well, have fun, darlin'. Einstein, come here! We have to finish our evening walk!"

Sunny walked back inside. She carried the wastebasket back to her bedroom.

Zach straightened as she tried to sidle past him unnoticed and caught hold of her. The next thing she knew, she was anchored against him, hip to breast. He was grinning down at her, evidently enjoying the perfect way their bodies meshed, and in no hurry at all to let her go.

"Nervous, aren't you?" he said softly.

"I don't—"

"It's okay. I am, too. And I know why. Sometimes

in medicine the cure is worse than the disease. And sometimes in romance the anticipation of a situation is more unnerving than the actual event. So maybe we should just get this over with,'' he said, and then his mouth came down to cover hers.

Caught off guard, she felt her mouth soften beneath his. Not again, she thought, alarmed. But even as her mind was telling her no, her body was already saying yes....

The kiss in the church had been properly restrained. This kiss was claiming her as his woman, Sunny noted, as Zach began a deep, achingly sweet exploration of her mouth.

And claim her he did, his mouth moving possessively over hers, his tongue coaxing her lips apart, drawing her deeper and deeper into the sensual battle, until she was no longer sure of anything but his strong arms and body, and the wonder of his mouth, and his sizzling, yet tender kiss.

Excitement pouring through her, Sunny wreathed her arms about Zach's neck. Surrendering to his will, she surged against him and felt her knees turn to butter. Murmuring his encouragement, he gathered her closer, enveloping her masterfully in his warmth and strength. He kissed her again, long and deeply, the hunger inside him matching hers. And though it warmed her, it left her feeling hollow, too. Wanting more...needing... Sunny thought dizzily—she wasn't quite sure what.

Reveling in the sheer intensity and wonder of their embrace, she sighed her pleasure softly. Zach's hand slid down her back, guiding her nearer. Sunny's breasts were crushed against the hardness of his chest. Lower still, she felt the unmistakable proof of his desire, the rock-hard brace of his thighs. With a start, she realized where things were headed if she didn't halt this forward pass of his right now.

It didn't matter how accomplished a lover Zach Grainger was. She had no intention of making this a real honeymoon.

Hand to his chest, she broke off the sizzling embrace. "What was that for?" she gasped.

"Because you look so good in those yellow sweats," he murmured, ducking his head once again.

Sunny sucked in another quick breath and wrested herself from his embrace. Heart pounding, she smoothed her tousled hair from her face. "You can't...I never said I'd—damn it, Zach, what do you think you're doing?"

He gently traced her cheekbone with his thumb, then bent to kiss her temple. "I'm making life more interesting."

"I don't want my life to be more interesting," Sunny insisted.

"That's not what your lips said when you were kissing me just now," he teased, his clear blue eyes glinting with humor. "It's not what your lips said when you kissed me back after the ceremony."

"That was all for show," Sunny huffed.

"Keep putting on a show like that and no one will believe our claims of annulment later on." Arms folded in front of him, he leaned close, his eyes twinkling. "And besides, if you didn't want me to notice you, how come you're wearing a different perfume tonight than you were this afternoon?"

"I'm notoriously absentminded when I have a lot of work to do," Sunny fibbed.

"Funny," Zach drawled, giving her the slow, sensual

once-over. "You strike me as a woman who'd be in perfect control of her faculties all the time."

That had been true, Sunny thought. Until Zach had charged into her life. "Well, I am. Absentminded. Sometimes. I mean."

"Hmm." He rubbed his jaw contemplatively. "I guess I'll have to take your word for that."

"Not to worry, Zach," Sunny assured him, feeling yet again as if she were in an "I Love Lucy" episode. "It won't happen anymore!"

His expression was one of comically exaggerated misunderstanding. "No more perfume?" he asked sadly.

Sunny flushed, aware he had gotten under her skin in a way no man ever had. "No more anything!" she said firmly.

"Now, Sunny," he teased, his gaze sliding over her, "don't make any promises you can't keep. Especially since we have the rest of our honeymoon weekend ahead of us."

Sunny tossed her hair. "I've never made any promises I couldn't keep," she vowed hotly. "Furthermore, you're the one who is in for a surprise! Now, out!" Her pulse pounding as she half anticipated another kiss, she pushed him out of her bedroom and slammed the door.

From the other side of the door, Zach chuckled softly, victoriously, then sauntered away. Sunny waited for his footsteps to recede all the way down the hall, then let go of the breath she had been holding. Her knees were so weak and trembly she nearly collapsed against the door. Leaning against it, she knotted her damp hands in front of her and briefly closed her eyes.

Zach could call this whatever he liked, but now that she'd had a moment to contemplate it, she knew darn well what this newfound behavior of his was all about. It wasn't so much desire as his payback to her for having been forced by her family and friends into marrying her. Obviously he blamed her for their predicament. Hence, he intended to extract his own style of vengeance by torturing her with kisses and treating her like a real wife and potential lover every chance he got.

Well, Sunny surmised grimly, her usual confidence returning, Zach was fooling himself if he thought he was going to get the best of her. She could torture him, too…simply by turning herself into the kind of wife he *wouldn't* want.

Chapter Three

Take Me as I Am

If he didn't know better, Zach thought, as he awoke to the delicious smells of blueberry muffins and hot coffee, he'd think he'd fallen into a velvet-lined trap. Here he was, in Carlisle less than three weeks, and he had a beautiful wife who even cooked him breakfast.

Not that he had ever expected to find himself in this position. He had figured that the scandal would die down if he just imposed an iron will and stayed away from her. And, Zach admitted honestly, it had taken all his strength to stay clear of the local angel with the red-gold hair.

But the uproar over Sunny's compromising hadn't died down. And that was her fault, too. After all, he might have been a virtual newcomer, but she resided in town. She should never have stripped down out there in the country or induced him to do the same no matter how skunky their clothes had been. She should have known the odds were they'd get caught sneaking back into town. Particularly since her grandfather had worried when she hadn't shown up for dinner and had been out looking for her.

Which brought him to the marriage. He had agreed to it, but that didn't mean he'd had to like it. He hated losing control of his life. But he had tried to make the best of this mutually bad situation they found themselves in by taking the supper to her the evening before. He hadn't anticipated kissing her; that had just happened. And though he had no plans of staying in Carlisle, he did want to make love to her. And if their lovemaking was even one-tenth as sweet as their kisses had been, well, who knew what would happen after that? Zach mused happily as he rolled out of bed and grabbed a robe.

Her fixing breakfast for them *had* to be a good sign. It meant she was willing to meet him halfway on this. Zach's smile faded as soon as he walked into the kitchen.

Sunny sat at the kitchen table. Her gorgeous hair was wrapped in curlers. She had something that looked like whipped cream smeared all over her face. She was wearing an oversize man's shirt that was stained with paint. Her jeans were old and ripped at the knees. The kitchen was a huge mess. The muffin tin stood empty.

Trying hard not to laugh—for Sunny could not be anything but beautiful to him, no matter how she outfitted herself—Zach strolled over to pour himself some coffee. He wasn't surprised to find the carafe was bone-dry.

"There aren't any more muffins," she said.

Zach's glance roved her slender figure in a sensual way designed to annoy her. "You ate a dozen muffins all by yourself?" he asked mildly.

"I only made two." Wielding a pair of scissors, she continued cutting out big patches of the morning paper.

Zach noted with chagrin she had done particular damage to the sports page. He could get another newspaper. He could also easily make another pot of coffee. The muffins were another matter. "I didn't know you could make just two muffins," he said casually.

"I cut the recipe down to size."

If she could do it, he could, too. He began to look around for a recipe and ingredients.

"I also used up the last of the blueberries." She hid her grin behind her full coffee cup.

Zach knew she was giving him hell. Whether it was to punish him for kissing her the night before or discourage him from doing it again didn't really matter. He could handle her. In fact, as she would soon find out, he could dish it out, as well. Sunny, the darling princess of Carlisle, might be used to having her own way all the time, but that was going to change.

"I think I'll go back upstairs and get dressed," Zach announced laconically.

"You do that," Sunny murmured in an unconcerned voice as she buried her nose in the morning paper.

"You just wait, honey," he whispered, a smile of anticipation on his lips. "I'll best you yet."

SUNNY WANTED to leave the face mask on all day, just to irritate Zack, but she was afraid of what would happen to her skin, so she rinsed it off in the kitchen sink and replaced it with a thick coating of winter-strength moisturizer. Satisfied her face had a disgusting oily gleam to it that would be bound to discourage any further kisses from her new husband, she went back to cutting more holes in the morning paper.

Seconds later, loud footsteps sounded on the stairs. Zach walked into the kitchen. Sunny never would have believed it, but the rascal had outdone her.

He was dressed in a white undershirt that was ripped down the center, white socks, black shoes and high-water pants. She wasn't sure what he had put on his hair, but he had fixed it with numerous cowlicks spiked up in the back. He hadn't shaved and the morning beard gave him a piratical look.

Zach cleared a place on the counter with a swipe of his arm that sent even more flour flying. "Think I'll fix me a little breakfast," he said.

Taking that to be her cue to leave, Sunny slipped out of the kitchen and back up the stairs. Now what? she wondered as she barricaded herself in her bedroom. She had wanted him to know this marriage, temporary or not, was going to be no picnic with free sex. She hadn't counted on him trying to outdo her.

If she backed off now—by acting and dressing normally—he would think he had won. Therefore, Sunny decided, she would just have to tough out the rest of the weekend. She only had twenty hours and forty-three minutes left before she could go to work again.

The rest of the morning passed quickly. She had a few bad moments when she smelled the hash brown potatoes cooking. That was, after all, her favorite dish. But she forced herself to stay in her bedroom and get some more Carlisle-company work done. It was the sound of the baseball game on the radio that eventually drew her out. It was loud enough to be heard in every room of the house, and worse, it was a doubleheader, which meant it would be on for hours.

Wanting something to eat, she ambled on back downstairs.

Squelching the urge to ask him to turn the radio down, she headed for the kitchen. It was in an even bigger mess than she had left it. Zach walked in behind her. His closeness made her senses spin.

"Where do you keep your spittoon?" he asked in an innocent voice.

Hanging on to her temper with effort, Sunny whirled to face him. Like her, he had done nothing to improve his appearance. They looked like characters in a comedy show.

Ignoring the sudden heavy jump in her pulse, she smiled at him firmly. "I don't have a spittoon," she replied calmly.

Zach slowly ripped open a pouch of chewing tobacco. "Then where am I going to put my spit?"

Sunny had put up with a lot, but there were limits, even if she had to sacrifice a little pride to enforce them. "You are not doing that in my house," she announced firmly.

"It's our house now, sugar," he corrected, patting her rollers condescendingly with the flat of his hand. "And don't worry about not having a spittoon for me right off the bat. I forgive you."

"You are so—" As Sunny sputtered for words that would be precise yet ladylike, Zach edged closer. As he neared her, the room seemed to do a half spin.

"What?" Zach's eyes took on a predatory gleam.

"Thoughtful," Sunny said.

"Aren't I?" He turned away from her and opened the cupboard. "I suppose I could put a teacup in every room and use that in lieu of a spittoon."

Sunny slipped between Zach and her teacups and crossed her arms in front of her. "Over my dead body."

"Is that a challenge?"

Sunny's temper began to flame. "Babe," she drawled, "it's an ultimatum."

Zach grinned at her and plucked a big wad of tobacco from the pouch. "Don't you dare," she said. "Zach, I swear—"

He kept going anyway. She grabbed for the pouch with one hand and knocked the pinch from his fingers with the other. Loose tobacco sprayed the floor at the exact moment he stepped forward, trapping her against the counter. "Give me my tobacco back," he ordered mildly, one hand braced on either side of her.

Sunny's heart pounded at his proximity. Even in the outrageous getup he was enormously attractive. But she was *not* giving in. "If you want to do something that disgusting, you can do it outside," she said, clutching the pouch and trying not to think about the intimate way his muscled thighs were now pressing against hers.

Zach's dimples deepened. "What if I want to do something even more disgusting inside?" he whispered.

The way he dipped his head toward her mouth caused a distinct melting sensation in her knees.

Oh, no. He was going to kiss her again. Sunny sucked in a breath, determined not to let him make her feel all weak and hot and compliant again, and turned her head to the side. Her eyes widened as she saw Aunt Gertie, Matilda and a very pregnant Rhonda-Faye Pearson on the other side of the screen door. Sunny exchanged mortified glances with Rhonda-Faye, knowing that if anyone could understand even an inkling of what was going on here, it would be her best friend. And even that, Sunny thought, studying Rhonda-Faye's stunned expression, would be a stretch.

"Oh, dear," Gertie said, shifting the foil-wrapped casserole dish in her hand.

The sole proprietor of the town's only department store, Gertie felt it her duty to dress with perfect panache and style all the time. Her polished appearance only made Sunny feel all the more comically disheveled.

"It appears we've come at an inopportune time," Gertie said.

The forty-five-year-old Matilda was not only Sunny's friend and nearest neighbor, but also a key employee over at the furniture factory. "We rang the bell, dear," she said, putting a plump hand to her cheek.

"I guess you all didn't hear since the radio was on so loud," Rhonda-Faye added, looking resplendent in a white maternity outfit.

"So we came around to the back," Gertie continued, flattening one white-gloved hand over the signature pearl necklace around her neck. "We brought you some dinner so you wouldn't have to cook while you were on your honeymoon. But I can see that you two already have been cooking."

Sunny was so embarrassed she wanted to sink right through the floor. She never had a messy kitchen!

And as for their appearances, she recollected in silent misery, this was going to be all over town in no time.

"Thank you so much. Zach and I were just goofing around, weren't we, honey?" Sunny elbowed him in the ribs.

"It's been a barrel of laughs so far," he said.

Sunny turned to Zach and gave him a glare only he could see. *Help me out here,* she ordered with her eyes.

"Well, we'll be going, dear. If you're sure that everything is okay?" Gertie said, taking in their mutually comical state.

Rhonda-Faye giggled and backed out the door. "I think we ought to leave, ladies, and let these two get back to whatever it was they were doing."

"Thanks for the food. If Sunny doesn't eat it all herself, I'll be in seventh heaven," Zach said.

Sunny gave him another elbow as the ladies laughed. When they were alone again, she faced Zach. Unlike him, she wasn't laughing. "We are in so deep now," she moaned miserably. "You have no idea."

ZACH OPENED the clinic at 9:00 a.m. Monday. Sunny's grandfather marched in at 9:02. Zach eyed her protector with courtesy and respect, hoping this was a professional visit. "What can I do for you, Mr. Carlisle?" he asked politely.

"You can call me 'Augustus', now that we're related," he said, fastening his piercing eyes on Zach. "And there's nothing wrong with me—today anyway— so you can put that darn stethoscope away. I just came in to talk."

Zach had been afraid of that. "About what?"

"Sunny, what else. I heard what went on over at your home yesterday."

Zach had had a feeling it would get all over town. He had not expected to have to endure any lectures on his behavior.

"If you sincerely want to make a go of your marriage to my granddaughter, son, you are going to have to work a little harder."

Had the marriage to Sunny been a real one, Zach would have worked hard.

"You do want to make a go of this marriage, don't you?" Augustus persisted.

It was funny. The day he had agreed to marry Sunny, making a go of the ill-advised union had been the last thing on his mind. Seeing her in a wedding dress, holding her in his arms, kissing her, had softened his resistance somewhat. To his surprise, her orneriness had appealed to him even more. Zach liked the idea of a little mischief in his wife.

"Of course I want what's best for Sunny," Zach said honestly, aware Augustus was still waiting for an answer.

"Yes, well, Sunny is more fragile than she appears," Augustus warned.

"She seems inordinately strong willed to me," Zach disagreed.

"About business, yes. But her personal life hasn't always been easy."

"Are you taking about her broken engagement again?" he asked.

Augustus frowned and held up a warning hand. "I've said too much as it is. If Sunny wants you to know about her life before she came to Carlisle, she'll tell you. In the meantime, if you plan to stay married to my granddaughter, you need to shave, even on weekends."

"Yes, sir."

Augustus looked Zach up and down. "You be good to my granddaughter, you hear? I expect you to treat her with the love and respect she deserves."

Again Zach nodded. He didn't mind the lecture nearly as much as he expected. Maybe because he saw the love Augustus felt for Sunny. As for the marriage, he knew he should have minded that more than he did, even if it was only a temporary social fix for a local scandal. He needed to be careful not to get too involved here. He had his own life to live.

"SUNNY, I AM SORRY, but I will never get the hang of this new computer," Matilda said late Monday afternoon.

"Yes, you will. Just give it time."

"I have. But I just can't remember anything that Chuck Conway told me to do," Matilda said with a sigh.

"Then maybe he needs to come back and show you how to work this new order-entry system again," Sunny said. "I'll call him right now and set up a time."

No sooner was Sunny off the phone than Aunt Gertie appeared in the doorway to Sunny's office. "May I have a word with you, sugarplum?"

"Sure." Sunny knew it had to be important. Otherwise Gertie never would have left Carlisle Department Store during business hours.

She came in, shut the door behind her and inched off her gloves. "Sugarplum, I am gonna be frank with you. I don't know what your mama and daddy told you about marriage—"

"Gertie, this isn't a sex talk, is it?"

"Well. Sort of. I mean I—I expect you know about the birds and bees."

"Yes, ma'am, I do."

"But there's a lot more to sex and marriage than just the birds and the bees," Gertie continued seriously.

Sunny tried, but could not contain a flush of embarrassment. "Aunt Gertie, I love you for trying to help me out on this, but we couldn't save this talk for another time?"

Gertie patted Sunny's shoulder fondly. "Sugarplum, after what I saw at your home yesterday morning, I think we need to have this talk now, before any more damage is done to this sweet new union of yours."

Sunny could see there was going to be no getting out of this lecture. When Aunt Gertie had something on her mind, she did not rest until she had said it. Sunny sat down. Gertie took her hand in hers.

"First of all, technically speaking, you are still on your honeymoon. And it's important for you to act like a newlywed. And not wear curlers in your hair and goo on your face and old clothes. Even on weekend mornings."

Her embarrassment fading, Sunny folded her arms in front of her. "I'm not going to pretend to be something I'm not," she told her aunt stubbornly.

"Good. Because you're not the kind of woman who goes around with curlers in your hair. Unless, of course, you're trying to send that new husband of yours a message that you aren't interested in him sexually."

"Aunt Gertie!" Her face flaming, Sunny bolted up off the sofa.

Gertie patted her own perfect bob of red-gold curls. "We may as well speak frankly, sugarplum. I know this marriage of yours was more or less arranged."

"Against my will and better judgment, I might add," Sunny interjected, as she paced back and forth.

"But that young man of yours is quite a catch. He's a doctor, he's kind and good-looking and your age and he's from Tennessee."

"But he's not going to stay in Carlisle," Sunny said, deciding now was as good a time as any to lay the groundwork for her and Zach's eventual annulment. Sunny planted her feet firmly on the carpet and regarded her great-aunt willfully. "I am."

"He'll be here for two years. Who knows what can happen in that time? You might have a baby. He might change his mind about leaving."

"It's still an arranged marriage," Sunny persisted,

trying not to let herself get sidetracked with idyllic images of Zach and a baby.

"Oh, I know arranged marriages aren't really an 'in' thing these days, but they do work. My own marriage to your uncle Fergus was arranged, and we've been married for nearly forty years now."

"I know, and I'm glad you're happy, but—"

A knock sounded on the door. Matilda poked her head in. She was beaming. Sunny frowned, instantly knowing from the excitement crackling in the air that something was up.

"We're ready," Matilda sang out.

A group of women burst through the doors to Sunny's office. They were all carrying gaily wrapped gifts. Matilda came last, wheeling in a pink-and-white cake in the shape of a wedding bell and a crystal bowl of pink-lemonade punch.

"Surprise!" everyone shouted.

"We're giving you a wedding shower," Rhonda-Faye said.

"Rhonda-Faye made the cake over at the diner."

Sunny smiled at her friends. This was what she liked about living in Carlisle. The closeness and camaraderie. The way everyone watched out for everyone else. She had never had that growing up and she had missed it dearly.

"This is wonderful! Thank you!" She hugged everyone in turn and then settled in to enjoy the party.

It was only after the gifts had been opened, the games played and the cake eaten that Gertie stood to make an announcement. "We have one last present for you, Sunny."

"I can't imagine what," Sunny joked. "You've already given me everything but the kitchen sink. Cookbooks, nightgowns, several bottles of blackberry wine.''

"But this is something really special," Gertie said.

"Yes," Matilda added. "We all know how you love to learn, Sunny."

"So we pitched in and hired an instructor for you," Gertie said.

"An instructor on what?" Sunny asked, visions of Masters and Johnson textbooks dancing in her head.

"On how to be happily married, of course," Gertie explained.

Matilda leaned forward excitedly. "The course tells you everything you need to know about being a good, loving wife in five easy lessons that are spaced out over a period of two weeks."

Oh, my gosh. "This is so sweet, really—" Sunny began.

"Honey, you don't have to be embarrassed," Aunt Gertie soothed. "We know the newlywed phase isn't easy."

The very pregnant Rhonda-Faye nodded. "We've all been there. And we all feel we have something to learn, too." She leaned forward earnestly. "I mean, what marriage couldn't be made better?"

"What are you saying?" Sunny asked with trepidation.

"We all signed up to take the course with you," Rhonda-Faye replied, her excitement about the endeavor evident.

"So what do you say?" Matilda asked enthusiastically. "Are you ready for your first lesson?"

Chapter Four

That Kind of Girl

"Getting pretty busy here, aren't you, Doc," Fergus Walker said when he came in to have his blood pressure checked the next day.

That was a matter of opinion. Zach wasn't doing nearly as much for the community as he could, given half a chance. "I've seen four patients here today," Zach said dryly, noting it was nearly 6:00 p.m., closing time for the clinic. "I think I'm setting a record."

"Now, now, don't you fret none," Fergus said as he pushed up the light blue sleeve of his post-office uniform. Fergus watched as Zach fitted the blood-pressure cuff around his upper arm. "As word filters out around the mountain that you done right by Sunny, folks will be lining up to see you, 'cause it's either that or a sixty-mile trip to the nearest doctor."

"Sixty-five," Zach corrected absently, already pumping air into the cuff.

Fergus was silent as Zach read his blood pressure. "So how am I doing, Doc?"

Not as good as he would have liked, considering Sunny's uncle was only fifty-five. "How long have you been on your current medication?'' Zach asked, pulling the stethoscope from his ears.

Fergus stroked the handlebars of his thick black mustache. ''About two years now, I reckon.''

''And the dosage is—?''

Fergus told him. ''Why do you ask?''

Zach went to the cupboard and pulled out a sample packet of pills. ''Your blood pressure is a little high. I think you might do better on this.''

Fergus shrugged uninterestedly. ''Whatever you think, Doc, will be fine. Now, back to that new bride of yours—''

''I wasn't aware we were discussing Sunny,'' Zach said, already writing out a prescription.

Fergus stroked the ends of his mustache. ''C'mon, Doc, don't mess with me. I know what happened over the weekend. Hell, everybody in town knows.''

''Well, that makes me feel better,'' Zach drawled. Not that he was surprised about this. Fergus was married to Gertie—one of the eyewitnesses.

Fergus stabbed a finger at Zach. ''And I know you're probably wondering what you've done, marrying a beautiful gal like that. But I am here to reassure you that damn near anyone can be a good husband. All it takes is a little work.''

Zach ripped the prescription off his pad and handed it to Fergus. ''Is that so?'' he asked blandly.

He knew he should have minded this advice from Fergus more than he did, even if his marriage to Sunny was only temporary. And that puzzled Zach, too. Sunny Carlisle was still a virtual stranger to him. Why should he have cared whether she was happy or not?

''Yes, sirree. Nevertheless, you're going to have to

work a little harder if you want to make a go of this marriage. You do want to, don't you, Doc?''

Zach wouldn't mind making love with Sunny, but as for the rest…the idea of being married to anyone at this point made him feel as though he were suffocating. "To tell you the truth, Mr.—"

"Call me 'Fergus.'"

"I'm not all that sure I'm the marrying kind," Zach confessed.

Fergus's affable grin widened. He clapped Zach on the shoulder. "Then it's high time we changed all that. Now, do you want to do something that will make Sunny sweet on you? 'Cause, if so, I've got just the thing."

ZACH WAS STILL mulling over Fergus's suggestion as he locked up the clinic and drove home. Fergus had had a good idea, although a little corny, but Zach didn't know if he wanted to follow through on it. He didn't really need to get more involved with Sunny than he already was, or make their relationship any more intimate or romantic. Besides, Zach mused as he parked his truck in front of her house, got out and started up the walk, did he want her to think he was the kind of guy who could be pushed, coerced and generally led around by the nose?

Zach heard the temperamental banging of kitchen-cupboard doors from halfway up the walk. He found Sunny in the kitchen, scowling as she slid a plate of food into the microwave. "What's got you in a lather?" he asked.

"I don't want to talk about it!"

But she needed to, he thought. When no other information was forthcoming, he shrugged. "Fine. I'll just call the town grapevine and ask for details there." He pivoted toward the phone on the wall, knowing just about anyone would do, since everyone knew everyone else's business in Carlisle.

Sunny caught up with him as he lifted the receiver from the cradle. Her hand tightened on his wrist, forcing the phone back down.

"Don't."

Zach sucked in a silent breath and tolerated the sizzling warmth of her touch. "Then start speaking," he said gruffly.

Sunny's lower lip pushed out petulantly as she dropped first her gaze, then her hand. "I suppose you'll hear about it anyway."

Briefly she told him about the belated bridal shower the ladies had held for her and their mutual gift. Zach tried to hold in his amusement, but the look of righteous indignation on her face sent him over the edge. He laughed until tears streamed from his eyes and he was doubled over at the waist.

"You, in a class on how to be a loving wife?"

"It's not funny! I am not looking forward to this."

"Oh, but I am," he teased.

"Don't think I am going to turn into some mousy little thing who lives and breathes to do your bidding," Sunny warned.

Zach clapped his palm to his chest in a parody of hopefulness. "I can dream, can't I?"

Sunny removed his hand from his chest and forced it back down to his side. "I'm serious, Zach," she stormed. "I am not looking forward to this."

He appreciated the rosy color in her cheeks and the indignant sparkle in her whiskey-colored eyes more than he knew he should. "So don't go through with it," he advised. "Tell them thanks, but no thanks."

Sunny paced away from him, her hips swaying sexily beneath her trim black skirt.

"I can't do that, either."

"Why not?"

Sunny whirled to face him in a drift of flowery perfume. She pushed the red-gold curls from her face with the heel of her hand.

"Because I'd hurt their feelings. They put a lot of thought into that gift."

"The wrong kind of thought." Zach got a plate out and dipped a generous heap of Gertie's mostaccioli casserole on it. "You're setting a dangerous precedent, allowing them to meddle in our lives this way. Furthermore, I don't know how you tolerate the intrusive behavior of our neighbors."

Sunny watched as he added tossed green salad to a bowl, then Italian dressing. "If you are referring to the other morning, you're lucky it wasn't Gramps who walked in on us."

Zach shrugged. Deciding Sunny needed a salad to round out her meal, he dipped some for her, too. "We have a right to behave any way we want in our own home."

"My home," Sunny corrected, taking the salad he handed her. She carried it to the table. "And maybe we do…but they also had a point. If you and I are going to stay married, even for a little while, we need to do better, Zach. The other morning we both behaved ridiculously."

"Oh, I don't know." Unable to resist teasing her just a little, he sauntered nearer and gave her the once-over.

"I kind of like dressing up—or down, as the case may be—every once in a while."

Sunny's chin set stubbornly as she added a pitcher of freshly brewed iced tea to the center of the table. "Well, I don't like being embarrassed." She waved her arms at him, agitatedly punctuating each and every word she spoke. "And I felt like a fool, being caught in that get-up, with my kitchen a mess."

Zach shook his head at her and gave her a censuring glance. "You care too much about what the neighbors think."

"And you don't care enough."

Her words were casually—maybe even gently—spoken, but they hit a nerve. It bothered him, too, but he was not able to change the way he felt. Right now he wanted a wall around his heart. Which was yet another reason he never should have let himself be talked into this temporary marriage.

Silence fell between them as Sunny removed her dinner from the microwave and carried her plate to the table. Zach popped his dinner in and pushed buttons. As he waited for it to heat, he regarded her curiously, realizing she was as much a mystery to him as he was to her. "Why doesn't all this bother you?"

Sunny sat down at the table, spread her napkin on her lap, then waited for him to join her. "Maybe because I know what it's like to have the shoe on the other foot."

Zach stared at her. "You mean you were ostracized for something else?"

"No, silly," she said as the microwave buzzer sounded. "I mean I didn't always live here."

Zach carried his plate over and joined her at the table. "Where did you live?"

"Various European countries. My parents are both international-law attorneys. They specialize in helping U.S. companies expand their operations overseas and are generally involved in the setup and so on. It's difficult, demanding work."

"So you moved around a lot as a kid."

"At least once a year. Sometimes more."

"That sounds exciting."

Sunny stared down at her half-eaten casserole. "I suppose it had its advantages," she said carefully.

Zach read between the lines. "But you didn't see what those advantages were at the time, did you?" he said softly.

Again she was silent. Zach could tell he was probing too fast and hard. He would have to back off. At least a little. He tried again. "Aren't you bored living in a small mountain community?"

Sunny shook her head, her love of her surroundings shining through. "I love the warmth and the sense of community here in Carlisle."

"Is that the only reason you stay? For family?"

"My grandfather needs me to help run his business," she said.

"Surely he could hire a plant manager."

"He doesn't have to, not when he has family." Sunny got up and retrieved the peach cobbler Matilda had baked for them. "Do you want ice cream with this?" she asked.

Zach knew exactly what his new bride was doing. "Waiting on me, or just trying to change the subject?" he drawled.

Sunny flushed. She stacked two desert plates on top of the ice cream, picked up the cobbler with her other hand and carried it all to the table. "I don't see you volunteering much about yourself,'' she asserted as she sat down again.

"That's because your life sounds like more fun," Zach said as he finished his dinner and helped himself to dessert. "So, tell me more about this class. What are you going to learn?"

Sunny toyed with the cobbler on her plate. "I don't know yet."

Leaning close, Zach noticed the faint blush of freckles across her nose. "Why would they think you need it?"

Sunny rolled her eyes and dropped her fork. "You have to ask after those getups they caught us in?"

Zach grinned at the exasperation in her tone. He knew how much the locals loved Sunny. This gift was something special. Obviously they had given it to her for a reason. "You haven't answered my question," he teased.

"They know I love to learn."

"And how do they know that?"

She drew a deep breath and looked him straight in the eye. "Because I delayed taking over my grandfather's company for two years, until I had gone back to school and earned an M.B.A."

"You didn't feel comfortable taking it over with just him to guide you?"

"No. I'm the kind of person who likes to be well versed in whatever subject I tackle before I dive into it."

"Hmm...I'm just the opposite. I tackle something first, then read the directions only if I can't figure it out on my own."

"I figured as much."

"So how long is this class going to take?" Zach

didn't want it to take up too much of her time, since she already seemed quite busy at the factory. Besides, the house was lonely without her.

"I have five lessons and a graduation party, spread out over the next couple of weeks. Each class is supposed to be an hour or so in length."

"You're going alone?" If it was down the mountain somewhere, maybe he could drive her.

"No. Five other women have signed up to take it, too."

"Don't they already know how to be loving wives?"

"They hope to learn something. And so do I," she said firmly.

"To use on me?" Zach asked hopefully.

"No way." Sunny rose gracefully and carried her dishes to the sink. "I signed up to learn something that will help me when I really give my heart to someone and get married."

That wasn't the welcome prospect it should have been, Zach thought as he began to take care of his own dinner dishes. Instead of feeling relieved to know that she one day intended to end this farce of a marriage to him, as promised, he felt a flash of jealousy. Determinedly he pushed the feeling away. What she did was no business of his. He'd been hurt to the quick when Lori had died; his pain had intensified when he'd become involved with Melody; he wasn't going to open himself up to that kind of pain again. Not for Sunny, not for anyone.

"Is EVERYONE ready for lesson number one?" the instructor asked.

As ready as I'll ever be, Sunny thought, settling into a folding chair in the community church basement.

Booklets stamped *How to be a Loving Wife* were passed out. Sunny stared at the cover, taking in the photo of a bride being scooped up in her husband's arms. If only married life were that simple, she thought wistfully. She sighed. Life with Zach was much more complicated than she had anticipated.

"Sunny, what did you and your husband have for dinner tonight?"

Sunny offered a mortified smile. "Casserole that was brought to us over the weekend."

"Describe how the table was set, what your centerpiece was and any special touches you added, like sprigs of mint."

Sunny shrugged. "I didn't set the table. We took what we needed to the table with us. And each did our own dishes afterward."

A gasp of dismay was uttered by the entire group. Sunny looked at them. "I am not waiting on him hand and foot."

"Then how do you expect him to ever want to wait on you?" the instructor asked gently.

"I don't!" Sunny said, flushing all the more as she recalled Zach bringing her the supper tray up to her room the first night they were married. She had yet to pay him back for his thoughtfulness. And that made her feel guilty.

"One kindness begets another, Sunny," the instructor said sternly. "Now, please, try to keep an open mind...."

ZACH AWOKE the next morning to the delicious smells of bacon and hot coffee. He shifted onto his stomach, his arms and legs hanging off the rollaway bed, and buried his face in the pillow. No doubt Sunny had made just enough for herself again. "She sure knows how to torture a man," he grumbled to himself.

"I beg your pardon?"

Zach rolled over with a start. Sunny was standing in the doorway with a tray in her hands. He shook his head to clear it, sure he must be dreaming. "Breakfast in bed?"

"Well, I'm in a hurry. I have to get to the office, and you weren't up yet," Sunny explained. She marched in as crisply as her fuzzy bunny slippers would allow.

Zach caught a drift of her perfume—it was lemony this morning—as she bent to help him put a pillow behind his head and settle the tray on his lap. She looked very sexy in a business suit. "Did something happen I'm not aware of?" he asked.

"If you think this is payment for staying out half the night, you're wrong," she said.

Was that a tinge of jealousy in her voice? "I was over at the clinic, reading files. Now that people are coming to see me, I figured I should be more up on patient history."

"Sure you just didn't want to avoid seeing me?"

Zach shrugged, aware she was looking at his bare chest and the sheet that came *almost* to his waist. He knew what she was thinking: he wasn't wearing much. Considering the way his body was reacting to her nearness, Zach shared her wish that he had on more than his glen-plaid boxer shorts. He yanked the sheet up to cover his navel and ran his hands through his hair. "I wasn't sure what kind of mood you'd be in after you took that class, so I thought I'd make myself scarce."

"As you can see, Zach, my mood is fine."

That was a question open for debate. She was serving him breakfast in bed, but she didn't look happy about it. "So why are you waiting on me hand and foot all of a sudden?" And why did she look so damn cuddly and kissable, even in her ultraconservative business attire?

"Can't you guess?" Sunny took a small notepad from the pocket of the frilly gingham apron she had tied around her waist. "It's an *assignment*."

"Oh." Zach's spirits took a nosedive. He had hoped that she had done this out of the goodness of her heart. In retrospect, he could see how irrational that hope was. Sunny didn't believe they were really married any more than he did. She wasn't interested in playing house, either. Never mind having the kind of hot, passionate fling with him that he wanted to have with her.

"So?" Sunny stood poised with her pencil over the pad. She eyed him expectantly.

Zach nudged his sheet a little higher, so it rested against his ribs. He leaned back against the pillow and the wall casually. "So what?"

Color stealing into her cheeks, Sunny blew out an exasperated breath. "Make some inane comment about what I've just served you, Zach."

He looked down at the tray and couldn't help but be pleased by what he saw. The French toast was golden brown, perfectly prepared and dusted with confectioner's sugar. The bacon was crisp, the orange juice chilled, the coffee black, strong and steaming. She had even put a flower from her garden out back in a vase. "Breakfast looks wonderful, Sunny," he said softly, meaning it.

"'Breakfast…looks…wonderful…Sunny,'" she murmured as she wrote. Finished, she gazed at him and offered an officious smile.

"Now what are you doing?" he asked dryly.

"Making notes, of course, for my report back to the class. I found out last night that every lesson has a homework assignment. We all have to do them and report back to the class on the results of our assignment."

Now, this, Zach thought, sounded like trouble. "What other kind of assignments are you going to be asked to do?"

Sunny looked bewildered. "I don't know."

"Give me a hint." Zach cut into his French toast.

"I wish I could, but I truly don't have a clue. Our instructor wants to surprise us. Now, do you have any other comments to make about breakfast?"

"For you to write down?" he asked, feeling a wave of orneriness coming on.

"Yes," she said primly, her pen at the ready.

"Well, the food is delicious."

"'The…food…is…delicious….'"

"But it doesn't look—"

"'Doesn't look—'" Sunny was so busy writing she didn't see him get out of bed.

"Nearly as delicious as you," Zach said, taking her into his arms, so that her hands and the notepad were trapped between them. She smelled and felt as delicious as she appeared.

"Zach—" Sunny's soft voice carried a warning, as did her stiff, unrelenting posture.

"Hmm?" he asked. Taking advantage of her inability to move, he feathered light kisses down her nape.

"Don't." She shifted against him restlessly, her breath hitching in her chest.

Zach's heart started a slow, heavy beat as he studied her upturned face. "Why? Going to put this in your report, too, Sunny?" he asked, hoping he could make her understand how foolish and invasive of their privacy this class was.

Sunny drew an indignant breath and stomped on his bare foot with her bunny slipper. He let her go. Grinning, he got back into bed. Sunny in a temper was something to see.

"You think I won't write this down, don't you?" she said sweetly.

"Which part? Where I kissed your neck or you stomped on my foot?"

"I'm writing them *both* down."

Oh, no. Zach could feel another lecture from a well-meaning patient coming on. "Both?" he croaked unhappily.

"Of course my stomping on your foot was done accidentally—" Sunny continued blithely.

Like hell it was, Zach thought. Not about to let her know she was getting to him, he kept his face expressionless. "Accidentally on purpose, you mean," he corrected.

"But—" Sunny ignored him and kept writing furiously "—it was enough to spoil the mood." Finished, she grinned victoriously. "There. I completed my assignment. It didn't work, despite my very best efforts, which you, Zach, can attest to if asked. And our marriage is still doomed! Perfect!"

Zach shook his head. "You want to fail?"

"Of course," Sunny said smugly, closing her notebook with a snap. "Don't you?"

ZACH WAS STILL asking himself that question as he let himself into the clinic. He knew he should want to fail at this marriage business. Failing at it would give him and Sunny both an easy out. But failing—at anything—

went against his grain. He didn't like playing games. Whereas like a chameleon, Sunny excelled at them. He wondered why she would put up with this, then determined he would find out.

In the meantime, it wouldn't hurt to keep her off her guard, Zach thought. She'd caught him by surprise, serving him breakfast in bed. He could do the same, too. Put her in a position where she didn't know what to think, either. Besides, if she could tell everyone he had sent her flowers, maybe the nosy townsfolk would get the idea that things between Sunny and him were fine and they would stop pushing them to become the perfect newlywed couple. It was worth a try anyway, Zach thought.

He reached for the phone book on his desk and thumbed through the Yellow Pages. There were three florists in the vicinity. He was trying to decide which one to use, when the door to his office banged open. Sunny's grandfather stood in the portal. As usual, he was dressed in his fishing apparel.

"I ought to shoot you on sight," Augustus Carlisle said.

"What for this time?" Zach asked.

"Breaking my granddaughter's heart—that's what!"

Zach frowned. "What are you talking about?"

Augustus shook his finger at Zach. "She's over at the factory right now, locked in her office, and she won't come out, and all on account of you."

"Did she say what I'd done?" Zach asked curiously as he folded his hands behind his head. No doubt about it. Sunny was a woman who was full of surprises.

"No. But it was clear to the women who work with her that it had something to do with that class on marriage they're all taking down at the church." Augustus peered at him suspiciously. "One of them said she mighta been trying out some sort of lesson on you. Did she?"

"I think that's a private matter, best left between Sunny and me," Zach said calmly.

Augustus sent a fulminating glance at Zach, then just as abruptly became more reasonable. "I understand that Fergus was over here yesterday, offering you some advice."

Zach took his feet off the edge of his desk and put them back on the floor. "He told me to send her flowers."

"And did you do it?" Gramps pressed.

"No." Not then, Zach added, but right now he had been about to order some. And not because Fergus had told him to do so.

"So what stopped you?"

Zach shrugged. "Unlike Sunny, I don't like to be told what to do," he said emphatically. "*Especially* in my private life."

Augustus's eyes narrowed to slits. "You know, I should have taken my shotgun to you while I had the chance. But for whatever reason my granddaughter has taken a shine to you, and the two of you are married, so I won't."

"Gee, thanks," Zach said sarcastically.

"I will, however, insist you do something to cheer her up. We can't run a business if she is locked in her office."

Then maybe you should take that up with Sunny, Zach thought as the outer door to the reception area opened. Zach saw a mother with twin babies troop in. Deciding the only way to get rid of Augustus Carlisle was to agree with him, he said impatiently, "Look, I'll order flowers and give them to her this evening."

Augustus assessed Zach with a frown. "You'd better do it right, son," he warned.

Zach gave Augustus a flip look. "Is there any other way?"

Augustus scowled. "In the meantime, I have something to discuss with you. Do you still want to give me a physical?"

"Yes."

"Then let's get down to it."

Augustus was already unzipping his fishing vest. Zach led the way to an examining room. The next twenty minutes were spent obtaining a complete medical history, the fifteen after that doing an exam.

"So how am I?" Augustus asked when Zach had finished listening to his heart and lungs.

"On the surface, everything's fine, but something has to be causing these chest pains you've been having."

"How do you know I'm still having pains?"

"I know because you're here, asking me to examine you. If you weren't, you'd likely put it off another month or two." Augustus said nothing to disagree. "So when were the last ones?" Zach asked.

"Last night, when I got back from the stream. I was cleaning some fish for dinner and the pain went from here—" Augustus pointed to his chest "—all the way down my left arm into my hand."

"Sounds scary," Zach said.

"It was. *Is.*"

"How long did the pains last?"

"Only about five or ten minutes. They quit after I went over and sat down."

"What about the fish?"

"I put it away, to finish up later. I figured maybe I'd overdone things, so I went to bed early. I felt a lot better when I got up this morning."

"But you're scared the pains will come back."

Augustus nodded grimly. "That's why I'm here. What do you think it could be? Angina?"

"It's possible. To say for sure, we'd need to admit you to a hospital and do a complete series of tests."

Augustus vetoed that. "I don't want Sunny upset."

"We can do this without her knowing," Zach said calmly.

Augustus hesitated. "You promise you won't breathe a word of this to my granddaughter?" Zach nodded. "Okay, then do it," Augustus said.

Zack picked up the phone and began to make arrangements. Half an hour later, it was all set. Augustus would have the necessary tests done at a hospital in Knoxville, the following week. A physician friend of Zach's would personally oversee Augustus's care. Sunny would never know anything, at least while the tests were being done. Afterward, when a diagnosis was made, Zach would use every means at his disposal to persuade Augustus to tell Sunny what was going on.

Zach spent the day seeing a steady stream of patients. By the time five o'clock rolled around, he was pleasantly tired. He hadn't felt such a sense of satisfaction since arriving in Carlisle, he thought, as he took off his lab coat and loosened his tie. The only thing he hadn't done was call the florist. But he figured they had to have something in stock. When he reached the door to the florist, he swore softly in frustration. A big Closed sign hung on the door. Zach peered inside. The lights were off. The building appeared empty. Now what? he wondered.

It was too late in the day to order from the two other florists on the mountain, and they were probably closed up, too.

Augustus drove up in his big black Cadillac sedan. He rolled down a window on the passenger side. "I figured you'd forget," he said.

"I didn't realize the florist closed so early." Even as Zach said it, he knew it was a lame excuse. He should've taken care of this earlier.

"Yeah, well, I owe you a favor anyway." Augustus thrust a large ribbon-wrapped box at Zach. "Sunny's favorite—yellow roses." He rolled up his window and roared off.

Zach went back to his brand-new pickup truck and drove home. Sunny was dropped off right after him. She got out of Matilda's car, briefcase in hand, then waved as Matilda drove off. She looked tired and frazzled after a day at the office. She saw the florist's box and instantly became wary. Zach suddenly felt as tongue-tied as any kid. Wordlessly he handed the box to her.

"Where did this come from?" she asked, in a voice that sounded oddly rusty.

You don't want to know, he thought guiltily, and wished like hell he had followed through on his initial instincts and done this himself early that morning. But he hadn't, so he would just have to make the best of it. "Open it and see," he said.

Sunny put down her briefcase and struggled with the ribbon. She gasped as she pried off the lid and saw the two-dozen roses inside. "Oh, Zach," she said, her voice choking up even more. She looked up at him, eyes glistening. "Yellow roses are my absolute favorite! How did you know?"

Zach shrugged, feeling even guiltier. "Your grandfather.'' And that was true, he reassured himself. There was no way he wanted Sunny to know how she had really happened to get this beautiful bouquet tonight.

''I'll take them inside and put them in water,'' she said.

''Want to go out to the diner to eat?''

Again she looked surprised. ''Well…I guess we could. Zach, are you sure? Eating out is going to be like being on public display again.''

''We don't have anything to hide,'' he said gruffly. ''Besides, maybe it's time people got used to seeing us together.'' Maybe it was time he and Sunny got used to being together.

''Well, all right, but I want to change into something more comfortable first.'' Sunny flushed the moment the words were out.

For once Zach passed up the opportunity to put a sexy twist on her utterance. He nodded. ''I'll go out and get your mail for you.''

He was surprised to find his own mail in the box, as well. He hadn't changed any of his addresses. Leave it to Fergus to go ahead and do it anyway, Zach thought.

Minutes later, Sunny bounded down the stairs in jeans, sneakers and a white long-sleeve T-shirt. She had a pretty blue sweater tied around her neck, to ward off the chill of the spring evening. She had taken her hair down, and it fell over her shoulders in a riot of glorious red-gold curls. Irritated to find his heart slamming against his ribs, Zach stood and offered her a casual smile. ''Ready to go?''

''Yep. I just want to run the casserole dish over to Matilda before we go, okay? You can wait for me in your truck. And grab up my mail, will you? I want to read it on the way to the diner.''

"Pretty good at giving orders, aren't you?"

"You could say that!" Sunny bounded out the kitchen. The back door slammed.

Zach locked up and went out the front. He slid behind the wheel and waited. To his relief, she wasn't long in returning. To his dismay, she no longer looked the least bit happy. In fact, he thought as she neared, there was a decidedly militant edge to her posture. "What happened?" he asked as she climbed in stiffly beside him.

Sunny swiveled to face him. "What do you think happened?" she shot back, so angry she was trembling. "I know the truth about the flowers, Zach!"

Chapter Five

Roses in the Fire

"Zach, how could you?" Sunny stormed.

He braced one hand on the steering wheel and cautioned her with the other. "Whoa, now. Just hold on. It wasn't my idea."

Sunny lifted a brow skeptically, recalling, Zach supposed, just how difficult it was to get him to do anything against his will. "Well, it was and it wasn't," he amended hastily. "I was going to send you flowers—"

"Because Fergus told you to send them," Sunny declared sagely.

Zach paused. "You know about that, too?"

"Aunt Gertie can't keep her mouth shut—never could. And what do you mean do I know about that, too? What else should I know?"

Zach swore and said nothing. He was in up to his neck now.

"Zach, you better tell me. If I find out any other way—" Sunny warned, eyes flashing.

Zach knew there would be hell to pay. "I got the flowers from your grandfather to give to you."

"So they weren't from you after all." Sunny's expression saddened even more.

"No."

"So why did you pretend they were?" she asked, visibly upset.

"Because sometimes honesty isn't the best policy."

"Oh, really." Sunny surveyed him with glacial cool.

Zach regarded her in exasperation. "Haven't you ever kept something—some bit of information—to yourself because you knew it would hurt the other person?"

His words struck a nerve. She had done just that the day she'd met Zach, in not admitting up-front that she knew who he was, which made her as guilty as he was.

"Besides, I didn't want to hurt your feelings, and you had already assumed that the flowers were from me before I got a word in edgewise, so I went along with it."

Just when Zach thought he was getting through to Sunny, she abruptly got angrier.

She shook her head at him and studied him grimly. "I can't believe it. I can't believe my past is repeating itself this way!" She slammed out of the truck.

Zach vaulted out after her and followed her halfway up the drive. "What are you talking about?"

Sunny stopped so suddenly their bodies nearly collided. She pivoted to face him. "My parents did the same thing to me." New color swept into her cheeks. "They had my nanny or their secretaries buy presents for me because they could never remember, or make the time, to go shopping themselves."

"They *told* you this?" Zach was shocked.

"No, of course not," she said, her eyes gleaming with suppressed hurt. "But I caught on eventually. Kids have a way of sensing things."

Zach couldn't imagine growing up like that. His parents had always taken special care choosing gifts and he had learned to do the same. Which made what he had done to Sunny even worse. There was only one remedy for this. He would have to find some way of doing something special for her...all on his own.

Zach took her hand and led her over to the front porch. "What happened when they realized you knew what was going on?"

"They stopped pretending and gave me money, instead, to spend as I chose." Sunny sat down on the steps.

Zach followed suit and took her into the curve of his arm. "Did that make it easier? Or worse?"

"A little of both, I suppose." She rested her head on his shoulder. "It was a relief knowing I didn't have to pretend they'd put any thought into anything. But it hurt knowing they couldn't spare the time."

"I'm sorry," Zach said. Sorry he'd taken the easy way out with the flowers.

Sunny straightened and shook off his sympathy, her expression determined. "I shouldn't complain. My parents are good people and they work very hard. If they'd had less-demanding jobs, maybe it would have been different for me."

And maybe it wouldn't have, Zach thought. Maybe this was the key to Sunny's heart and soul, the reason she not only tolerated, but seemed to relish, the community's interference in their lives. "Tell me how it was," he encouraged softly, lifting her chin to his, wanting to know more about what had caused the glimmer of hurt in her eyes.

She looked deep into his eyes. "What do you want to know?"

"Were you an only child?"

Sunny nodded, still holding his gaze.

"You said you had a nanny," Zach continued softly, covering both her hands with one of his.

"A succession of them, actually, from the time I was born." She tightly enmeshed her fingers with his, then went back to resting her head on his shoulder.

"Why more than one?" Zach used his free hand to stroke her hair. It felt like silk beneath his fingertips.

Sunny snuggled closer. "We moved around a lot. You name it, I've lived there. They could never find a governess willing to travel around with us for more than a year or so at a time, so when one left, another came in to replace her."

"How long did that continue?" he asked quietly.

"Until I was twelve. Then I went to boarding school in Switzerland."

"Where did you go to college?" Zach asked, liking the way she felt in the curve of his arm.

"Where my mother went for undergrad, Smith. Wharton School of Business, for my M.B.A."

"Prestigious schools," he commented, impressed. "Your parents must be very proud of you."

Sunny shrugged. Lifting her head, she drew back again. "I really don't want to talk about this any longer."

He could see the walls around her heart going up again. It surprised him how much he wanted to tear them down. Usually he took his cues from other people. If they didn't want to talk, he didn't push it. But with Sunny, he couldn't help it; he had to be closer. "Why not?" he asked.

His question was met with silence. With every second that passed, Zach could feel her drifting further away from him. He wanted desperately to keep her near, so he tried once more. "What's your relationship with your parents like these days?"

"I'm not close to them, okay? Now, can we just leave it at that?" she asked impatiently, aware she was trembling with unresolved emotion.

Zach's expression was concerned. "On one condition," he drawled, as the two of them squared off.

Sunny lifted her chin contentiously. "What condition?"

He smiled and took her hand in his. Time to enact part two of figuring out what made his new wife tick. "That you have dinner with me tonight, just as we planned."

"THIS ISN'T going to work!" Sunny said outside the diner. She didn't even know why she had agreed to come here with him, after the flower fiasco, except that dining out would be much less intimate than eating at home.

"Sure it'll work. All we have to do is pretend to be cooing lovebirds and word will get out that we don't need any more help in the romance department. Everyone will back off. Then we won't have any more problems like the one we had today with the flowers," Zach said.

He was doing it again, Sunny thought. Realizing intuitively where she was vulnerable, then attempting to somehow attend to all her hurts, past and present. Because he was a healer by profession? Or because there was something special between them? She only knew for sure that the more he learned, the closer she felt to him. If they kept on this path she was going to have a hard time resisting him when he did make his move for

her. And she felt sure that it would be very soon. Sunny
backed up slightly on the sidewalk. "I'm no good at
acting."

"So don't act," Zach said with a shrug. "Just be nice
and remember the way you looked and felt when I
kissed you the other night."

That was the problem, Sunny thought. She couldn't
get those kisses out of her mind!

"Okay, so wing it," Zach advised cheerfully under
his breath.

"Better." That matter settled, she breezed through
the diner doors.

Rhonda-Faye looked up from behind the counter.
Sunny knew, from the flushed, yet pale, color in her
friend's face that something was wrong. She slipped
onto a stool in front of Rhonda-Faye. "You feeling
okay?"

Rhonda-Faye nodded. "Just a little backache—that's
all."

Zach sat down beside Sunny in a drift of wintry co-
logne. Suddenly he was all physician. "Any contractions?" he asked.

"No. Besides, I'm not due for another week, Doc."

Zach quirked a brow. "Babies have been known to
come early."

Rhonda-Faye rubbed at her lower back. "Truth to
tell, I wouldn't mind having the birth over with, but I'm
not in labor, not yet anyway."

"Think George is going to do any better this time?"
Sunny asked, recalling how excited Rhonda-Faye's husband tended to be at times like this.

Rhonda-Faye shook her head. "Heaven only knows.
Though he's promised me this time he is going to stay
calm."

Zach frowned. "Isn't this your fourth child?"

"Yes, and you'd think George would be used to the whole birth process by now," Rhonda-Faye drawled affectionately. "But you never know."

Sunny grinned. If Zach was around for the birthing of the baby, he was in for a real surprise. "You seem to need to get off your feet anyway," Sunny said. "Why don't you go on home and let me take over tonight?"

"What do you know about running a diner?" Zach interrupted.

Sunny gave him an incensed look. "I've helped out before. Haven't I, Rhonda-Faye?"

"You saved my life last Labor Day weekend, when two of my high schoolers came down with chicken pox at the same time. But really—the two of you being newlyweds and all—I couldn't impose."

"Sure you can," Zach said genially. "You go home and rest and Sunny and I will take over here. I'm sure we can handle it."

Rhonda-Faye squeezed Zach's arm and leaned over and gave Sunny a hug. "I'll pay you back," she promised. With a grateful nod at them both, she grabbed her sweater and slipped out the back door.

"Mighty sweet of you," Zach said, stepping behind the diner counter.

Sunny tied on an apron as two families with young children walked in. "You ain't seen nothing yet." She met Zach's eyes, stunned at the easy way she and he had slipped into couple mode. "You want to take the orders, while I fill the plates?"

Zach grinned. "Only if you promise not to break any over my head."

"Very funny. The booster chairs are in the back."

The next few minutes were a flurry of activity. Sunny was surprised to see that Zach was no novice when it came to waiting tables. He got the two families situated and took their orders in a jiff.

Circling back around to the grill, he said, "Two burger platters, cremated, extra grass. Both kids want short stacks and Grade A and their mom insists on side dishes of whatever fruit we've got to go with it."

Sunny poured silver dollar-size puddles of pancake batter onto one end of the griddle, then added two hamburgers to the other. "Applesauce and milk are in the fridge."

He whisked over to give the family their drinks, the kids their dishes of fruit, then swaggered back to Sunny's side, looking as at home in an apron as he did in a white lab coat.

"We're running a little low on draw one," Zach reported softly. "Harlan down at the end is going to be wanting more." His breath brushed her hair as he watched her slide perfectly made pancakes onto two kid-size platters, then reach over and flip the sizzling burgers.

"Harlan always wants more coffee," Sunny said. "He works the night shift at the factory." She handed the kiddie platters over to Zach, unable to help but be both pleased and surprised at the eager way he had pitched in. She never would've expected it of him. But then, maybe she just hadn't given him a chance. She had to admit the skunk incident had gotten them off on the wrong foot. And that in turn made her wonder what their relationship would have been like if they had met some other way.

The bell over the door tinkled as another group of customers walked in, pulling Sunny from her trance.

Telling herself sternly that this was no time to start getting warm, fuzzy feelings about her new husband, she forced herself to snap out of it and said, "The coffee is down below the coffeemaker."

"No problem," Zach said.

He chucked her under the chin, then bent to press a light, fleeting kiss on her lips. Her mouth was still tingling as he drew back.

Eyes still holding hers, he said softly, "I'll get the fire going under it right away."

The coffee wasn't the only thing with a fire under it, Sunny thought with a rueful grin, as she continued to run the grill while Zach waited tables.

When closing time rolled around, she was pleasantly exhausted. Zach pulled the shades, switched off the outside lights and locked the door, as Sunny dished up the last of the day's chili, two generous salads and warmed a slab of Rhonda-Faye's homemade sourdough bread. She settled in a booth in the back, while Zach dimmed the lights and fed quarters into the jukebox. Seconds later, the lively sound of Robben Ford and The Blue Line singing "Start It Up" filled the room.

The music Zach had played made her want to get up and dance. She was tapping her foot to the jazzy rhythm as he brought two frosty mugs of root beer to the table and set them down.

Before she knew what he was doing, he had pulled her up out of the booth, and they were jitterbugging to the bluesy beat. Eyes locked, bodies moving in synch, they spun their way through the song.

Breathlessly they returned to the booth.

"Thanks for helping out," Sunny said, as she slid in opposite him. "I'm sure Rhonda-Faye appreciated it."

Zach nudged her foot with his. "What about you?"

"Fishing for a compliment?" she teased.

"More like trying to find out if you're still mad at me over the flower business."

"Ah, yes, the yellow roses." She squeezed his hand. "What do you say we go home and throw them in the trash and start over, as friends this time?"

Sunny knew she wanted to give him a second chance. "But if we're going back to square one, we don't know very much about each other," she said cautiously, aware her heart was thundering against her ribs.

He focused on the turbulence in her eyes. "What do you want to know?"

Everything, she thought. Sunny smiled. "Have you ever been tied to a community before?"

He pinned her with a look. "I have a fondness for Murfreesboro, where I grew up, and Nashville—because I went to med school and did my residency there—but I don't particularly need to live in either place to be happy, if that's what you're asking," he said.

It was. Sunny suppressed her relief. "What about your romantic past? Have you ever been deeply involved?"

He nodded grimly. "Like you, I was engaged once."

Compassion welled up inside her. "What happened?"

"I knew from the beginning that Melody was close to her family. In fact, her abiding love for them was one of the things that attracted me to her. What I didn't realize until after we became engaged was how totally dependent she was on them. Everything that happened in our life together was somehow dictated by her family. She couldn't buy groceries without consulting her mother first. Needless to say, planning the wedding was a nightmare, finding a place to live even worse. I realized I couldn't live that way. I needed a wife who would put our relationship first, a woman who would make our marriage a priority and not just a convenience. With Melody, it was never going to be like that, so we broke it off.''

Sunny knew firsthand how devastating it was to end an engagement, even when you were sure you had no choice. ''That must have been a difficult time for you,'' she said sympathetically.

Zach nodded. ''My own parents understood, of course. Hers didn't.''

Sunny grinned. ''Another sign you weren't meant to be together, I guess.'' She lifted the mug of root beer to her lips. ''I think I'm going to like being friends,'' she said softly. She certainly understood him a lot better.

''Me, too,'' Zach said quietly. He leaned back against the booth and studied her.

Sunny knew he was thinking about kissing her again. Unbidden, the image of Zach as he had been that morning came to mind. Wearing nothing but his glen-plaid boxer shorts, his long, strong body stretched out sexily on his uncomfortably small bed. Just looking at him had made her heart pound and her mouth go dry. When he'd kissed her, her senses had gone into an uproar. They were still topsy-turvy every time she was near him.

As for her fantasies, Sunny knew she didn't need to be asleep to dream of what it would be like to be led down that forbidden path and be made love to by Zach.

Sunny drew a tranquilizing breath. With effort, she forced herself to put her daydreams aside and concentrate on the reality of the situation, which was that he didn't love her. And without love, any passion they shared would be meaningless.

She had waited too long to indulge in meaningless sex—with anyone, even her husband. She cleared her throat, determined to keep them on the right track. "Zach—"

"I know."

He touched her face with the palm of his hand, and it was all she could do not to lean into the incredible warmth and gentleness of his caress.

"Friends," he said, keeping his eyes locked on hers. "For now."

The way things were going, Sunny wondered how long they would stay that way. Because despite their efforts to keep theirs a marriage in name only, they were getting closer to making love every moment they were together.

EXHAUSTED FROM her impromptu stint at the diner, Sunny was sound asleep when the telephone rang. Groggily she pulled the receiver into bed with her and mumbled a sleepy hello. "Sunny? It's George! Get Zach on the line! Quick!"

"Hold on." Recognizing the panic in George's voice, she put the receiver down and stumbled into Zach's room across the hall.

Hand clamped to the smooth, warm skin of his muscular shoulder, she shook him out of what appeared to be a sound sleep. "Zach, wake up! Rhonda-Faye's husband is on the phone."

"Thanks, Sunny." Clad only in his boxer shorts, he shot out of bed and moved across the hall. "George, what is it?" He listened intently, then said, "Calm down. Everything is going to be fine. Just get Rhonda-

Faye in the car…no, don't bother to get her dressed…
and meet me at the clinic as soon as you can. I'll be
there in five minutes. Bye.''

"Rhonda-Faye is in labor?"

Zach nodded, already striding back across the hall to
retrieve his pants. "Apparently her water broke about
fifteen minutes ago. The contractions have been going
on ever since. George says they are about a minute and
a half apart."

"A minute and a half!"

"Yeah, I know. At that rate, they'll never make it
down the mountain to the hospital. Looks like I may
have to deliver her baby in the clinic." Zach tugged his
zipper up, slid his feet into his Topsiders and pulled on
a shirt.

Sunny grabbed the clothes she'd worn earlier and
slipped on her shoes. "You'll need help." Her clothing
bundled in her arm, she raced down the stairs after him.
"I'm going with you."

Sunny dressed in the pickup on the way over. They
had just opened up the clinic when George pulled up in
his Suburban. "Where's Rhonda-Faye?" Sunny asked,
since George appeared to be alone.

"Maybe lying down in back?" Zach suggested with
a shrug, already circling around to help.

George grabbed a suitcase and hopped out. He was
red in the face and completely out of breath. "I got here
as soon as I could!" he yelled.

"You did fine," Zach said. He peered into the middle
seat. It was also empty. "Where's Rhonda-Faye?"

George looked inside the vehicle, then back at Zach.
His expression was panicked. "Oh, my God—"

"You forgot to bring her?" Zach guessed.

George nodded. "I was in such a hurry to get here—"

"Calm down, George," Sunny said.

"It's going to be fine," Zach reassured him. "You drive back and get her and Sunny and I will go into the clinic and call Rhonda-Faye to let her know you're on your way."

George nodded, still looking completely in a dither. "Right." He put the suitcase back in the car, climbed behind the wheel and took off.

"The way George is acting, you'd think he was a first-time father," Zach mused, swiftly unlocking the clinic door.

Sunny grinned. "Rhonda-Faye says she gets more worried about him than delivering the baby."

Zach chuckled and shook his head as he headed for the phone. "Rhonda-Faye? Doc Grainger here. George is on his way back to get you. How are you doing? Every minute and fifteen seconds now, hmm? How long are the contractions lasting? Three minutes. Yeah, I agree—it'd be ridiculous to try to make the trip to the hospital at this point. No problem. Sunny's here with me, so she can help handle George. I'll see you in a few minutes." Zach hung up. "Looks like we're going to deliver a baby."

While Sunny kept an eye out for George and Rhonda-Faye, Zach spread out the sterile sheets and brought out the emergency incubator. Sunny gasped as the Suburban pulled up. "Zach, Rhonda-Faye is driving!"

Zach rushed out with her. George was sitting in the passenger seat beside his wife, a bloody cloth pressed to his head.

"He fell!" Rhonda-Faye said.

"I was running up the front steps to get her," George explained through gritted teeth.

Zach helped Rhonda-Faye step down from behind the wheel. Perspiration matted the hair on her forehead. She was pale and trembling. "Ohhhhhh," she moaned, doubling over as another contraction hit her.

"Rhonda-Faye, honey?" George said, sounding even more panicked as he stepped down, too.

"Zach's got her," Sunny said. She wrapped a steadying arm about his burly waist. "Let's just get you both inside."

No SOONER were they both inside than Rhonda-Faye let out a yelp. "The baby's coming!"

"Now?" George said, looking as if he were going to faint.

Sunny pushed him into one examining room, while Zach helped Rhonda-Faye into the other. There was another scream from Rhonda-Faye. George went even paler. Sunny guided him to the examining table. "Lie down before you fall down, George."

He groaned, even as he complied. "Rhonda-Faye—"

"Zach's got her. I'm sure they're doing fine." Struggling to recall what first aid she could, Sunny removed the bloody cloth from George's temple. The bleeding had stopped, but it was clear from the depth of the cut that he was going to need stitches.

She reached for a packet of sterile gauze and ripped it open. "I'm going to put a bandage on your head and then I'm going to go in and see if Zach needs any help. Okay?"

"Okay."

"You just stay here until Zach can get to you."

Hurriedly Sunny covered the gash on George's forehead. She patted his arm reassuringly, then dashed into the other examining room just as Rhonda-Faye let out another strangled sound. A sterile surgical gown tossed on over his clothes, Zach was sitting on a stool in front of Rhonda-Faye.

"Now," Zach said calmly, "one more push. C'mon, Rhonda-Faye. You're doing fine. Help me out here. Push...."

Rhonda-Faye bore down with all her might. The next thing Sunny knew Zach was holding a new baby in his hands. Sunny's eyes filled with tears as the baby let out a healthy squall of outrage.

"It's a girl, Rhonda-Faye," Zach said, laying the feisty newborn on the sterile cloth draped across her mother's stomach.

"Oh, she's beautiful," Rhonda-Faye gasped, gathering her close.

"That she is," Sunny agreed emotionally, as Zach swiftly cut the cord. Sunny grabbed a sterile gown to wrap the baby in, while Zach tended to his patient. "And she'll be even prettier once we get her cleaned up."

"One bath and a set of soft, warm clothes coming up," Zach promised.

"Oh, take her in to let George see first," Rhonda-Faye asked.

Zach smiled at Sunny and nodded his approval.

"Time to go see your daddy," Sunny said. Gently she lifted the baby in her arms. She carried the bundle in to George. He took one look at his beautiful new daughter, then fainted dead away.

"YOU SURE you're doing okay now, George?" Zach asked as he and Sunny escorted the trio out to the Suburban, where a neighbor was waiting to drive the happy family home.

"You mean except for the splitting headache and the six stitches in my temple?" George asked, tongue in cheek. Now that all the excitement was over, he had calmed down swiftly.

"I don't know why he fainted," Rhonda-Faye said. "It's not as if we haven't been through all this before."

"I think it was the way the baby looked," George said. "All that goo she had on her—"

"That was the vernix caseosa," Zach explained. "It covers the skin and protects the baby in the womb." Zach paused. "You were never in the delivery room before?"

"He was afraid he would faint," Rhonda-Faye said, and they all laughed.

"You call me if you have any problems today, and I'll stop by your house this evening to check on you all," Zach said.

"Thanks, Doc," Rhonda-Faye said.

"Thank God you were here tonight," George said. "We sure are lucky to have you here."

"I'm glad I was here, too," Zach said.

Zach and Sunny waved as the couple drove off. Together they walked back into the clinic and began to clean up and tidy everything. When they were finished, Zach put a pot of coffee on. They each filled a mug and went outside to sit on the back steps. Five in the morning, the stars and the moon were still visible. Sunny was as charged up as he could ever remember seeing her. Zach was wired, too.

It wasn't supposed to be like this. They weren't supposed to act like two members of a well-rehearsed team. They had signed on for a marriage of convenience with little or no exchange of feelings, yet almost from the moment he'd met her, his emotions had soared out of control. The medical emergency tonight had shown him yet another side of her.

She would, Zach decided, someday make some man a very good marriage partner. The only problem was, he realized uncomfortably, that he didn't want to think of her married to anyone but him.

His feelings puzzled him. After his engagement to Melody had ended, he had sworn never to get involved with a woman who put friends and family ahead of her relationship with him. Yet there he was, getting more and more tied to Sunny with every second that passed, knowing all the while that she cared every bit as much about the opinions, needs and wants of her family and friends as Melody had. Knowing that, he should have been running as fast and as far away as he could, but he didn't want to lose or halt what had begun between them.

"Is that the first time you've ever seen a baby born?" he asked. She was sitting so close to him he could feel her body heat.

"Yes. It was amazing, wasn't it?" As Sunny turned partway to face him, she nudged his muscular thigh with her knee. Her eyes were bright with wonder. "I mean, you always hear about the miracle of birth and all that, but to actually see it, be a part of it..." Aware she was rambling, Sunny stopped. Aware her knee was touching him, she pulled back.

Zach didn't want them to stop touching. He smiled at her and linked hands so that their fingers were intertwined. It was all he could do not to pull her into his arms and make love with her then and there. "I feel the same way," he admitted huskily. "Life is very precious." Drawing a breath, he gazed at the ever-lightening sky overhead. "I don't think any of us ever realize how much so except for times like this, when we're witness to a new life or—" Zach blinked and his voice thickened revealingly as pain exploded deep inside him "—we see one taken away."

"It must be hard for you when a patient dies," she said softly.

Zach nodded. He pushed the difficult memories away. "Losing someone close to you is hard on everyone," he said huskily. But he didn't want to talk about that, he thought as he wrapped an arm affectionately about her shoulders, squeezed and pressed a kiss into the fragrant softness of her red-gold hair. "Thanks for helping me out tonight. I don't know what I would have done without you."

"All a part of being a doctor's wife, I guess," Sunny said. "At least, a doctor's wife in a small town," she amended hastily, then paused.

Leaning her head on his shoulder, she noticed that Zach was still looking extraordinarily thoughtful, almost moody, tonight. She wondered if he was thinking about another patient of his, one he perhaps hadn't been able to help.

Straightening, Sunny took another sip of the hot coffee. Cupping both hands around the stoneware mug for warmth, she asked, "Did you mean what you said to George and Rhonda-Faye earlier—about being glad you were here?" *With them and with me?*

Zach turned to her. He knew a lot was riding on his answer. The first pearly-gray lights of dawn filtered over the horizon, illuminating his handsome face. The brooding look of moments before vanishing, he cupped her face in his hand. "Yes," he said, brushing her lips with a brief, all-too-fleeting kiss. "I did."

Chapter Six

Better Your Heart than Mine

"No, I understand, Gramps. Of course I can ask Zach."
I just don't want to, Sunny thought. This morning, in
front of the clinic, Zach had almost kissed her. If he
had, she was sure they would have succumbed to the
passion simmering between them and made love. He'd
known it, too. He'd also probably known the reckless,
highly romantic nature of their moods had come not
from the joy they were finding in being with each other
or their pretend marriage, but from the romance and
excitement of delivering a baby into this world. And
that excitement would fade, Sunny told herself severely.
And when it did they would still have to live in the
same house every day. And they would still be married.

"Yes. I'll see you in your office around ten. And I'll
have the sample pages for the new mail-order catalog
with me."

Sunny hung up the phone. She turned, to find Zach
lounging in the doorway of the kitchen. He was dressed
for work in shirt, tie and jeans.

"Ask me what?" he said.

"Nothing."

"C'mon, Sunny," he demanded impatiently.

"Gramps can't give me a ride into work, and it's so late that Matilda has already left."

"And you still can't drive your Land Rover because the skunk smell is still in it."

"Right."

Exasperation glimmered in his eyes. "If you need a ride, why didn't you say so?"

Because I'm beginning to feel too close to you, Sunny thought, a little desperately. "I didn't want to impose."

"You wouldn't be imposing."

The look in his eyes almost had her believing it. Sunny tapped a high-heeled foot against the parquet floor. "I need to fix that skunk smell."

Zach's expression softened sympathetically. "You've already tried damn near everything, haven't you?"

Sunny nodded, embarrassed. Zach had been right about that; they shouldn't have gotten into her vehicle until they had rid themselves of the smell. She shrugged and held the sample pages of the catalog to her chest. "Everyone says to just give it time."

"Time can work wonders in lots of areas," Zach agreed with a teasing grin, as his gaze roved her slender form.

He was thinking about kissing her again. Sunny could tell by the gleam of anticipation in his eyes. Her heart racing, she sidestepped the sensual embrace she sensed was coming if they dallied any longer. She was *not* going to be foolish enough to fall in love with him, not when she knew he couldn't wait for this farce of a marriage to end. Keeping her back to him, she gathered up her belongings. "I'm in a hurry, Zach," she said impatiently.

When she looked around at him again, he grinned, not the least bit put off by the edginess in her tone.

"And testy, too."

"I can't help it." Picking up where she'd left off when the phone had rung, Sunny swept a brush through her hair with long, practiced strokes. "It's aggravating me to no end not having a car to drive. I'm used to being completely self-sufficient."

Zach watched as she clipped her hair at the nape with a gold-filigreed barrette. "I know what you mean. I'm a pick-up-and-go type of person myself. In med school, my ability to leave town for a weekend now and then was the only thing that saved my sanity. I still like to get away for a weekend when I can."

"Where's your favorite place to go?" Sunny asked curiously, applying lipstick to her lips.

"I like water. Lakes and streams over beaches, generally. They're less crowded and I prefer the country to the city any day when looking for a little R and R." Zach watched as if mesmerized as she pressed her lips together to set the lipstick. "What about you?" His eyes trekked slowly back to hers.

"I don't know." His face was inches from hers as she recapped her lipstick and put it back in her purse. "I never really take vacations per se." Although Zach was making her regret that, too.

"How come?" He stepped behind her. Placing his palms on her shoulders, he kneaded the tenseness from her shoulders.

Sunny leaned into his soothing touch and briefly closed her eyes as his stroking, massaging fingers worked their magic. "Habit, I guess. As a kid, I saw plenty of the world, since my parents worked all over Europe, but every trip was always combined with work somehow. They'd go off to meetings. I'd either tag along and read a book while they labored and negotiated, or go tour a museum with my nanny. Either way, it seemed more like an extension of my education than a vacation.'' Relaxed now, she leaned against him.

Zach's hands stilled and he pressed a kiss in her hair. ''Maybe that's why you're so crazy about those old 'I Love Lucy' reruns, like the ones you were watching last night before bed. If there was any fun to be had within a hundred miles, Lucy would find it,'' he said as he wrapped an arm around her waist and held her near.

Sunny grinned, enjoying the warmth and gentleness he exuded. ''You're right about that.''

His arm still hooked around her waist, Zach turned her to face him. ''A little zaniness is good for the soul,'' he said, looking down at her affectionately.

Sunny felt her resistance to their marriage fading, inch by precious inch, even as they strayed into uncharted territory. Zach was becoming genuinely fond of her, as she was of him; that was not her imagination. ''And you're the expert on zaniness, I suppose?'' she teased back, thinking that if ever she had longed for her Ricky Ricardo, she had found him in Zach.

''Damn straight I am. Furthermore, one of these days I'll show you how to take a long, lazy weekend where nothing at all productive gets done.''

''Sounds fun.''

''In the meantime, I'll drop you at work,'' he said, handing her her purse and briefcase and tucking her arm in his.

Sunny looked up at him and saw something—a feeling, an emotion—that she couldn't analyze. ''Don't you have to be at the clinic?''

Zach's eyes glinted with good humor. ''I think I can

be fifteen minutes late arriving one morning. I'll just put a note on the clinic door telling people when to expect me.''

He was still going way out of his way. Sunny dug in her heels, afraid that if he evidenced much more kindness she really would be head over heels in love with him. "You don't have to do this for me, Zach.''

"Yes, I do, Sunny,'' he replied, tightening his hold on her possessively. "You're my wife.''

"WHAT'S GOING ON?'' Zach asked as he pulled his pickup into the Carlisle Furniture Factory parking lot.

Sunny groaned as she looked at the fifty or so employees scattered in front of the building, now interestedly gazing their way. "I completely forgot. It's Earth Day and the local chapter of the Sierra Club always comes out and celebrates by planting a tree.''

Zach didn't mind the two of them being seen together. In fact, he was beginning to kind of like it. But it was apparent Sunny did mind. He brought the truck to a halt. Leaving the engine running, he put the vehicle in park, then turned to her. "Looks like we have quite an audience,'' Zach murmured mischievously, unable to resist teasing her. Maybe it was time he stopped fighting it and played his husband act to the hilt. As long as they were together, they might as well have a little fun, he thought.

"Well, not to worry. There's not going to be anything for them to see,'' Sunny announced.

"On the contrary, Sunny,'' Zach drawled as he gave in to the temptation that had been plaguing him all morning and took her by the shoulders and kissed her soundly. Finished, he lifted his lips from hers and sifted a hand through her hair, knowing even as he did that he would never get enough to satisfy him, not even if he kissed her a thousand times. "I think there should be quite a lot for them to see. We are newlyweds, after all."

Sunny regarded him with a steamed glance, resenting, Zach supposed, the easy way she surrendered to him whenever he took her into his arms. What she didn't realize was that the feeling—of surrendering beyond their will—was mutual and just as difficult for him to fight. "I should have known you'd take advantage," she huffed.

Zach raised his brow, his desire to possess her, heart and soul, growing all the stronger. "Sunny, honey, that wasn't taking advantage," he murmured playfully. "This is."

Before Sunny had a chance to draw a breath, he had pulled her back into his arms and slanted his mouth over hers. Their kiss was hot and sweet and completely overwhelming in its intensity. Apparently forgetting her decision not to give an inch where he was concerned, she wreathed her arms around his neck and met him halfway. Engulfed by a wave of passion and need long held at bay, she let him pull her closer, deepen the kiss to tempestuous heights. Time lost all meaning as emotions swirled, and still it wasn't enough, Zach thought, amazed and shaken. It would never be.

He hadn't meant for this to happen. But now that it had, he was having a difficult time stopping himself. Only the thought that they had an audience kept him walking the straight and narrow. With difficulty, he ended the kiss, and lifted his lips from the tantalizing softness and warmth of hers.

She released a shaky breath. "You're not playing fair," she accused, her eyes shooting indignant sparks while she gave him an otherwise adoring look that was strictly for the benefit of their audience.

She wanted to talk about fair? Zach thought, still caught up in the moment and the essence that was her. There was nothing fair about this situation they found themselves in. Nothing easy about the circumstances that were compelling him to fall in love with her.

He cupped a hand under her chin, enjoying the slightly bedazzled state she was now in as much as he had loved leading her there. He tweaked her on the nose. "I never play fair, Sunny."

"WELL, LADIES, ready for lesson number two?" the instructor asked.

"If you ask me, Sunny's lessons are already working," Matilda said. "You should have seen that kiss Zach gave her in front of the factory this morning. Whoo-eee! It nearly knocked my socks off!"

"Thank you, Matilda," Sunny said dryly. She felt herself flushing bright red.

"Now, Sunny, don't you go getting embarrassed on us," Aunt Gertie counseled. "What you and Zach have is something to be proud of, to savor!"

"I agree," the instructor said, "and that is the basis for your next lesson. There is nothing sexier or more compelling to a man than the feeling of being the lord and master of his own castle. I am telling you, ladies, let your man take charge on the home front, and he will reward you with kisses galore."

"That's ridiculous," Sunny said.

"I don't like the sound of that, either," Matilda said.

"Let's put it to the test and then see," the instructor said. "Here is your assignment. I want all of you to give your husband free reign over his home for a period of six hours, starting tomorrow evening after work. His every wish is to be your command. You are to anticipate his every need. And most important of all, you are *not* to tell him or anyone else what you are doing or why. Not even a hint.''

"Why?''

"Because if we tell them, they'll take advantage of us,'' Rhonda-Faye grumbled.

"Close, but no cigar,'' the instructor said. "Quite simply, if your husband thinks this is a game, he will treat it as a game. And this is serious, ladies. I am teaching you a whole new way of life.''

"I don't know about the rest of you, but I did not sign on to learn how to become slave labor,'' Sunny said.

"I don't want you to be a slave,'' the instructor corrected. "I want you to treat your husband like a king. And when you do, you will find out that he will of his own volition treat you like his queen. Naturally, I'll expect you to keep a diary of your efforts and the results. During the next lesson we will share them with the class.''

Sunny groaned, anticipating Zach's reaction. Could it get any worse?

SUNNY EMERGED from the kitchen just as Zach walked in the front door. His glance slid over the navy silk lounging outfit she had just put on, then moved to the yellow roses prominently displayed on the pedestal table in the front hall.

"Are those my flowers?''

"Yes. They are.''

He narrowed his eyes at her. "I thought you were going to throw them out.''

"I decided it's the thought that counts," Sunny said cryptically. In this case, she wanted everyone to think she cherished the flowers. Whereas in truth, she was using them for a little visual on-site reality check. No more getting caught up in the idea of playing husband and wife the way she had in front of the factory this morning. No more steamy kisses. No more pent-up desire. No more falling in love with Zach! She was going to forget what they were teaching her in that class and live in the real world. And the reality was, no matter how tantalizing the idea of being really married to Zach or making wild, reckless, passionate love with him, neither thing was going to happen. Therefore, the only way to protect her heart was to keep her emotional distance.

Zach set down his medical bag with a thud. "What's going on here, Sunny?"

She regarded Zach innocently. "I'm trying to be nice," she said breezily. "So play along with me. Now, what would you like for dinner?"

"You're offering to cook for me?" He regarded her skeptically.

Sunny felt ridiculous, like a character out of some fifties sitcom trying to please her man. She wet her lips. "If you like." She was hoping desperately he had other plans.

"Uh-huh. What are my choices?"

Sunny shrugged, the irony of the situation not lost on her. She was married to the man and she had no idea what he liked. "Fried chicken. Steak on the grill."

Zach's lips compressed into a thoughtful line. "Fried chicken takes a while, doesn't it?" he prodded.

"Yes."

He faced her, an eyebrow raised in question. "Aren't you tired?"

Never too tired to make you happy, dear—at least, for the next six hours. "It'd be my pleasure," Sunny said, sidestepping his question altogether.

"To serve me?" Zach countered with a penetrating look. "I don't think so," he said drolly. "What's going on, Sunny?" He closed the distance between them and pointed to the yellow roses. "Are you trying to pay me back for the flowers mistake?"

"No, of course not." Sunny flushed.

"Then why the sudden eagerness to please me?" Zach towered over her. "Gramps going to pop in or something?"

"Not to my knowledge," she said truthfully, then pivoted. "I'll go start dinner."

Hand on her shoulder, he tugged her back to his side and gently spun her around. "I haven't decided what I want yet."

"Oh." Sunny folded her hands primly in front of her and took a deep, calming breath. "Right."

His eyes gleamed with mischief. "You know what? I think I'd like prime rib."

Leave it to Zach to make things more difficult, she thought. "I don't have any, but I think I can get to the market before closing. Unfortunately," she murmured, "it's not the sort of thing our butcher usually carries."

"I guess fried chicken will have to do, then," Zach drawled.

Sunny smiled and didn't comment. Every time she commented she got herself into trouble. Deciding this assignment would be a lot easier if they spent a few minutes apart, she said, "The newspaper is in the living room, dear."

Zach gave her a testing glance. "My slippers, too?" he asked innocently.

Sunny paused. As far as she knew, he did not wear slippers. But she supposed, for the sake of the class, she could give the idea some play. "I haven't seen your slippers."

"If you had, would you go get them?"

This assignment was a killer. "If you needed me to get them," Sunny specified sweetly. She couldn't think of a single reason where that would be the case.

Aware he was still ruminating over the sudden change in her behavior, Sunny slipped into the kitchen.

To her chagrin, he joined her there.

While he removed his tie and unfastened the first two buttons on his blue-and-white striped cotton dress shirt, Sunny got out the chicken.

He watched as she rinsed and patted it dry, pulled out the seasoned flour, then beat an egg and milk into a frothy mixture.

Zach poured himself a glass of iced tea as she prepared the chicken.

"You've done this before, I presume?" he said finally.

Sunny nodded, not shy about admitting, "Many times."

"Who taught you?" he asked softly, drawing closer.

"I taught myself by reading cookbooks."

His eyebrows lifted. "Julia Child?"

Sunny's mouth curved wryly as she added oil to the skillet and waited for it to heat. "Try Betty Crocker, Fannie Farmer, Pillsbury and anyone else who specializes in home-style cuisine. Since my parents preferred nouvelle cuisine and continental fare, I wanted pizza, hog dogs, fried chicken, grits and so on."

"Naturally." Zach grinned.

"What did you grow up eating?"

"Home-style American cuisine."

Sunny dropped pieces of chicken into a black cast-iron skillet. "What did you want?"

Zach stood looking over her shoulder. "Home-style American cuisine."

Satisfied the chicken was cooking nicely, Sunny went over to the pantry. She contemplated various side-dish possibilities. "Mashed potatoes okay with you?"

"As long as you make gravy. I can't eat mashed potatoes without gravy."

Sunny chuckled at the absurdity of that. Finally a character flaw she could identify with, she thought. She had begun to think Zach hadn't a whimsical bone in his body.

"Want me to make a salad to go with it?" He started for the refrigerator.

Sunny intercepted him midway. Zach's helpfulness was not in her lesson plan. "No. I have to do it," she said quickly, before she could think.

Some of the pleasure left his eyes. It was replaced swiftly by hurt. Sunny could have shot herself for the slip.

Zach folded his arms in front of him calmly. He quirked a brow. "What do you mean you have to do it?" he echoed.

Sunny flushed. Now that he was alerted to her deceptiveness where the evening was concerned, he would never just let it go. Nevertheless she tried to bluff her way out of trouble. "You know what I mean."

"I'm starting to." He trapped her against the refrigerator door. An arm on either side of her, caging her in, he murmured silkily, "If I didn't know better, I'd think you'd do just about anything to please me tonight."

Sunny inhaled jerkily. Unable to move without bringing them into closer contact, she remained motionless and held her ground.

"That's it. Isn't it?" Zach asked.

Their earlier camaraderie vanished. Hurt shimmered in his eyes, turning them an even darker blue.

"This is some sort of lesson...an experiment for your class."

"Now, Zach, I'm just trying to be cordial," Sunny said breathlessly.

He studied her. "Suppose I told you I'd changed my mind about the chicken and now I wanted steak."

Sunny kept her eyes on his. "Then I'd finish the chicken, save it for tomorrow and heat up the grill in the meantime."

"Hmm." Zach strode away from her and retrieved his glass of iced tea. "I think I will read that paper."

Sunny couldn't believe he was just going to walk away from her, now that he knew what her task was, but he did. Heart pounding, she waited for him to come back, to deliver the next zinger. He did neither, and she spent the next hour in the kitchen alone, preparing dinner, while he watched the television news and read the paper.

This proves he is definitely not husband material. No, she corrected herself wearily, her innate sense of fairness coming to the fore. It just proves he doesn't like to be a lab rat for some how-to-be-happily-married class. And for that, Sunny couldn't blame him.

"You really outdid yourself with dinner," Zach said, after they had finished their strawberry shortcake and coffee. And that was a surprise. He had half expected her to ruin it on purpose, after he'd caught on to the reason behind her sudden change of heart.

Fool that he was, he had thought it was due to the passionate kisses they'd shared, the fact that they were getting to know each other and more often than not now liking what they found. He should have known that the idea of Sunny meeting him halfway to try to make this temporary marriage of theirs work was too good to be true. She had been forced into it, too. She also had to deal with that class. But that didn't excuse what she'd done this evening, raising his hopes unfairly by dressing in that silky navy blue outfit that made the most of her slender curves.

"Thank you," Sunny said politely. "I'm glad you enjoyed dinner."

Not as much as I'm going to enjoy this, Zach thought. Deliberately he let his eyes drop to her breasts before returning to her face. "You know what I really feel like doing?"

Sunny flushed. "The dishes?"

"No, Sunny," he drawled, sitting back in his chair. He folded his arms in front of him. "I think the dishes can wait indefinitely, don't you?"

Her tongue snaked out to wet her lower lip. "What did you have in mind, then?" She kept her eyes on his.

"I want to play a little game," Zach said, testing her reaction, and finding it every bit as uncertain and off kilter as he'd hoped.

"I've got Scrabble upstairs," Sunny said, already jumping up to get it.

Zach caught her wrist as she passed by. "I want to play Simon Says," Zach announced. He tugged her down onto his lap. "And I want to be Simon."

"That's a child's game."

"Not the way I intend to play it."

Muttering something indecipherable, Sunny attempted to vault off his lap but was held in place by his arms. "Darn you." She tried to release his arms from her waist. Failing at that, as well, she wiggled around to free herself, then stopped seconds later, apparently realizing what her subtle shifting was doing to his already much-aroused lower half. She drew a deep breath, the silk shifting beneath her thighs, and began in a much more reasonable tone, "Zach. I don't think—"

He touched a gentle hand to her lips, silencing her. He was aching all over and was sure he would pay for this hours later in terms of pent-up need, but he was not willing to stop until he had given Sunny a taste of her own medicine. "So you're refusing to do what I say— is that it?" he asked mildly. He knew how she liked to succeed at whatever she did, even the meddlesome class. In fact, he was counting on that trait in her to get them back to a level playing field, where honesty of feelings and not silly games prevailed.

Sunny flushed guiltily. She drew another bolstering breath, glanced down at her watch, as if contemplating how much time she had left on this particular assignment. "I thought you might want to rent a movie," she said finally.

Zach shook his head. Watching a video would do nothing to get Sunny to drop the compliant-wife act. "I think I'd prefer the game."

She bit her lip and looked up at him. He knew what she was thinking—that Simon Says, in the hands of a lascivious male, could be dangerous. "Shall we give it a try?" he asked softly, in a tone meant to incense her. "Or are you afraid to play games with me?"

Her temper visibly igniting, Sunny glared at him. "I am not afraid," she announced loftily.

"Good, then let's give it a try," he said, ready to get down to business. "Simon says put your arms around Zach's neck."

Sunny's eyes darkened angrily, as they always did when she was forced to do something she did not want to do, but she followed his instructions.

Zach smiled. Lucky for her, he had scruples. "Simon says close your eyes."

Rebellious color flooded her pretty cheeks, but she reluctantly lowered her thick red-gold lashes anyway, closing them almost all the way.

Zach frowned. "Are you cheating?"

"What?"

"Sunny, c'mon. Close those eyelashes all the way, now," he commanded sternly. "If you're going to play this game with me you have to play it right."

Murmuring a protest, she frowned nervously and started to shut her eyes completely. "Aha," Zach announced victoriously, "caught you!"

"Caught me!" Sunny echoed, incensed, as her eyelids flew open.

Zach shook his head at her in mocking report. "Simon never said you could open your eyes, either," he teased.

Her cheeks burning as she realized she'd been duped, Sunny pummeled his chest with her fist in aggravation. "This isn't fair!"

"No, Sunny, it's the way the game is played." Zach put his hands around her waist and started to shift her off his lap before any real damage could be done, any real temptation succumbed to. "You lose." *In fact, because of your playacting tonight, we both do.*

To his surprise, she refused to move in the direction he wanted her to go. Instead she remained squarely on his lap. Her lower lip was thrust out in a seductive pout. Her breasts were rising and falling seductively with each breath she took.

"I want another turn," she demanded stubbornly.

As Zack felt the warm, silk-clad weight of her settle in more comfortably on his lap, it was all he could do not to groan aloud in frustration. He had known all along how she hated to lose. He had even suspected she might purposely lose the game quickly, just as a way of getting out of having to play. He hadn't figured she would get genuinely flustered so soon, lose and then insist on playing another round.

"Sure now?" Zach taunted, no more willing to lose face than she was. "I could confuse you even worse this time," he warned.

"Just start playing!" she ordered bad-temperedly. "Now!"

"Okay." He grinned, keeping his hands around her slender waist, as he orchestrated a quick end to the game. "Simon says touch your lips to mine." His whole body throbbing, he waited for her to leap off his lap.

But this time, to his dismay, Sunny kept her cool. She quirked a brow. "You think I won't do it, don't you?"

Zach ignored the urgent demands of his body and gave her a look. "Babe, I know you won't do it."

"Ha! Just goes to show what you know!" Sunny muttered. Anger sparking in her eyes, she leaned forward and lightly touched her lips to his.

Zach knew what she was expecting. She was expecting him to play around a little more.

In truth, he had initially intended to do just that. But there was something about the softness of her lips against his, the cozy feeling of having her on his lap, that sent the rules of the game—and caution—to the wind.

He knew he shouldn't do it. He no longer gave a damn. Wrapping a hand around the back of her neck, he tilted her head beneath his. Their lips fused. He felt the need pouring out of her, mingling with the desire and the temper. And beneath that, he felt the tenderness that was so much a part of her, too. His need to be close to her was as overwhelming as it was magical. He threaded his fingers through her red-gold hair, tipped her head up to allow himself greater access, and claimed her as his.

As her mouth opened to his, he kissed her long and hard and deep. He kissed her until she moaned softly and melted in his arms. Until it felt as if they were both on a long magic-carpet ride. Realizing it was either stop now or take her to bed—and she wasn't ready to be made love to, at least not yet—Zach slowly, reluctantly, drew the kiss to an end.

His mouth tingling, his whole body trembling, he moved back slightly. He expected to see fury in her face. And he saw it, but only after the wonder and the stars in her eyes faded. "Guess I got a little carried away," he drawled.

"I guess you did," Sunny said, almost too sweetly.

And once again, to Zach's acute disappointment, she reined her feelings in.

"But then," she continued, gazing up at him with all-too-innocent eyes, "that kiss you gave me is nothing that can't be remedied."

"Remedied?" He did not like the sound of that.

"Sure," Sunny said, as she slid gracefully off his lap. "Because now it's my turn to play Simon."

Zach shrugged. "Give it your best shot."

"Simon says stand on one foot."

Zach rolled to his feet and stood on one foot.

"Put both feet on the floor."

His expression benign, he remained on one foot.

She looked him up and down, like a farmer examining a prize bull at market. Zach's feelings of unease increased. He sensed she was about to order him to take a long walk off a short pier.

"Simon says...turn toward the back door."

Keeping his shoulders loose and relaxed with effort, Zach turned casually toward the back door. No need to let her see she was getting to him, he thought.

Her smile widening, Sunny dropped her voice a seductive notch. "Simon says turn toward the sink."

He turned toward the sink.

"Simon says wash the dishes!"

It was all he could do not to groan. There were a lot of dishes.

"And Simon says don't stop until you're done!"

Sunny threw a napkin at him and stomped out of the room.

His body still humming with unslaked desire, Zach watched the provocative sway of her retreating backside. Maybe he had overdone it, but it sure had been fun while it lasted.

Chapter Seven

Ain't Misbehavin'

Zach awoke at dawn to the sound of water hitting metal. He looked outside to see Sunny in cutoffs and an old Smith College sweatshirt, hosing down the *inside* of her Land Rover. Finished, she tugged a red bandanna bandit-style over her mouth and nose, picked up a bucket of soapy water and a scrub brush and leaned into the Land Rover.

Pulling on a pair of running shorts, T-shirt and shoes, he headed downstairs. He heard Sunny swearing her displeasure as he neared. The top half of her was inside the truck; her bottom half extended out of it. As Zach neared her, he couldn't help but notice what spectacular legs she had. Or how much he liked seeing her in those Daisy Mae short-shorts she was wearing.

Sunny let out another litany of swear words as she continued to scrub her vehicle's interior carpet.

"Need any help?" he asked.

She started, and would have bumped her head if Zach hadn't caught her in time. She pivoted toward him, her bare legs rubbing up against the length of his. "Must you always sneak up on me like that?" she demanded.

"Do you have any idea what time it is?" Zach countered, his nose wrinkling at the pungent smell.

"Six-fifteen." Sunny shot him a look that told him she still hadn't forgiven him for kissing her so thoroughly during their Simon Says game.

Aware he wasn't due over at the clinic until nine, he stuck his hands in his pockets and lounged against the side of the truck. "Don't you have to go to work today?"

"Don't you?" she retorted, without bothering to answer his question.

So she wasn't going to make it easy on him. Zach rubbed at the stubble on his unshaven jaw. He felt just a little contrite, even though he didn't really believe he had anything to apologize for. Sunny had only gotten what she'd had coming to her for trying to put one over on him. But, as always, she didn't see it that way.

Aware the silence between them was growing, he drawled, "So what are you doing out here?"

"Trying to get the skunk smell out of my Land Rover. What are you doing out here?" she asked in a muffled voice.

Enjoying the view, Zach thought. Trying to make peace. "Checking up on you."

"Well, as you can see," she said temperamentally, letting go of the bandanna, so that it fell around her neck, "I'm fine!"

Zach didn't think so. He pushed away from the rear of the vehicle and ambled closer. "Need a hand?"

Sunny shrugged. "Be my guest and scrub away."

"What are you using this time?" he asked. She had done this at least every other day since they'd imbued her Land Rover with the fragrance of skunk. She had also air-dried it in the sun repeatedly, also to no avail.

"I think a more apropos question is what haven't I used. Today it is a solution of detergent and water."

Zach wrinkled his nose. "I hate to say this, but so far it doesn't seem to be working."

Sunny scowled and dipped her brush back in the bucket. "You got any better ideas?"

"Actually...yes."

She straightened, hands on her hips, and gave him an expectant look. "I'm all ears, husband dear."

"What do you say we hand wash the whole interior in tomato juice?"

"Because the tomato juice would also stain the carpet."

"So rip out the carpet and forget about it. The seats are leather, so the tomato juice will rinse right off."

Sunny studied the sudsy carpet on the floor of her truck. "I don't know, Zach. It seems like a waste."

Zach understood her reluctance to spend money unnecessarily. He also knew, in this case, that it was going to be inevitable. "Have you tried your insurance?" he asked.

Sunny nodded unhappily. "My policy only covers theft, wrecks and natural disasters involving fire or flood."

"A skunk isn't a natural disaster?"

Sunny made a face. "Only to you and me."

Zach regarded her Land Rover. "Thought about driving it off a cliff? Then you could collect."

"Very funny and the answer is yes, numerous times." Sunny kicked at a tire. "Dammit Zach, I want a vehicle to drive!"

"You could borrow mine," he suggested gently.

Sunny shook off the offer. "You need it for house calls."

Zach sighed. "True."

She gave him another droll look. Moving several feet away from her vehicle, she fingered the bandanna she still had looped around her neck. "I think now is the point where you're supposed to say something soothing," she remarked, tongue in cheek.

Zach searched his mind for a comforting bromide to fit the bill. He couldn't come up with much. "Well, look at it this way, Sunny," he said sagely at last. "No good smell stays forever, so no bad smell can stay forever, either."

Sunny tilted her chin and kept her eyes on his. "Meaning what, exactly?"

Zach shrugged. "In a year it should smell better?"

Sunny closed her eyes and silently counted to ten. Finally she opened them again. "That's not helping," she said flatly.

Zach grinned down at her. "Then maybe this will."

He swung her up into his arms and carried her, protesting loudly all the way, over to her front porch. He set her down on the narrow steps.

"What do you think you are doing?" she demanded.

Zach touched the tip of her nose with his index finger, amazed at how much she had come to mean to him in so short a time and how dull his life was going to seem if he was ever without her again. "I'll continue scrubbing—it will be my good deed for the day. Now, sit here and be quiet for all of five minutes, okay?"

"I saw Zach carrying you around this morning. My, the two of you certainly have a lot of energy," Matilda said, as she drove Sunny to work an hour and a half later.

Sunny knew she shouldn't have been laboring over

her truck again before work, but she'd had to do something to use up the excess adrenaline pouring through her veins. She had barely slept at all last night, just thinking about Zach's kisses. Which were getting more and more frequent and potent all the time. She was beginning to seriously contemplate making love with him...to live dangerously for a change. She and Zach would never really be man and wife. They were just too different. But they could have a wild, reckless, passionate love affair....

A love affair she'd remember and cherish the rest of her life. More important, she knew by the way he was kissing her, that he wanted to make love to her, too. So what was stopping her?

"Sunny?" Matilda said loudly, breaking into her thoughts. "You haven't heard a word I've said, have you?"

Sunny blinked. "Hmm?"

"Whatever are you thinking about?"

Zach, and how much I am beginning to care for him, Sunny thought.

"And why do you have that silly besotted look on your face?" Matilda continued, as she turned off Main Street and onto the two-lane highway that led to the factory.

"I—" Sunny brought herself up short. "I don't know." She frowned. "I'm just worried about so many things." *Like getting out of this marriage with my heart and soul intact.*

Needing to change the subject, Sunny sniffed the inside of her wrist. "Do I smell like skunk?"

Matilda shook her head. "Apricot bath soap."

Now, there was a possibility she hadn't yet considered. "Hmm. Maybe I should try that on the interior of my car," Sunny mused.

"Maybe. Although I'm with Zach that nothing will get rid of a skunk odor when it gets on cloth or anything," Matilda said.

"We'll see," Sunny said.

Matilda gave Sunny a bluntly assessing look. "So how did your assignment go last night?" she asked casually.

Recalling how it had felt to sit on Zach's lap, her arms wreathed around his neck, and kiss him like there was no tomorrow, Sunny flushed. "We're not supposed to talk about it until class, remember?"

Matilda grinned. "He liked being king of his own castle, hmm?"

Heavens, yes! Sunny thought.

She turned toward Matilda, wondering if everyone else had gotten the same results from the experiment. "Did Slim?"

"He didn't notice anything different. That newlywed husband of yours apparently did," Matilda said with a sly look.

"That's because Zach notices everything." Even more telling, Sunny thought, was the fact that she noticed everything about him, as well. Including the fact that he was much too big for that rollaway bed he was sleeping on in the guest room.

Knowing he was uncomfortable every night made her feel so guilty she'd begun to consider solutions. And she knew what Zach wanted, of course—to move into her bedroom.

ZACH REALIZED something was going on the moment he walked in that evening and saw the disassembled cardboard furniture boxes littering the front hall. He took the stairs two at a time, strode past the folded-up rollaway bed he had been sleeping on and skittered to a halt in the guest bedroom doorway.

Sunny was home and still dressed in the tailored green tunic and black skirt she'd worn to work. Oblivious to his presence, she was standing next to a maple bedstead that dominated the entire guest room, calmly unfolding a white cotton mattress pad.

Looking at the bed, Zach couldn't help smiling. "What's going on?" he asked laconically as he went to give her a hand.

"I know how uncomfortable you've been sleeping on the rollaway bed. And I've been meaning to do something about it," she explained, avoiding his eyes as she smoothed the mattress pad onto the bed, covering the gathered elastic corners on her side, while Zach wordlessly covered the corners on his side.

"So I brought home a new bed for you," Sunny said. "It's a double bed, which should be large enough for you to sleep comfortably on, I think. If you're sleeping alone, that is."

Enjoying the easy way they were able to work together, Zach helped her cover the mattress pad with a set of sage green cotton sheets. "How about if I'm not sleeping alone?"

Sunny gave him a droll look and tossed him a pillow. "Then it might be a little crowded," she said dryly.

She was determined, Zach thought, not to be anything more than politely friendly to him this evening. No matter what they had been through together bringing Rhonda-Faye and George's baby into the world, or the closeness they had shared afterward, or the way they had teased each other the night before. She was backing away again. Zach was not going to let her do that, even if he had to tease her mercilessly to draw her out of the cocoon she had woven for herself.

Anyone could know Sunny the public person. No one knew the private one. At least not the way Zach wanted and intended to know her.

He watched as she covered one pillow with a sage green case, then followed suit.

"Oh, I don't know. I think we could cuddle up on it quite nicely," Zach drawled. In fact, he could easily imagine making love to her on the thick new mattress.

Sunny sent him a sassy glance. "Dream on."

"Trust me. I intend to."

He dropped his pillow onto the left side of the bed. She dropped hers on the right.

"Okay if I try it out?" he asked casually, watching the way the late-afternoon sunlight drifted in through the windows, setting fire to her red-gold hair.

"Sure. I guess so. In fact, it's probably a good idea."

Zach kicked off his shoes and stretched out on the crisp, fresh-smelling sheets. Aware Sunny was watching his reaction to the bed closely, he frowned and asked, "Is this bed from the factory?"

"Yes."

Her expression became sober. Her teeth sliced into her soft, bare lower lip. For the first time since he had walked into the house tonight, she looked uncertain. He wondered if she was reevaluating the boundaries they had set out for their relationship, just as he was. He wondered, too, if she was beginning to feel as married as he was beginning to feel.

"It's one of the floor models for a discontinued Hearthside line," Sunny continued.

"Hmm." Zach closed his eyes and concentrated on

the enormously comfortable feel of the bed beneath him. There was only one thing he needed to make this bed complete now.

He folded his hands behind his head and continued to study her. "What about the mattress and box springs?"

"They're from the factory, too. I bought the whole set at an employee discount." She leaned toward him to remove a tag that was still looped around the knobs on the headboard. As she moved, he was inundated with the fresh floral scent of her perfume. It was all he could do not to groan.

Tag in hand, Sunny straightened. She looked down at him, her eyes all at once businesslike and solicitous. Once again, he was struck by her innocence, and the lack of it in himself. It was impossible to go through what he had, not to mention what he had seen in the emergency rooms, and still retain any semblance of culpability. There was no fate or grand plan. Life was random. People did and said foolish things. And it was true, the worst things happened to the best people. Which was all the more reason he should have fun now, while he could, Zach thought, his playful mood returning full force.

"Why do you ask where the bed came from?" she inquired quietly.

"I don't know." Zach hesitated. Watching her, he could see she was determined to prove she could be in his presence and not react. Just as he was determined to prove that when in each other's presence, they couldn't help but react.

"I hate to say anything," he continued in a way he knew would provoke her curiosity and keep her there with him a little longer.

Sunny frowned. A tiny pleat formed between her eyes. "If there's something wrong with the bed you need to tell me, Zach."

He worked to suppress a wicked grin. He doubted she would like his analysis of what his new bed needed.

"Maybe you should just try it and see what you think," he said. Maybe then she would come to the same conclusion he had.

Ever the devoted businesswoman, Sunny assumed a worried look. She kicked off her shoes hurriedly and sat down on the edge of the bed, then, apparently unable to tell anything from that, rested her head on the pillow and stretched out. She wiggled her shoulders and hips slightly, testing the mattress beneath her for flaws. Finally she said briskly, "My side of the bed feels fine."

"Good."

"How about yours?"

"I don't know. I think there's something wrong."

"Where?"

Zach turned toward her a bit and patted the space next to him solemnly. "Here. Right in the middle."

"Are you serious?" Sunny sat up with a jolt. The idea that there might be something wrong with a product her furniture company manufactured was very alarming.

Zach shrugged in a way that allowed he was no expert when it came to furniture. "Maybe it's just me," he said. "You try it." He patted the mattress center. "Tell me what you think."

With a frown, Sunny scooted toward him a little more. Shoulders stiff, she lay back down. Again she wiggled her hips and shoulders, getting settled.

Watching her, Zach felt his mouth go dry. The loneliness he'd been feeling for months now intensified in a solid ache around his heart. He had never wanted to reach out to a woman more than he did at that moment.

"You know you're right, Zach." Oblivious to the swirl of feelings in his heart, Sunny stared up at the ceiling. "It is a little stiff," she decreed finally.

She wasn't kidding, he thought, as the ache in his lower half intensified by leaps and bounds.

A contemplative grin tugging at the corners of her soft lips, Sunny propped her head on her bent elbow and rolled toward Zach a little, so they were lying face-to-face. "But with any new bed there's always that breaking-in stage," she continued with the soothing zeal of a good furniture salesperson. Her eyes danced as she related, "Did you know that it can take up to three months to get to feeling really comfortable in a new bed?"

Zach grinned and Sunny blushed as they both became aware of the double meaning of her words.

"Oh, I don't know. I think I'm comfortable now," he drawled. "I think," he said as he gave in to temptation, pulled her into his arms and bent his head toward her softly parted lips, "all I needed—all I ever needed—was this."

Zach bent his head for a kiss. The feel of her lips beneath his was sweet, soft and all too intoxicating.

All too soon, Sunny broke off the kiss, her hand to his chest.

"Now, just hold on there a moment, lover boy," she drawled, gasping for breath. "This was not part of the deal."

But she liked it just the same. "I know." Zach grinned. "But maybe it's time we rethink our situation," he said.

Sunny regarded him suspiciously. "Rethink it how?"

Zach lay back on the pillow. He folded his hands beneath his head. "Maybe we should stop fighting what we're feeling."

For a second, Sunny looked tempted. She braced a forearm on his chest and rolled so that she was lying across him. "And what are we feeling, Zach?" she asked very, very softly.

He knew much depended on his answer. "For starters, a very strong, very undeniable attraction to each other." Unable to resist touching her again, he wound a curl of her silky red-gold hair around his fingertip.

Sunny leaned into his touch instead of away from it.

"I admit there's some chemistry," she said, surprising him with her honesty.

She looked down at his chest and tightened her fingers on the ends of his striped necktie. "But that doesn't mean we have to act on it."

Zach considered the way his lower body felt, the way she had responded to his kiss, trembling at just the mere touch of his lips to hers. They were fooling themselves if they thought they were going to keep this marriage of theirs platonic. It was time Sunny dealt with that fact, too.

He slid his hand beneath the veil of her hair and gently caressed her nape with his thumb. "We may not be able to help it, Sunny."

She bit into her lower lip tremulously, then gave him a smug look. "Oh, I think we will."

Zach felt another battle coming on, one he anticipated greatly.

"I don't know." He shook his head in exaggerated confusion, then teased, "We're living in extreme proximity, Sunny. We're married. Heck, who knows? Some night we might even find ourselves doing some lesson for one of your classes that involves us sharing the same bed.''

The notion of them sharing the covers was apparently as disturbing to her as it was to him. Pink color climbing from her neck into her face, Sunny sat up. Swinging her legs over the edge of the bed, she turned her back on him. The fabric of her skirt pulled against her trim hips as she bent to retrieve her heels.

''I think I could get around any such lesson my instructor might cook up. Besides, I only have a few left.''

Not ready to let her go just yet, Zach pried the suede shoes from her hand and shifted her so she was prone again and they were touching in one long, tensile line. ''All the more reason we need to take things a step or two further and begin to explore some of what we've both been feeling,'' Zach said. ''Because there's so much I want to learn about you, Sunny. So very, very much.''

She was prepared to be drawn into his arms and kissed once more, but what she wasn't ready for was how fast she went from simply being kissed to kissing in return. She didn't even know how he did it. All she knew was that her world was taken over by the taste and touch and smell of him, that she'd never been so excited and that she felt wild and free and womanly for the first time in her life.

Giving in to the subtle pressure and gentle wooing of his lips, Sunny opened her mouth to the rapaciousness of his tongue and returned every touch and pressure tenfold. Before she knew it, one kiss had turned into many. It no longer mattered, she thought dizzily, as the yearning inside her, the sensation of being cherished, intensified into a fierce, unquenchable ache. All that mattered was that this touching, this tenderness, this gentle loving, never stop.

Zach groaned as she kissed him deeply.

Feeling the hypnotic stroke of his hands as they swept over her, Sunny started to succumb to whatever it was that came next. Then realized, as Zach began to unbutton her tunic, that no matter what he wanted, no matter how much she ached to be one with him, she couldn't give her body without also giving her heart.

For Zach, she feared, it was *not* the same. All too aware of the thundering of his heart and the rigid tension in his thighs, she tore her mouth from his and put a staying hand on his. "Zach, no. I—" The right time might come, but it wasn't here yet.

He sighed and released his hold on the button he'd been about to undo. "I was afraid you were going to say that," he murmured as he let her go.

Sunny studied him. Even though she'd said no to lovemaking, it was clear he was not giving up.

Zach touched a finger to her lips and gently wiped away the dewy residue of their kiss. He surveyed her tenderly. "You expect me to be angry with you for putting on the brakes, don't you?"

That was usually the drill, she thought. Say no to a man and he flew into a rage.

"Aren't you?" she asked curiously, still testing his reaction to her denial.

"No." Zach shook his head, his eyes glowing with pleasure. "I see this as a very necessary first step."

Sunny took a deep, hitching breath. A very necessary first step. To making their marriage a real one? "That sounds ominous," she quipped, aware her hands were trembling.

"Pleasurable," he corrected huskily with an unabashed grin. "And it will be, I promise."

Sunny was afraid of that, too.

She was irritated by the way she kept melting in his arms, despite all her intentions to the contrary. "I know you think so," she said tartly. She had yet to see. Yet to be brave enough…to go all the way. But Zach didn't know any of that. And she wasn't about to tell him. Her lips still tingling from his kisses, Sunny slipped away from him.

He relaxed against the pillows, making no move to follow her. "One of these days I'm going to get you back in this bed and we're going to find out what we've been missing," he teased. They were going to be together. It was only a question of when.

Chapter Eight

A Little Less Talk
and a Lot More Action

"Yes, sir. Absolutely. We'll have it to you within the month!" Sunny promised with a smile, then hung up the phone.

Matilda set a neatly typed list of new orders on Sunny's desk. "Good news?" she asked as she popped the lid on a can of diet cola.

"The best. Where's Gramps?"

Matilda picked up her steno pad. "Last I saw he was in his office, preparing for the sales meeting in the showroom this afternoon. After that, he's going fishing. You ready to dictate those letters yet?"

"Not quite. I want to tell Gramps my news first."

"Okay. I'll go back to figuring that new computer out. Now, that's a chore that should last me the rest of my life."

Sunny patted her assistant on the shoulder. Chuck Conway had been out three times to work with Matilda in the past two weeks, but she was still struggling to make the transition from one order-entry system to another. "Just keep at it. You'll get the hang of it yet."

"That I don't know about," Matilda murmured. "'Course, it might help if I actually read the instruction manual from cover to cover."

Sunny lifted a brow. "Any particular reason you haven't?"

"Yes. It's written in technogibberish. I don't understand a word of it."

Sunny grinned. "Think it'd be better if we hired Chuck to come in for a solid week, work with you and make up an emergency manual for you in language you do understand?"

"Maybe." Matilda tapped her pen against her steno pad. "I mean, I always get it when he's here. It's only when I try to work it on my own that I seem to get confused about what I'm doing and muck things up."

"I'll call Chuck again today," Sunny promised.

Sunny finished up her business with Matilda, then dashed off in search of her grandfather. Though she was now officially running the company, he still came in for a few hours every morning to lend a hand and answer any questions she might have. And the truth was, she liked having him around. He lent her plenty of moral support, and he believed in her gut instincts when it came to business, and her ability to manage the company. He also felt she was doing work she should be proud of. Sunny sighed, wishing everyone in her family felt the same way.

Her grandfather's door was slightly ajar. He had his back to her, but Sunny could see he was on the phone. Not wanting to interrupt, she lingered in the hallway.

While she waited patiently for him to finish, his voice floated out to Sunny. "That boy has a responsibility to this community, never mind my granddaughter! I don't want another doctor in Carlisle!"

Another doctor! she thought, straightening abruptly. Was Zach going somewhere? She could not recall ever seeing her grandfather look so angry.

Gramps glared up as Sunny slipped inside his office. He frowned. "I'm going to have to hang up. Yes, later." He put the receiver in its cradle. "What is it, darlin'?"

Sunny shut the door behind her. She stepped around the fishing gear that seemed to go everywhere with Gramps since his semiretirement. Hands shoved in the pockets of her trousers, she approached her grandfather's desk. "We won the bid. Carlisle Furniture is going to supply the beds, bureaus, tables and chairs for all the rooms of the new Southern Hospitality Inn in Nashville."

Gramps beamed and leaned over to give her a hug. "Congratulations, honey. I knew you could do it."

So had Sunny. If only her parents had the same confidence in her ability, she thought wistfully. "What was that all about—on the phone just now?"

"Nothing."

Sunny sent her grandfather a brief, dissenting glance. "It's not nothing if it's about my husband," she remarked sagely.

Gramps studied her. Without warning, his expression grew exceedingly grim. "You don't know what that rascal's up to now, do you?"

Sunny lifted her shoulder in an eloquent shrug. "How could I unless you tell me?"

"He asked for a transfer out of Carlisle."

The news hit her like a sharp blow to her chest, but she kept her demeanor impassive. "When?" Sunny asked quietly.

"A day after the two of you got caught draped in nothing but a chamois and a checkered tablecloth."

That fast, Zach had wanted the hell out of Carlisle. She had realized he had been unhappy about their predicament even before the two of them had been forced to marry. She hadn't realized he had put in for a transfer.

"And?" Sunny pressed for more details.

"And the person in charge of the physician recruitment program for rural areas called me to say they're still working on finding one."

"Why call you?"

"Because Carlisle Furniture chipped in on the moving costs for the new doc, remember? We'd have to pay moving and living for the new doctor. Not to mention recall the selection committee to review another round of appointments."

"Oh. Right."

Gramps stepped forward. "Everything okay?"

"Everything's fine," Sunny said, though she felt as though her whole world were coming apart.

"I take it Zach didn't mention this to you."

"No," she admitted tightly, doing her best to hide her inner misery. "He didn't."

"Yet another reason to wring his fool neck," Gramps muttered.

"Don't you dare," Sunny warned hot-temperedly. "I'll handle my new husband."

"Sure?" Gramps picked up the fishing lure he'd been working on while he was on the phone. He bent his head over it again. "I could talk some sense into him," Gramps offered slyly.

Sunny was hoping that wouldn't be necessary. "It

may be he has already changed his mind about staying,'' she said optimistically.

Gramps's hands stilled and he looked up. "And if he hasn't?'' he prodded with a frown, pausing absently to massage his left shoulder and the center of his chest.

Sunny drew a deep breath. "Then that's his decision.'' She wasn't about to force Zach into anything. Her parents had imposed their will on her; she was still reeling from the pressure. She wouldn't do the same to Zach.

Gramps surveyed her distressed expression. He set the lure in his left hand on his desk. "This is ridiculous. I'm going to call and tell them to cancel his transfer request.''

Sunny lifted a staying hand. "No. I don't want you to interfere.''

Gramps frowned unhappily. He looked around his desk until he found a roll of antacid tablets. "Why the devil not?'' he demanded as he popped one into his mouth.

"Because you've done quite enough already in forcing Zach to marry me.''

Gramps chased the antacid tablet with a gulp of water. "No one held a gun to his head.''

"Close enough,'' Sunny said ruefully. "Besides, this is his decision.''

"You mean that, don't you?'' Gramps said.

Sunny nodded. She took a closer look at her grandfather. He seemed a little pale. "Say, are you feeling okay?''

He waved off her concern. "Too much spicy food for lunch. It was Mexican Day over at the diner. Listen, I forgot to mention it, but I'd like to go off on a fishing trip for a few days. That okay with you?''

Sunny nodded. "Of course."

"Are you sure?" Without warning, he looked a little anxious. "'Cause I could cancel it if you need me here."

"Don't be silly. You just go off and have fun. I'll hold the fort down." And wait for Zach to make a decision and retract the transfer. Sunny could only hope he would make the right decision for both of them. Their marriage had started out for all the wrong reasons, but now that they were married, they were growing closer day by day, maybe even falling in love. She wanted a chance to see their relationship through. She didn't want to look back later and think they might have had something really special if only they'd given themselves the chance.

"YOUR MAMA IS just going to kill me," Gertie told four-year-old Toby as she ushered him into the Carlisle Clinic.

Toby looked at Zach, then Gertie. "Did you swallow a marble, too?" Toby asked Gertie.

"Toby swallowed a marble?" Zach interrupted.

Gertie wrung her hands. "That's what he said. I didn't even know he had any marbles with him."

"I always keep them in my pocket, right here," Toby said importantly. He patted the front right pocket on his child-size jeans, then reached inside and pulled out a white-and-green marble. "See?" He held it up for both adults. "It was just like this one and I put it in my mouth—"

"No!" Gertie and Zach said in unison when Toby started to demonstrate how he had swallowed the first marble.

"Here, honey, let me hold that for you," Gertie said

as perspiration broke out on her brow. She placed the marble in her purse.

"When did you realize he had swallowed a marble?" Zach asked, perplexed because Toby was showing none of the expected signs of respiratory distress or physical discomfort.

"When he told me, about ten minutes ago," Gertie said, looking as if she might burst into tears at any second.

"Where's Rhonda-Faye?"

"At home with the new baby, asleep. She was up all night and I told her that I would take Toby this morning while the others went to school, since it's my day off."

"That was nice of you," Zach said.

"Rhonda-Faye will not think so when she finds out what happened," Gertie said, nervously fingering the strand of pearls around her neck. "She will think I am a complete novice with kids."

"She doesn't know what happened?"

"After all she's been through with George and the baby coming early, I thought I'd better find out how bad it was, first. How bad is it?"

Zach touched Gertie's shoulder reassuringly as Toby gravitated to the box of toys and books in the far corner of the room. "There's one way to find out."

"So you'll take a quick look at him before we call Rhonda-Faye or George and tell them?" Gertie said.

Zach paused, watching as Toby tried out a child-size chair and seemed to like it. What Gertie was asking of him was highly unusual. "Normally, I need a parent's verbal or written permission to treat a child."

"What about on an emergency basis?" Gertie pressed.

"Then treatment can be rendered after getting express permission from the adult caring for the child," Zach said.

"Which is me," Gertie interrupted.

"Right."

"So what do you say?" she asked anxiously.

Zach smiled. "Under the circumstances, I think it would be permissible to find out what kind of shape Toby's in before we call his folks. There's no use upsetting them unnecessarily."

"And you know how excited George gets in any medical emergency," Gertie murmured.

Zach nodded. "We don't want him having another accident trying to make it to the clinic." One set of stitches had been enough.

Zach stepped closer to his young patient, who, unlike Gertie, was remarkably calm. "Toby, how about coming into an examining room so I can listen to your lungs?" Zach said.

Toby moved away from the box of toys in the corner of the waiting room. He had a storybook in his hand. "Can I bring this with me, Dr. Zach?"

"Sure." Zach grinned. "So how do you like your new sister?"

Toby made a face. "She cries a lot and she goes to the bathroom in her pants."

"Diapers," Zach corrected.

"Whatever," Toby said, climbing up onto the pediatric table with Zach's help. "It's disgusting. All my brothers think so."

"I bet."

"Sounds like sibling rivalry," Gertie said.

Zach nodded. He helped Toby pull off his shirt, then looked into his young patient's throat. "Say 'ahhh.'"

"Ahh."

Zach listened to Toby's chest. "Are you sure you swallowed that marble? That it didn't just fall out of your mouth—maybe on the floor somewhere?"

"I swallowed it all right. It hurt a little when it went down, too," Toby declared.

"Does it hurt now?" Zach asked.

"No. But it did then," Toby said.

Zach took another long careful look at the boy's throat. He could find no evidence that the four-year-old had swallowed anything. "If he did swallow a marble, it appears to have gone into his stomach," Zach told Gertie.

Gertie looked as if she were going to burst into tears any second. "Can't you find it?"

"Not so far, but to be on the safe side, we'll do an X ray and see if we can locate it that way," Zach told her.

"It's not there," he said, fifteen minutes later as the three of them studied the X rays.

"But how is that possible?" Gertie cried, looking all the more upset.

Zach wondered the same thing. He turned to Toby, who was looking sideways at the pictures of his insides. "Toby, when did you swallow the marble? Was it before or after Gertie picked you up?"

"Before."

"How long before?"

"I dunno." Toby shrugged his small shoulders.

"This morning?" Zach pressed.

Toby shook his head. "Last Christmas."

"Last Christmas," Zach echoed as he and Gertie shared a relieved laugh.

"Yeah." Toby appeared confused. He did not get what they were chuckling about.

"Did you tell your mom and dad you swallowed this marble?" Zach asked.

"Nope."

"Why not?"

"I dunno. I forgot, I guess. Christmas is a pretty busy time. Can I have a sticker now?" Toby asked hopefully.

"Sure." Zach got out a whole box of them from the cabinet. "You were such a good patient, you may have two."

"Okay, but can I look through all of them first before I have to pick?" he asked.

"Take your time," Zach said.

Gertie turned to Zach. "I suppose it's safe to assume the marble went the way of everything else Toby ingests but doesn't need?"

Zach nodded.

"I'm so embarrassed," Gertie said, covering her eyes with her white lace hankie.

"Been there," Zach said.

Gertie grinned at him. "I suppose you have. So, how are you enjoying married life?"

Zach hesitated. What could he say to that? He liked being with Sunny. But marriage...what kind of marriage was it when the vows were not taken seriously and the couple didn't even share the same bed?

"Just what I thought," Gertie said. "The two of you still have the honeymoon blues."

"Honeymoon blues?" Zach asked.

"You know. The getting-adjusted-to-everything blues. But take it from me, Zach—" Gertie patted his arm reassuringly "—I know just what the two of you need."

"NEED A RIDE?"

The low, familiar voice sent shudders of awareness

down her spine. "Zach." Sunny flushed as she clasped her clipboard to her chest and turned to face him. He was wearing a blue chambray dress shirt, red tie and jeans. His hair was wind tossed and sexy, his jaw freshly shaven and scented with the after-shave she liked. "What are you doing here?"

"Enjoying the scenery." Looking relaxed and at ease, he stepped away from the entrance to the factory display room and closed the short distance between them.

Her shoulder nudging his, Sunny said, "There is no scenery in here."

He chucked her on the chin and grinned down at her. "Gotta differ with you there, babe. There's plenty of scenery in this room."

The compliment was as heartfelt as it was teasing. Response trembled along her skin. "The new display rooms are nice, aren't they?" Sunny said, being deliberately obtuse.

Zach nodded and cast an admiring glance around. The room they were standing in featured living room furniture, done in a timeless traditional style.

"Yes, it's very nice. I noticed, coming in, that the rooms are really put together down to the last detail. Having the right accessories makes the furniture look even classier."

Sunny nodded. "I know. I've been thinking the same thing. That's why I'm trying to get my grandfather to enlarge our operation here and sell accessories—like quilts and pictures and lamps. Maybe even a line of coordinating, custom-made draperies."

"Going to turn Carlisle's into the next Sears Roebuck?"

"More like an L. L. Bean Furniture store and catalog. Our look will stay pure Tennessee."

He took her hand in his and tugged her over to the red-and-green plaid sofa. "None of that eclectic post-modern stuff for you, hmm?"

Sunny made a face. "No way."

"How come?" He sat down next to her.

Sunny sat back against the cushions. "Because I love what warm, cozy furniture can do to a room—transform it from a utilitarian space to a place to regroup, and replenish the soul."

"Old-fashioned furniture for an old-fashioned girl."

"Absolutely. Does that bother you?"

"Just makes me curious. You seem so open-minded about everything else. Why not with modern furniture, too?" Zach's eyes locked on hers.

Sunny shrugged. He was seeing too much again. Zeroing in on her vulnerable side without half trying. "That's all we ever had in our home, growing up. There's something very cold about it, at least for me. And I just don't like it, so I'm not going to make it, and I'm not going to sell it."

Zach wondered if she was talking about furniture now or her parents. "Sorry. I didn't mean to upset you."

"No." Sunny shook her head and ran a hand through her hair. "I'm sorry for snapping at you. It's just been a long day."

Gertie had been right. Sunny did need some tender, loving care. Fortunately, he was just the man to give it to her, Zach thought, as he walked her out to his pickup.

Sunny stopped short when they reached the door and she looked inside. "What's all this?" she asked, pointing to the wicker picnic baskets, blankets and thermos.

"Supper. I thought maybe you'd take me up to the top of the mountain so we could enjoy the view."

"You haven't been there yet?" As she gazed up at him, her breath was uneven, shivers raced along her spine.

"No. And I've been told it's the greatest place to watch the sunset."

"It is." It was also highly romantic. For that reason alone, Sunny told herself she should not go there with him. She turned and stepped up into the truck. Aware she felt happy and sad simultaneously, she asked, "Why are you doing this?"

Zach leaned in to assist her with her seat belt. He smiled at her, his blue eyes dazzling in their intensity.

"You pampered me," he said softly, pausing to kiss her temple. "I thought it was high time I did the same for you."

One kindness begets another...wasn't that what they'd taught in her marriage class? Was it possible the theory worked, even in their case? Sunny wondered, amazed as Zach drove the short distance to their picnic site and parked the truck at the end of the old gravel logging road.

"You're awfully quiet," he said. He got out, grabbed the picnic gear and circled around to her side.

Sunny was wishing she were not nearly so susceptible to him. She was also wishing she had her tennis shoes instead of her flats. She was lucky, though, that she had on trousers instead of a dress. "I was thinking about the bid we won today," Sunny fibbed. As they spread out the blankets, she told him about it.

"The Southern Hospitality Inn is part of a big hotel chain, isn't it?" Zach asked as he brought out beef-brisket sandwiches, potato salad.

Sunny nodded. "They've got four-star hotels in practically every major city of the country."

"So this could lead to other jobs and really put Carlisle Furniture on the map," Zach said as he added zesty vinegar slaw, homemade dill pickles and an assortment of black and green olives to their plates.

Sunny poured them each generous glasses of iced tea. "We hope it leads to more work." Famished, she bit into her sandwich.

"If that happens, would you move the factory elsewhere, open a second one or expand here?"

"I think I'd try to expand here," she said cautiously. She settled in beside him, appreciating the quiet beauty of their surroundings and the intimacy of being with him. Zach had put a lot of thought into the evening, and she had needed to get away from it all, more than she had realized.

"Bringing a lot of people in would change the community."

"I know, and that worries me." Sunny set her plate aside. She brought her knees up to her chest and wrapped her arms around them. "I like living in a small town."

Zach looked out at the countryside below. Carlisle was visible in the distance, rooftops popping up between the trees on peaceful shady streets. Old-fashioned but neatly kept, the town resembled something out of a Norman Rockwell painting. And though it was beautiful, it was also dull. "You don't think you'll get bored here eventually? Carlisle is awfully small."

Sunny's jaw set stubbornly. "I need more than an intellectual challenge to keep me happy. I need the feeling of belonging and closeness, of community, that living here gives me."

"Your parents didn't feel the same way, I guess."

"No, they didn't. For all their lawyerly brilliance, they are never going to understand why I care so much about the people in this town, or why I want to take care of the business and keep it growing and thriving so the town can still exist. The employees aren't numbers to me. They're people, with faces and names and personalities and families to support. I like knowing everyone here. I like knowing that what I do is making a tremendous difference in their lives and in the overall soundness of Gramps's company."

"Taking care of people is very satisfying."

Sunny gazed into his eyes, saw the compassion there, and knew he really did understand. More so than she had expected that he would. "You're speaking as a physician."

Zach shrugged. For an instant he was moodily silent, pulling away from her. "And a member of my own family."

His brooding look gone almost as soon as it appeared, Zach lifted a forkful of potato salad to her lips. "Recognize the recipe?"

Sunny smiled. "Gertie's."

"Right." Zach fed her another forkful of potato salad. "She cooked the whole meal for us."

"That was sweet of her. I'll have to thank her."

He smiled at her warmly as she took another bite of her sandwich. "I already did, for both of us."

He was acting as if they were a real couple, she thought. Or maybe he was just getting into the swing of pretending, for as long as he was there.

The sandwich suddenly turning to sawdust in her throat, Sunny swallowed. She felt angry and hurt, and she had no right to feel either, she told herself sternly.

He wasn't breaking any promises to her, because he'd never made any commitment.

Around them, the sunlight faded to a dusky romantic glow. Zach paused to light an outdoor candle in a mason jar.

"You don't mind that I agreed to let her cook for us, do you?" he said, his expression concerned.

"No, of course not," Sunny said, sitting Indian-style again. *I mind that you are trying to leave here, and you haven't even bothered to tell me. Despite the fact that I am your wife!* Then again, she thought, he wasn't acting like a man with one foot out the door tonight. And Gramps had succeeded in blocking his transfer, at least temporarily. Thinking of Gramps, she wondered if he still had his indigestion tonight. He had left the factory early to pack for his trip, which was slated to begin that evening.

"Sunny?" Zach touched her hand. "You look... upset. Is everything okay?"

She slipped her hand in his, glad she had him to confide in. "It's Gramps," she said, swallowing around the lump in her throat. "I don't think he was feeling all that well today."

Zach grew very still. "What seemed to be the matter?"

"He was rubbing his shoulder and guzzling antacids."

Zach's eyes darkened. "Did he say he was in pain?"

"No." She lifted her face to his. Without warning, her heart was pounding. "Why would you ask that?"

"Because I'm a doctor." Zach regarded her patiently. "Those are the kinds of questions I'm supposed to ask."

"Oh." Sunny forced herself to calm down. "No, he

just seemed…I don't know…generally uncomfortable, a little anxious and upset.''

Zach looked down at his plate. ''He's taking a few days off to go fishing, isn't he?'' he said casually.

Sunny nodded, not sure why but she felt something was amiss here. ''How did you know that?''

''He mentioned it to me last week.''

''So you don't think I should worry?''

Zach shifted restlessly on the blanket beside her. ''I don't think Augustus would go off on a three-day fishing trip if he were ill, do you?''

''No.'' Sunny forced herself to relax. ''You're right. He wouldn't. I guess I'm just overreacting—that's all. Gramps means so much to me.'' Her voice caught. ''He's the only one who's ever believed in me.'' Tears stung her eyes. ''I don't know what I'd do without him.''

Zach reached over to squeeze her hand. ''Luck willing, he'll be with us a long time to come, but if it will make you feel any better, I'll check up on him, too.''

''Thanks, Zach. I appreciate it.''

''Is everything okay with you?'' he continued. ''You look a little stressed out tonight, too.''

Sunny shook off her confusion. It was going to be dark soon, and with the stars and the moon overhead, oh, so romantic. ''I'm just tired—that's all,'' she said. And that was true. She didn't want to talk about his transfer request or what Gramps had done to block it. She smiled at Zach encouragingly. ''How was your day?''

At the mention of his work, Zach broke into a wide grin. ''I saw one of Rhonda-Faye and George's little boys.'' He recounted the marble incident in great detail.

By the time he had finished, Sunny was laughing right along with him.

"Toby is something else," she murmured sympathetically, pleased that Zach had such a sense of humor about the whole incident and that he was quickly warming to the people in the community.

Zach shook his head. "I should have asked the little tyke *when* he swallowed the marble right off."

Sunny shrugged. "Live and learn." And that could be said about everything.

They both smiled. He leaned over in the picnic basket and brought out another container. "And now for the pièce de résistance," he said with a flourish. "Double-chocolate walnut brownies."

Sunny groaned in feigned ecstasy. "My favorite."

"I can think of something I like better," Zach murmured as he started to take her in his arms.

Her heart racing, Sunny flattened a palm against his chest to keep him from coming any closer. She wanted him, and she didn't. "No, Zach. No kissing," she said breathlessly.

He fastened his eyes on hers as he teased, "Not even just one?"

She shook her head firmly, ignoring his obvious disappointment—and hers. "Not even one."

SUNNY'S LOW melodious voice floated out into the backyard as Zach headed toward the door, sack of groceries in his arms.

"Matilda's really having trouble." Sunny laughed softly, then continued speaking into the phone. "Easy for you and me, but we grew up using computers. She didn't. I think it would be a good idea if you came back and stayed until she has the hang of the entire order-entry system.'' She paused, head bent, listening intently. ''I know it'll be expensive, but it'll be worth it.'' Sunny paused again, then laughed softly. ''I really appreciate it, Chuck. I consider it a personal favor. Right. See you then. Looking forward to it.''

Sunny hung up the phone and turned around to see Zach lounging in the kitchen doorway. From the expression on her face, he guessed she had been wondering how much he had overheard of her telephone conversation. Enough to make him damn jealous, Zach thought. Never mind that the emotion was completely irrational; it was there.

''Back already?'' she asked lightly.

He nodded, trying hard not to notice how much she wanted to get rid of him this evening, or how much it stung to realize she felt that way. He carried the single bag of groceries into the kitchen and set it down on the counter, next to the fridge. ''Milk, cereal and a fresh loaf of bread, just like you asked.'' He began putting them away. ''And I also checked on Gramps—'' who was now in the Knoxville hospital, undergoing tests ''—and he's fine.''

''Thank you,'' Sunny said gratefully.

Zach nodded. He just wished he could tell her everything about her grandfather.

Noting the coffee had stopped brewing, Sunny poured herself a mug. She had work papers scattered over the kitchen table. ''And thanks for getting the groceries, too. Normally I wouldn't ask you to run an errand, but I have so much to do tonight. And I didn't want you to wake up to an empty refrigerator and no breakfast.''

''Sounds like those how-to-be-a-loving-wife lessons are really sinking in,'' he teased.

Sunny's jaw set rebelliously even as she studiously avoided his eyes. Zach stepped closer and took her into his arms. She splayed a hand across his chest to prevent him from coming any nearer. Hurt and wariness glimmered in her eyes.

Suddenly Zach knew he had to ask. "What's wrong, Sunny?" Acquiescing to her obvious wishes, he dropped his hands from her shoulders. "You've been acting funny all evening."

She stepped back and tossed her head. "I'm a regular laugh riot, aren't I?" she retorted sadly.

Zach struggled against the urge to bury his hands in the shimmering softness of her red-gold hair. He lounged against the counter, instead, bracing a hand on either side of him. "Have I done or said something to make you uncomfortable?"

She regarded him indifferently. "What would make you think that?"

"The fact that you wouldn't stay and watch the sunset with me at the top of Carlisle Mountain."

Sunny shrugged. She picked up her coffee mug again and took a sip. "The roads get dangerous after dark."

Zach knew an excuse when he heard one. It infuriated him to see her putting up barriers between them, just when he'd begun to tear them down. "Ten to one it never bothered you before."

She flushed guiltily, confirming his suspicions that she was trying hard to keep them from getting any closer. "And then there is the quick way you sent me off to the store, the determined way you are immersing yourself in your work."

Sunny tightened her hands around her mug. "I have things to do tonight, Zach."

He sensed her work was nothing that couldn't wait

until morning. "You're hiding something from me, Sunny."

"Because I didn't want to kiss you tonight?" she said coolly.

"That's part of it," he said slowly, knowing in his gut there was more to the sudden distrust in her eyes. If he'd done something to annoy her, he wanted to know about it.

Sunny released a troubled sigh. Confusion colored her low voice. "I don't want to play house with you, Zach."

"Is that what you think we've been doing?" *He* thought they'd been building something important here, growing closer.

Sunny raked her teeth across her lip. "I don't know what we've been doing. Or even how or why I allowed myself to get sucked into this. All I know is that our marriage is only a temporary arrangement, Zach, one we both entered into for all the wrong reasons."

He couldn't dispute that. But he thought that they'd been making progress by the way she kissed him and melted in his arms at the slightest touch, that she wanted to make love as much as he did. Apparently he'd been wrong. "Meaning what?" Zach returned, unable to keep his disappointment in check. "That our marriage is going to remain one in name only?"

"Of course." Sunny planted her hands on her hips and regarded him exasperatedly. "Why would you ever have expected anything else?"

Chapter Nine

Woman, Walk the Line

"I'm glad you're back," Zach told Gramps several days later, when he stopped by the clinic upon his return.

Augustus handed over copies of his files, sent by the Knoxville Hospital. "So am I. If I'd had to pretend to be on a fishing trip much longer, Sunny would've gotten suspicious."

Zach had already been informed of the test results by phone, but he welcomed the chance to look at the lab reports himself. "How are you feeling?"

Augustus sank into a chair. "Better than I have in weeks, though why that should be after three days of lying around in a hospital bed is a mystery, to be sure."

"The rest in between tests probably did you good."

"Made me antsy is more like it. When will I know what's causing my chest pains?" he asked, frowning anxiously.

"I'm not sure," Zach said honestly, wishing he had better news to relate. Augustus's symptoms still had them all baffled. "So far all we've managed to do is rule things out. Your heart and lungs are fine. The dentist says there's no sign you've been grinding your teeth, which is something that can also cause chest pain. And your GI series was fine. Of course, the pain you've been experiencing could still be indigestion and linked to something you're eating, a particular spice or food. It just didn't show up as inflammation or anything serious in the tests.'' And Zach was relieved about that. Whatever was going on, Augustus was not dying.

"So what next?" Augustus asked with a relieved sigh.

Zach picked up a pencil and turned it end over end. "There's got to be a pattern to these episodes. It's up to us to play medical detective and track it down. So the moment you have chest pain," Zach admonished seriously, "I want you to drop everything and come and see me. I don't care what time of day or night it is. We will figure this out."

Augustus nodded. "In the meantime, is it all right if I go fishing—for real this time? I've missed my rod and reel."

"Sure. As long as you don't overdo."

"I won't. Sunny doesn't suspect a thing, does she?"

"No," Zach said. And he felt bad about keeping it from her. He'd wanted to confide in her the other night so much. These days, he didn't want anything between them holding them apart, not even her grandfather's secret.

"So what do you think, Doc?" Matilda said, showing Zach her red, blistered hands.

"I think you've got one of the worst cases of contact dermatitis I've ever seen. What have you been doing?"

"I've been washing dishes over at the diner and filling in for Rhonda-Faye, who's still out with her new baby."

"Well, you need to wear gloves when you put your hands in water, and apply this cream to your hands four times a day in the meantime."

"Will do. And Doc?"

"Yes, Matilda?"

"About those classes Sunny has been taking. She's really been putting her heart into them."

This was news to Zach.

"The only thing is, and I don't know quite how to say this and still be tactful."

"Just spit it out, Matilda."

"Well, judging by the reports Sunny has been giving back to the group, the other ladies and I feel that you may not be doing your part in return."

"Let me get this straight." Zach tamped down his anger with effort. "Sunny has been telling your group that I'm a bad husband?"

"Oh, no. Sunny would never say that, Doc. It's just sometimes when she's making her reports I get the feeling she's kind of disappointed in the way things have worked out. Don't get me wrong. She puts on a brave front and speaks in a cheerful tone, but underneath…well, I think in her heart she was wishing you all had had a more conventional or romantic start."

She wasn't the only one, Zach thought.

"But I think she really is trying. I think she wants this marriage of yours to work." Matilda pressed a hand to her ample bosom. "Oh, dear, I can see I've offended you with all my frank talk, haven't I?"

"It does seem like a violation of privacy, knowing what's going on in our marriage is being reported back to that class," Zach said.

"Slim doesn't like it, either," Matilda freely admitted. "And some of the lessons have given us rather

confounding results. But overall he likes the changes
the class is bringing to our marriage. And the same goes
for all the other husbands. Why, we haven't paid this
much attention to each other in years!'' Matilda said.
''If you would just give the class—and Sunny—a
chance, Zach, I know the two of you could be happy,''
she said kindly.

Could they? he wondered, a little guiltily. He knew
he hadn't given the relationship or Sunny a chance initially, but lately they had become a lot closer anyway.
Was it possible that she was more serious than he'd
been led to believe? Was it possible she wanted to make
their marriage a real one, too? And that her testy behavior was due to her disappointment in him rather than
her chafing at the increasingly intimate situation in
which they found themselves? If that was the case, if
Sunny was really trying to make this marriage of theirs
work in her own convoluted way, Zach saw he owed
her an apology.

''Furthermore, I know how you can make it up to
her. Slim and the boys have all offered to help,'' Matilda continued exuberantly.

Making up with Sunny seemed like a good idea. Having the whole community in on the plan did not. ''Help
me how?'' Zach asked warily.

''Why, help make Sunny feel better,'' Matilda said.
''All you have to do is show up at our house, say around
9:00 p.m.?''

''YOU'RE WHERE?'' Sunny gasped into the telephone.
She had expected her parents to be angry with her, not
rush to her side.

''About ten minutes away from your house,'' her

mother replied. "You had to know that as soon as we received your letter we'd want to see you."

Suddenly her desire to get even with her parents for trying to dupe her into marrying Andrew did not seem like such a good idea. "You're planning to stay with Gramps, aren't you?" Sunny asked nervously.

"Honey, we want to stay with you. We want to get to know your husband and well...help you straighten things out. Oh, your father's waving at me. Gotta run."

Sunny stared at the phone. Her parents there in ten minutes? Heart pounding, she raced for the stairs. Grabbing a stack of Zach's clothes and medical journals, she tossed them about the master bedroom, then raced back to the guest room to get the rest of his stuff. Her parents mustn't guess this was a marriage in name only or she'd never hear the end of her foolhardiness. And considering the way things were turning out, Sunny thought, as she wiped a stream of perspiration from her brow, she knew they would be right.

Finished moving most of his stuff, she put a set of clean sheets on the bed in the master bedroom, hung fresh towels in the bathroom, tidied the sink and then raced for the linen closet again. She had just picked out a set of fresh sheets for the guest-room bed, when she heard it. The unmistakable sound of Slim's fiddle, Fergus's guitar, George's banjo and Gramps's harmonica! And a familiar voice singing..."Love Me Tender"?

She swore again. She didn't know what Zach was up to now, but his timing couldn't be worse.

ZACH FELT LIKE a fool standing in front of Sunny's stoop, a bunch of daisies in hand, singing love songs off-key. Worse, the racket he and the band were making was causing quite a commotion. Doors and windows were opening all over the neighborhood. Including Sunny's.

A come-hither smile on her face, she sauntered out to greet him. "Welcome home, sweetheart," she purred, lacing her arms about his neck. Standing on tiptoe, she kissed him soundly on the lips.

Telling himself the best way to end the impromptu concert was to act as if he and Sunny had much better things to do than stand out there singing all night, Zach wrapped both arms about her waist and shifted her close. Ignoring the way she stiffened in surprise, he gave the kiss all he had and then some.

Male laughter sounded behind him. Then applause.

"See, Zach?" Slim said. "Told you that serenading her with love songs would work."

"Always does," George agreed.

"I think you fellas better let me take my husband inside," Sunny crooned. "Before we really put on a show."

Zach inclined his head in Sunny's direction. "You heard the woman, fellas." He was glad he didn't have to do any more singing.

"We'll let y'all cook while the griddle's hot," Fergus said with a naughty wink. "But if you need us to come back, so Zach can do some more singing, y'all just holler."

"Will do," Sunny promised, wrapping her slender arm about Zach's waist. She rested her head against his chest.

Zach liked the feel of having her so close. They waited on the sidewalk and waved goodbye as the fellas all drove off. "Thanks for rescuing me," Zach said with a sigh of relief.

Sunny stayed where she was as yet another car drove

up. "We're not rescued yet," she murmured. "Far from it. So play along with me. Mom, Dad!" she said as an elegantly dressed couple in their fifties emerged from the rented Lincoln. "I'm so glad you could come!"

"YOU DIDN'T TELL ME we were having company," Zach whispered in Sunny's ear.

"That's because I didn't know myself until ten minutes ago," she whispered back.

"So this is your husband," Sunny's dad said, giving Zach the once-over as Sunny moved out of Zach's arm and into his.

Zach immediately snapped to attention, while Sunny hugged her folks.

"Sir." He shook hands with her father. Somehow meeting Sunny's folks made their marriage all the more real. He nodded at her mother, not sure what was expected of him, only knowing he wanted things to go smoothly for Sunny's sake. "Mrs. Carlisle."

"Please, Zach. Call us Elanore and Eli."

"You should have let us know you were coming," Sunny said as they started up the steps.

Zach had never seen Sunny's cheeks so pink, her eyes so vulnerable. He wanted to wrap her in his arms and hold her close, reassure her everything was going to be all right.

"How about some coffee?" Sunny said the minute they got in the door.

"Actually, sweetheart, we'd like to talk with you alone, if you don't mind," Eli said.

Zach excused himself. Sunny sat down on the living room sofa. "What is it?"

"You married him to get even with us, didn't you?" her father said.

"It would serve you right if I had," Sunny retorted, folding her arms in front of her. "I still can't believe you actually sent Andrew Singleton here!"

"Andrew's a nice man," Elanore said.

"Oh, please! He wanted a merger, not a marriage!" Sunny shouted back. "And to think I almost fell for it."

"What happened?" Zach appeared in the doorway, a grim look on his face. Sunny could tell he'd heard everything.

"Zach, this is none of your concern," Elanore said.

"He's my husband. Of course it's his concern," Sunny interrupted, motioning Zach into the living room. "My parents set me up with the son of a fellow attorney shortly after I moved here. He pretended to be vacationing. He was really sent here on a mission to sweep me off my feet and get me out of Carlisle permanently. It would have worked if I hadn't figured out the connection as we started to make our wedding plans."

"Sunny confronted Andrew about the situation," Elanore continued. "And the wedding was off. She's still angry with us, which is why, no doubt, she did not let us know about your wedding in time for us to attend."

Sunny thrust out her chin stubbornly. "I didn't want you to try to stop it."

"You're saying it should have been stopped?" Eli retorted.

"Eli, dear, we did not come here to fight with Sunny. We came here to make up with her and lend whatever assistance she needs." Elanore cast a glance at Zach, who was hovering protectively at Sunny's side. "Perhaps she doesn't need as much help as we thought. At any rate, this is probably something best talked out in the morning.''

Eli sighed. ''I guess you're right. We have been on our feet for twenty-two hours straight now.''

They did look exhausted, Sunny noted. Maybe they cared about her more than she'd thought. ''I've already made up your room. You can have ours,'' she said.

Her parents said good-night and went quietly up the stairs. Zach waited until he heard the bedroom door shut, then took her by the hand and led her out onto the front porch. ''Did you marry me to get back at them?'' he asked grimly.

''It started out that way.'' Sunny swallowed, knowing she owed him honesty and a lot more. ''But now it's turned into so much more than that, Zach. And furthermore,'' she said, her heart beating wildly, ''I don't care what my parents think about my marrying you the way I did. They are not going to interfere in my relationship with you and that's final!''

Zach realized Sunny was offering him what he had always wanted in a relationship. ''I'm glad to hear that,'' he said with a grin, ''because those are my sentiments exactly.''

''YOU DIDN'T TELL them the truth about our marriage, did you?'' Zach asked as he and Sunny made up the bed in the guest room.

Sunny paused to look at Zach. For a person who hated familial interference, he was taking this all remarkably well. ''They already think my moving to Tennessee was a mistake.''

''How come?''

Sunny poured her heart out to him. ''Because in their opinion, there's nothing for me here.'' She plumped a pillow almost violently. "They saw I had the very best education. Now they want me to put it to better use," she confided bitterly, as she plopped down on the edge of the half-made bed.

Zach sat down beside her. He wrapped a comforting arm around her shoulders and pulled her close. "They don't know you at all, do they?" he commiserated softly.

Sunny rested her face on his shoulder. She loved the way he felt, so warm and solid and strong. "They never have," she admitted sadly. "I used to think it was my fault, but now I know that's not true. They love me in their own way. But it's in a detached way one moment, a smothering way the next. There's never any happy medium with them."

He held her closer. "I'm sorry." He rubbed her arm consolingly and turned toward her.

"Why?" Loving their intimacy, Sunny buried her face in the curve of his neck.

"Because living that way has obviously been very tough on you."

Sunny luxuriated in the brisk wintry scent that was him, then drew back to look at him seriously. "Are you close to your folks?" she asked quietly at length, wondering if he'd had a happier childhood than she had.

Zach nodded, all too willing to admit it as he squeezed her hand in his. "I can tell them just about everything."

The edges of her lips began to curl. "Except that we're married," she said, taking a guess.

Zach nodded. He looked deep into her eyes. "But only because they'd worry about me if they knew it wasn't a real marriage, and they'd want to celebrate with me if they thought it was. I felt we already had enough interference in our lives as it was.''

Sunny breathed a shaky sigh of relief. ''I'll second that,'' she said with a light laugh. She didn't know what she would do if they had another set of parents on their doorstep.

Turning slightly toward him, so their knees were touching, Sunny rested the palm of her hand just above his knee. ''Do you have any brothers and sisters?''

''It's just me, my mom and dad now,'' Zach said, a brooding look appearing suddenly on his face. ''I had a sister who died,'' he said quietly after a moment.

But to Sunny's increasing disappointment, he didn't continue. He climbed in on his side of the bed, turned his back to her and shut his eyes. Seconds later, he was asleep.

Sunny lay staring at the ceiling, thinking of all the kisses they'd shared, and the ones they hadn't. So much for her worrying about her virtue, she thought. Even in the same bed, married to the man, she couldn't have been safer. It was turning out to be exactly what she wanted, a night that was affable enough to fool her parents into thinking everything was fine between her and Zach. So why was she feeling so disappointed?

ZACK AWOKE at the first light of dawn to find a stack of pillows and a rolled-up blanket between Sunny and him. He eased from the bed, grabbed a robe and headed downstairs. He wouldn't be able to dress for work until he could get to his clothes, which Sunny had stuffed in her closet. And he wouldn't be able to do that until her parents were awake.

To his surprise, Eli and Elanore were already in the

kitchen. They had made a pot of coffee and were working on a thick stack of legal papers.

"We're still on European time," Elanore explained.

Zach nodded. "I saw the packed suitcases in the front hall," he said. He wondered how Sunny would react to that.

"We've got a meeting in New York late this afternoon," Eli explained. "We're flying out of Memphis-Nashville at 1:00 p.m."

Which meant they would have to leave in a few hours, Zach thought. Sunny was going to be so disappointed.

"So where did you go to med school, Zach?" Eli asked.

"Vanderbilt," he said, knowing the third degree had a purpose. They wanted to know if he was good enough for their daughter.

Eli and Elanore beamed their approval at his alma mater.

"Good school. Very prestigious," Eli said.

"So how did you end up here?" Elanore asked.

Zach resented the implication that Carlisle was somehow less important because it was a rural location. "I had a contract with the state. They paid my tuition. In turn, I promised two years of service in a rural area."

"Of your choice?"

"Actually, it was a little more complicated than that. I applied to a number of places and then was assigned," Zach said. Which reminded him, he should check and see how his transfer request was going. Not that he was so inclined to leave now that he was beginning to get settled in at the clinic and he and Sunny had declared a truce. In fact, were things to progress to the point where he and Sunny became lovers he wasn't sure he would want to leave at all. Until his two-year assignment in Carlisle was up, of course.

"Well, Sunny had an excellent education, too," Elanore said.

"Her mother and I really think she is going through a phase and that she'll live up to her potential as soon as she gets this sojourn here out of her system," Eli said. "It probably had something to do with all those sociology classes she took at Smith."

"My being here has nothing to do with all the classes I took at college," Sunny said angrily. She stormed into the kitchen, hair in disarray, her terry-cloth robe wrapped tightly around her waist. "Furthermore, I resent your telling Zach that is the case."

"Now, Sunny," Elanore said with a beleaguered sigh. "It's not that we want to fight with you."

Sunny spread her hands. Her eyes sparkled with tears. "Then why did you come here? Why are you saying all these things?"

"Because we feel you're wasting your potential here," Eli explained gently. "With your education and credentials, you could be working for a top Fortune 500 company."

"I'm a CEO here," Sunny stressed.

"Of a regional furniture company, honey!" Eli shot back.

To Zach's surprise, Sunny kept quiet about her plans to expand Carlisle Furniture with a mail-order catalog business.

She folded her arms in front of her. "Why don't you just say it?" she retorted thickly. "The fact that I've come back here to live and work is embarrassing you in front of all your colleagues and friends."

"It's just that you're capable of so much more," Elanore said gently.

Eli nodded in affirmation. "We've got friends in influential places. We could call in a few markers and get you a job on the fast track, in Europe or here in the States."

Sunny swept a hand through her hair. Her mouth tightened. She stared at her parents in exasperation, then looked at Zach.

He knew she needed him. "I think Sunny is happy right where she is," he said firmly, moving to stand beside his wife and lace an arm about her shoulders. "And as far as I'm concerned, that's all that matters."

"THANKS FOR helping out like that," Sunny said after her parents had left, and they were both upstairs getting ready to go to work. "Though given the way you feel about living in Carlisle yourself, I'm not sure why you did."

"You've got to make your own decisions, Sunny. Although their remarks did leave me with a few questions of my own."

"Such as?"

She plugged in her curling iron and sat down at the vanity table next to the bathroom sink. She was dressed in a mint green shirtdress with a cinched-in waist and a long swirling skirt. She looked beautiful in a hands-off sort of way...and was also highly emotional. So much so, in fact, that Zach wished he could take the day off work and spend it just being with her, offering her what comfort he could.

"Have you ever had any second thoughts about settling here permanently?" he asked as he smoothed shaving cream on his face.

"Let me guess," Sunny said grimly as she began to brush her hair. "You think I'm wasting my time, too."

Zach began to shave with long, smooth strokes. He hadn't agreed with Elanore and Eli's approach, but he knew they did have some valid points that should be considered. "You are well educated, with a lot of business savvy. Your parents are right. There probably are a lot of other opportunities out there for you."

Sunny leaned toward the mirror as she curled her bangs. "Living in Carlisle is like being part of one big family, and I adore it." Finished, she set her curling iron down and swiveled toward him. "Maybe if I hadn't already lived in Europe I'd want to see more of the world. But thanks to my parents, I've already seen and done so much. Right now what I want is a home, pure and simple, and I've got that here."

Zach rinsed and towel-dried his face. "Carlisle is a friendly town—I'll give you that. Everyone cares about everyone else."

"But—?"

Zach shrugged as he reached for his dress shirt and slipped it on. "I don't like having to fight for control of my own life."

Sunny raised a lecturing finger his way. "If your life is out of control, it is not because you're living in Carlisle, Zach."

He reached for his tie and put it around his neck. "Then what is it?"

Sunny brushed past him in a drift of cinnamon-scented perfume.

"Maybe the close quarters and intense public scrutiny have just forced you to really examine your life for the first time. Maybe you're uncomfortable because you don't like what you find."

Zach followed her into her bedroom. He watched as she tossed shoes out of her closet, finally settling on a pair of ivory flats. "Hey, I've got nothing to feel ashamed about. I'm working in a noble profession. I've devoted my life to caring for other people."

"But what about your private life, Zach?" Sunny asked as she slipped on her shoes. "Take it from me, there's got to be more than meaningful work to make you happy. You've got to have a personal life, too."

Zach steadied her with a hand on her waist. "That's kind of hard to do when I'm married to a woman who barely gives me the time of day." He touched a gentle hand to the side of her face. "Unless, of course, that is going to change, and we're going to have some sort of private life together?"

Sunny extricated herself from his light, possessive hold and stepped aside. Her shoulders were stiff as she turned away from him. "You knew what the terms of this arrangement were going to be when we got together, Zach."

Yes, he had. He just hadn't realized it was going to be so hard living with her and not loving her. He wondered if she was feeling as deprived of intimacy and affection as he was. "Unless you're prepared to renegotiate our agreement—" he countered hopefully.

Her eyes lit up like firecrackers. "If you're talking about sex—" Sunny warned.

Zach grabbed his billfold off the bureau and slid it in his back pocket. He figured, as long as they were laying everything on the line, they might as well be honest and up-front about this, too. "What else?"

Love, Sunny thought. *I want love. I won't settle for anything else.* "Well," she said with an arch expression, "there's cooking and cleaning—"

"Forget that," Zach grumbled. That sounded like another have-to lesson from her class on marriage.

Sunny gave him a chastising look. He wanted to make her his, all right, she mused, but only in a physical sense. "That's what I thought," she stated grimly.

"What?" Zach followed her out the bedroom and down the stairs.

She picked up a pair of gold earrings on a downstairs hall table and clipped them on her ears. "You're not interested in an equal-opportunity marriage." Her jaw set in silent censure.

Zach lounged against the banister, watching Sunny. He wasn't pleased to be sparring with her this morning. He'd much rather spend his time loving her. But at least their latest battle of the sexes had gotten her mind off her parents.

It had also brought excited color to her cheeks and a sparkle to her eyes. "Of course, I might be interested in a more chore-equitable arrangement," he teased, unable to help himself from provoking her a little more. "Providing the price was right."

Sunny shot him a look meant to cool his jets. "For instance?"

"I can see us doing the dishes together if we cozied up afterward."

Sunny knew he could. Worse, she thought, she could imagine cuddling with Zach, too. But the easy, vivid images that came to mind would not keep her heart from being broken. Only she could do that. Slowing her pulse with effort, she looked at her watch. "I've got to get going. Matilda's waiting to give me a lift to work."

"What time do you think you'll be home tonight?" he asked. Maybe the two of them could drive down the mountain, go out to dinner…

"I don't know." Sunny frowned. "I've got a full day ahead of me, plus a supper-hour meeting with the catalog photographer and a marriage class after that. And I want to stop by and see Gramps this evening and catch him up on what's been happening at the factory since he got back from his fishing trip."

Zach shifted uncomfortably. Sunny was going to be furious when she found out where Augustus had really been.

"Don't look so upset," she scolded, misinterpreting the reason behind his dismay. "I really do have a lot to do."

Zach didn't doubt that. He also knew it wasn't his imagination. She was avoiding him like the plague. "You'll be home late, then?" he said grimly. And wondered what the men in the community would advise him to do about that. Put his foot down or weather the storm?

Sunny nodded, her expression brisk and businesslike as she picked up her briefcase. "Don't wait dinner for me."

ZACH SLID his TV dinner in the oven as the front door slammed with hurricane force. Seconds later, Sunny was framed in the kitchen doorway.

"How could you not have told me my grandfather was just hospitalized!" she stormed.

Zach swore. "How'd you find out?"

"The hospital. They called Personnel because there was a question about his insurance."

"Have you talked to him?"

"He's out fishing!"

Zach steered her resisting body into a chair. "Sit

down and I'll explain." Minutes later, when he'd finished, she stared at him, looking even more upset.

"And there's still no diagnosis?" she asked, her lower lip trembling.

"No. There isn't. But we're working on it and I'm sure—" Zach's eyes tracked the sound of a car in the driveway. He looked out the window, to see a black Cadillac in the drive. Augustus got out of the car, winced as he moved toward the house. Sunny and Zach were outside in a flash. Together they helped him into the house.

"When did it start?" Zach asked. It was obvious Augustus was in pain.

"While I was fishing."

"Tell me exactly what you were doing," Zach ordered.

"Nothing to tell." He demonstrated with his left hand. "I was casting my line in the stream—" Augustus winced as he moved his arm above his head. "Damn, there it goes again."

And suddenly Zach knew what it was.

"Bursitis!" Augustus said minutes later when Zach had finished his exam and had injected steroid medication and local anesthetic into the painful joint. Together he and Sunny packed Augustus's shoulder in ice.

"All that fly-fishing you've been doing since you semiretired has aggravated your shoulder joint. The pain you felt originated there, then spread out into your chest and down your arm, mimicking heart pains or angina," Zach said. "We didn't pinpoint the source because up until now there's been no swelling or inflammation in the joint."

"But it's there now," Augustus said.

"Yes. Very visible, too. Which means you are going

to have to lay off the fishing for a couple of weeks, until you heal.''

"Okay," Augustus said. He blew out a weary breath. "Thanks, Zach."

"You're welcome," Zach said with a smile. He felt as relieved as Augustus looked. Sunny was not nearly as happy. She let him have it after they saw her grandfather home.

"I can't believe you kept that from me," she said tersely, marching back to Zach's truck, her hands balled into fists at her side.

"I had no choice." He walked along beside her, his shoes crunching on the gravel drive. "Augustus was my patient. And he did not want you to know."

"But what if something had happened? What if he'd been in the hospital and—" Sunny whirled to face him at the truck door. "You still should have told me. Dropped a hint. Something! I'm your wife!" Her voice was choked as she regarded him tearfully. "I thought we were close," she whispered.

"We are," Zach insisted, aware that she looked more hurt and confused than he had ever seen her.

But she only shook her head at him in a way that let him know she was comparing his machinations with Augustus to those of her parents. They had deliberately conspired to keep her in the dark.

"Not close enough, apparently," she said grimly.

His own frustration and disappointment boiling over, Zach studied her upturned face. As he had feared, Augustus's secret had driven a wedge between them. It was going to be a while before Sunny forgave him. If she did at all.

"YOU RENTED a what for us?" Zach asked Friday afternoon, when he arrived home to find Sunny lugging a suitcase down from the attic.

"I rented a houseboat for the weekend," she explained patiently, avoiding his eyes all the while.

Had she done this because she wanted to be close to him, Zach would've been exultant. But it was all too clear from the determined expression on her face that this was not the case. She was still as confused as ever, wanting to trust him, not quite sure she should. But that was something, Zach assured himself firmly, that could be overcome.

"Let me guess what prompted this," he said dryly, giving her a hand with the suitcase. "Your class, right?"

Sunny popped the case open and began filling it with clothing. "My assignment was to plan something special for just the two of us," she admitted sheepishly, pausing to look up into his face. He could tell, even if she wasn't quite ready to admit it yet, that she wanted to make up with him, too.

She wet her lips and continued softly, still holding his eyes, "I remembered what you said once about going away for the weekend being your salvation in med school and thought it might be nice to try it. That is…if you don't mind."

"I don't mind," Zach said, already anticipating their time alone, away from the prying eyes of the community. This was his chance to make amends with her.

As he pictured Sunny in a bikini, sunbathing on the deck of the boat, it was all he could do not to groan. The close quarters were going to be murder, just as not making love to her was going to be sheer torture. But he was looking forward to spending time with her alone, he realized, as he began to pack, also. And he could no longer deny that he did not want this marriage of theirs to end.

Chapter Ten

This Can't Be Love

"Maybe we should turn back," Sunny suggested, peering at the gray sky overhead.

"After we drove two hours to get here?" Zach said, striding down the dock. He tossed their suitcases onto the deck of their rented houseboat, then returned for the cooler full of ice and soft drinks. "Not on your life, Sunny."

She grabbed a sack of groceries from the front seat of his pickup. "What if it rains?" She didn't know why, but suddenly she was very nervous about spending the entire weekend alone with Zach. Maybe because he looked so incredibly sexy and at home on the shores of the Tennessee lake.

Zach swaggered back to her side, happier than he had been in weeks. He grabbed the last two sacks of groceries, a portable stereo and a first-aid kit. "Then we'll throw out our fishing lines and stay inside the boat."

"I don't know." Sunny continued to drag her feet. What if she found herself succumbing to the heat and passion of his kisses? A lot could happen in forty-eight hours.

Zach dumped the rest of the stuff on the deck, then turned and put his hands on her shoulders. He gazed down at her warmly. "Sunny, trust me. Everything is going to be fine. A little rain never hurt anything. Besides, the forecast calls for bright and sunny skies tonight and tomorrow. We're going to be fine."

He was right. She was being silly. "If it rains I'll just work on the catalog."

Zach lifted his brow, suddenly a lot less happy. "You brought work with you?"

"In my suitcase," Sunny confirmed. Her work had sustained her on more than one occasion. This would be no exception, she told herself firmly.

"Gonna tell your class that when you get back?" Zach teased as he gave her a hand onto the deck of the houseboat.

Sunny blushed. She could imagine the lectures she would get if she did. "That'll have to be our little secret, Zach."

"I don't know, Sunny," he drawled, rubbing his jaw.

He gave her a temptation-laced glance that set her heart to pounding.

"I'm not very good at keeping secrets."

Nor was he any good at hiding his growing desire for her, Sunny thought. "Well, try," she advised airily, aggravated to find she was blushing all the harder. Zach was acting as if this trip were going to be the honeymoon they'd never had. And damned if his feelings weren't just a bit contagious.

She had to stop thinking like this. Had to get busy.

"I'll put the galley in order," Sunny said with an outward calm she couldn't begin to feel. Aware of Zach's eyes on her, lovingly tracing every inch of her, she grabbed the groceries and slipped inside the houseboat.

Out on deck, Zach leaned over the bow of the thirty-two-foot boat and brought up anchor. Seconds later, they were on their way.

By the time they had reached the middle of the lake, the clouds had rolled in. Thirty minutes later, it began to sprinkle. Two hours later, fat raindrops thudded on the deck and roof of the houseboat.

Sunny groaned. She should have known the weather would work against them. She should have listened to the regional forecast before she'd left. Now it was too late. They were here and would just have to muddle through as best they could.

That, too, became more of a test than she'd expected as visibility soon dropped to ten feet. Swearing at the treacherous conditions, Zach steered the boat over to a secluded cove surrounded by a thick forest of trees and a steep, rocky shore. He cut the motor, then turned to face her.

"Don't suppose you located a rain slicker or umbrella anywhere in the cabin?" he asked languidly.

Sunny shook her head, aware he was going to have to leave the cabin and go out on deck to secure the boat. "Sorry."

"No problem," he said.

Sunny watched him stride out into the pouring rain. He moved around the rear of the boat. By the time he had dropped anchor and come back inside the cabin, his shirt and shorts were soaked clear through to the skin.

Sunny handed him a towel.

"Thanks," he said.

Mouth dry, she watched as he stripped off his shirt and headed into the bedroom to change. He came back out in shorts and a polo shirt, his hair slicked back from his face.

Rain pounded overhead, so loudly they had to shout to be heard. "The storm'll pass soon," Zach promised, as Sunny handed him a cup of coffee.

But the rain didn't stop. And that was when the real trouble began.

LIGHTNING SHIMMERED above, followed by a nearly simultaneous crack of thunder. Four o'clock in the afternoon, and the sky was nearly pitch-black. It was getting very scary, Sunny thought nervously as she peered out the windows for the thousandth time. In fact, it looked like tornado weather.

She paced back and forth in the small interior of the cabin, the galley on one side of her, the booth where Zach lounged on the other. Great gusts of wind rocked the boat, while rain still pounded on the roof overhead.

"You're not supposed to be in water during a thunderstorm," Sunny said shakily.

"We're not in the water. We're in a boat."

"A boat that's on water," Sunny said pointedly, wringing her hands in front of her.

"Please relax, will you?" Zach said as another jagged fork of lightning exploded in the sky. He stood impatiently. "It's just a storm. It'll be over soon."

"Just a storm," she muttered, covering her ears as another crack of tremendous thunder sounded overhead and another gust of wind shook the boat. Up above them on the bluff, lightning sliced into a towering walnut tree. A flash of fire followed, then the branch went tumbling down into the water ten feet from the bow of the houseboat. Above them, the trunk continued to smoke. The only thing that saved it from leaping into flames was the continuous downpour of rain.

Sunny shook her head, trembling over the close call. "Okay, that does it. I'm getting us out of here." She went to the captain's wheel and reached for the key in the boat ignition.

Zach was by her side in an instant. "What the hell do you think you're doing?"

"Getting us out of here." She started the boat with a roar.

He covered her hand with his and just as decisively turned the motor off. "I dropped anchor, remember?"

Fuming, Sunny whirled on him. "Then pull it up," she ordered anxiously. They were going to die out there and it was going to be all his fault.

"We're safe here in this cove," Zach said.

His implacable certainty infuriated her even more. "The only way we'll be safe is if we're back on land. Now, are you going to pull up that anchor or not?" she asked, frustrated beyond belief.

"Not." Zach took the key from the ignition, pocketed it and sat down grimly.

"Fine." Sunny leapt off the captain's seat. Her mind made up, she headed for the sliding-glass door at the front of the boat, which led out to the covered deck. He might be fool enough to want to die on this stupid boat, but that did not mean she had to join him.

Zach vaulted after her. "Come back here!" he shouted.

Sunny was already struggling around the side of the boat. The wind blew her back. She landed in Zach's arms. He clamped his arms around her decisively. "Come back inside, Sunny!" he ordered.

Bristling at the cool decisiveness in his voice, she pushed against his chest. "No!"

"You're hysterical," he shouted in her ear, holding her all the firmer.

"No, I am not, but I will be screaming if you don't let me get us out of here!" she shouted back.

Again he refused to let her go, merely turned her around so she was facing him. Arms locked around her middle like a vise, he commanded, "Stop fighting me and come back into the cabin!"

It wasn't only Zach she was fighting. It was the idea of them being alone, the thought that something terrible might happen now, this very afternoon, and her life would be all over, and she would never have known. She had to get out of there. Pulse pounding, she twisted in his arms. Swearing at her lack of cooperativeness, Zach held her all the tighter and dragged her toward the door, regardless of her feelings. The next thing she knew, she and Zach landed in a heap on the wet deck.

Still, rain pounded them, the wind roared. In the distance, Sunny saw what she had feared. The tail end of a funnel cloud touching down on the opposite side of the lake. "Oh, God, Zach!" Shaking, she pointed in the opposite direction.

His arms tightened protectively around her as he saw the tornado, too. In terrified silence, they watched it head across the lake, in a path parallel to them.

"Let's go into the cabin now," Zach said. He helped her up from the deck. They scrambled inside, both of them soaked to the skin.

The tornado continued on across the lake, touching down occasionally, sending debris flying in its wake. Finally it passed out of sight. The storm quieted somewhat. Sunny stared at the horizon for long minutes afterward, still shaking badly. "Now can we get out of here?" she said, distressed tears filling her eyes.

Zach looked at the storm around them. "I know it's bad, Sunny. I'm sorry. But we're still safer where we are," he said.

Sunny pushed the damp hair off her face. "What if another tornado comes?"

"We're still better off here than out on the lake," Zach said. He narrowed his eyes at her. "I don't suppose you brought any liquor with you?"

She shook her head mutely.

"Then we'll just have to use what we've got to calm you down," Zach said. Before she had time to resist, he scooped her up in his arms and carried her back to the bedroom...and the queen-size pull-down bed. He set her down next to it. "You're still shaking," he said, already rummaging through the clothes she'd hung up in the tiny closet. "You need to get out of those wet clothes."

"So do you." Sunny winced as lightning illuminated the curtained windows and thunder flashed overhead. But she noted the rain pounding against the windows was finally abating, the wind dying down, just a little.

He tossed her a robe and slipped out of the bedroom with his in hand. When he returned seconds later, her shorts and top were draped over the closet door to dry and she was wrapped in white terry cloth from neck to ankle. Zach was wearing a brown velour monk's robe.

"I wish the storm would end," she said miserably, glancing anxiously out the window one more time.

"So do I." Zach took her hand and led her toward the bed, while lightning flashed outside. "But since we have no control over that, we'll just have to talk until it ends."

His manner resolute, Zach guided her down and stretched out beside her. Lying back on the pillows, he dragged her wordlessly into his arms and held her close.

Sunny figured if she was going to die, she might as well go happy.

"Now, tell me," he said as he stroked his hand through her hair, "why are you so afraid of storms?"

Sunny buried her head in his chest. She felt safer with his arms around her, as though nothing could hurt her, not as long as he was there. "It goes back to the summer I was five," she said in a muffled voice, clinging to his warmth and strength. She closed her eyes, trying to relax. "We were living in Greece."

"Sounds exciting," Zach said, now stroking her hair with the flat of his hand.

"Not really," she murmured, recalling that for her the time had been anything but that. "My parents were working on an important international merger, and we were living in a villa along the coast."

"Big or little?"

"Huge. Old. Scary. Anyway, they hired this governess to take care of me. She seemed ancient at the time, but looking back, I think maybe she was only middle-aged."

"Not very nice, I guess?"

"She could put on the charm for my parents."

"But not for you?" Zach asked sympathetically.

Sunny nodded. Getting caught up in the past, she paid less and less attention to the storm outside. "Mrs. Miniver didn't believe in coddling children, and I was a kid who needed a lot of attention."

"Because you spent so much time away from your parents?" Zach said, taking a guess.

"Yes. So one night when a really bad storm blew in

off the sea, Mrs. Miniver decided I needed to learn to handle my fear of thunder and lightning. So she put me in my bedroom upstairs, turned out all the lights on the floor and went back downstairs.'' Sunny shook her head in abject misery, remembering. ''The storm went on forever, and I cried and cried. When my parents got home around two in the morning, they found me under the bed. She got fired, of course. But my fear of storms has remained. I know it's irrational, but I really hate them.'' Sunny shuddered, clinging to Zach all the harder as he wrapped his arms around her tightly. ''I can't stand feeling as if my life might be blown apart at any minute. I can't stand not feeling safe.''

''I know what you mean,'' he said, stroking her hair. ''Safety is important to me, too,'' he said softly. There was a heartbeat of silence. ''There's nothing worse than seeing someone you love hurting and not being able to do anything to change it,'' he said softly.

''You talk as if you've been in a similar situation,'' she said.

Zach nodded, his expression grave. ''When we found out my sister, Lori, was terminal, I tried to be there for her as much as I could. It was still one of the worst times in my entire life,'' he said thickly. ''When she died, I made a vow to myself that I would never feel that helpless again. And as you can see,'' he remarked with dark humor, exerting incredible self-control over his emotions, as another rumble of thunder sounded overhead, ''I haven't made much, if any, progress on that score. But what the hell,'' he concluded with a rueful shrug and a bittersweet smile, ''I'm trying my best to control the universe.''

''I've noticed,'' she said dryly.

''Yep, I bet you have,'' he drawled back.

Silence fell between them once more. He grinned at her. Sunny met his smile with one of her own. It was important to her that he had confided in her. It meant a lot to be able to confide in him.

His gaze turned gentle. He traced the curve of her mouth with his fingertip, the fragile caress heating her blood.

"Feeling better?" he asked softly.

Yes and no, Sunny thought. She wanted to make love with him so badly she ached. The edges of reality and fantasy were blurring. She was beginning to feel really married to Zach, committed to him, even though she knew that was not the case. And until it was, maybe it would be better if she put some distance between them.

"You don't seem as frightened as you were," Zach continued.

The truth was, when she was in his arms, she wasn't scared at all, Sunny realized. The problem came in how she would feel when he was gone. If he left. She was still working on somehow inducing him to say.

"You know, I am feeling better, now that the worst of the storm seems to be past us," she admitted on a ragged breath, aware that wise or not, it wouldn't take much convincing at all to get her to surrender everything to him. "In fact, I think I can get up now," she said briskly, deciding the inevitable could be postponed for just a little while longer.

"Not yet," he murmured gently, rolling so she was beneath him, framing her face with his hands. He looked down at her, his eyes glowing with love. "Not until I tell you how I feel." His voice caught. "If something had happened just now, Sunny. If that tornado had hit us. If I'd lost you—"

"I know, Zach, I know. I felt the same." She held

on to the edge of his robe, the raw vulnerability in his face giving her the courage to say what was in her heart, had been there all along. "But we are here. And we're together and safe."

In that instant, the world fell away, and it was just the two of them. She knew, more than anything, what she wanted. The love and closeness that had always eluded her, the desire only Zach could give.

Eyes darkening, he lowered his mouth to hers. His tongue parted her lips and swept inside her mouth. With a moan, she wreathed her arms around his neck and clasped him to her and felt his body and hers heat instantly in response.

In a haze, she let him open her robe. His hands skimmed her breasts, sensitizing the curves, until she thought she might die from the pleasure of it. Needing, wanting, more intimate contact, Sunny arched into his touch. She trembled beneath his questing fingertips, caught up in the intensity of what she was feeling, all they had become to each other and all they could be, if only they took that giant leap of faith and made their marriage a real one.

"Oh, Sunny, I want so much to make you mine." He caressed the side of her face with his thumb. "I want so much to stop thinking and just feel…to stop planning so damn much and take a chance."

She knew exactly what he meant. "So do I, Zach." Her arms about his neck, she fitted her mouth to his and kissed him deeply, tenderly. She didn't know what the rest of her life held. And right now, selfish or not, she didn't care. She knew only that she had the chance to have a wild, reckless, incredibly passionate love affair. The chance to be with Zach like this might never come again. If she didn't take advantage of it, she would regret not making love with him the rest of her life. And she didn't want any regrets where he was concerned. She wanted only love and sweet, wonderful memories.

"Sunny, are you sure?" Zach asked, as his hands skimmed lower, slipping between her thighs. He touched her intimately, the heat of his caress sending her arching up into his questing hand.

"Yes, Zach, I'm sure," she said huskily, knowing if they weren't together now she would die.

Zach looked down into her eyes. He caressed her face lovingly, first with his eyes, then his fingertips and finally his lips. "Then I'm going to show you what love really is," he said softly, already working the robe from her shoulders, shrugging off his.

The light in the cabin was dim, but Sunny could see the beauty of his masculine shape. He was hard all over and lower still, below the waist, aroused beyond belief. Her heart pounding, the need in her an incessant ache, she closed her eyes, afraid she would lose her nerve if she thought about the enormity of the situation too much. She gripped his shoulders and took a deep breath. "All right if I let you lead the way?" she asked tremulously, never needing or wanting him more than she did at that moment, knowing what was at stake.

Zach sifted his fingers through her hair, his expression fierce with longing and the primal need to possess. Cupping her head in his hands, he angled her chin up to his. "I wouldn't have it any other way," he whispered, lowering his mouth to hers again.

His kisses melted one into another. She returned them passionately, her body feeling as if it were on fire from the inside out. She arched against his hands, yearning fervently. Sensations hammered at her. She strained against him, her body moving in undulations. "Now," she said softly, clutching at his shoulders. She was only sure she couldn't bear any more of this. She had to find a way to reach fulfillment. She had to find a way to be closer to him.

"Sunny—" He spoke as if in a haze, the hot, heavy fullness of him straining against her closed thighs.

"I want you, Zach." She slipped her hands around his hips and guided him lower still, so he was positioned precisely where he should be. She was trembling with a fierce, unquenchable ache. "I want you so much." More than she could ever have imagined. "Please. Now."

"I want you, too." He turned the words against her lips. Then he was pushing her thighs apart with his knees, stroking her gently. Sunny arched again, his name tumbling from her lips as he surged against her, penetrating the final barrier. Eyes full of wonder and fierce possessiveness, he stared down at her...and knew what she hadn't told him. "Oh, God. Sunny—" he breathed.

"Just love me, Zach," she whispered, bringing his mouth back to hers for another slow, searing, sensual kiss. "Just love me," she said again. And love her he did. His hands touched every inch of her, until she was weak with longing, overwhelmed with sensation. She surged up against him, every inch of her wanting every part of him.

ZACH LAY on his back, Sunny sprawled against his chest, her head on his shoulder. Outside, the storm had abated. Inside, as he wrapped his arms around Sunny and held her close, the storm was just beginning. In retrospect, he could see the signs had been there all along. He just hadn't wanted to deal with them because he had wanted her so much. Not just as a lover. But as his wife. "Why didn't you tell me?" he asked, stroking his hand over her slender shoulders.

Sunny snuggled against him contentedly. "Because it wasn't important." Her voice was muffled against his chest.

Like hell it wasn't. Zach was surprised by the fierce possessiveness welling inside him. He wanted only the best for Sunny. What had just happened did not fall into that category.

"Besides, I know how gallant you are at heart. You've demonstrated it many times. If I had, you would've—" She stopped, as if abruptly deciding she'd revealed too much.

Needing to see her face, he rolled so that she was beneath him. He cupped her shoulders warmly as his gaze roved her flushed features and kiss-swollen lips. "You're right, Sunny. I never would have made love to you if I'd guessed—"

She traced idle patterns on his chest. "That I was a virgin?"

Zach nodded, feeling even worse now that she had said it. "Yes." He had handled this situation all wrong, let his feelings for her carry him away. He wasn't used to being out of control; the knowledge that he could be, under any circumstances, was hard to handle.

Sunny shrugged, as if it were no big deal. "Well, now I'm experienced," she said cavalierly.

Zach released a frustrated breath. "That's not funny, Sunny," he said, chastising bluntly, as guilt flooded him again. He had taken something precious from her, something that couldn't just be given back. And that in turn made their relationship even more complicated than it already had been. And dammit all, she had known that.

"Look, Zach, it had to happen sometime," she reassured him gently, her fingertips stroking his chest, making him want her all over again.

Zach scowled. Once again, Sunny was too naive for her own good. She should have had a real marriage, and until he'd come along she'd held out for just that, he admitted grimly to himself. But maybe it wasn't too late. "I'll make it up to you," he said softly, realizing he was more of an old-fashioned guy than he'd thought. "I promise."

Sunny's face flamed, as she mistakenly took his concern for her as rejection. Before he could correct her misimpression, she pushed away from him and sat up, dragging the sheet over her breasts. Her eyes flared with a temper she was working very hard to subdue.

"Listen, Zach," she lectured. "I never asked you to hold the key to my chastity belt. In fact, if you want to get technical about it, the way things were going…you had every right to expect we'd eventually make love."

No, Zach thought, he hadn't. He'd only hoped.

"This doesn't have to change anything," she persisted willfully.

He shook his head at her, amazed at her innocence once again. "You're wrong, Sunny," he said gently. "What happened between us just now changes everything." Because she had given her heart to him—body and soul—and now their marriage was a real one in every respect.

SUNNY VAULTED from the bed, the sheet draped about her like a long white toga. She couldn't believe he was filled with ambivalence about the most wonderful thing that had ever happened in her life. Now reality was sinking in. "Why does it have to change everything, Zach?" she asked coolly, slipping out of the bedroom and into the galley. She bent to extract a can of icy lemonade from the cooler and settled into the booth. Outside, the storm had passed. Only a gentle rain remained.

"Because it does," he insisted.

Sunny watched as Zach wrapped himself in his robe. His straight ash blond hair all tousled, his face shadowed with just a hint of evening beard, he had never looked sexier. "You don't have to feel guilty," Sunny said quietly. *You don't have to feel trapped.*

"How do you expect me to feel?" He got himself a cold soda and joined her in the tiny vinyl booth. Maybe if he got her talking, he'd find out how she was feeling about all this, too.

How about pleased, instead of horrified, Sunny thought, taking a long sip of her lemonade. But seeing that wasn't about to happen, at least not today, she shrugged. "Sexually satisfied, I guess." She turned to look at him and said slyly, "You were satisfied, weren't you?"

Zach swore, the heat of his embarrassment and chagrin moving from his neck into his face. He looked heavenward for his answers. "Why me?"

Sunny grinned, enjoying his discomfiture. It wasn't often the tables were turned. "That's no answer, Zach," she answered with an inner steeliness she couldn't begin to feel.

He leveled his glance back at her. "You know I…was," he said thickly.

"How would I know?" she shrugged. "It's not like

I've had a lot of experience in the area, you know,'' she said dryly.

"Yes, I know," Zach drawled.

His blue eyes glimmered as if he had every intention of making her his again. But not before they'd talked, Sunny surmised.

"And now that we're on the subject—" he captured her bare legs beneath the table and shifted them onto his lap "—why haven't you had a lot of experience?"

She closed her eyes and didn't answer. Zach stroked her legs, from ankle to knees. "You wanted the first time to be with your husband, didn't you?" Not just someone who was pretending to be your husband, he thought, then swore inwardly again. Maybe if they'd agreed to stay married and make their union a lasting one, it would have been different. But they hadn't. So he'd have to convince her...to make their marriage last, not just for a short time, but forever.

Sunny ignored the tingles starting beneath his caressing fingertips. She stared at the tabletop, beginning to get embarrassed now despite herself. "I waited because I wanted it to be special," she admitted reluctantly, not meeting his eyes.

"And it wasn't," Zach interrupted, with a self-effacing sigh.

She glanced up. He was so hard on himself sometimes. "What makes you think that?" she asked curiously. For her, it had been very special.

"Because it just wasn't—that's all." At least not special enough to make her want to stay married to him, Zach thought, his determination growing. "But it could be," he said as he took her hand and pulled her out of the booth.

"Zach—"

He wrapped her in his arms and pressed his lips into the fragrant softness of her hair. "Sunny, we can't leave it like this."

Sunny shook her head. Through the opening of his robe, she could see the suntanned column of his throat, muscled chest and crisp golden brown hair. She pressed the flat of her palm on his skin. Confusion clouded her eyes. "I haven't the slightest idea what you're talking about."

Zach's heart thudded heavily beneath her hand.

"Precisely my point," he said dryly.

Sunny sighed and ran her hand up to his shoulder. "I think what happened was wonderful." She couldn't ever remember feeling as loved as she had when he'd made her his for the very first time.

Zach traced the swell of her breasts, above the tucked-in sheet. "You're right—it was great—but it could have been a lot better."

Sunny tilted her head back to better see his face. Zach was half teasing, half serious. "What do you mean?" she said softly, wondering all the while if he was falling in love with her as hard and fast as she was with him. Had it not been for the crazy way they'd gotten together, would he have been this open with her?

Zach raked his fingers through her thick red-gold hair. "If I'd known you were a virgin, I would have gone about it very differently," he said gently. "You'll just have to trust me on the fact that your introduction to lovemaking could have been a lot more...um... enticing. Fortunately," he teased, sifting his hands through her hair and giving her a decidedly sensual glance, "it's not too late for me to make amends."

But did he love her? she wondered. Or was he just

trying, once again, to right another wrong? Until she knew for sure… "Zach, I—I'm tired," Sunny fibbed.

Just as he'd suspected, Zach thought, she already had one foot out the door again. He quirked a brow. "Too tired to see what else you've been missing all this time?"

Sunny hesitated. He would have to point that out. She had always been curious about what it would be like to have a lover. She studied his face, liking the rapt adoration she saw there beneath his overriding concern, loving even more the idea of making love with him all night. Though she couldn't imagine it being any more enticing…

The temptation to find out what else she'd been missing was great, but so was her anxiety, and right now, she felt she and Zach were poised on the brink of either total happiness or disaster. "If I'd known this was what we were going to be doing on this boat, I would have brought some champagne with us," Sunny groaned. "Anything to help me relax."

He massaged her shoulders. "You are a little tense."

"Now that I'm thinking about what's going to happen, Zach, I'm getting nervous about it again."

Zach paused. He dropped his hands. "Then maybe we should put it off a little while," he suggested.

Sunny wavered between relief and disappointment. It seemed he was full of surprises today. One minute possessive, the next willing to let her go her own way.

"The rain's stopped," he continued affably. "We could take a break, go on deck and enjoy the sunset. After all, we've got all weekend to perfect our lovemaking skills."

Sunny sighed. She had her reprieve. She just wasn't sure she wanted it.

"TRUST ME, Sunny. There's nothing like sleeping under the stars."

Sunny stood motionless beside Zach. She'd waited for him to make his move, and he hadn't. Not during dinner. Not after. Not at all.

She looked at the foot-high solid white Plexiglas railing on top of the houseboat. "At least we don't have to worry about falling off in our sleep. But if it rains, we're in trouble."

"It's not going to rain," he said firmly.

"If my memory serves me correctly, that's exactly what you said before," Sunny remarked sagely.

"Yeah, well, this time it wouldn't dare," Zach said as he dragged the mattress up on top of the sun deck, atop the houseboat cabin. Together he and Sunny spread out blankets, sheets and pillows. He took her hand and tugged her down beside him. They were both clad in menswear pajamas, thick cotton socks and deck shoes. "Trust me, Sunny, this will be a great place to spend the evening."

"I admit it's cozy up here," she said, looking up at the stars and the moon overhead. "Kind of like camping out, only better."

"It seems we're the only two on the lake tonight, doesn't it?" Zach said.

"Probably the only two people fool enough to be out here after that storm we had this afternoon," she joked, settling back on the pillows, her hands folded beneath her head.

"Yeah, well, there's something to be said for

storms," Zach said softly, drawing an imaginary line down her middle.

"Oh, yeah?" Sunny teased, as the warm rain-scented air blew over them.

"The storms in your eyes are magnificent to see." He reached over and began to undo her pajama top.

She inhaled a shaky breath. "Zach—"

"Relax, Sunny."

He turned her on her side; she was nestled against his warmth, so she could see the gentle, serious light in his eyes.

"We've got all night." He cupped a hand behind her head and kissed her slowly, deliberately. "And I intend to take my time."

Where before there had been passion and urgency, there was only tenderness and care. He undressed her one button, one snap at a time.

He lingered over her breasts and her thighs and every sweet inch between. He kissed her repeatedly, languid kisses that were as intimate as his caresses. He kissed her in ways that revealed his soul. And she loved him back, starting shyly, growing more and more bold. Spearing her hands through his hair, across his shoulders, down his torso to his thighs, she offered him whatever he wanted from her, whatever he needed. And this time, she took, too.

She was lost in him. She was in love with him. And she needed him. Oh, Sunny thought, surging toward the outer limits of her control, how she needed him... needed this...wanted to feel loved...and so incredibly cherished.

ZACH PARKED in the driveway and cut the motor. Wordlessly he snapped off his seat belt and hers, dragged

Sunny across the bench seat of his pickup into his arms and settled her on his lap.

"What are you thinking?"

She sighed wistfully, not sure when she had ever felt so content or so loved. "That what happened this weekend changes everything."

"For the better," Zach agreed as she laid her head on his shoulder. He chuckled softly. "Living with you and not loving you was getting to be damn hard."

Sunny stroked his chest with long, soothing strokes. She sensed he was delaying going back inside for the same reason she was. "Now that we're home again, Zach—" she began.

Reading her mind, he touched a fingertip to her lips. "I want to share your bed every night. Or you can come to mine. It doesn't matter, as long as we're together."

Sunny drew a deep breath. She could feel the thundering of his heart beneath her palm. "So this wasn't a fling?"

Zach shook his head. "We're married partners involved in a full-fledged love affair." He paused, studying her face in the moonlight. "How does that set with you?"

It frightened and thrilled her all at once. "I think I can live with it," she said cautiously, curling her fingers in the fabric of his shirt. *As long as it doesn't ever end.*

Zach smiled, his happiness as potent as hers. "So it's settled," he said, running a possessive hand down her spine. "From now on, we'll be together every night."

"Yes," Sunny said softly. They would make love endlessly and sleep wrapped in each other's arms. And for once, she wouldn't worry so much about the future.

Zach's eyes darkened passionately. He cupped the

back of her head and kissed her gently. Within seconds, they were both trembling.

"If we stay out here much longer, we're going to end up giving the neighbors a show," he teased.

Sunny grinned, unable to imagine a time when she wouldn't want to make love with him over and over again. "You always did look cute wrapped in nothing but a chamois loincloth," she murmured.

"Not to mention what you do for a red-and-white checkered tablecloth," Zach quipped back, as they drew apart reluctantly and she slid off his lap. "But if we're going to play Nature Walk dress-up, we'll have to do it inside the house this time."

He hopped down and circled around the truck to help Sunny down. She paused as her feet hit the ground, frowning as she caught sight of her Land Rover. She was sure she'd left it parked out back. It was now next to the house and sporting a huge red ribbon across the top. Sunny glanced at Zach. He was grinning complacently. "Do you know anything about that?"

Zach gave her an aw-shucks look. "I just might." He set down their bags and took her hand. "Let's go see."

"It smells like...pine!" Sunny said in unmitigated delight, once they'd opened the door and the interior light had come on. "And is that new carpet on the floor?" Her vehicle looked brand-new again inside.

"Yep."

"Zach, how did you manage this?"

"I enlisted a chemist friend of mine from Vanderbilt. He was able to treat the leather seats, but he feared the carpet would be a lost cause, just as I did, so I had the local garage rip it out and replace it with new."

"I can't believe it!" Sunny stuck her head inside the

truck. "No skunk smell! I can drive my Land Rover again!"

Zach pulled her against him, so they were both still facing her vehicle and touching front to back in one long, tensile line. "No more bad memories?" he said, clasping his hands in front of her.

Sunny grinned up at him. "From now on, Zach, the only memories we have of skunk are the funny ones."

"Good. Now there's only one thing left to do," he said, scooping her up into his arms. Holding her against his chest, he strode toward the front door of her house.

"And what is that?" she asked, her heart thudding heavily against her ribs.

Zach winked at her. Pausing on the steps, he bent his head to give her a slow, leisurely kiss that sent fire sizzling through her in waves. "Make some new memories," he said.

Chapter Eleven

Hearts in Armor

"That must have been some vacation you and Zach took," Gramps said slyly. "You haven't stopped glowing all morning!"

Sunny flushed. She had been afraid it would show. But she couldn't help it. She had never felt more loved in her life, even if Zach hadn't yet said the words.

"He even carried her up the steps and through the front door upon their return, honeymoon-style," Matilda added, as she joined the conversation around the coffeemaker.

Sunny's eyes widened in surprise.

"Sorry, honey," Matilda continued, "but the two of you are the talk of the town. It does all our old hearts good to see you two young-uns looking so happy."

"Especially mine," Gramps said. "I knew Zach was the man for you all along."

Sunny had known it, too; she just hadn't wanted to admit it to herself. And she wasn't going to confide it to Gramps, either, at least not yet. "I'm glad you all are so happy," she said dryly, "but now it's time to get back to business. Has Chuck Conway arrived yet?"

"He's supposed to be here any minute to work with me on the new computer system," Matilda said.

"Please ask him to stop by my office and see me when he's through," Sunny said. "I've got a few questions of my own to ask him."

"Will do," Matilda said.

"Well, I'm going to check out the new designs and then go fly-fishing," Gramps said.

Sunny kissed his tanned cheek. "Enjoy yourself. You've earned it."

Gramps grinned back at her. He patted her shoulder affectionately. "Thanks, I will."

Sunny spent the rest of the morning in her office. Around noon, Chuck Conway appeared in her door. The thirty-year-old software engineer was wearing a gray herringbone suit that looked brand-new. An overabundance of after-shave clung to his jaw. "Hey, Sunny," he said as he breezed in. "Heard you wanted to see me."

"Yes, I did, Chuck. Come on in."

He shut the door behind him and strolled closer, running a hand through his slicked-back brown hair.

Sunny noted he appeared more self-conscious than usual.

"So what's up?" Chuck asked, his eyes glued to her face.

Sunny got up from her desk and motioned him closer. Chuck's voice carried and she didn't want anyone overhearing what she was about to say. "Do you think Matilda can handle that new system you installed for us?" she asked.

Shoving both hands in his trousers, Chuck shrugged. "I think so."

Sunny bit her lip. "You're sure we don't need something simpler?" she insisted worriedly.

He shook his head. "Something simpler wouldn't meet your needs, Sunny. Therefore it'd be a bad business decision."

She sighed and looked into Chuck's eyes. She wanted him to understand. "Making Matilda feel incompetent because she can't understand the complicated system you installed is bad business, too."

"You could always hire someone else to help you out with it," he said. "Someone younger. And assign Matilda to something else."

"No, I don't think so."

"Well, then." Chuck grinned as if she'd given him an unexpected Christmas gift. "I guess I'll just have to come up here every day and see you all until we get things squared away," he said, stepping even closer.

Again he looked at her funny.

"Is everything okay?" Sunny asked, puzzled by the way he was peering at her.

"It will be," he said. "Once I get this over with."

Before Sunny could guess what he was going to do, he had bear-hugged her around the middle. Knowing he was about to kiss her, she shoved her elbows into his ribs. His legs got tangled up with hers.

He tripped and they both went sprawling, with Sunny crashing sideways into the display of untreated wood samples. She gasped as the soft pine splintered beneath her weight, ripping her panty hose and embedding in her skin.

"What the hell's going on in here?" George came crashing into the office. "Sunny, are you all right?" George stepped over Chuck to get to Sunny. He helped her to her feet.

She looked down at her burning thigh and groaned. "Oh, no."

"You want to tell me how you got this injury?" Zach said.

"Not particularly," Sunny replied breezily. She kicked off her shoes, rolled down her panty hose. Hiking up her skirt, she carefully climbed up on the examining table and rolled onto her side. "However, if you must know, I crashed into a display and fell on some wood."

Zach narrowed his eyes at her, his proprietary male side coming to the fore. "It's not like you to be clumsy."

How well Sunny knew that. But she hadn't expected Chuck Conway's five-year crush to suddenly manifest itself in a pass today. In retrospect, she could see she never should have called him at home after-hours, asked him to meet with her alone. All had been "clues" he had added up the wrong way.

Both irritated and embarrassed to find herself in this situation, she propped her head on her hand and grumbled, "Can't you hurry it up with the medical treatment? I need to get back to the office."

Zach treated the area with antiseptic. "I'd love to oblige you, but these splinters are going to take time to get out."

Sunny groaned. She couldn't think of a more ridiculous and humiliating position to be in, though Zach didn't seem to mind the work, or the fact that she'd had to take off her panty hose and hike her skirt nearly to her waist.

"So. How has your day been?" she asked, in an effort to keep her mind off what he was doing.

"Busy. I saw fifteen patients this morning, and I have a nearly full appointment book this afternoon, too."

Sunny winced as he removed a splinter and put it in the basin beside him. "Word's spreading."

"You can say that again," Zach agreed. "And not just about my skills as a physician." He paused to take out two more splinters, then gave her an interested glance. "Do you know people saw me carry you across the threshold last night?"

Sunny blushed, even as she noticed how good he looked in a white lab coat. "It was mentioned to me, too."

Zach's face split into a grin. "Everyone thinks we're on a honeymoon," he reported, his voice dropping to a sexy whisper.

"It feels that way to me, too," she said. Which was another reason she didn't want to spoil the current romantic mood with stories about Chuck and his hopelessly misguided attempt to kiss her. In this instance, what Zach didn't know wouldn't hurt him, she decided.

"I'm glad to hear that you feel that way," he said. Finished taking out the splinters, he treated the area with antiseptic cream.

"Why?" Sunny asked, watching as he expertly bandaged her thigh, then ripped off his surgical gloves.

Zach leaned over her, caging her against the examining table. "'Cause this honeymoon of ours is not over yet," he warned in a voice that made her heart pound all the harder. "Not by a long shot," he promised as he pressed his lips to hers and delivered a long, leisurely kiss.

Sunny was trembling when he finally lifted his head. She knew if they hadn't been in the clinic, he would have made love to her then and there. With effort, she marshaled her thundering pulse.

"I've got a class tonight after work, but I'll try to be home as soon as I can after that. Maybe by around seven-thirty," she promised.

"I'll be home as soon as I can, too," he told her, looking as if he were anticipating their reunion after a day spent apart every bit as much as she was. "Unfortunately, tonight is my night to make house calls on the shut-ins in the area, so you'll probably beat me home. But not by much if I have anything to do with it," he vowed softly.

"WHAT A beautiful baby," Zach said, as he finished examining Heidi Pearson later that same day. He had stopped by their house at the end of his house calls to save Rhonda-Faye and George a trip to the clinic. Now, inside their warm cozy home, which was brimming with kids, he was glad he had.

"I didn't think physicians were supposed to be partial to their patients," Rhonda-Faye said, bundling her newborn daughter back up in swaddling clothes.

Zach winked at Rhonda-Faye and stepped over one of Toby's toys. "I won't tell if you won't."

"Are you going to have babies with Sunny anytime soon?"

Good question, Zach thought. Maybe it was time to start a family.

"Hi, Doc." George came into the room.

"Ready to get those stitches on your forehead out?" Zach asked.

"Sure thing." George sat down in the chair Zach indicated as Rhonda-Faye slipped from the room, Heidi in her arms. "Sorry about the way I acted when

Rhonda-Faye went into labor,'' George said. "I get a little crazy whenever our kids are born.''

"So I heard.'' Zach grinned.

"Think you'll do the same?'' George asked.

That, Zach didn't know. "I consider myself to be pretty calm during medical emergencies,'' he said finally.

"You're pretty calm about what happened to Sunny today, too,'' George remarked casually, surprised.

"You mean about the splinters?'' Finished taking out the stitches, Zach cleaned his scissors and tweezers thoroughly with alcohol.

"Yeah, the way it happened and all,'' George said matter-of-factly.

Once again, Zach had the feeling Sunny was deliberately shutting him out. Ever so casually, he replaced his scissors and tweezers back in his medical bag. Time to go on a fishing expedition. "What did you think about what happened?'' Zach asked, folding his arms in front of him.

"Well, I know Sunny didn't see it coming, but I knew he'd make a pass at her eventually.''

Zach froze. "What was the guy's name again?''

"Conway. Chuck Conway.''

The same guy she had talked to on the phone. "I've never met him,'' Zach said benignly. "What's he like?''

George ran a hand over his hair. "Harmless. Nerdy. Kind of clueless, if you know what I mean.''

I'm beginning to. "So he's had a crush on Sunny for a long time?'' Zach asked.

"Yeah. I don't think she was even aware of it. You know how Sunny is. She doesn't see stuff like that, but me and the other guys did.''

Then how come you didn't stop it? Zach tamped

down his anger deliberately. "How was she at the time it happened?" Zach asked, then explained, "She was calm when she got here. She had kind of shrugged it off."

George rubbed at his jaw thoughtfully. "I think she was shocked, but she didn't take offense. She just figured it was a misunderstanding, that Conway read her wrong, which isn't surprising, 'cause like I said, the nerd's clueless."

Sunny should have told me this! Zach thought.

"Ticks you off, doesn't it, Doc?" George stared with a provoking grin.

"Well…" Zach shrugged. "She is my wife."

"So naturally you feel protective of her," George continued affably.

"Naturally."

"Want my advice?"

Zach knew he was going to get it anyway. Maybe George knew how to handle a situation like this. "Sure," Zach said.

"A woman likes a man to take charge. This Chuck Conway incident, for instance. Sunny would probably never admit it in a million years, but she probably secretly wanted you to go all jealous on her and get upset and so forth."

Zach didn't have to pretend to feel that way. He was upset. And Sunny was going to know it!

"I CAN'T DO THAT!" Sunny told her marriage class.

"Honey, with a body like yours, you've got nothing to hide," Gertie said.

"Right. It's the rest of us that ought to be worried about greeting our husbands at the door covered in nothing but plastic wrap!" Matilda said.

"Particularly me, since I just had a baby," Rhonda-Faye said, patting her ever-flattening tummy. "And can't participate in the…um…follow-through yet."

"Rhonda-Faye, you have permission to delay this particular exercise until your physician gives you the okay to resume relations," the instructor said.

"Seems fair," Matilda commented.

"Speaking of fairness," Sunny interrupted. "Can't we amend the lesson a bit?" she asked. "Forget the plastic wrap and just dress in a suggestive manner and greet our husbands at the door? For instance, I have a beautiful negligee I got as a wedding gift that I haven't even worn—"

"Sunny Carlisle, why ever on earth not?" Gertie demanded.

Sunny blushed. "I was waiting for the right occasion."

"That was for your wedding night!" Gertie said.

"Well, I uh—"

"What she's trying to say is she didn't need it on her wedding night," Matilda broke in, in an attempt to save the day. "And even if she had put it on, that cute young husband of hers probably would've taken it right off…so why not save it for later, when the love life got a little dull? But so far there hasn't been time for it to get boring, right, Sunny?"

Sunny knew she was blushing to the roots of her hair. She sank down in her chair, covering her red face with her hand.

All the women laughed. "I think you hit the nail right on the head," Rhonda-Faye drawled. "Not that it's surprising. Sunny and Zach are both young and gorgeous, and at that age where their hormones are in full bloom.

They'd have to be monks not to appreciate each other, especially in this newlywed phase.''

''Back to my question,'' Sunny said as she doodled aimlessly on the notepad in front of her. ''Couldn't I just greet Zach at the door in that negligee? Maybe with some champagne?''

Maybe if she did, he would forget to ask more questions about how she'd gotten those splinters in her thigh earlier today, Sunny thought.

''All right, Sunny, if you'd be more comfortable, you can wear a negligee instead of plastic wrap. But the rest of the assignment still stands. And we want a full report during the next and last class!''

SUNNY LOOKED at herself in the mirror and shook her head. The negligee she was wearing was made of pale peach silk. The bodice was low-cut and clinging, the fabric blissfully opaque.

She wore matching peach silk mules and a matching peignoir. Had it not been for the weekend they'd spent together on the boat, she would have felt ridiculous. But now that they were lovers, she felt nothing but anticipation. Last night, making love to Zach in their bed, in their own home, had been wonderful. Tonight, Sunny decided as she poured two brimming glasses of champagne, would be beautiful, too.

A car engine sounded in the driveway. That had to be Zach, and he was right on time.

Picking up the glasses of champagne, Sunny switched on the stereo and floated to the front door. Looking through the front screen, she did not see Zach. Instead she saw two people she had never met. She hadn't a clue who they were, but from the looks on their faces they apparently knew just who she was.

"You must be Sunny Carlisle," the woman said.

Sunny set down the champagne. She drew the edges of her peignoir together, a little embarrassed to be caught in a nightgown during the dinner hour. "And you are?" she asked, already afraid she knew.

"Nate and Maxine Grainger, Zach's parents." Zach's father held out his hand.

Sunny shook it warmly.

"He didn't tell me you were coming," she said nervously, glancing at the wood-paneled station wagon in her driveway.

Zach's mother smiled. Petite, blond, she was dressed in a long-sleeved knit blouse, denim wraparound skirt and sneakers. She had the same Nordic good looks and blue eyes Zach did. "That's because he didn't know," she said kindly.

His dad, who was as tall and fit as Zach was, added, "We wanted to surprise him."

"Well, you've certainly done that." Sunny opened the screen door to let them inside.

"But why did you come here looking for him?" she asked. Zach had not told his parents he was married as far as she knew. "I mean, I—we—"

Zach's father held up a hand. "No need to pretend, Sunny. Maxine and I don't want to pry, but we might as well tell you the secret is out of the bag. We found out on Saturday, when we called the clinic looking for him. The answering service operator told us he was out of town with *his new wife.*"

"Naturally—" Maxine picked up the story where Nate had left off "—we were shocked to find out he had married without even telling us. So we decided to drive on up here today, after we finished teaching school, and find out for ourselves what was going on."

Sunny blushed. She wished Zach were there to take the heat right along with her. "I don't know what to say," she murmured. This was *so embarrassing*.

Fortunately she was saved the trouble as Zach turned his pickup into the drive. She pointed behind the Graingers and smiled cheerfully, unable to completely disguise her relief. "There's Zach now."

"He has a lot to answer for," Nate said, pulling a pair of glasses out of the pocket of his seersucker shirt.

Zach bounded out of the truck, his medical bag in hand. He grinned wickedly as he caught a glimpse of Sunny's outfit, then bounded across the yard and up onto the porch, where he hugged his mother and father warmly. "I guess you know," he said finally.

"I guess we do," Maxine said.

The trio looked at one another with so much affection it made Sunny tingle.

"I was going to tell you," Zach said eventually.

"Why didn't you?" Maxine said.

Sunny held her breath. She didn't know why exactly, but she hoped he would not tell his parents their marriage was a fake and that they were forced into it by the well-meaning members of the close-knit, but old-fashioned, community.

Zach shrugged and wrapped a possessive arm around Sunny's shoulders. "Isn't it obvious? I wanted to keep my beautiful wife to myself. Besides," he continued in a more serious tone, "I thought you might object to my hasty wedding."

Maxine leveled an admonishing finger at her son. "The only thing I object to is you not inviting us to the wedding."

Zach shrugged and said with a careful honesty Sunny

applauded, "It was one of those affairs that was thrown together at the last minute."

"I see." Nate regarded his son with a combination of sternness and love.

Sunny felt a lecture coming on. "I think I'll go upstairs and change," she said, eager to take off the negligee.

"I REALLY AM sorry that you got the news about my marriage to Zach the way you did," Sunny told Maxine as the two of them whipped up a salad for dinner.

"No need to apologize, dear," Maxine said as she rinsed the lettuce leaves and then placed them in a colander to drain. "I think I know why Zach didn't tell us. He probably thought we'd make a fuss, which we would have. And he probably felt he couldn't handle the emotional aspects of it."

"I don't understand," Sunny said slowly.

Maxine drew a breath. "Because of Lori. He took her death very hard. We all did, and since then big family gatherings and holidays have been hard on the three of us. Zach's wedding would have been bittersweet. He probably thought—erroneously, I might add—that he was protecting us by not including us."

Sunny didn't know about that, but it did explain Zach's distance from other people and the walls he had put up between himself and the community.

"He loved Lori a lot, didn't he?" Sunny said, wishing Zach would talk about his kid sister's death with her as freely as his mother did.

Maxine nodded. "The two of them were extremely close. I don't think they had any secrets from each other." Maxine teared up, and she had to pause to wipe her eyes, as she confessed thickly, "Zach sacrificed so much of his own life, just to be with her. And then he took her death very hard. I don't think he has really let anyone close to him since. Oh, he has plenty of friends, both male and female, but I think there's been a fence around his heart ever since then. Until you, of course. You must have really thrown him for a loop.''

"I think that goes both ways," Sunny said. He had certainly thrown her feelings into turmoil. She had never been so simultaneously happy and sad as she was right now.

"Perhaps we should talk about something else," Maxine said.

Sunny nodded. She and Zach would work this out. It would just take a little more time for him to get his life back on track. When he did, he would see there was no reason for him to keep from getting close to those around him.

Sunny sliced carrots with a vengeance, aware she wanted Zach as she had never wanted anyone or anything else. How she wished theirs were a normal marriage.

"YOU AND MY MOM were in the kitchen a long time tonight," Zach said as he and Sunny got ready for bed.

Sunny slipped a long white nightgown over her head and sat down on the bed. As she brushed her hair, she lifted her eyes to his. "She told me about Lori, Zach."

Somehow, he had figured that was the case.

He kept his glance level. "She did."

"She thinks Lori is the reason you never married until now."

Zach tensed. "She's probably right," he said in a matter-of-fact tone. Clad only in pajama bottoms, he eased down beside her. "Lori's death took everything out of me that I had to give. I had enough left over for patients, but that was all.''

Sunny clasped his hand tightly in both of hers. ''Tell me about her.''

Zach stared down at their entwined hands. Talking about what happened to Lori made his gut twist, but he knew it was past time he started talking about his loss. There was no one he wanted to confide in more than Sunny.

Marshaling his inner strength, Zach looked into Sunny's eyes. The compassion and understanding he saw there gave him the courage to continue. ''Lori was two years younger than me. From as far back as I can remember, it was always my job to protect her. And I did until she was thirteen, and she got leukemia. She was sick off and on for the next twelve years. She suffered through three all-too-brief remissions before finally dying of the disease two years ago. I was her cheerleader, her patient advocate. I did everything I could think of to help her get better, including a lot of research on my own.'' He sighed wearily. ''I was so sure we could beat the cancer if we went after it together.''

''I suppose she had all the newest treatments?''

Zach nodded, recalling with difficulty how hard it had been on his sister. And through it all, she'd been such a trooper, never complaining, never giving up, even at the bitter end. His eyes welled with tears; determinedly he blinked them back. ''I even gave her a bone-marrow transplant,'' he said thickly. ''It didn't help.'' He gripped his hands in front of him until the skin around his knuckles turned white. ''Nothing did.''

''Is that why you became a doctor?'' Sunny asked

gently, covering his hands with the warmth of hers. "Because of what happened to your sister?"

He nodded slowly. "I went to the hospital with her every time she needed chemo. The more I learned about her disease and what they could and couldn't do for her in terms of treatment, the more I wanted to know."

Sunny put her hairbrush aside. "Your mom said you sacrificed much of your own life to be with her."

"I don't think it was such a big deal. Although—" Zach grinned, recalling what a stir that had caused "—I think Mom's still mad at me for skipping out on my senior prom."

"You didn't go?"

"Lori was sick and was in St. Jude's hospital. How could I have had a good time, knowing what kind of shape she was in? So I canceled and spent the night at her bedside."

Sunny released an unsteady breath. She was looking at him as if he were some sort of a saint, Zach thought uncomfortably.

When in truth, all he could focus on was the fact that he had failed his sister.

"I wish I had known her," Sunny said finally.

Funny, Zach could imagine the two of them together. It was a poignant vision. "I do, too," Zach said softly. "I think she would've liked you.

"And she would've especially liked," Zach added, simultaneously blinking back tears and laughing lightly, "the way you don't hesitate to give me hell when you think I need it."

Sunny's lips curved in a teasing grin. "Let me guess," she deadpanned. "Lori gave you hell, too?"

Zach nodded, the good memories crowding out the bad once again. "You bet she did. Lori read me the riot act all the time, as any good kid sister would. She wanted to bring me up right she always said. And in her opinion, Mom and Dad were both too soft on me.''

Sunny smiled. ''You really have a loving family.''

Zach nodded, shifting his grip so that he held both of Sunny's hands in his. He knew how lucky he was, never more so than now. ''I'm glad you like them,'' he said. ''They've taken to you, too.'' Just as he had known they would. ''My mom said she really enjoyed talking with you tonight. And speaking of talking to someone,'' Zach said, reminded of what he had been waiting all evening to find out. ''What's this I hear about Chuck Conway putting the moves on you today?'' He was still surprised by the amount of jealousy that information had evoked in him.

Sunny flushed. ''How did you hear about that?'' she moaned, looking as though she wanted to die of embarrassment.

''Never mind how I found out,'' Zach said sternly, for once glad the efficient grapevine in Carlisle existed. ''Why didn't you tell me Chuck was the reason for your splinters?''

''Because I was afraid you'd react like a jealous husband,'' Sunny said, rolling her eyes.

He felt like a jealous husband. It didn't bother him as much as he would've expected. ''I don't want him putting the moves on you,'' Zach said firmly, meaning it. The next time he wouldn't let it go by without incident.

''It won't happen again,'' Sunny told him confidently as she slid beneath the covers and lay back against the pillows.

Zach slid in beside her, but delayed turning off the

light. "How do you know it won't happen again?" he said, studying her upturned face.

Sunny shifted onto her side and regarded him smugly. "Because I told him what no one else had bothered to report to him—that I am married now."

Zach shifted onto his side, too. "How could he not have known?"

"Chuck doesn't reside in Carlisle, Zach."

"Even so—" he began.

"I don't know." Sunny waggled her eyebrows at him teasingly. "Maybe he isn't as into gossip as everyone else, including you, in this town is."

"Very funny."

Sunny lifted a hand in warning. "Just don't go getting any ideas about fistfights on my behalf."

Zach grinned and began to unbutton her chaste white nightgown. "Only if you put that peach negligee on again."

"Zach!" She swatted at his hands.

He pushed her hands away and kept unbuttoning. "I mean it. My blood has been boiling ever since I caught a glimpse of you in it."

She nudged his thigh with her knee and whispered hoarsely, "Your parents are just across the hall."

Zach grinned, not the least bit upset. "They think we're newlyweds." And these days, he felt like one. "They won't mind."

Zach bent to kiss her. Her lips parted for him and she uttered a soft little groan in the back of her throat.

"What if they hear us?" Sunny said, worrying out loud.

Zach slid a hand inside her gown to cup her breast, and felt her nipple bud against his palm. "Then you had better be quiet, hadn't you?" he whispered back, dropping his palm lower, exalting in the way her soft curves heated beneath his touch.

"Mmmmm." Sunny moaned again, arching up against his questing fingers, even while she initiated a few clever moves of her own. "Gramps was right," she teased. "You *are* bad news...."

"You ain't seen nothing yet," he promised, and then set about divesting her of her nightgown and making her his all over again.

"If I'm going to be naked, you're going to be, too," Sunny declared, unsnapping his pajama bottoms.

"Sounds good to me." Fierce desire already swirling through him, Zach covered her with his body. Dipping his head, he kissed her thoroughly until she was feeling the same way and her lips were hot and wanting beneath his.

"Oh, Zach, you make me feel so good," Sunny murmured. She nestled against him, softness to hardness, their caresses flowing one into the next, until there was no ending, no beginning, only a sweet continuum of unrelenting pleasure that drove him on and on.

Slowly he filled her, and she received him, arching at the pleasure, taking him deeper and deeper inside.

Feeling as if he were drowning in her softness, the sweet solace her lips offered, he moved with her, molding the length of his body to hers.

They came together, the power and the emotion of the moment stunning him, leaving him lost and free all at once.

He had not ever imagined it could be like this. Sunny drew a passion and tenderness from him that he never would have dreamed possible. And she did it without half trying, Zach thought, holding her close and drinking in the soap and perfume scent that was uniquely her.

He knew this was love. But was it marriage? He sensed they would both find out soon enough. Whatever happened, he was not letting her go, not giving up. Life was too short, too precious, for them not to be together, he decided fiercely. The only question was, how was he going to convince Sunny of that? How was he going to make her believe that they needed to live their lives free of gossip and community pressure?

As strange as it was, she actually liked the interference.

"Zach?" Sunny said sleepily, cuddling close.

"Yeah?" He brought the covers up around them, his heartbeat settling down to a contented purr.

"I'm glad you told me about Lori."

"I'm glad, too." He stroked a hand through her hair, a wave of tenderness washing over him. "It felt good to talk about it. Maybe because I never do."

And it had brought them closer, Zach thought with a satisfied grin as he curled an arm possessively around her.

If everything continued to go right, the two of them might get past their shaky beginning and make a real marriage of this yet.

Chapter Twelve

I Don't Fall in Love So Easy

"How's the poison ivy, Slim?" Zach asked at the graduation party for Sunny's how-to-be-happily-married class.

"Lots better, thanks to the medicine you gave me," Slim said with a wink. "Though I gotta admit it's the first time I've ever had poison ivy where the sun don't shine."

Zach laughed softly. Slim was nothing if not honest. "Guess you appreciated the side benefits of having your wife take this class, hmm?"

"Didn't you?" Fergus asked, coming up to join the group. "It certainly brought a lot of zip to my marriage with Gertie, and that was something...well, let's just say after thirty-one years of marriage, I didn't expect it."

"What about you, Doc?" George asked, joining the men at the punch bowl. "Did this class lend any zip to your marriage or were you so deep in the honeymoon phase that you didn't even notice?"

It would have been hard not to notice Sunny in that peach silk negligee, Zach thought, the memory of the night they had spent in each other's arms after his parents had left still vivid in his mind. "Since I've never been married, that'd be kind of hard to know," he said.

"Got a point there, Zach," George agreed. He cast a fond look at his wife, who was cradling their new baby in her arms. "All I know is that I wouldn't trade Rhonda-Faye for any woman in this world, I love her and the kids so."

Zach knew how George felt. He didn't want to trade Sunny, either. And that had given him second thoughts about leaving Carlisle.

"WHAT DO YOU MEAN my transfer request was put on hold a long time ago?" Zach asked the clerk in charge of the outreach program incredulously.

"We had a call from the governor several weeks ago, right after your request came in. He said he had talked to your local sponsor, Augustus Carlisle, and that you had changed your mind. Something about you marrying his granddaughter Sunny and settling in there right fine."

"So you're telling me he canceled my request *for* me?" Zach asked.

"Well, yes." The clerk paused. "Does this mean you want to reinstate it?"

"Yes! No! I don't know," he said. "I'll have to get back to you." He hung up and charged out the door of the clinic. He and Augustus were going to have it out once and for all.

Unfortunately Augustus wasn't home, and he wasn't fishing, according to his housekeeper. He was at the factory with Sunny.

Zach thought about waiting, then decided this confrontation couldn't wait. Augustus had crossed the line for the very last time.

Zach stormed into the factory. Sunny and her grandfather were in the showroom with a group of prospective buyers. Sunny left her group and crossed to his side.

"Is everything okay, Zach?"

He didn't want to upset Sunny. This wasn't her fault. Like him, she knew nothing about it. "I just need to talk to your grandfather. Clinic business." Which was true, as far as it went.

Sunny turned. "Gramps, Zach needs to talk to you." With a dazzling smile, she rejoined her group. "Now, where were we?"

"What's so all-fired important?" Augustus said.

"This conversation needs to happen in private," Zach said grimly.

Gramps took a good look at his grandson-in-law's face. "No problem," he said smoothly. "We'll use my office."

They strode in silence to his office, a cubbyhole next to Sunny's executive-sized haven. Gramps shut the door behind him. He immediately faced off with Zach. "Let's have it, greenhorn."

"I just talked to the outreach office in charge of rural physician assignments."

"Oh." Augustus had the grace to look chagrined.

"Yes, 'oh'," Zach said heavily. "I notice you're not denying you called the governor?"

"I talk to him regularly. We're old friends."

"You put a halt on my request."

"What did you expect me to do? You had just married my granddaughter."

"I don't care," Zach said evenly. "That wasn't your call to make."

"I don't know what you're so all-fired upset about." Gramps was incensed. "It worked out in the end, didn't it? You and Sunny are as happy as can be."

"That's not the point," Zach roared, exasperated beyond belief. "You trapped me into marrying Sunny and then you manipulated me into staying well past what was necessary under the circumstances."

"Now you're talking nonsense," Augustus growled.

No, Zach thought, he wasn't. In fact, judging by the increasingly guilty look on Gramps's face, there might be even more to it than he'd originally realized.

"Who exactly was on the selection committee that brought me here?" Zach asked cordially.

Gramps blanched and didn't answer.

"Sunny was on the selection committee, wasn't she?" Zach pressed.

"So what if she was? A lot of other people were on it, too."

"Did she get to choose me, or was it more a group effort?" he asked.

"I don't know what you're talking about," Augustus returned hotly as he picked up a fishing lure from his desk. But he wouldn't meet Zach's eyes.

Barely able to believe how stupid and gullible he'd been, Zach stalked nearer. He planted his hands on Gramps's desk and leaned across it. "Are you denying that Sunny went through the files that were sent here, picking and choosing among the candidates?"

Gramps shrugged and looked all the guiltier as he tied a piece of line to a feather. "I admit she helped us try to find a good match by reading through the résumés right along with the rest of us. But that was all she did, Zach."

It was more than enough. His jaw clenched.

"The idea of us choosing you for some evil purpose is just ludicrous," Gramps continued.

Was it? "So why didn't you choose a woman physician?"

"Because we live so far out in the country, it made more sense to choose a man!"

"And I was the one Sunny was most interested in!" he said, guessing slyly.

"You had a fine résumé," Gramps retorted, exasperated. "A fine education."

Zach recalled how impressed Sunny's parents had been by his education background; he wondered if that had factored into the decision, too.

As he realized how well and easily he'd been duped, it was all Zach could do not to slam his fist into the wall. "So you admit you all lured me to the community with the idea of me marrying your granddaughter in mind!" he shouted back triumphantly.

"I wouldn't say we had the idea of marrying you two right off," Gramps said hotly.

Zach read between the lines, his experience with the wily old man telling him there was a lot more to this than what appeared at first glance. "But you did expect me to keep company with her!" he asserted baldly.

"Well, why not? The two of you were both well educated and among the few young unmarried people in this town. Sure, I hoped she might date you when she finally got to know you!!"

"Let's be honest," Zach said grimly. "This was all a plot from the beginning, wasn't it? You lured me to Carlisle so that your granddaughter would have a husband. You used me to keep Sunny here in Carlisle, make her happy and give you a grandson." Zach didn't know why he hadn't put it all together sooner. Now that he had, he felt like such a damn fool. "Well, the game's up!" he said furiously. "I'm through being caught in a snare!"

SUNNY STOOD outside Gramps's office, her face going alternately white and red. Reminded of how she and Zach had really gotten together, she wanted to die. There was no love involved here, only passion. She had been fooling herself into thinking there was.

Bracing herself for the battle to come, she opened the door and stepped inside.

Zach looked at her. "I heard everything," she told both men, her expression stony with resolve. "Including the fact that Zach thinks he's been had."

"Can you blame me for feeling I walked into a trap?" he asked.

Hell, yes, Sunny thought. But not about to let herself sink to the shouting level of the men, she shook her head and shut the door quietly behind her. "You're right, Zach," she said sweetly, moving closer to join them. She looked at him innocently. "It's all been a nefarious plot. I paid those skunks to trail me and made sure you were driving on that particular country road, on that day, at the precise time I was checking out the reforestation of that select slice of company-owned land. Then—and this was the truly difficult part—I somehow convinced those skunks to follow me, knowing all the while that you were bound to see me in danger and pull your pickup to the side of the road, leap over the fence in a single, soundless bound, creep up from behind and scare the life out of me and get us both sprayed with skunk. Then, not content with that, devious woman that I am, I made sure you were driving a brand-new truck that you would of course refuse to let us ride in. I had nothing in my knapsack but a table-cloth, and you nothing but a chamois—"

Zach silenced her with a look. "All right, all right. So maybe the skunks were an accident, but they played right into your grand plan," he asserted.

Sunny looked heavenward. "Right, Zach. I wanted to get caught by my grandfather and two policemen with me in nothing but a tablecloth and you in a chamois. I wanted to be humiliated beyond belief."

Zach's mouth tightened. Sunny knew she had finally gotten through to him; he knew how ridiculous he sounded, even if he wasn't about to forgive her or Gramps.

"You didn't object to marrying me!" Zach thundered.

"No," Sunny said very quietly as tears of frustration sparkled in her eyes. "But I should have. It was a bad idea."

"You two were happy the past few days," Gramps interrupted. "And you can't deny you were!"

No, Sunny couldn't deny that the past few days had been among the best of her life. But that was apparently where it stopped. "We were deluding ourselves!" she said miserably, blinking back her tears. "We got caught up in the honeymoon aspect of things, but we weren't dealing in reality. The reality is we got married for all the wrong reasons. It took us a while, but we have finally woken up. Now that we have, I want out, and so apparently does Zach. So you have your wish. I'll start divorce proceedings tomorrow. Gramps will call the governor back and ask him to expedite your transfer request. *Won't you, Gramps?*"

"Of course, Sunny."

"And in the meantime, Zach, you can sleep at the

clinic! Now, is everybody happy and satisfied?'' she asked with icy control. She knew she wasn't! Not waiting for an answer, she turned on her heel and stormed from Gramps's office.

''Sunny—'' Zach started after her. He caught up with her in the central bull pen. Disregarding the company employees gaping at them, she shrugged off the grip he had on her arm. ''Leave me alone, Zach. We have nothing further to discuss.''

''The hell we don't!'' He clamped a hand on her wrist and directed her into her office.

There was a murmur of approval and excitement behind them. Sunny ignored it. She waited until Zach had shut the door behind them and released her. ''I don't know what this is going to prove,'' she said, moving away from him defiantly.

He rounded on her. ''I want to know why you married me.''

She regarded him stonily, feeling as if her heart were encased in a block of ice. She let out a long breath and looked away.

Hands braced on his waist, he eyed her implacably. ''You regret it, don't you?''

''Yes. Because what's happened here today has made me realize that the marriage was a mistake. It was unnecessary. And I knew it in my heart all along.'' Sunny's lower lip trembled as she forced herself to admit. ''But I wanted to be with you, so I let them bully and talk me into it. Just as you did,'' she conceded miserably.

Zach nodded his understanding grimly. He pushed impatient fingers through his hair. ''So what now?''

Sunny knew they were at a turning point. This time

she was determined to make the right decision, to behave as an adult rather than a lovestruck teen.

She moved to the window and stood looking out at the Tennessee mountains she'd come to love. "I knew when I moved here that I was not going to put my energy into lost causes anymore. For years, I did everything positive to win my parents love and affection, and as you saw for yourself, they still barely know I'm alive. That isn't going to change. I'm not going to beat my head against the wall anymore, trying. And I'm not going to torture myself like that again. Especially when I know through my easy but newfound relationship with Gramps and everyone else in Carlisle that unconditional love does exist."

"Unconditional love, my shoe. He pressured you into marrying me, Sunny." And he could not forgive her grandfather for that.

Sunny raised her chin. "Yes, he did, because he was old-fashioned and hopeful enough to think that was the best thing for both of us to do under the circumstances. But had I stood up for myself and said no and meant it, he would have stopped pressuring me. He would not have stopped loving me then any more than he did just now when I read him the riot act."

Zach shook his head in silent censure of all that had happened. He felt as miserable as she did. "I can't live here anymore."

Sunny sighed. She was not surprised. Zach had wanted out of Carlisle almost from the moment he'd arrived. "I figured as much," she said tightly.

He gave her a long look, his expression stony. "So what about us?" he asked grimly.

If he had shown her the least sign, indicated he was in love with her or wanted to try again, Sunny would've moved heaven and earth to be with him. But he didn't. Instead he acted as though this were a business agreement in need of resolution, and nothing more. Well, she thought wearily, perhaps that was all it had ever been to him. A business deal, with passion thrown in. Initially that was all it had been with her, too. She'd just had the bad sense to fall in love with him.

"What about us?" Sunny echoed dispassionately. *Tell me it's not too late, Zach,* she pleaded silently.

He stared at the floor for a long moment. A muscle worked in his cheek. Finally he looked back at her, the expression in his eyes bleak and unforgiving. "You said you wanted to file for divorce?" he stated, very low.

She saw the guilt in his eyes, the regret. And suddenly she knew that he had only stayed as long as he had, tried as hard as he had, because he'd wanted to make a success of his career in Carlisle and thereby guarantee his future as a physician. "Yes, I'll handle the expense and paperwork involved in a divorce," Sunny said, knowing she couldn't bear this heartbreak for one more second. "You won't have to do a thing, Zach. You're free to go. Your life is your own again."

Chapter Thirteen

Life Is Too Short to Love like That

"I can tell from the heartbroken looks on your faces that you've heard the news, too," Sunny told her marriage class, as they gathered in Rhonda-Faye's diner after hours.

"It's true, then?" Rhonda-Faye said as she served strawberry sodas to everyone. "You and Zach are calling it quits?" She was incredulous.

Sunny put on her bravest face. "He thinks I brought him to Carlisle to trap and coerce him into marrying me, so I cut him loose."

"Oh, surely he knows that isn't true!" Matilda said, appearing as upset as Sunny and the rest of the group.

Sunny stirred her soda disconsolately. "The circumstantial evidence is running against me. He knows I went through the profiles of the various physician candidates with Gramps and said Zach's was interesting."

The ladies grinned as if that were proof Sunny had been head over heels in lust with Zach even then. "You can't fall in love with a picture," she said dryly.

"But you can fall in love with the flesh-and-blood reality of an intriguing picture," Matilda said slyly.

Sunny sipped her soda. It was delicious, but she could take no pleasure in it. "Whether I'm attracted to Zach isn't the issue here. He is through being used and wants out of Carlisle. Like it or not, my marriage is over," she reported dejectedly.

The ladies exchanged concerned looks.

Rhonda-Faye eyed Sunny seriously. "All I know is that a marriage takes work, even for the most in-love couple on earth."

"Rhonda-Faye's right. The two of you gotta break each other in," Aunt Gertie said. "And have a few tiffs as you settle into matrimony. That's all that's been going on between the two of you. You had a tiff. You told him to take a hike, more or less, exactly as you should have, under the circumstances. Now it's time to tell him that you forgive him for his stupidity—and that it's okay to come back to you. We've all done the same thing with our men, haven't we, ladies?"

The group nodded unanimously.

Her expression both serious and helpful, Matilda elaborated on Gertie's advice. "Sacrifice is the key here, Sunny," she said. "For you and for Zach."

"And let's not forget compromise," Gertie added. "You can't have a marriage without both those ingredients."

"You can't have a marriage without love, either," Sunny said morosely, staring into her strawberry soda. If Zach had really loved her, he would've known that she had never meant to trap him into marriage, and he never would have left.

"Oh, now, honey. Zach loves you!" Gertie said.

Rhonda-Faye nodded vigorously in agreement. "I've never seen a man so silly with it. He's head over heels in love with you."

He's head over heels in lust with me, you mean, Sunny thought. And they were not the same thing. "Then how come he never said so?" she asked the group belligerently.

"Maybe because of the way your marriage started— at the end of a shotgun," Rhonda-Faye said softly.

Sunny didn't want to admit it, but Rhonda-Faye had a point. Zach had been forced into this more or less against his will. The only way he'd been able to salvage his fierce pride and self-respect was to tell her repeatedly that he refused to give in to the social pressures being exerted on him. Admitting he loved her probably was tantamount to failure, at least in his view. At the very least, it was proof he'd lost his independence and done what everyone else had predicted would happen all along.

"Try reading his face instead of his lips," Matilda advised.

"Oh, I don't know," Aunt Gertie teased, "you can tell a lot from the way a man kisses, too. Tell me true, Sunny. Does Zach kiss you like he means it?"

And then some, Sunny thought wistfully.

"If there's love in his kiss, there's love in his heart."

No matter how much she tried to forget them, Aunt Gertie's words stayed with her the rest of the impromptu meeting. Zach did kiss her as though he loved her, she thought. And there had been other signs he cared about her, too. The way he'd fixed up her car, for instance, helping to get rid of the skunk smell. Then there was his jealous reaction to Chuck Conway's pass at her. The way he had comforted her after her parents' visit and protected her during the storm.

So what if he hadn't come right out and said the words? Neither had she. Yet she had felt his love. And would still be feeling it if she hadn't overheard his conversation with Gramps.

Was it too late for a second chance? She hoped not. All she had to do was swallow her pride, find Zach and try one more time to work things out. She knew that if she didn't, she would always regret it.

She left the diner and went straight to the clinic.

To her disappointment, the front door was locked. A Closed sign was in the window. Beneath that was a printed notice announcing that another doctor would be arriving to take Zach's place at the clinic just as soon as the state agency and the local selection committee could arrange it. Zach's truck was nowhere in sight.

Sunny blanched. Was it possible he had already left? Moved out and on?

Despondently she returned to her house. Her hopes rose as she saw his shiny new pickup sitting in her drive, then fell again as she noted the bed of the truck was filled with his belongings. Either he'd come home to her—which seemed damn unlikely, considering how they had left things between them—or he had just stopped in to talk legalities with her before he left town.

Aware her legs were shaking, Sunny stepped out of her Land Rover. She moved toward the house, the first few steps taking all the willpower she had. And that was when she saw him, slouched on the steps of her front porch. In jeans, dress shirt and tie, he had never looked more handsome. Or more unapproachable. She eyed him cautiously, unsure of his mood.

Zach unfolded himself and stood with a determined, lazy grace that quickened her heartbeat.

"About time you got home, woman," he said softly, curling his thumbs through the belt loops of his jeans.

Sunny stared at him, not sure whether to laugh or

burst into tears. She knew only that she had never felt more tense or uncertain or full of bittersweet anticipation in her life. And Zach, damn him, was to blame.

Pride stiffened her shoulders. "Since when did you turn into John Wayne?" she returned, regarding him with a coolness she couldn't begin to feel deep inside.

"Since I was cornered by Slim, Fergus, Gramps and George." He swaggered laconically down the porch steps like the hero in a Western movie, not stopping until he towered over her and they stood toe-to-toe. His blue eyes were shrewdly direct as they locked on hers.

"They think I handled you all wrong."

Sunny's lips curved sardonically. Whether he wanted to admit it or not, they had formed their own marriage-counseling service for men, although it was a little less organized. She folded her arms in front of her and adopted a contentious stance. "Well, it'll warm your heart to know that the women in the community think I've handled you all wrong, too."

Zach braced his hands on his waist. "Is that a fact," he drawled.

Sunny nodded, her temper soaring as all the things they had said to each other at their last meeting came rushing back to hit her square in the heart. Honestly, how could Zach ever have thought she had set him up for a shotgun wedding? Shouldn't he have known instinctively she was not to blame? And where did he get off acting all macho now? As if she were the one to blame!

"Furthermore," Sunny continued loftily, drawing her own line in the sand, "I think they're right," she fibbed, twisting things around for the sake of her own argument. "I think I should have kicked you out weeks ago!"

"Okay," Zach said, "that's it. I've heard quite enough for one evening." He scooped her up in his arms, carried her across the porch.

"Creating yet another scene for the neighbors to see?" she asked sweetly.

He shrugged as he entered the house. "It's not my fault there's nothing this entertaining on TV."

"Zach, I'm warning you. I am in no mood for games."

He paused just inside the threshold. Still holding her in his arms, he cradled her against his chest, the passion he'd always felt for her gleaming in his eyes.

"I don't want to play games, either, Sunny. I want to make things right."

Sunny's heart pounded at his proximity, but she refused to sacrifice her pride, when she'd already sacrificed so much. "By divorcing me?" she asked coolly.

"By loving you," Zach corrected as he slowly set her down so her feet touched the floor.

Sunny saw the intent look in his eyes. It kindled her own fires. Needing to clarify things for her sake, to make sure he was there because he loved her, she stepped back, announced defiantly, "Zach, I can't go back to having an affair with you, even if we are legally married."

Framing her face with his hands, he tilted it beneath his. "How about being my wife, then, in every sense?"

Unable to move without risking closer contact, Sunny held her ground. She wanted so much for them—a happy marriage, children and everlasting love. She wanted him to want them, too. "And how long is this offer good for, Zach—as long as you stay in Carlisle?"

"No, Sunny, as the vows said," he told her, blocking

her in place, when she would have tried to march past him once again, ''for as long as we both shall live.''

Sunny swallowed. She stared at his tie, her pulse racing; she was unwilling to admit how much just the thought of letting him go disturbed her. It appeared it was about to happen. ''So you're still planning to leave Carlisle, then?'' she asked, a little sadly, aware her mouth was dry and her palms were damp and that she'd never had so much at stake in her entire life.

''I received my official transfer.'' He gestured toward his truck matter-of-factly. ''As you can see, I even packed up and got ready to leave town.''

Unable to help herself, Sunny moved another half step closer, so they were standing just inches apart. ''What stopped you?'' She knew the answer she wanted to hear.

''You.'' Eyes darkening seriously, he dove his hands into her hair. ''I realized I not only didn't want to leave, Carlisle, I couldn't.'' His voice caught. After a moment in which he stared long and hard at the horizon, he forced himself to go on. ''The thought of a life without you is unbearable, Sunny.''

Her heart leapt at what he had just admitted. She tipped her head up to his. ''Because of the passion between us?'' she asked slowly, knowing that if they were going to be together again, their relationship had to be real, and it had to be right.

''I admit I love the way we make love, Sunny, but that's not what is keeping me here,'' he said hoarsely. ''I'm here because you hold the key to my happiness. I gave you my heart without ever knowing it. Just as you gave yours to me. I love you, Sunny,'' he said huskily. ''And I always will.''

Nothing he could have said would have pleased her

more. "Oh, Zach." She wrapped her arms about his neck and kissed him sweetly. "I love you, too," she whispered emotionally. "So very, very much." They kissed again, putting everything they felt into the caress. "But I want you to be sure this is what you want," Sunny said tremulously at last.

"It is. Although I regret to admit it's taken almost losing you to make me realize it. I know I've been unfair to you, to everyone." He paused and shook his head in silent admonishment. "Lori's death took so much out of me that I wasn't sure I had any love to give. And for a very long time I didn't want to find out if, or even when, that would change. And I sure as heck didn't want to fail anyone I cared about again," he finished fiercely.

Sunny hugged him hard as the rest of her doubts melted away. "Oh, Zach, you didn't fail Lori," she reassured him gently. She leaned back against the warm cradle of his arms to gaze into his face. "You did everything you could for her."

Zach's fingers tensed, then relaxed again as he talked openly about his pain. "Only it wasn't enough, and it damn near killed me. I didn't want to fail you, too." His eyes sobered. "But I realize now the only way I could fail you is by walking away."

Sunny swallowed. They had one more bridge to cross. "What about feeling trapped?"

Zach gave her a long, steady look and admitted on a rueful sigh, "The only trap I fell into was putting a fence around my heart. Coming to Carlisle, meeting you, set me free again."

Euphoric relief surged through her. Against all the odds, despite all the meddling, she and Zach had a future together. She had never felt more complete. "Big talk there, fella,'' Sunny teased, laying a hand over his heart. Beneath her fingers, she felt its strong, steady beat, and knew her world had righted once again.

"Yeah, but it's from the bottom of my heart," Zach said in a rusty, trembling voice. "All these how-to-be-a-proper-husband hints from the guys must've sunk in," he offered with a teasing wink.

"Must have. They're working on me, at any rate." Sunny wrapped her arms around his waist and leaned in close, savoring his warmth and his strength and the essence that was him.

Zach lifted the veil of her hair and kissed her exposed throat. "Does this mean you forgive me?"

"Guess so," Sunny quipped as her heart soared. Her eyes danced as they met his. "You're a hard man to stay mad at."

"Now, why is that, I wonder," Zach drawled, looking incredibly happy and content, too. He kissed her full on the mouth, a long, slow kiss that made her tremble.

"Maybe because I love you, too," she confessed. Surging into his embrace, she guided him back to her for another soulful touch. Finally they drew apart. "Zach?" Sunny said, her knees so weak and trembly she could barely stand. She knew where she wanted all this to lead.

"Hmm?" Once again sweeping her up into his arms, he carried her up the staircase.

"About our marriage—" she began.

"It's a real one, in every sense," he confirmed, striding unhurriedly down the upstairs hall. "Truth to tell, I think it has been for a long time." He put her down gently, then followed her down on the bed, kissing her long and slow and deep, drawing on all the power and the wonder of their love. Sunny had never been happier, or more replete.

"Zach?" she said breathlessly after a while, as she began to work off his tie and he undid her buttons.

"Hmm?" He slid a warm palm against her skin.

"About that baby we've both talked about in the hypothetical, the one we both want someday but have been afraid to plan on." Sunny caught her breath at what he was doing and looked into his clear blue eyes. She saw the promise of the future. "How about making it a real possibility?"

Zach paused, his face aglow with delight. For the first time, they really did have it all. "Sunny, love, you read my mind."

Silhouette Books presents a dazzling keepsake
collection featuring two full-length novels by
international bestselling author

DIANA PALMER

Brides To Be

(On sale May 2002)

THE AUSTRALIAN
*Will rugged outback rancher Jonathan Sterling
be roped into marriage?*

HEART OF ICE
*Close proximity sparks a breathtaking attraction between a
feisty young woman and a hardheaded bachelor!*

You'll be swept off your feet by Diana Palmer's BRIDES TO BE.

Don't miss out on this special two-in-one volume, available soon.

*Available only from Silhouette Books
at your favorite retail outlet.*

Where love comes alive™

Visit Silhouette at www.eHarlequin.com

MONTANA
Bred

From the bestselling series

MONTANA MAVERICKS

Wed in Whitehorn

Two more tales that capture living and loving
beneath the Big Sky.

JUST PRETENDING by Myrna Mackenzie

FBI Agent David Hannon's plans for a quiet vacation
were overturned by a murder investigation—and by
officer Gretchen Neal!

STORMING WHITEHORN by Christine Scott

Native American Storm Hunter's return to Whitehorn
sent tremors through the town—and shock waves of
desire through Jasmine Kincaid Monroe....

V *Silhouette*®
™ *Where love comes alive*™

Visit Silhouette at www.eHarlequin.com   PSBRED

Silhouette® —

where love comes alive—online...

eHARLEQUIN.com

buy books

♥ Find all the new Silhouette releases at everyday great discounts.

♥ Try before you buy! Read an excerpt from the latest Silhouette novels.

♥ Write an online review and share your thoughts with others.

online reads

♥ Read our Internet exclusive daily and weekly online serials, or vote in our interactive novel.

♥ Talk to other readers about your favorite novels in our Reading Groups.

♥ Take our Choose-a-Book quiz to find the series that matches you!

authors

♥ Find out interesting tidbits and details about your favorite authors' lives, interests and writing habits.

♥ Ever dreamed of being an author? Enter our Writing Round Robin. The Winning Chapter will be published online! Or review our writing guidelines for submitting your novel.

All this and more available at
www.eHarlequin.com

SINTB1R2

If you enjoyed what you just read,
then we've got an offer you can't resist!

Take 2
bestselling novels FREE!
Plus get a FREE surprise gift!

Clip this page and mail it to The Best of the Best™

IN U.S.A.	IN CANADA
3010 Walden Ave.	P.O. Box 609
P.O. Box 1867	Fort Erie, Ontario
Buffalo, N.Y. 14240-1867	L2A 5X3

YES! Please send me 2 free Best of the Best™ novels and my free surprise gift. After receiving them, if I don't wish to receive anymore, I can return the shipping statement marked cancel. If I don't cancel, I will receive 4 brand-new novels every month, before they're available in stores! In the U.S.A., bill me at the bargain price of $4.74 plus 25¢ shipping and handling per book and applicable sales tax, if any*. In Canada, bill me at the bargain price of $5.24 plus 25¢ shipping and handling per book and applicable taxes**. That's the complete price and a savings of over 20% off the cover prices—what a great deal! I understand that accepting the 2 free books and gift places me under no obligation ever to buy any books. I can always return a shipment and cancel at any time. Even if I never buy another The Best of the Best™ book, the 2 free books and gift are mine to keep forever.

185 MEN DNUX
385 MEN DNUY

Name	(PLEASE PRINT)	
Address	Apt.#	
City	State/Prov.	Zip/Postal Code

* Terms and prices subject to change without notice. Sales tax applicable in N.Y.
** Canadian residents will be charged applicable provincial taxes and GST.
All orders subject to approval. Offer limited to one per household and not valid to current The Best of the Best™ subscribers.
® are registered trademarks of Harlequin Enterprises Limited.

BOB02   ©1998 Harlequin Enterprises Limited

ANN MAJOR
CHRISTINE RIMMER
BEVERLY BARTON

cordially invite you to attend the year's most exclusive party at the **LONE STAR COUNTRY CLUB!**

Meet three very different young women who'll discover that wishes *can* come true!

LONE STAR
COUNTRY CLUB:
The Debutantes

Lone Star Country Club: Where Texas society reigns supreme—and appearances are *everything*.

Available in May at your favorite retail outlet, only from Silhouette.

Silhouette®
Where love comes alive™

Visit Silhouette at www.eHarlequin.com   PSLSCCTD